D0441867

New York Times bestselling author **Maisey Yates** lives in rural Oregon with her three children and her husband, whose chiseled jaw and arresting features continue to make her swoon. She feels the epic trek she takes several times a day from her office to her coffee maker is a true example of her pioneer spirit.

USA TODAY bestselling author **Naima Simone**'s love of romance was first stirred by Johanna Lindsey, Sandra Brown and Linda Howard many years ago. Well, not that many. She is only eighteen...ish. Though her first attempt at a romance novel starring Ralph Tresvant from New Edition never saw the light of day, her love of romance, reading and writing has endured. Published since 2009, she spends her days—and nights—writing sizzling romances with a touch of humor and snark. She is wife to Superman, or his non-Kryptonian, less-bulletproof equivalent, and mother to the most awesome kids ever. They all live in perfect, sometimes domestically challenged bliss in the southern United States.

New York Times Bestselling Author

MAISEY YATES

HOLD ME, COWBOY

HARLEQUIN
BESTSELLING
AUTHOR
COLLECTION

**HARLEQUIN®
BESTSELLING
AUTHOR
COLLECTION**

Recycling programs
for this product may
not exist in your area.

ISBN-13: 978-1-335-40627-9

Hold Me, Cowboy
First published in 2016. This edition published in 2021.
Copyright © 2016 by Maisey Yates

Black Tie Billionaire
First published in 2019. This edition published in 2021.
Copyright © 2019 by Naima Simone

This edition published by arrangement with Harlequin Books S.A.

For questions and comments about the quality of this book, please contact us at CustomerService@Harlequin.com.

Harlequin Enterprises ULC
22 Adelaide St. West, 41st Floor
Toronto, Ontario M5H 4E3, Canada
www.Harlequin.com

Printed in U.S.A.

CONTENTS

HOLD ME, COWBOY

Maisey Yates

To KatieSauce, the sister I was always waiting for.
What a joy it is to have you in my life.

Chapter 1

"Creative photography," Madison West muttered as she entered the security code on the box that contained the key to the cabin she would be staying in for the weekend.

She looked across the snowy landscape to see another home situated *far* too close to the place she would be inhabiting for the next couple of days. The photographs on the vacation-rental website hadn't mentioned that she would be sharing the property with anyone else.

And obviously, the example pictures had been taken from inventive angles.

It didn't matter. Nothing was going to change her plans. She just hoped the neighbors had earplugs. Because she was having sex this weekend. Nonstop sex.

Ten years celibate, and it was ending tonight. She had finally found *the one*. Not the one she was going to marry, obviously. *Please*. Love was for other people. People who hadn't been tricked, manipulated and humiliated when they were seventeen.

No, she had no interest in love and marriage. But she had abundant interest in orgasms. So much interest. And she had found the perfect man to deliver them.

All day, all night, for the next forty-eight hours.

She was armed with a suitcase full of lingerie and four bottles of wine. Neighbors be damned. She'd been hoping for a little more seclusion, but this was fine. It would be fine.

She unlocked the door and stepped inside, breathing a sigh of relief when she saw that the interior, at least, met with her expectations. But it was a little bit smaller than it had looked online, and she could only hope that wasn't some sort of dark portent for the rest of her evening.

She shook her head; she was not going to introduce that concern into the mix, thank you very much. There was enough to worry about when you were thinking about breaking ten years of celibacy without adding such concerns.

Christopher was going to arrive soon, so she figured she'd better get upstairs and start setting a scene. She made her way to the bedroom, then opened her suitcase and took out the preselected bit of lace she had chosen for their first time. It was red, which looked very good on her, if a bit obvious. But she was aiming for obvious.

Christopher wasn't her boyfriend. And he wasn't going to be. He was a very nice equine-vitamin-supplement salesman she'd met a few weeks ago when he'd come by the West estate. She had bought some products for her horses, and they'd struck up a conversation, which had transitioned into a flirtation.

Typically, when things began to transition into flirtation, Maddy put a stop to them. But she hadn't with him. Maybe because he was special. Maybe because ten years was just way too long. Either way, she had kept on flirting with him.

They'd gone out for drinks, and she'd allowed him to kiss her. Which had been a lot more than she'd allowed any other guy in recent years. It had reminded her how much she'd enjoyed that sort of thing once upon a time. And once she'd been reminded…well.

He'd asked for another date. She'd stopped him. Because wouldn't a no-strings physical encounter be way better?

He'd of course agreed. Because he was a man.

But she hadn't wanted to get involved with anyone in town. She didn't need anyone seeing her at a hotel or his house or with his car parked at her little home on her parents' property.

Thus, the cabin-weekend idea had been born.

She shimmied out of her clothes and wiggled into the skintight lace dress that barely covered her backside. Then she set to work fluffing her blond hair and applying some lipstick that matched the lingerie.

She was not answering the door in this outfit, however.

She put her long coat back on over the lingerie, then gave her reflection a critical look. It had been a long time since she had dressed to attract a man. Usually, she was more interested in keeping them at a distance.

"Not tonight," she said. "*Not* tonight."

She padded downstairs, peering out the window and seeing nothing beyond the truck parked at the small house across the way and a vast stretch of snow, falling harder and faster.

Typically, it didn't snow in Copper Ridge, Oregon. You had to drive up to the mountains—as she'd done today—to get any of the white stuff. So, for her, this was a treat, albeit a chilly one. But that was perfect, since she planned to get her blood all heated and stuff.

She hummed, keeping an eye on the scene outside, waiting for Christopher to pull in. She wondered if she should have brought a condom downstairs with her. Decided that she should have.

She went back upstairs, taking them two at a time, grateful that she was by herself, since there was nothing sexy about her ascent. Then she rifled through her bag, found some protection and curled her fingers around it before heading back down the stairs as quickly as possible.

As soon as she entered the living area, the lights flickered, then died. Suddenly, everything in the house seemed unnaturally quiet, and even though it was probably her imagination, she felt the temperature drop several degrees.

"Are you kidding me?" she asked, into the darkness.

There was no answer. Nothing but a subtle creak from the house. Maybe it was all that heavy snow on the roof. Maybe it was going to collapse. That would figure.

A punishment for her thinking she could be normal and have sex.

A shiver worked its way down her spine, and she jolted.

Suddenly, she had gone from hopeful and buoyant to feeling a bit flat and tragic. That was definitely not the best sign.

No. She wasn't doing this. She wasn't sinking into self-pity and tragedy. Been there, done that for ten years, thank you.

Madison didn't believe in signs. *So there.* She believed in fuses blowing in bad weather when overtaxed heaters had to work too hard in ancient houses. Yes, *that* she believed in. She also believed that she would have to wait for Christopher to arrive to fix the problem.

She sighed and then made her way over to the kitchen counter and grabbed hold of her purse as she deposited the two condoms on the counter. She pulled her phone out and grimaced when she saw that she had no signal.

Too late, she remembered that she had thought the lack of cell service might be an attraction to a place like this. That it would be nice if both she and Christopher could be cut off from the outside world while they indulged themselves.

That notion seemed really freaking stupid right now. Since she couldn't use the phone in the house thanks to the outage, and that left her cut off from the outside world all alone.

"Oh no," she said, "I'm the first five minutes of a crime show. I'm going to get ax-murdered. And I'm going to die a born-again virgin."

She scowled, looking back out at the resolutely blank landscape. Christopher still wasn't here. But it looked like the house across the way had power.

She pressed her lips together, not happy about the idea of interrupting her neighbor. Or of meeting her neighbor, since the whole point of going out of town was so they could remain anonymous and not see people.

She tightened the belt on her coat and made her way slowly out the front door, bracing herself against the arctic wind.

She muttered darkly about the cold as she made her

way across the space between the houses. She paused for a moment in front of the larger cabin, lit up and looking all warm and toasty. Clearly, this was the premium accommodation. While hers was likely beset by rodents that had chewed through relevant cords.

She huffed, clutching her coat tightly as she knocked on the door. She waited, bouncing in place to try to keep her blood flowing. She just needed to call Christopher and find out when he would be arriving and, if he was still a ways out, possibly beg her neighbor for help getting the power going. Or at least help getting a fire started.

The front door swung open and Madison's heart stopped. The man standing there was large, so tall that she only just came up to the middle of his chest. He was broad, his shoulders well muscled, his waist trim. He had the kind of body that came not from working out but from hard physical labor.

Then she looked up. Straight nose, square jaw, short brown hair and dark eyes that were even harder than his muscles. And far too familiar.

"What are *you* doing here?"

Sam McCormack gritted his teeth against the sharp tug of irritation that assaulted him when Madison West asked the question that had been on his own lips.

"I rented the place," he responded, not inviting her in. "Though I could ask you the same question."

She continued to do a little bounce in place, her arms folded tight against her body, her hands clasped beneath her chin. "And you'd get the same answer," she said. "I'm across the driveway."

"Then you're at the wrong door." He made a move to shut said door, and she reached out, stopping him.

"Sam. Do you always have to be this unpleasant?"

It was a question that had been asked of him more than once. And he gave his standard answer. "Yes."

"*Sam,*" she said, sounding exasperated. "The power went out, and I'm freezing to death. Can I come in?"

He let out a long-suffering sigh and stepped to the side. He didn't like Madison West. He never had. Not from the moment he had been hired on as a farrier for the West estate eight years earlier. In all the years since he'd first met Madison, since he'd first started shoeing her horses, he'd never received one polite word from her.

But then, he'd never given one either.

She was sleek, blonde and freezing cold—and he didn't mean because she had just come in from the storm. The woman carried her own little snow cloud right above her head at all times, and he wasn't a fan of ice princesses. Still, something about her had always been like a burr beneath his skin that he couldn't get at.

"Thank you," she said crisply, stepping over the threshold.

"You're rich and pretty," he said, shutting the door tight behind her. "And I'm poor. And kind of an ass. It wouldn't do for me to let you die out there in a snowdrift. I would probably end up getting hung."

Madison sniffed, making a show of brushing snowflakes from the shoulders of her jacket. "I highly doubt you're poor," she said drily.

She wasn't wrong. A lot had changed since he'd gone to work for the Wests eight years ago. Hell, a lot had changed in the past year.

The strangest thing was that his art had taken off, and along with it the metalwork and blacksmithing business he ran with his brother, Chase.

But now he was busier coming up with actual fine-art pieces than he was doing daily grunt work. One sale on a piece like that could set them up for the entire quarter. Strange, and not where he'd seen his life going, but true.

He still had trouble defining himself as an artist. In his mind, he was just a blacksmith cowboy. Most at home on the family ranch, most proficient at pounding metal into another shape. It just so happened that for some reason people wanted to spend a lot of money on that metal.

"Well," he said, "perception is everything."

She looked up at him, those blue eyes hitting him hard, like a punch in the gut. That was the other obnoxious thing about Madison West. She was pretty. She was more than pretty. She was the kind of pretty that kept a man up all night, hard and aching, with fantasies about her swirling in his head.

She was also the kind of woman who would probably leave icicles on a man's member after a blow job.

No, thank you.

"Sure," she said, waving her hand. "Now, I *perceive* that I need to use your phone."

"There's no cell service up here."

"Landline," she said. "I have no power. And no cell service. The source of all my problems."

"In that case, be my guest," he responded, turning away from her and walking toward the kitchen, where the lone phone was plugged in.

He picked up the receiver and held it out to her. She eyed it for a moment as though it were a live snake, then snatched it out of his hand. "Are you just going to stand there?"

He shrugged, crossing his arms and leaning against the doorframe. "I thought I might."

She scoffed, then dialed the number, doing the same impatient hop she'd been doing outside while she waited for the person on the other end to answer. "Christopher?"

The physical response Sam felt to her uttering another man's name was not something he ever could have anticipated. His stomach tightened, dropped, and a lick of flame that felt a hell of a lot like jealousy sparked inside him.

"What do you mean you can't get up here?" She looked away from him, determinedly so, her eyes fixed on the kitchen floor. "The road is closed. Okay. So that means I can't get back down either?" There was a pause. "Right. Well, hopefully I don't freeze to death." Another pause. "No, you don't need to call anybody. I'm not going to freeze to death. I'm using the neighbor's phone. Just forget it. I don't have cell service. I'll call you if the power comes back on in my cabin."

She hung up then, her expression so sharp it could have cut him clean through.

"I take it you had plans."

She looked at him, her eyes as frosty as the weather outside. "Did you figure that out all by yourself?"

"Only just barely. You know blacksmiths aren't known for their deductive reasoning skills. Mostly we're famous for hitting heavy things with other heavy things."

"Kind of like cavemen and rocks."

He took a step toward her. "Kind of."

She shrank back, a hint of color bleeding into her cheeks. "Well, now that we've established that there's basically no difference between you and a Neanderthal, I better get back to my dark, empty cabin. And hope that you aren't a secret serial killer."

Her sharp tongue left cuts behind, and he had to admit he kind of enjoyed it. There weren't very many people who sparred with him like this. Possibly because he didn't talk to very many people. "Is that a legitimate concern you have?"

"I don't know. The entire situation is just crazy enough that I might be trapped in a horror movie with a tortured artist blacksmith who is also secretly murdery."

"I guarantee you I'm not murdery. If you see me outside with an ax, it will only be because I'm cutting firewood."

She cocked her head to the side, a glint in her blue eyes that didn't look like ice making his stomach—and everything south of there—tighten. "Well, that's a relief. Anyway. I'm going. Dark cabin, no one waiting for me. It promises to be a seriously good time."

"You don't have any idea why the power is out, or how to fix it?" he asked.

"No," she said, sounding exasperated, and about thirty seconds away from stamping her foot.

Well, damn his conscience, but he wasn't letting her go back to an empty, dark, cold cabin. No matter that she had always treated him like a bit of muck she'd stepped in with her handmade riding boots.

"Let me have a look at your fuse box," he said.

"You sound like you'd rather die," she said.

"I pretty much would, but I'm not going to let *you* die either." He reached for his black jacket and the matching black cowboy hat hanging on a hook. He put both on and nodded.

"Thank you," she muttered, and he could tell the little bit of social nicety directed at him cost her dearly.

They headed toward the front door and he pushed it open, waiting for her to go out first. Since he had arrived earlier today, the temperature had dropped drastically. He had come up to the mountain to do some planning for his next few art projects. It pained him to admit, even to himself, that solitude was somewhat necessary for him to get a clear handle on what he was going to work on next.

"So," he said, making conversation not so much for the sake of it but more to needle her and see if he could earn one of her patented death glares, "Christopher, huh? Your boyfriend?" That hot spike drove its way through his gut again and he did his best to ignore it.

"No," she said tersely. "Just a friend."

"I see. So you decided to meet a man up here for a friendly game of Twister?"

She turned slightly, arching one pale brow. "Yahtzee, actually. I'm very good at it."

"And I'm sure your...*friend* was hoping to get a full house."

She rolled her eyes and looked forward again, taking quick steps over the icy ground, and somehow managing to keep sure footing. Then she opened the door to her cabin. "Welcome," she said, extending her arm. "Please excuse the shuddering cold and oppressive darkness."

"Ladies first," he said.

She shook her head, walking into the house, and he followed behind, closing the door against the elements. It was already cold in the dark little room. "You were just going to come back here and sit in the dark if I hadn't offered to fiddle with the circuit breaker?"

"Maybe I know how to break my own circuits, Sam. Did you ever think of that?"

"Oh, but you said you didn't, Madison."

"I prefer Maddy," she said.

"Sorry, Madison," he said, tipping his hat, just to be a jerk.

"I should have just frozen to death. Then there could have been a legend about my tragic and beautiful demise in the mountains." He didn't say anything. He just looked at her until she sighed and continued talking. "I don't know where the box thingy is. You're going to have to hunt for it."

"I think I can handle that." He walked deeper into the kitchen, then stopped when he saw two purple packets sitting on the kitchen counter. That heat returned with a vengeance when he realized exactly what they were, and what they meant. He looked up, his eyes meeting her extremely guilty gaze. "Yahtzee, huh?"

"That's what the kids call it," she said, pressing her palm over the telling packets.

"Only because they're too immature to call it fucking."

Color washed up her neck, into her cheeks. "Or not crass enough."

In that moment, he had no idea what devil possessed him, and he didn't particularly care. He turned to face her, planting his hands on the countertop, just an inch away from hers. "I don't know about that. I'm betting that you could use a little crassness in your life, Madison West."

"Are you trying to suggest that I need *you*?" she asked, her voice choked.

Lightning streaked through his blood, and in that moment, he was lost. It didn't matter that he thought she was insufferable, a prissy little princess who didn't appreciate any damn thing she had. It didn't matter that he'd come up here to work.

All that mattered was he hadn't touched a woman in a long time, and Madison West was so close all he would have to do was shift his weight slightly and he'd be able to take her into his arms.

He looked down pointedly at her hand, acting as though he could see straight through to the protection beneath. "Well," he said, "you have a couple of the essential ingredients to have yourself a pretty fun evening. All you seem to be missing is the man. But I imagine the guy you invited up here is *nice*. I'm not very nice, Madison," he said, leaning in, "but I could damn sure show you a good time."

Chapter 2

The absolute worst thing was the fact that Sam's words sent a shiver down her spine. Sam McCormack. Why did it have to be Sam McCormack? He was the deadly serpent to her Indiana Jones.

She should throw him out. Throw him out and get back to her very disappointing evening where all orgasms would be self-administered. So, basically a regular Friday night.

She wanted to throw herself on the ground and wail. It was not supposed to be a regular Friday night. She was supposed to be breaking her sex fast. Maybe this was why people had flings in the spring. Inclement weather made winter flings difficult. Also, mostly you just wanted to keep your socks on the whole time. And that wasn't sexy.

Maybe her libido should hibernate for a while. Pop up again when the pear trees were blooming or something.

She looked over at Sam, and her libido made a dash to the foreground. That was the problem with Sam. He irritated her. He was exactly the kind of man she didn't like. He was cocky. He was rough and crude.

Whenever she'd given him very helpful pointers about handling the horses when he came to do farrier work at the estate, he was always telling her to go away and in general showing no deference.

And okay, if he'd come and told her how to do her job, she would have told him where he could stick his hoof nippers. But still. Her animals. So she was entitled to her opinions.

Last time she'd walked into the barn when he was doing shoes, he hadn't even looked up from his work. He'd just pointed back toward the door and shouted, *out!*

Yeah, he was a jerk.

However, there was something about the way he looked in a tight T-shirt, his muscles bulging as he did all that hard labor, that made a mockery of that very certain hatred she felt burning in her breast.

"Are you going to take off your coat and stay awhile?" The question, asked in a faintly mocking tone, sent a dart of tension straight down between her thighs.

She could *not* take off her coat. Because she was wearing nothing more than a little scrap of red lace underneath it. And now that was all she could think of. About how little stood between Sam and her naked body.

About what might happen if she just went ahead and dropped the coat now and revealed all of that to him.

"It's cold," she snapped. "Maybe if you went to work getting the electricity back on rather than standing there making terrible double entendres, I would be able to take off my coat."

He lifted a brow. "And then do you think you'll take me up on my offer to show you a good time?"

"If you can get my electricity back on, I will consider a good time shown to me. Honestly, that's all I want. The ability to microwave popcorn and not turn into a Maddycicle."

The maddening man raised his eyebrows, shooting her a look that clearly said *Suit yourself*, then set about looking for the fuse box.

She stood by alone for a while, her arms wrapped around her midsection. Then she started to feel like an idiot just kind of hanging out there while he searched for the source of all power. She let out an exasperated sigh and followed his path, stopping when she saw him leaning up against a wall, a little metal door fixed between the logs open as he examined the small black switches inside.

"It's not a fuse. That means there's something else going on." He slammed the door shut. Then he turned back to look at her. "You should come over to my cabin."

"No!" The denial was a little bit too enthusiastic. A little bit too telling. "I mean, I can start a fire here—it's going to be fine. I'm not going to freeze."

"You're going to curl up by the fire with a blanket? Like a sad little pet?"

She made a scoffing sound. "No, I'm going to curl up by the fire like the Little Match Girl."

"That makes it even worse. The Little Match Girl froze to death."

"What?"

"How did you not know that?"

"I saw it when I was a kid. It was a *cartoon*. She really died?" Maddy blinked. "What kind of story is that to present to children?"

"An early lesson, maybe? Life is bleak, and then you freeze to death alone?"

"Charming," she said.

"Life rarely is." He kept looking at her. His dark gaze was worrisome.

"I'm fine," she said, because somebody had to say something.

"You are not. Get your suitcase—come over to the cabin. We can flip the lights on, and then if we notice from across the driveway that your power's on again, you can always come back."

It was stupid to refuse him. She knew him, if not personally, at least well enough to know that he wasn't any kind of danger to her.

The alternative was trying to sleep on the couch in the living room while the outside temperatures hovered below freezing, waking up every few hours to keep the fire stoked.

Definitely, going over to his cabin made more sense. But the idea filled her with a strange tension that she couldn't quite shake. Well, she knew exactly what kind of tension it was. *Sexual tension.*

She and Sam had so much of it that hung between them like a fog whenever they interacted. Although, maybe she read it wrong. Maybe on his end it was just irritation and it wasn't at all tinged with sensual shame.

"Why do you have to be so damned reasonable?" she asked, turning away from him and stalking toward the stairs.

"Where are you going?"

She stopped, turning to face him. "To change. Also, to get my suitcase. I have snacks in there."

"Are snacks a euphemism for something interesting?" he asked, arching a dark brow.

She sputtered, genuinely speechless. Which was unusual to downright unheard of. "No," she said, her tone sounding petulant. "I have *actual snacks*."

"Come over to my place. Bring the snacks."

"I will," she said, turning on her heel, heading toward the stairs.

"Maybe bring the Yahtzee too."

Those words hit her hard, with all the impact of a stomach punch. She could feel her face turning crimson, and she refused to look back at him. Refused to react to that bait at all. He didn't want *that*. He did not want to play euphemistic board games with her. And she didn't want to play them with him.

If she felt a little bit…on edge, it was just because she had been anticipating sex and she had experienced profound sex disappointment. That was all.

She continued up the stairs, making her way to the bedroom, then changed back into a pair of jeans and a sweatshirt as quickly as possible before stuffing the little red lace thing back in the bag and zipping everything up.

She lugged it back downstairs, her heart slamming against her breastbone when Sam was in her line of sight again. Tall, broad shouldered and far too sexy for his own good, he promised to be the antidote to sexual disappointment.

But an emotionless hookup with a guy she liked well enough but wouldn't get emotionally involved with was one thing. Replacing him at the last moment with a guy she didn't even like? No, that was out of the question.

Absolutely and completely out of the question.

"Okay," she said, "let's go."

By the time she got settled in the extra room in the cabin, she was feeling antsy. She could hide, but she was hungry. And Maddy didn't believe in being hungry when food was at hand. Yes, she had some various sugar-based items in her bag, but she needed protein.

In the past, she had braved any number of her father's awkward soirees to gain access to bacon-wrapped appetizers.

She could brave Sam McCormack well enough to root around for sustenance. She would allow no man to stand between herself and her dinner.

Cautiously, she made her way downstairs, hoping that maybe Sam had put himself away for the night. The thought made her smile. That he didn't go to bed like a normal person but closed himself inside…not a coffin. But maybe a scratchy, rock-hewn box that would provide no warmth or comfort. It seemed like something he would be into.

In fairness, she didn't really know Sam McCormack that well, but everything she did know about him led her to believe that he was a supremely unpleasant person. Well, except for the whole him-not-letting-her-die-of-frostbite-in-her-powerless-cabin thing. She supposed she had to go ahead and put that in the Maybe He's Not Such a Jackass column.

Her foot hit the ground after the last stair silently, and she cautiously padded into the kitchen.

"Looking for something?"

She startled, turning around and seeing Sam standing there, leaning in the doorway, his muscular arms crossed over his broad chest. She did her best to look cool. Composed. Not interested in his muscles. "Well—" she tucked her hair behind her ear "—I was hoping to find some food."

"You brought snacks," he said.

"Candy," she countered.

"So, that made it okay for you to come downstairs and steal my steak?"

Her stomach growled. "You have steak?"

"It's *my* steak."

She hadn't really thought of that. "Well, my...you know, *the guy*. He was supposed to bring food. And I'm sorry. I didn't exactly think about the fact that whatever food is in this fridge is food that you personally provided. I was protein blind." She did her best to look plaintive. Unsurprisingly, Sam did not seem moved by her plaintiveness.

"I mean, it seems cruel to eat steak in front of you, Madison. Especially if I'm not willing to share." He rubbed his chin, the sounds of his whiskers abrading his palm sending a little shiver down her back. God knew why.

"You *would* do that. You would... You would tease me with your steak." Suddenly, it was all starting to sound a little bit sexual. Which she had a feeling was due in part to the fact that everything felt sexual to her right about now.

Which was because of the other man she had been about to sleep with. Not Sam. Not really.

A slow smile crossed his face. "I would never tease you with my steak, Madison. If you want a taste, all you have to do is ask. Nicely."

She felt her face getting hotter. "May I please have your steak?"

"Are you going to cook it for me?"

"Did you want it to be edible?"

"That would be the goal, yes," he responded.

She lifted her hands up, palms out. "These hands don't cook."

His expression shifted. A glint of wickedness cutting through all that hardness. She'd known Sam was mean.

She'd known he was rough. She had not realized he was wicked. "What do those hands do, I wonder?"

He let that innuendo linger between them and she practically hissed in response. "Do you have salad? I will fix salad. *You* cook steak. Then we can eat."

"Works for me, but I assume you're going to be sharing your candy with me?"

Seriously, everything sounded filthy. She had to get a handle on herself. "Maybe," she said, "but it depends on if your behavior merits candy." That didn't make it better.

"I see. And what, pray tell, does Madison West consider candy-deserving behavior?"

She shrugged, making her way to the fridge and opening it, bending down and opening the crisper drawer. "I don't know. Not being completely unbearable?"

"Your standards are low."

"Luckily for you."

She looked up at him and saw that that had actually elicited what looked to be a genuine grin. The man was a mystery. And she shouldn't care about that. She should not want to unlock, unravel or otherwise solve him.

The great thing about Christopher was that he was simple. He wasn't connected to her life in any way. They could come up and have an affair and it would never bleed over to her existence in Copper Ridge. It was the antithesis of everything she had experienced with David. David, who had blown up her entire life, shattered her career ambitions and damaged her good standing in the community.

This thing with Christopher was supposed to be sex. Sex that made nary a ripple in the rest of her life.

Sam would not be rippleless.

The McCormack family was too much a part of the

fabric of Copper Ridge. More so in the past year. Sam and his brother, Chase, had done an amazing job of revitalizing their family ranch, and somewhere in all of that Sam had become an in-demand artist. Though he would be the last person to say it. He still showed up right on schedule to do the farrier work at her family ranch. As though he weren't raking in way more money with his ironwork.

Sam was… Well, he was kind of everywhere. His works of art appearing in restaurants and galleries around town. His person appearing on the family ranch to work on the horses. He was the exact wrong kind of man for her to be fantasizing about.

She should be more gun-shy than this. Actually, she had spent the past decade being more gun-shy than this. It was just that apparently now that she had allowed herself to remember she had sexual feelings, it was difficult for her to turn them off. Especially when she was trapped in a snowstorm with a man for whom the term *rock-hard body* would be a mere description and not hyperbole.

She produced the salad, then set about to preparing it. Thankfully, it was washed and torn already. So her responsibility literally consisted of dumping it from bag to bowl. That was the kind of cooking she could get behind. Meanwhile, Sam busied himself with preparing two steaks on the stovetop. At some point, he took the pan from the stovetop and transferred it to the oven.

"I didn't know you had actual cooking technique," she said, not even pretending to herself that she wasn't watching the play of his muscles in his forearms as he worked.

Even at the West Ranch, where she always ended up sniping at him if they ever interacted, she tended to linger around him while he did his work with the horses because his arms put on quite a show. She was hardly going to turn away from him now that they were in an enclosed space, with said arms very, very close. And no one else around to witness her ogling.

She just didn't possess that kind of willpower.

"Well, Madison, I have a lot of eating technique. The two are compatible."

"Right," she said, "as you don't have a wife. Or a girl-friend…" She could have punched her own face for that. It sounded so leading and obvious. As if she cared if he had a woman in his life.

She didn't. Well, she kind of did. Because honestly, she didn't even like to ogle men who could be involved with another woman. Once bitten, twice shy. By which she meant once caught in a torrid extramarital affair with a man in good standing in the equestrian community, ten years emotionally scarred.

"No," he said, tilting his head, the cocky look in his eye doing strange things to her stomach, "I don't."

"I don't have a boyfriend. Not an actual boyfriend." Oh, good Lord. She was the desperate worst and she hated herself.

"So you keep saying," he returned. "You really want to make sure I know Christopher isn't your boyfriend." She couldn't ignore the implication in his tone.

"Because he isn't. Because we're not… Because we've never. This was going to be our first time." Being forth-right and making people uncomfortable with said forth-rightness had been a very handy shield for the past decade, but tonight it was really obnoxious.

"Oh really?" He suddenly looked extremely interested.

"Yes," she responded, keeping her tone crisp, refusing

to show him just how off-kilter she felt. "I'm just making dinner conversation."

"This is the kind of dinner conversation you normally make?"

She arched her brow. "Actually, yes. Shocking people is kind of my modus operandi."

"I don't find you that shocking, Madison. I do find it a little bit amusing that you got cock-blocked by a snowbank."

She nearly choked. "Wine. Do you have wine?" She turned and started rummaging through the nearest cabinet. "Of course you do. You probably have a baguette too. That seems like something an artist would do. Set up here and drink wine and eat a baguette."

He laughed, a kind of short, dismissive sound. "Hate to disappoint you. But my artistic genius is fueled by Jack." He reached up, opening the cabinet nearest to his head, and pulled down a bottle of whiskey. "But I'm happy to share that too."

"You have diet soda?"

"Regular."

"My, this *is* a hedonistic experience. I'll have regular, then."

"Well, when a woman was expecting sex and doesn't get it, I suppose regular cola is poor consolation, but it is better than diet."

"Truer words were never spoken." She watched him while he set about to making a couple of mixed drinks for them. He handed one to her, and she lifted it in salute before taking a small sip. By then he was taking the steak out of the oven and setting it back on the stovetop.

"Perfect," he remarked when he cut one of the pieces of meat in half and gauged the color of the interior.

She frowned. "How did I never notice that you aren't horrible?"

He looked at her, his expression one of mock surprise. "Not horrible? You be careful throwing around compliments like that, missy. A man could get the wrong idea."

She rolled her eyes. "Right. I just mean, you're funny."

"How much of that whiskey have you had?"

"One sip. So it isn't even that." She eyeballed the food that he was now putting onto plates. "It might be the steak. I'm not going to lie to you."

"I'm comfortable with that."

He carried their plates to the table, and she took the lone bottle of ranch dressing out of the fridge and set it and her drink next to her plate. And then, somehow, she ended up sitting at a very nicely appointed dinner table with Sam McCormack, who was not the man she was supposed to be with tonight.

Maybe it was because of the liquored-up soda. Maybe it was neglected hormones losing their ever-loving minds in the presence of such a fine male specimen. Maybe it was just as simple as want. Maybe there was no justification for it at all. Except that Sam was actually beautiful. And she had always thought so, no matter how much he got under her skin.

That was the honest truth. It was why she found him so off-putting, why she had always found him so off-putting from the moment he had first walked onto the West Ranch property. Because he was the kind of man a woman could make a mistake with. And she had thought she was done making mistakes.

Now she was starting to wonder if a woman was entitled to one every decade.

Her safe mistake, the one who would lift out of her life, hadn't eventuated. And here in front of her was one that had the potential to be huge. But very, very good.

She wasn't so young anymore. She wasn't naive at all. When it came right down to it, she was hot for Sam. She had been for a long time.

She'd had so much caution for so long. So much hiding. So much *not doing*. Well, she was tired of that.

"I was very disappointed about Christopher not making it up here," she said, just as Sam was putting the last bite of steak into his mouth.

"Sure," he said.

"Very disappointed."

"Nobody likes blue balls, Maddy, even if they don't have testicles."

She forced a laugh through her constricted throat. "That's hilarious," she said.

He looked up at her slowly. "No," he said, "it wasn't."

She let out a long, slow breath. "Okay," she said, "it wasn't that funny. But here's the thing. The reason I was so looking forward to tonight is that I hadn't had sex with Christopher before. In fact, I haven't had sex with anyone in ten years. So. Maybe you could help me with that?"

Chapter 3

Sam was pretty sure he must be hallucinating. Because there was no way Madison West had just propositioned him. Especially not on the heels of admitting that it had been ten years since she'd had sex.

Hell, he was starting to think that *he* was the celibacy champion. But clearly, Maddy had him beat. Or she didn't, because there was no way in hell that she had actually said any of that.

"Are you drunk, Madison?" It was the first thing that came to mind, and it seemed like an important thing to figure out.

"After one Jack Daniel's and Coke? Absolutely not. I am a West, dammit. We can hold our liquor. I am... reckless, opportunistic and horny. A lot horny. I just... I need this. Sam, do you know what it's like to go *ten years* without doing something? It becomes a whole thing. Like, a whole big thing that starts to define you, even if it shouldn't. And you don't want anyone to know. Oh, my gosh, can you even imagine if my friends knew that it has been ten years since I have seen an actual...?" She took a deep breath, then forged on. "I'm rambling and I just *really* need this."

Sam felt like he had been hit over the head with a metric ton of iron. He had no idea how he was supposed to respond to this—the strangest of all propositions—from a woman who had professed to hate him only a few moments ago.

He had always thought Madison was a snob. A pain in his ass, even if she was a pretty pain in the ass. She was always looming around, looking down her nose at him while he did his work. As though only the aristocracy of Copper Ridge could possibly know how to do the lowly labor he was seeing to. Even if they hadn't the ability to do it themselves.

The kinds of people who professed to have strengths in "management." People who didn't know how to get their hands dirty.

He hated people like that. And he had never been a fan of Madison West.

He, Sam McCormack, should not be interested in taking her up on her offer. No, not in any way. However, Sam McCormack's dick was way more interested in it than he would've liked to admit.

Immediately, he was rock hard thinking about what it would be like to have her delicate, soft hands skimming over him. He had rough hands. Workman's hands. The kind of hands that a woman like Madison West had probably never felt against her rarefied flesh.

Hell, the fact that it had been ten years since she'd

gotten any made that even more likely. And damn if that didn't turn him on. It was kind of twisted, a little bit sick, but then, it was nothing short of what he expected from himself.

He was a lot of things. Good wasn't one of them.

Ready to explode after years of repressing his desires, after years of pushing said desire all down and pretending it wasn't there? He was that.

"I'm not actually sure you want this," he said, wondering what the hell he was doing. Giving her an out when he wanted to throw her down and make her his.

Maddy stood up, not about to be cowed by him. He should have known that she would take that as a challenge. Maybe he had known that. Maybe it was why he'd said it.

That sounded like him. That sounded a lot more like him than trying to do the honorable thing.

"You don't know what I want, Sam," she said, crossing the space between them, swaying her hips just a little bit more than she usually did.

He would be a damn liar if he said that he had never thought about what it might be like to grab hold of those hips and pull Maddy West up against him. To grind his hardness against her soft flesh and make her feel exactly what her snobby-rich-girl mouth did to him.

But just because he'd fantasized about it before, didn't mean he had ever anticipated doing it. It didn't mean that he should take her up on it now.

Still, the closer she got to him, the less likely it seemed that he was going to say no.

"I think that after ten years of celibacy a man could make the argument that you don't know what you want, Madison West."

Her eyes narrowed, glittering blue diamonds that looked like they could cut a man straight down to the bone. "I've always known what I wanted. I may not have always made the best decisions, but I was completely certain that I wanted them. At the time."

His lips tipped upward. "I'm just going to be another *at the time*, Maddy. Nothing else."

"That was the entire point of this weekend. For me to have something that didn't have consequences. For me to get a little bit of something for myself. Is that so wrong? Do I have to live a passionless existence because I made a mistake once? Am I going to question myself forever? I just need to… I need to rip the Band-Aid off."

"The Band-Aid?"

"The sex Band-Aid."

He nodded, pretending that he understood. "Okay."

"I want this," she said, her tone confident.

"Are you…suggesting…that I give you…sexual healing?"

She made a scoffing sound. "Don't make it sound cheesy. This is very serious. I would never joke about my sexual needs." She let out an exasperated sigh. "I'm doing this wrong. I'm just…"

Suddenly, she launched herself at him, wrapping her arms around his neck and pressing her lips against his. The moment she did it, it was like the strike of a hammer against hot iron. As rigid as he'd been before—in that moment, he bent. And easily.

Staying seated in the chair, he curved himself around Madison, wrapping his arms around her body, sliding his hands over her back, down to the sweet indent of her waist, farther still to the flare of those pretty hips. The hips he had thought about taking hold of so many times before.

There was no hesitation now. None at all. There was only this. Only her. Only the soft, intoxicating taste of her on his tongue. Sugar, Jack Daniel's and something that was entirely Maddy.

Too rich for his blood. Far too expensive for a man like him. It didn't matter what he became. Didn't matter how much money he had in his bank account, he would always be what he was. There was no escaping it. Nobody knew. Not really. Not the various women who had graced his bed over the years, not his brother, Chase.

Nobody knew Sam McCormack.

At least, nobody alive.

Neither, he thought, would Madison West. This wasn't about knowing anybody. This was just about satisfying a need. And he was simple enough to take her up on that.

He wedged his thigh up between her legs, pressing his palm down on her lower back, encouraging her to flex her hips in time with each stroke of his tongue. Encouraging her to satisfy that ache at the apex of her thighs.

Her head fell back, her skin flushed and satisfaction grabbed him by the throat, gripping him hard and strong. It would've surprised him if he hadn't suspected he was the sort of bastard who would get off on something like this.

Watching this beautiful, classy girl coming undone in his arms.

She was right. This weekend could be out of time. It could be a moment for them to indulge in things they would never normally allow themselves to have. The kinds of things that he had closed himself off from years ago.

Softness, warmth, touch.

He had denied himself all those things for years. Why not do this now? No one would know. No one would ever have to know. Maddy would see to that. She would never, no chance in hell, admit that she had gotten down and dirty with a man who was essentially a glorified blacksmith.

No way in hell.

That made them both safe. It made this safe. Well, as safe as fire this hot could be.

She bit his lip and he growled, pushing his hands up underneath the hem of her shirt, kissing her deeper as he let his fingertips roam to the line of her elegant spine, then tracing it upward until he found her bra, releasing it with ease, then dragging it and her top up over her head, leaving her naked from the waist up.

"I…" Her face was a bright shade of red. "I… I have lingerie. I wasn't going to…"

"I don't give a damn about your lingerie. I just want this." He lowered his head, sliding his tongue around the perimeter of one of her tightened nipples. "I want your skin." He closed his lips over that tight bud, sucking it in deep.

"I had a seduction plan," she said, her voice trembling. He wasn't entirely sure it was a protest, or even a complaint.

"You don't plan passion, baby," he said.

At least, he didn't. Because if he were thinking clearly, he would be putting her top back on and telling her to go back to her ice-cold cabin, where she would be safe.

"I do," she said, her teeth chattering in spite of the fact that it was very warm in the kitchen. "I plan everything."

"Not this. You're a dirty girl now, Madison West," he said, sliding his thumb over her damp nipple, moving it in a slow circle until she arched her back and cried out. "You were going to sleep with another man this weekend, and you replaced him so damn easily. With me. Doesn't even matter to you who you have. As long as you get a little bit. Is that how it is?"

She whimpered, biting her lip, rolling her hips against him.

"Good girl," he said, his gut tightening, his arousal so hard he was sure he was going to burst through the front of his jeans. "I like that. I like you being dirty for me."

He moved his hands then, curving his fingers around her midsection, his thumbs resting just beneath the swell of her breasts. She was so soft, so smooth, so petite and fragile. Everything he should never be allowed to put his hands on. But for some reason, instead of feeling a bolt of shame, he felt aroused. Hotter and harder than he could ever remember being. "You like that? My hands are rough. Maybe a little bit too rough for you."

"No," she said, and this time the protest was clear. "Not too rough for me at all."

He slid his hands down her back, taking a moment to really revel in how soft she was and how much different he must feel to her. She squirmed against him, and he took that as evidence that she really did like it.

That only made him hotter. Harder. More impatient.

"You didn't bring your damn candy and forget the condoms, did you?"

"No," she said, the denial coming quickly. "I brought the condoms."

"You always knew we would end up like this, didn't you?"

She looked away from him, and the way she refused to meet his eyes turned a throwaway game of a question into something deadly serious.

"Madison," he said, his voice hard. She still didn't look at him. He grabbed hold of her chin, redirecting her face so that she was forced to make eye contact with him. "You knew this would happen all along, didn't you?"

She still refused to answer him. Refused to speak.

"I think you did," he continued. "I think that's why you can never say a kind word to me. I think that's why you acted like a scalded cat every time I walked into the room. Because you knew it would end here. Because you wanted this. Because you wanted me."

Her expression turned even more mutinous.

"Madison," he said, a warning lacing through the word. "Don't play games with me. Or I'm not going to give you what you want. So you have to tell me. Tell me that you've always wanted me. You've always wanted my dirty hands on you. That's why you hate me so damn much, isn't it? Because you want me."

"I…"

"Madison," he said, his tone even more firm, "tell me—" he rubbed his hand over her nipple "—or I stop."

"I wanted you," she said, the admission rushed but clear all the same.

"More," he said, barely recognizing his own voice. "Tell me more."

It seemed essential suddenly, to know she'd wanted him. He didn't know why. He didn't care why.

"I've always wanted you. From the moment I first saw you. I knew that it would be like this. I knew that I would climb up into your lap and I would make a fool of myself

rubbing all over you like a cat. I knew that from the beginning. So I argued with you instead."

He felt a satisfied smile that curved his lips upward.
"Good girl." He lowered his hands, undoing the snap on
her jeans and drawing the zipper down slowly. "You just
made us both very happy." He moved his fingertips down
beneath the waistband of her panties, his breath catching
in his throat when he felt hot wetness beneath his touch.
It had been way too long since he felt a silky-smooth de-
sirable woman. Had been way too long in his self-imposed prison.

Too long since he'd wanted at all.

But Madison wasn't Elizabeth. And this wasn't the
same.

He didn't need to think about her. He wasn't going to.
Not for the rest of the night.

He pushed every thought out of his mind and instead
exulted in the sound that Madison made when he moved
his fingers over that place where she was wet and aching
for him. When he delved deeper, pushing one finger inside
her, feeling just how close she was to the edge, evidenced
by the way her internal muscles clenched around him. He
could thrust into her here. Take her hard and fast and she
would still come. He knew that she would.

But she'd had ten years of celibacy, and he was pushing on five. They deserved more. They deserved better.
At the very least they deserved a damn bed.

With that in mind, he wrapped his arms more tightly
around her, moving his hands to cup her behind as he
lifted her, wrapping her legs tightly around him as he carried them across the kitchen and toward the stairs.

Maddy let out an inelegant squeak as he began to ascend toward the bedrooms. "This is really happening," she said, sounding slightly dazed.

"I thought you said you weren't drunk."

"I'm not."

"Then try not to look so surprised. It's making me question things. And I don't want to question things. I just want you."

She shivered in his hold. "You're not like most men I know."

"Pretty boys with popped collars and pastel polo shirts? I must be a real disappointment."

"Obviously you aren't. Obviously I don't care about men in pastel polo shirts or I would've gotten laid any number of times in the past decade."

He pushed open the bedroom door, threw her down over the simply appointed bed that was far too small for the kind of acrobatics he wanted to get up to tonight. Then he stood back, admiring her, wearing nothing but those half-open jeans riding low on her hips, her stomach dipping in with each breath, her breasts thrust into greater prominence at the same time.

"Were you waiting for me?" He kept the words light, taunting, because he knew that she liked it.

She had always liked sparring with him. That was what they'd always done. Of course she would like it now. Of course he would like it now. Or maybe it had nothing to do with her. Maybe it had everything to do with the fact that he had years' worth of dirty in him that needed to be let out.

"Screw you," she said, pushing herself back farther up the mattress so that her head was resting on the pillow.

Then she put her hands behind her head, her blue gaze sharp. "Come on, cowboy. Get naked for me."

"Oh no, Maddy, you're not running the show."

"Ten years," she said, her gaze level with his. "Ten years, Sam. That's how long it's been since I've seen a naked man. And let me tell you, I have never seen a naked man like you." She held up a finger. "One man. One insipid man. He wasn't even that good."

"You haven't had sex for ten years and your last lover wasn't even good? I was sort of hoping that it had been so good you were waiting for your knees to stop shaking before you bothered to go out and get some again."

"If only. My knees never once shook. In fact, they're shaking harder now and you haven't even gotten out of those pants yet."

"You give good dirty talk."

She lifted a shoulder. "I'm good at talking. That's about the thing I'm best at."

"Oh, I hope not, baby. I hope that mouth is good for a lot of other things too."

He saw her breasts hitch. Her eyes growing round. Then he smiled, grabbing hold of the hem of his shirt and stripping it off over his head. Her reaction was more satisfying than he could've possibly anticipated. It'd been a long time since he'd seen a woman looking at him that way.

Sure, women checked him out. That happened all the time. But this was different. This was raw, open hunger. She wasn't bothering to hide it. Why would she? They were both here to do this. No holds barred, no clothes, no nothing. Why bother to be coy? Why bother to pretend this was about anything other than satisfying lust. And if that was all it was, why should either of them bother to hide that lust.

"Keep looking at me like that, sweetheart, this is gonna end fast."

"Don't do that," she said, a wicked smile on her lips. "You're no good to me in that case."

"Don't worry, babe. I can get it up more than once."

At least, he could if he remembered correctly.

"Good thing I brought about three boxes of condoms."

"For two days? You did have high hopes for the weekend."

"Ten years," she reiterated.

"Point taken."

He moved his hands down, slowly working at his belt. The way that she licked her lips as her eyes followed his every movement ratcheting up his arousal another impossible notch.

Everything felt too sharp, too clear, every rasp of fabric over his skin, every downward flick of her eyes, every small, near-imperceptible gasp on her lips.

He hadn't been in a bedroom alone with a woman in a long damn time. And it was all catching up with him now.

Shutting down, being a mean bastard who didn't let anyone close? That was easy enough. It made it easy to forget. He shut the world out, stripped everything away. Reverted back to the way he had been just after his parents had died and it had been too difficult to feel anything more than his grief.

That was what he had done in the past five years. That was what he had done with his new, impossible loss that never should have happened. Wouldn't have if he'd had a shred of self-control and decency.

And now, tonight, he was proving that he probably still didn't have any at all. Oh well, just as well. Because he was going to do this.

He was going to do her.

He pushed his jeans down his lean hips, showing her the extent of his desire for her, reveling in the way her eyes widened when he revealed his body completely to her hungry gaze.

"I have never seen one that big before," she said.

He laughed. "Are you just saying that because it's what you think men need to hear?"

"No, I'm saying that because it's the biggest I've ever seen. And I want it."

"Baby," he said, "you can have it."

Maddy turned over onto her stomach and crawled across the bed on all fours in a move that damn near gave him a heart attack. Then she moved to the edge of the mattress, straightening up, raking her nails down over his torso before she leaned in, flicking her tongue over the head of his arousal.

He jerked beneath her touch, his length twitching as her tongue traced it from base to tip, just before she engulfed him completely in the warm heat of her mouth. She hummed, the vibration moving through his body, drawing his balls up tight. He really was going to lose it. Here and now like a green teenage boy if he didn't get a grip on himself. Or a grip on her.

He settled for the second option.

He reached back, grabbing hold of her hair and jerking her lips away from him. "You keep doing that and it really will end."

The color was high in her cheeks, her eyes glittering. "I've never, ever enjoyed it like that before."

She was so good for his ego. Way better than a man like him deserved. But damned if he wasn't going to take it.

"Well, you can enjoy more of that. Later. Right now? I need to be inside you."

"Technically," she said, her tone one of protest, "you were inside me."

"And as much as I like being in that pretty mouth of yours, that isn't what I want right now." He gritted his teeth, looking around the room. "The condoms."

She scrambled off the bed and shimmied out of her jeans and panties as she made her way across the room and toward her suitcase. She flipped it open, dug through it frantically and produced the two packets he had seen earlier.

All things considered, he felt a little bit triumphant to be the one getting these condoms. He didn't know Christopher, but that sad sack was sitting at home with a hardon, and Sam was having his woman. He was going to go ahead and enjoy the hell out of that.

Madison turned to face him, the sight of that enticing, pale triangle at the apex of her thighs sending a shot straight down to his gut. She kept her eyes on his as she moved nearer, holding one of the condoms like it was a reward he was about to receive.

She tore it open and settled back onto the bed, then leaned forward and rolled it over his length. Then she took her position back up against the pillows, her thighs parting, her heavily lidded gaze averted from his now that she was in that vulnerable position.

"Okay," she said, "I'm ready."

She wasn't. Not by a long shot.

Ten years.

And he had been ready to thrust into her with absolutely no finesse. A woman who'd been celibate for ten years deserved more than that. She deserved more than one orgasm. Hell, she deserved more than two.

He had never been the biggest fan of Madison West, but tonight they were allies. Allies in pleasure. And he was going to hold up his end of the bargain so well that if she was celibate after this, it really would be because she was waiting for her legs to work again.

"Not quite yet, Maddy," he said, kneeling down at the end of the bed, reaching forward and grabbing hold of her hips, dragging her down toward his face. He brought her up against his mouth, her legs thrown over his shoulders, that place where she was warm and wet for him right there, ready for him to taste her.

"Sam!" Maddy squeaked.

"There is no way you're a prude, Maddy," he said. "I've had too many conversations with you to believe that."

"I've never… No one has ever…"

"Then it's time somebody did."

He lowered his head, tasting her in long, slow passes, like she was an ice-cream cone that he just had to take the time to savor. Like she was a delicacy he couldn't get enough of.

Because she was.

She was all warmth and sweet female, better than he had ever remembered a woman being. Or maybe she was just better. It was hard to say. He didn't really care which. It didn't matter. All that mattered was this.

If he could lose himself in any moment, in any time, it would be this one.

It sure as hell wouldn't be pounding iron, trying to hammer the guilt out of his body. Certainly wouldn't be in his damn sculptures, trying to figure out what to make next, trying to figure out how to satisfy the customer. This deeply personal thing that had started being given to the rest of the world, when he wasn't sure he wanted the rest of the world to see what was inside him.

Hell, *he* didn't want to see what was inside him.

He made a hell of a lot of money, carving himself out, making it into a product people could buy. And he sure as hell liked the money, but that didn't make it a pleasant experience.

No, none of that mattered. Not now. Not when there was Maddy. And that sweet sugar-whiskey taste.

He tasted her until she screamed, and then he thrust his fingers inside her, fast and rough, until he felt her pulse around him, until her orgasm swept through them both.

Then he moved up, his lips almost touching hers. "Now," he said, his voice husky, "now you're ready."

Chapter 4

Maddy was shaking from head to toe, and she honestly didn't know if she could take any more. She had never—not in her entire life—had an orgasm like that. It was still echoing through her body, creating little waves of sensation that shivered through her with each and every breath she took.

And there was still more. They weren't done. She was glad about that. She didn't want to be done. But at the same time she wasn't sure if she could handle the rest. But there he was, above her, over her, so hot and hard and male that she didn't think she could deny him. She didn't want to deny him.

She looked at him, at the broad expanse of his shoulders and chest, the way it tapered down to his narrow waist, those flat washboard abs that she could probably actually wash her clothes on.

He was everything a man should be. If the perfect

fantasy man had been pulled straight out of her deepest fantasies, he would look like this. It hit her then that Christopher had not even been close to being a fantasy man. And that was maybe why he had been so safe. It was why Sam had always been so threatening.

Because Christopher had the power to make a ripple. Sam McCormack possessed the power to engulf her in a tidal wave.

She had no desire to be swept out to sea by any man. But in this instance she had a life preserver. And that was her general dislike of him. The fact that their time together was going to be contained to only this weekend. So what did it matter if she allowed herself to get a little bit storm tossed. It didn't. She was free. Free to enjoy this as much as she wanted.

And she wanted. *Wanted* with an endless hunger that seemed to growl inside her like a feral beast.

He possessed the equipment to satisfy it. She let her eyes drift lower than just his abs, taking in the heart, the unequivocal evidence, of his maleness. She had not been lying when she said it was the biggest one she'd ever seen. It made her feel a little bit intimidated. Especially since she had been celibate for so very long. But she had a few days to acclimate.

The thought made her giddy.

"Now," she said, not entirely certain that she was totally prepared for him now but also unable to wait for him.

"You sure you're ready for me?" He leaned forward, bracing his hand on the headboard, poised over her like the very embodiment of carnal temptation. Just out of reach, close enough that she did easily inhale his masculine scent. Far enough away that he wasn't giving her what she needed. Not yet.

She felt hollow. Aching. And that, she realized, was

how she knew she was going to take all of him whether or not it seemed possible. Because the only other option was remaining like this. Hollowed out and empty. And she couldn't stand that either. Not for one more second.

"Please," she said, not caring that she sounded plaintive. Not caring that she was begging. Begging Sam, the man she had spent the past several years harassing every time he came around her ranch.

No, she didn't care. She would make a fool out of herself if she had to, would lower herself as far down as she needed to go, if only she could get the kind of satisfaction that his body promised to deliver.

He moved his other hand up to the headboard, gripping it tight. Then he flexed his hips forward, the blunt head of his arousal teasing the slick entrance to her body. She reached up, bracing her palms flat against his chest, a shiver running through her as he teased her with near penetration.

She cursed. The sound quivering, weak in the near silence of the room. She had no idea where hard-ass Maddy had gone. That tough, flippant girl who knew how to keep everyone at a distance with her words. Who knew how to play off every situation as if it weren't a big deal.

This was a big deal. How could she pretend that it wasn't? She was breaking apart from the inside out; how could she act as though she weren't?

"Please," she repeated.

He let go of the headboard with one hand and pressed his hand down next to her face, then repeated the motion with the other as he rocked his hips forward more fully, entering her slowly, inch by tantalizing inch. She gasped when he filled her all the way, the intense stretching sensation a pleasure more than it was a pain.

She slid her hands up to his shoulders, down his back, holding on to him tightly there before locking her legs around his lean hips and urging him even deeper.

"Yes," she breathed, a wave of satisfaction rolling over her, chased on the heels by a sense that she was still incomplete. That this wasn't enough. That it would never be enough.

Then he began to move. Ratcheting up the tension between them. Taking her need, her arousal, to greater heights than she had ever imagined possible. He was measured at first, taking care to establish a rhythm that helped her move closer to completion. But she didn't need the help. She didn't want it. She just wanted to ride the storm.

She tilted her head to the side, scraping her teeth along the tendon in his neck that stood out as a testament to his hard-won self-control.

And that did it.

He growled low in his throat. Then his movements became hard, harsh. Following no particular rhythm but his own. She loved it. Gloried in it. He grabbed hold of her hips, tugging her up against him every time he thrust down, making it rougher, making it deeper. Making it hurt. She felt full with it, full with him. This was exactly what she needed, and she hadn't even realized it. To be utterly and completely overwhelmed. To have this man consume her every sensation, her every breath.

She fused her lips to his, kissing him frantically as he continued to move inside her and she held on to him tighter, her nails digging into his skin. But she knew he didn't mind the pain. She knew it just as she didn't mind it. Knew it because he began to move harder, faster, reaching the edge of his own control as he pushed her nearer to the edge of hers.

Suddenly, it gripped her fiercely, down low inside her, a force of pleasure that she couldn't deny or control. She froze, stiffening against him, the scream that lodged itself in her throat the very opposite of who she usually was. It wasn't calculated; it wasn't pretty; it wasn't designed to do anything. It simply was. An expression of what she felt. Beyond her reach, beyond her completely.

She was racked with her desire for him, with the intensity of the orgasm that swept through her. And then, just as she was beginning to find a way to breathe again, he found his own release, his hardness pulsing deep inside her as he gave himself up to it.

His release—the intensity of it—sent another shattering wave through her. And she clung to him even more tightly, needing him to anchor her to the bed, to the earth, or she would lose herself completely.

And then in the aftermath, she was left there, clinging to a stranger, having just shown the deepest, most hidden parts of herself to him. Having just lost her control with him in a way she never would have done with someone she knew better. Perhaps this was the only way she could have ever experienced this kind of freedom. The only way she could have ever let her guard down enough. What did she have to lose with Sam? His opinion of her was already low. So if he thought that she was a sex-hungry maniac after this, what did it matter?

He moved away from her and she threw her arm over her face, letting her head fall back, the sound of her fractured breathing echoing in the room.

After she had gulped in a few gasps of air, she removed her arm, opened her eyes and realized that Sam wasn't in the room anymore. Probably off to the bathroom to deal with necessities. Good. She needed some space. She needed a moment. At least a few breaths.

He returned a little bit quicker than she had hoped he might, all long lean muscle and satisfied male. It was the expression on his face that began to ease the tension in her chest. He didn't look angry. He didn't look like he was judging her. And he didn't look like he was in love with her or was about to start making promises that she didn't want him to make.

No, he just looked satisfied. A bone-deep satisfaction that she felt too.

"Holy hell," he said, coming to lie on the bed next to her, drawing her naked body up against his. She felt a smile curve her lips. "I think you about blew my head off."

"You're so romantic," she said, smiling even wider. Because this was perfect. Absolutely perfect.

"You don't want me to be romantic," he returned.

"No," she said, feeling happy, buoyant even. "I sure as hell don't."

"You want me to be bad, and dirty, and to be your every fantasy of slumming it with a man who is so very beneath you."

That, she took affront to a little bit. "I don't think you're beneath me, Sam," she said. Then he grabbed hold of her hips and lifted her up off the mattress before bringing her down over his body. A wicked smile crossed his face.

"I am now."

"You're insatiable. And terrible."

"For a weekend fling, honey, that's all you really need."

"Oh, dammit," she said, "what if the roads open up, and Christopher tries to come up?"

"I'm not really into threesomes." He tightened his grip on her. "And I'm not into sharing."

"No worries. I don't have any desire to broaden my experience by testing him out."

"Have I ruined you for him?"

The cocky bastard. She wanted to tell him no, but she had a feeling that denting the masculine ego when a man was underneath you wasn't the best idea if you wanted to have sex with said man again.

"Ruined me completely," she responded. "In fact, I should leave a message for him."

Sam snagged the phone on the nightstand and thrust it at her. "You can leave him a message now."

"Okay," she said, grimacing slightly.

She picked up the phone and dialed Christopher's number quickly. Praying that she got his voice mail and not his actual voice.

Of course, if she did, that meant he'd gone out. Which meant that maybe he was trying to find sex to replace the sex that he'd lost. Which she had done; she couldn't really be annoyed about that. But she had baggage.

"Come on," she muttered as the phone rang endlessly. Then she breathed a sigh of relief when she got his voice mail. "Hi, Christopher, it's Madison. Don't worry about coming up here if the roads clear up. If that happens, I'm probably just going to go back to Copper Ridge. The weekend is kind of ruined. And…and maybe you should just wait for me to call you?" She looked up at Sam, who was nearly vibrating with forcibly contained laughter. She rolled her eyes. "Anyway, sorry that this didn't work out. Bye."

"That was terrible," he said. "But I think you made it pretty clear that you don't want to hear from him."

"I said I would call him," she said in protestation.

"Are you going to?"

"*Hell* no."

Sam chuckled, rolling her back underneath him, kissing her deep, hard. "Good thing I only want a weekend."

"Why is that?"

"God help the man that wants more from you."

"Oh, please, that's not fair." She wiggled, luxuriating in the hard feel of him between her thighs. He wanted her again already. "I pity the woman that falls for you, Sam McCormack."

A shadow passed over his face. "So do I."

Then, as quickly as they had appeared, those clouds cleared and he was smiling again, that wicked, intense smile that let her know he was about ready to take her to heaven again.

"It's a good thing both of us only want a weekend."

Chapter 5

"How did the art retreat go?"

Sam gritted his teeth against his younger brother's questioning as Chase walked into their workshop. "Fine," he returned.

"Fine?" Chase leaned against the doorframe, crossing his arms, looking a little too much like Sam for his own comfort. Because he was a bastard, and he didn't want to see his bastard face looking back at him. "I thought you were going to get inspiration. To come up with the ideas that will keep the McCormack Ranch flush for the next several years."

"I'm not a machine," Sam said, keeping his tone hard. "You can't force art."

He said things like that, in that tone, because he knew that no one would believe that cliché phrase, even if it was true. He didn't like that it was true.

But there wasn't much he was willing to do about it either.

"Sure. And I feel a slight amount of guilt over pressuring you, but since I do a lot of managing of your career, I consider it a part of my job."

"Stick to pounding iron, Chase—that's where your talents lie."

"I don't have talent," Chase said. "I have business sense. Which you don't have. So you should be thankful for me."

"You say that. You say it a lot. I think mostly because you know that I actually shouldn't be all that thankful for your meddling."

He was being irritable, and he knew it. But he didn't want Chase asking how the weekend was. He didn't want to explain the way he had spent his time. And he really didn't want to get into why the only thing he was inspired to do was start painting nudes.

Of one woman in particular.

Because the only kind of grand inspirational moments he'd had were when he was inside Maddy. Yeah, he wasn't going to explain that to his younger brother. He was never going to tell anybody. And he had to get his shit together.

"Seriously, though, everything is going okay? Anna is worried about you."

"Your wife is meddlesome. I liked her better when she was just your friend and all she did was come by for pizza a couple times a week. And she didn't worry too much about what I was doing or whether or not I was happy."

"Yeah, sadly for you she has decided she loves me. And by extension she has decided she loves you, which means her getting up in your business. I don't think she knows another way to be."

"Tell her to go pull apart a tractor and stop digging around in my life."

"No, thanks, I like my balls where they are. Which means I will not be telling Anna what to do. Ever."

"I liked it better when you were miserable and alone."

Chase laughed. "Why, because you're miserable and alone?"

"No, that would imply that I'm uncomfortable with the state of things. I myself am quite dedicated to my solitude and my misery."

"They say misery loves company," Chase said.

"Only true if you aren't a hermit."

"I suppose that's true." His brother looked at him, his gaze far too perceptive for Sam's liking. "You didn't used to be this terrible."

"I have been for a while." But worse with Maddy. She pushed at him. At things and needs and desires that were best left in the past.

He gritted his teeth. She pushed at him because he turned her on and that made her mad. He... Well, it was complicated.

"Yes," Chase said. "For a while."

"Don't psychoanalyze me. Maybe it's a crazy artist thing. Dad always said that it would make me a pussy."

"You aren't a pussy. You're a jerk."

"Six of one, half dozen of the other. Either way, I have issues."

Chase shook his head. "Well, deal with them on your own time. You have to be over at the West Ranch in less than an hour." Chase shook his head. "Pretty soon we'll be released from the contract. But you know until then we could always hire somebody else to go. You don't have to do horseshoes if you don't want. We're kind of beyond that now."

Sam gritted his teeth. For the first time he was actually tempted to take his brother up on the offer. To replace his position with someone else. Mostly because the idea of seeing Madison again filled him with the kind of reckless tension that he knew he wouldn't be able to do anything about once he saw her again.

Oh, not because of her. Not because of anything to do with her moral code or protestations. He could demolish those easily enough. It was because he couldn't afford to waste any more time thinking about her. Because he couldn't afford to get in any deeper. What had happened over the past weekend had been good. Damn good. But he had to leave it there.

Normally, he relished the idea of getting in there and doing grunt work. There was something about it that fulfilled him. Chase might not understand that.

But Sam wasn't a paperwork man. He wasn't a business mind. He needed physical exertion to keep himself going.

His lips twitched as he thought about the kind of physical exertion he had indulged in with Maddy. Yeah, it kind of all made sense. Why he had thrown himself into the blacksmithing thing during his celibacy. He needed to pound something, one way or another. And since he had been so intent on denying himself female companionship, he had picked up a hammer instead.

He was tempted to back out. To make sure he kept his distance from Maddy. He wouldn't, because he was also far too tempted to go. Too tempted to test his control and see if there was a weak link. If he might end up with her underneath him again.

It would be the better thing to send Chase. Or to call in and say they would have to reschedule, then hire somebody else to take over that kind of work. They could more than afford it. But as much as he wanted to avoid Maddy, he wanted to see her again.

Just because.

His body began to harden just thinking about it.

"It's fine. I'm going to head over. You know that I like physical labor."

"I just don't understand why," Chase said, looking genuinely mystified.

But hell, Chase had a life. A wife. Things that Sam was never going to have. Chase had worked through his stuff and made them both a hell of a lot of money, and Sam was happy for him. As happy as he ever got.

"You don't need to understand me. You just have to keep me organized so that I don't end up out on the street."

"You would never end up out on the streets of Copper Ridge. Mostly because if you stood out there with a cardboard sign, some well-meaning elderly woman would wrap you in a blanket and take you back to her house for casserole. And you would rather die. We both know that."

That made Sam smile reluctantly. "True enough."

"So, I guess you better keep working, then."

Sam thought about Maddy again, about her sweet, supple curves. About how seeing her again was going to test him in the best way possible. Perhaps that was why he should go. Just so he could test himself. Push up against his control. Yeah, maybe that was what he needed.

Yeah, that justification worked well. And it meant he would see her again.

It wasn't feelings. It was just sex. And he was starting to think just sex might be what he needed.

"I plan on it."

Maddy took a deep breath of clean salt air and arena dirt. There was something comforting about it. Familiar. Whenever things had gone wrong in her life, this was what she could count on. The familiar sights and sounds of the ranch, her horses. Herself.

She never felt stronger than when she was on the back of a horse, working in time with the animal to move from a trot to a walk, a walk to a halt. She never felt more understood.

A funny thing. Because, while she knew she was an excellent trainer and she had full confidence in her ability to keep control over the animal, she knew that she would never have absolute control. Animals were unpredictable. Always.

One day, they could simply decide they didn't want to deal with you and buck you off. It was the risk that every person who worked with large beasts took. And they took it on gladly.

She liked that juxtaposition. The control, the danger. The fact that though she achieved a certain level of mastery with each horse she worked with, they could still decide they weren't going to behave on a given day.

She had never felt much of that in the rest of her life. Often she felt like she was fighting against so much. Having something like this, something that made her feel both small and powerful had been essential to her well-being. Especially during all that crap that had happened ten years ago. She had been thinking more about it lately. Honestly, it had all started because of Christopher, because she had been considering breaking her celibacy. And it had only gotten worse after she actually had. After Sam.

Mostly because she couldn't stop thinking about him. Mostly because she felt like one weekend could never be enough. And she needed it to be. She badly needed it to be. She needed to be able to have sex with a guy without having lingering feelings for him. David had really done a number on her, and she did not want another number done on her.

It was for the best if she never saw Sam again. She knew that was unlikely, but it would be better. She let out a deep breath, walking into the barn, her riding boots making a strident sound on the hardpacked dirt as she walked in. Then she saw movement toward the end of the barn, someone coming out of one of the stalls.

She froze. It wasn't uncommon for there to be other people around. Her family employed a full staff to keep the ranch running smoothly, but for some reason this felt different. And a couple of seconds later, as the person came into view, she realized why.

Black cowboy hat, broad shoulders, muscular forearms. That lean waist and hips. That built, muscular physique that she was intimately acquainted with.

Dear Lord. Sam McCormack was here.

She had known that there would be some compromise on the never-seeing-him-again thing; she had just hoped that it wouldn't be seeing him now.

"Sam," she said, because she would be damned if she appeared like she had been caught unawares. "I didn't expect you to be here."

"Your father wanted to make sure that all of the horses

were in good shape before the holidays, since it was going to delay my next visit."

Maddy gritted her teeth. Christmas was in a couple of weeks, which meant her family would be having their annual party. The festivities had started to become a bit threadbare and brittle in recent years. Now that everybody knew Nathan West had been forced to sell off all of his properties downtown. Now that everyone knew he had a bastard son, Jack Monaghan, whose existence Nathan had tried to deny for more than thirty years. Yes, now that everybody had seen the cracks in the gleaming West family foundation, it all seemed farcical to Maddy.

But then, seeing as she had been one of the first major cracks in the foundation, she supposed that she wasn't really entitled to be too judgmental about it. However, she was starting to feel a bit exhausted.

"Right," she returned, knowing that her voice sounded dull.

"Have you seen Christopher?"

His question caught her off guard, as did his tone, which sounded a bit hard and possessive. It was funny, because this taciturn man in front of her was more what she had considered Sam to be before they had spent those days in the cabin together. Those days—where they had mostly been naked—had been a lot easier. Quieter. He had smiled more. But then, she supposed that any man receiving an endless supply of orgasms was prone to smiling more. They had barely gotten out of bed.

They had both been more than a little bit insatiable, and Maddy hadn't minded that at all. But this was a harsh slap back to reality. To a time that could almost have been before their little rendezvous but clearly wasn't, because his line of questioning was tinged with jealousy.

"No. As you guessed, I lied to him and didn't call him."

"And he call you?'"

Maddy lifted her fingernail and began to chew on it, grimacing when she realized she had just ruined her manicure. "He did call," she said, her face heating slightly. "And I changed his name in my phone book to Don't Answer."

"Why did you do that?"

"Obviously you can't delete somebody from your phone book when you don't want to talk to them, Sam. You have to make sure that you know who's calling. But I like the reminder that I'm not speaking to him. Because then my phone rings and the screen says Don't Answer, and then I go, 'Okay.'"

"I really do pity the man who ends up wanting to chase after you."

"Good thing you don't. Except, oh wait, you're here."

She regretted that as soon as she said it. His gaze darkened, his eyes sweeping over her figure. Why did she want to push him?

Why did she always want to push him?

"You know why I'm here."

"Yes, because my daddy pays you to be here." She didn't know why she said that. To reinforce the difference between them? To remind him she was Lady of the Manor, and that regardless of his bank balance he was socially beneath her? To make herself look like a stupid rich girl he wouldn't want to mess around with anyway. Honestly, these days it was difficult for her to guess at her own motives.

"Is this all part of your fantasy? You want to be…taken by the stable boy or something? I mean, it's a nice one, Maddy, and I didn't really mind acting it out with you last weekend, but we both know that I'm not exactly the stable boy and you're not exactly the breathless virgin."

Heat streaked through her face, rage pooling in her stomach. "Right. Because I'm not some pure, snow-white virgin, my fantasies are somehow wrong?" It was too close to that wound. The one she wished wasn't there. The one she couldn't ignore, no matter how much she tried.

"That wasn't the point I was making. And anyway, when your whole fantasy about a man centers around him being bad for you, I'm not exactly sure where you get off trying to take the moral-outrage route."

"I will be as morally outraged as I please," she snapped, turning to walk away from him.

He reached out, grabbing hold of her arm and turning her back to face him, taking hold of her other arm and pulling her forward. "Everything was supposed to stay back up at those cabins," he said, his voice rough.

"So why aren't you letting it?" she spat. Reckless. Shaky. She was a hypocrite. Because she wasn't letting it rest either.

"Because you walked in in those tight pants and it made it a lot harder for me to think."

"My breeches," she said, keeping the words sharp and crisp as a green apple, "are not typically the sort of garment that inspire men to fits of uncontrollable lust." Except *she* was drowning in a fit of uncontrollable lust. His gaze was hot, his hands on her arms even hotter. She wanted to arch against him, to press her breasts against his chest as she had done more times than she could count when they had been together. She wanted… She wanted the impossible. She wanted more. More of him. More of everything they had shared together, even though they had agreed that would be a bad idea.

Even though she knew it was something she shouldn't even want.

"Your pretty little ass in anything would make a man lose his mind. Don't tell me those breeches put any man off, or I'm gonna have to call you a liar."

"It isn't my breeches that put them off. That's just my personality."

"If some man can't handle you being a little bit hard, then he's no kind of man. I can take you, baby. I can take all of you. And that's good, since we both know you can take all of me."

"Are you just going to be a tease, Sam?" she asked, echoing back a phrase that had been uttered to her by many men over the years. "Or is this leading somewhere?"

"You don't want it to lead anywhere, you said so yourself." He released his hold on her, taking a step back.

"You're contrary, Sam McCormack—do you know that?"

He laughed. "That's about the only thing anyone calls me. We both know what I am. The only thing that confuses me is exactly why you seem surprised by it now."

She was kind of stumped by that question. Because really, the only answer was sex. That she had imagined that the two of them being together, that the man he had been during that time, meant something.

Which proved that she really hadn't learned anything about sexual relationships, in spite of the fact that she had been so badly wounded by one in the past. She had always known that she had a hard head, but really, this was ridiculous.

But it wasn't just her head that was hard. She had hardened up a considerable amount in the years since her relationship with David. Because she'd had to. Because within the equestrian community, she had spent the years following that affair known as the skank who had seriously jeopardized the marriage of an upright member of the community. Never mind that she had been his student. Never mind that she had been seventeen years old, a virgin who had believed every word that had come out of the esteemed older man's mouth. Who had believed that his marriage really was over and that he wanted a life and a future with her.

It was laughable to her now. Any man nearing his forties who found himself able to relate to a seventeen-year-old on an emotional level was a little bit suspect. A married one, in a position of power, was even worse. She knew all of that. She knew it down to her bones. Believing it was another thing.

So sometimes her judgment was in doubt. Sometimes she felt like an idiot. But she was much more equipped to deal with difficult situations now. She was a lot pricklier. A lot more inured.

And that was what came to her defense now.

"Sam, if you still want me, all you have to do is say it. Don't you stand there growling because you're hard and sexually frustrated and we both agreed that it would only be that one weekend. Just be a man and admit it."

"Are you sure you should be talking to me like that here? Anyone can catch us. If I backed you up against that wall and kissed your smart mouth, then people would know. Doesn't it make you feel dirty? Doesn't it make you feel ashamed?" His words lashed at her, made her feel all of those things but also aroused her. She had no idea what was wrong with her. Except that maybe part of it was that she simply didn't know how to feel desire without feeling ashamed. Another gift from her one and only love affair.

"You're the one that's saying all of this. Not me," she said, keeping her voice steely. She lifted a shoulder. "If I didn't know better, I would say you have issues. I don't want to help you work those out." A sudden rush of heat took over, a reckless thought that she had no business having, that she really should work to get a handle on. But she didn't.

She took a deep breath. "I don't have any desire to help you with your issues, but if you're horny, I can help you with that."

"What the hell?"

"You heard me," she said, crossing her arms and giving him her toughest air. "If you want me, then have me."

Sam could hardly believe what he was hearing. Yet again, Madison West was propositioning him. And this time, he was pissed off. Because he wasn't a dog that she could bring to heel whenever she wanted to. He wasn't the kind of man who could be manipulated.

Even worse, he wanted her. He wanted to say yes. And he wasn't sure he could spite his dick to soothe his pride.

"You can't just come in here and start playing games with me," he said. "I'm not a dog that you can call whenever you want me to come."

He let the double meaning of that statement sit between them. "That isn't what I'm doing," she said, her tone waspish.

"Then what are you doing, Madison? We agreed that it would be one weekend. And then you come in here sniping at me, and suddenly you're propositioning me. I gave in to all of this when you asked the first time, because I'm a man. And I'm not going to say no in a situation like the one we were in. But I'm also not the kind of man you can manipulate."

Color rose high in her cheeks. "I'm not trying to manipulate you. Why is it that men are always accusing me of that?"

"Because no man likes to be turned on and then left waiting," he returned.

The color in her cheeks darkened, and then she turned on one boot heel and walked quickly away from him.

He moved after her, reaching out and grabbing hold of her arm, stopping her. "What? Now you're going to go?"

"I can't do this. I can't do this if you're going to wrap all of it up in accusations and shame. I've been there. I've done it, Sam, and I'm not doing it again. Trust me. I've been accused of a lot of things. I've had my fill of it. So, great, you don't want to be manipulated. I don't want to be the one that has to leave this affair feeling guilty."

Sam frowned. "That's not what I meant."

She was the one who was being unreasonable, blowing hot and cold on him. How was it that he had been the one to be made to feel guilty? He didn't like that. He didn't like feeling anything but irritation and desire for her. He certainly didn't want to feel any guilt.

He didn't want to feel any damn thing.

"Well, what did you mean? Am I a tease, Sam? Is that what I am? And men like you just can't help themselves?"

He took a step back. "No," he said. "But you do have to make a decision. Either you want this, or you don't."

"Or?"

"Or nothing," he said, his tone hard. "If you don't want it, you don't want it. I'm not going to coerce you into anything. But I don't do the hot-and-cold thing."

Of course, he didn't really do any kind of thing anymore. But this, this back and forth, reminded him too much of his interaction with Elizabeth. Actually, all of it reminded him a little bit too much of Elizabeth. This seemingly soft, sweet woman with a bit of an edge. Someone who was high-class and a little bit luxurious. Who felt like a break from his life on the ranch. His life of rough work and solitude.

But after too much back and forth, it had ended. And he didn't speak to her for months. Until he had gotten a call that he needed to go to the hospital.

He gritted his teeth, looking at Madison. He couldn't imagine anything with Madison ending quite that way, not simply because he refused to ever lose his control the way he had done with Elizabeth, but also because he couldn't imagine Maddy slinking off in silence. She might go hot and cold, but she would never do it quietly.

"Twelve days. There are twelve days until Christmas. That's what I want. Twelve days to get myself on the naughty list. So to speak." She leveled her blue gaze with his. "If you don't want to oblige me, I'm sure Christopher will. But I would much rather it be you."

"Why?" He might want this, but he would be damned if

he would make it easy for her. Mostly because he wanted to make it a little harder on himself.

"Because I planned to go up to that cabin and have sex with Christopher. I had to, like, come up with a plan. A series of tactical maneuvers that would help me make the decision to get it over with after all that time. You," she said, gesturing at him, "you, I didn't plan to have anything happen with. Ever. But I couldn't stop myself. I think at the end of the day it's much better to carry on a sex-only affair with a man that you can't control yourself with. Like right now. I was not going to proposition you today, Sam. I promise. Not today, not ever again. In fact, I'm mad at you, so it should be really easy for me to walk away. But I don't want to. I want you. I want you even if it's a terrible idea."

He looked around, then took her arm again, dragging her into one of the empty stalls, where they would be out of sight if anyone walked into the barn. Then he pressed her against the wall, gripping her chin and taking her mouth in a deep, searing kiss. She whimpered, arching against him, grabbing hold of his shoulders and widening her stance so that he could press his hardened length against where she was soft and sensitive, ready for him already.

He slid his hand down her back, not caring that the hard wall bit into his knuckles as he grabbed hold of her rear, barely covered by those riding pants, which ought to have been illegal.

She whimpered, wiggling against him, obviously trying to get some satisfaction for the ache inside her. He knew that she felt it, because he felt the same way. He wrenched his mouth away from hers. "Dammit," he said, "I have to get back to work."

"Do you really?" She looked up at him, her expression

so desperate it was nearly comical. Except he felt too desperate to laugh.

"Yes," he said.

"Well, since my family owns the property, I feel like I can give you permission to—"

He held up a hand. "I'm going to stop you right there. Nobody gives me permission to do anything. If I didn't want to finish the day's work, I wouldn't. I don't need the money. That's not why I do this. It's my reputation. My pride. I'm contracted to do it, and I will do what I promised I would. But when the contract is up? I won't."

"Oh," she said. "I didn't realize that."

"Everything is going well with the art business." At least, it would if he could think of something else to do. He supposed he could always do more animals and cowboys. People never got tired of that. They had been his most popular art installations so far.

"Great. That's great. Maybe you could…not press yourself up against me? Because I'm going to do something really stupid in a minute."

He did not comply with her request; instead, he kept her there, held up against the wall. "What's that?"

She frowned. "Something I shouldn't do in a public place."

"You're not exactly enticing me to let you go." His body was so hard he was pretty sure he was going to turn to stone.

"I'll bite you."

"Still not enticed."

"Are you telling me that you want to get bitten?"

He rolled his hips forward, let her feel exactly what she was doing to him. "Biting can be all part of the fun."

"I have some things to learn," she said, her blue eyes widening.

"I'm happy to teach them to you," he said, wavering on whether or not he would finish what they'd started here. "Where should I meet you tonight?"

"Here," she said, the word rushed.

"Are you sure? I live on the same property as Chase, but in different houses. We are close, but not that close."

"No, I have my own place here too. And there's always a lot of cars. It won't look weird. I just don't want anyone to see me…" She looked away from him. "I don't want to advertise."

"That's fine." It suited him to keep everyone in the dark too. He didn't want the kind of attention that would come with being associated with Madison West. Already, the attention that he got for the various art projects he did, for the different displays around town, was a little much for him.

It was an impossible situation for him, as always. He wanted things that seemed destined to require more of himself than he wanted to give. Things that seemed to need him to reach deep, when it was better if he never did. Yet he seemed to choose them. Women like Madison. A career like art.

Someday he would examine that. Not today.

"Okay," she said, "come over after it's dark."

"This is like a covert operation."

"Is that a problem?"

It really wasn't. It was hypocritical of him to pretend otherwise. Hell, his last relationship—the one with Elizabeth—had been conducted almost entirely in secrecy because he had been going out of town to see her. That had been her choice, because she knew her association with him would be an issue for her family.

And, as he already established, he didn't really want anyone to know about this thing with Maddy either. Still, sneaking around felt contrary to his nature too. In general, he didn't really care what people thought about him. Or about his decisions.

You're a liar.

He gritted his teeth. Everything with Elizabeth was its own exception. There was no point talking to anyone about it. No point getting into that terrible thing he had been a part of. The terrible thing he had caused.

"Not a problem," he said. "I'll see you in a few hours."

"I can cook," she said as he turned to walk out of the stall.

"You don't have to. I can grab something on my way."

"No, I would rather we had dinner."

He frowned. "Maddy," he began, "this isn't going to be a relationship. It can't be."

"I know," she said, looking up and away from him, swallowing hard. "But I need for it to be something a little more than just sex too. I just… Look, obviously you know that somebody that hasn't had a sexual partner in the past ten years has some baggage. I do. Shocking, I know, because I seem like a bastion of mental health. But I just don't like the feeling. I really don't."

His chest tightened. Part of him was tempted to ask her exactly what had happened. Why she had been celibate for so long. But then, if they began to trade stories about their pasts, she might want to know something about his. And he wasn't getting into that. Not now, not ever.

"Is there anything you don't like?"

"No," he said, "I'm easy. I thought you said you didn't cook?"

She shrugged a shoulder. "Okay, if I'm being completely honest, I have a set of frozen meals in my freezer that my parents' housekeeper makes for me. But I can heat up a double portion so we can eat together."

He shook his head. "Okay."

"I have pot roast, meat loaf and roast chicken."

"I'll tell you what. The only thing I want is to have your body for dessert. I'll let you go ahead and plan dinner."

"Pot roast it is," she said, her voice a borderline squeak.

He chuckled, turning and walking away from her, something shifting in his chest. He didn't know how she managed to do that. Make him feel heavier one moment, then lighter the next. It was dangerous. That's what it was. And if he had a brain in his head, he would walk away from her and never look back.

Sadly, his ability to think with his brain had long since ceased to function.

Even if it was a stupid idea, and he was fairly certain it was, he was going to come to Madison's house tonight, and he was going to have her in about every way he could think of.

He fixed his mouth into a grim line and set about finishing his work. But while he kept his face completely stoic, inside he felt anticipation for the first time in longer than he could remember.

Chapter 6

Maddy wondered if seductresses typically wore pearls. Probably pearls and nothing else. Maybe pearls and lace. Probably not high-waisted pencil skirts and cropped sweaters. But warming pot roast for Sam had put her in the mind-set of a 1950s housewife, and she had decided to go ahead and embrace the theme.

She caught a glimpse of her reflection in the mirror in the hall of her little house and she laughed at herself. She was wearing red lipstick, her blond hair pulled back into a bun. She rolled her eyes, then stuck out her tongue. Then continued on into the kitchen, her high heels clicking on the tile.

At least underneath the sweater, she had on a piece of pretty hot lingerie, if she said so herself. She knew Sam was big on the idea that seduction couldn't be planned, but Maddy did like to have a plan. It helped her feel more in control, and when it came to Sam, she had never felt more out of control.

She sighed, reaching up into the cupboard and taking out a bottle of wine that she had picked up at Grassroots Winery that afternoon. She might not be the best cook, or any kind of cook at all, but she knew how to pick a good wine. Everyone had their strengths.

The strange thing was she kind of enjoyed feeling out of control with Sam, but it also made her feel cautious. Protective. When she had met David, she had dived into the affair headlong. She hadn't thought at all. She had led entirely with her heart, and in the end, she had gotten her heart broken. More than that, the aftermath had shattered her entire world. She had lost friends; she had lost her standing within a community that had become dear to her... Everything.

"But you aren't seventeen. And Sam isn't a married douche bag." She spoke the words fiercely into the silence of the kitchen, buoyed by the reality of them.

She could lose a little bit of control with Sam. Even within that, there would be all of her years, her wisdom— such as it was—and her experience. She was never going to be the girl she had been. That was a good thing. She would never be able to be hurt like that, not again. She simply didn't possess the emotional capacity.

She had emerged Teflon coated. Everything slid off now.

There was a knock on her front door and she straightened, closing her eyes and taking a deep breath, trying to calm the fluttering in her stomach. That reminded her a bit too much of the past. Feeling all fluttery and breathless just because she was going to see the man she was fixated on. That felt a little too much like emotion.

No. It wasn't emotion. It was just anticipation. She was old enough now to tell the difference between the two things.

She went quickly to the door, suddenly feeling a little bit ridiculous as she pulled it open. When it was too late for her to do anything about it. Her feeling of ridiculousness only increased when she saw Sam standing there, wearing his typical black cowboy hat, tight T-shirt and well-fitted jeans. Of course, he didn't need to wear anything different to be hotter to her.

A cowboy hat would do it every time.

"Hi," she said, taking a step back and gesturing with her hand. "Come in."

He obliged, walking over the threshold and looking around the space. For some reason, she found herself looking at it through his eyes. Wondering what kinds of conclusions he would draw about the neat, spare environment.

She had lived out in the little guesthouse ever since she was nineteen. Needing a little bit of distance from her family but never exactly leaving. For the first time, that seemed a little bit weird to her. It had always just been her life. She worked on the ranch, so there didn't seem to be any point in leaving it.

Now she tried to imagine explaining it to someone else—to Sam—and she wondered if it was weird.

"My mother's interior decorator did the place," she said. "Except for the yellow and red." She had added little pops of color through throw pillows, vases and art on the wall. But otherwise the surroundings were predominantly white.

"Great," he said, clearly not interested at all.

It had felt weird, thinking about him judging her based on the space, thinking about him judging her circumstances. But it was even weirder to see that he wasn't even curious.

She supposed that was de rigueur for physical affairs. And that was what this was.

"Dinner is almost ready," she said, reminding them both of the nonphysical part of the evening. Now she felt ridiculous for suggesting that too. But the idea of meeting him in secret had reminded her way too much of David. Somehow, adding pot roast had seemed to make the whole thing aboveboard.

Pot roast was an extremely nonsalacious food.

"Great," he said, looking very much like he didn't actually care that much.

"I just have to get it out of the microwave." She treated him to an exaggerated wink.

That earned her an uneasy laugh. "Great," he said.

"Come on," she said, gesturing for him to follow her. She moved into the kitchen, grabbed the pan that contained the meat and the vegetables out of the microwave and set it on the table, where the place settings were already laid out and the salad was already waiting.

"I promise I'm not trying to Stepford-wife you," she said as they both took their seats.

"I didn't think that," he said, but his blank expression betrayed the fact that he was lying.

"You did," she said. "You thought that I was trying to become your creepy robot wife."

"No, but I did wonder exactly why dinner was so important."

She looked down. It wasn't as if David were a secret. In fact, the affair was basically open information. "Do you really want to know?"

Judging by the expression on his face, he didn't. "There isn't really a good way to answer that question."

"True. Honesty is probably not the best policy. I'll think you're uninterested in me."

"On the contrary, I'm very interested in you."

"Being interested in my boobs is not the same thing."

He laughed, taking a portion of pot roast out of the dish in the center of the table. "I'm going to eat. If you want to tell me…well, go ahead. But I don't think you're trying to ensnare me."

"You don't?"

"Honestly, Maddy, nobody would want me for that long."

Those words were spoken with a bit of humor, but they made her sad. "I'm sure that's not true," she said, even though she wasn't sure of any such thing. He was grumpy. And he wasn't the most adept emotionally. Still, it didn't seem like a very kind thing for a person to think about themselves.

"It is," he said. "Chase is only with me because he's stuck with me. He feels some kind of loyalty to our parents."

"I thought your parents…"

"They're dead," he responded, his tone flat.

"I'm sorry," she said.

"Me too."

Silence fell between them after that, and she knew the only way to break it was to go ahead and get it out. "The first guy…the one ten years ago, we were having a physical-only affair. Except I didn't know it."

"Ouch," Sam said.

"Very. I mean, trust me, there were plenty of signs. And even though he was outright lying to me about his intentions, if I had been a little bit older or more experienced, I would have known. It's a terrible thing to find out you're a cliché. I imagine you wouldn't know what that's like."

"No, not exactly. Artist-cowboy-blacksmith is not really a well-worn template."

She laughed and took a sip of her wine. "No, I guess not." Then she took another sip. She needed something to fortify her. Anything.

"But other woman that actually believes he'll leave his wife for you, that is." She swallowed hard, waiting for his face to change, waiting for him to call her a name, to get disgusted and walk out.

It occurred to her just then that that was why she was telling him all of this. Because she needed him to know. She needed him to know, and she needed to see what he would think. If he would still want her. Or if he would think that she was guilty beyond forgiving.

There were a lot of people who did.

But he didn't say anything. And his face didn't change. So they just sat in silence for a moment.

"When we got involved, he told me that he was done with her. That their marriage was a mess and they were already starting divorce proceedings. He said that he just wore his wedding ring to avoid awkward questions from their friends. The dressage community around here is pretty small, and he said that he and his wife were waiting until they could tell people themselves, personally, so that there were no rumors flying around." She laughed, almost because she was unable to help it. It was so ridiculous. She wanted to go back and shake seventeen-year-old her. For being such an idiot. For caring so much.

"Anyway," she continued, "he said he wanted to protect me. You know, because of how unkind people can be."

"He was married," Sam said.

She braced herself. "Yes," she returned, unflinching.

"How old were you?"

"Seventeen."

"How old was he?"

"Almost forty."

Sam cursed. "He should have been arrested."

"Maybe," she said, "except I did want him."

She had loved the attention he had given her. Had loved feeling special. It had been more than lust. It had been neediness. For all the approval she hadn't gotten in her life. Classic daddy issues, basically. But, as messed up as a man his age had to be for wanting to fool around with a teenager, the teenager had to be pretty screwed up too.

"How did you know him?"

"He was my… He was my trainer."

"Right, so some jackass in a position of power. Very surprising."

Warmth bloomed in her chest and spread outward, a strange, completely unfamiliar sensation. There were only a few people on earth who defended her when the subject came up. And mostly, they kept it from coming up. Sierra, her younger sister, knew about it only from the perspective of someone who had been younger at the time. Maddy had shared a little bit about it, about the breakup and how much it had messed with her, when Sierra was having difficulty in her own love life.

And then there were her brothers, Colton and Gage. Who would both have cheerfully killed David if they had ever been able to get their hands on him. But Sam was the first person she had ever told the whole story to. And he was the first person who wasn't one of her siblings who had jumped to her defense immediately.

There had been no interrogation about what kinds of clothes she'd worn to her lessons. About how she had behaved. Part of her wanted to revel in it. Another part of her wanted to push back at it.

"Well, I wore those breeches around him. I know they made you act a little bit crazy. Maybe it was my fault."

"Is this why you got mad about what I said earlier?"

She lifted a shoulder. "Well, that and it was mean."

"I didn't realize this had happened to you," he said, his voice not exactly tender but full of a whole lot more sympathy than she had ever imagined getting from him. "I'm sorry."

"The worst part was losing all my friends," she said, looking up at him. "Everybody really liked him. He was their favorite instructor. As far as dressage instructors go, he was young and cool, trust me."

"So you bore the brunt of it because he turned out to be human garbage and nobody wanted to face it?"

The way he phrased that, so matter-of-fact and real, made a bubble of humor well up inside her chest. "I guess so."

"That doesn't seem fair."

"It really doesn't."

"So that's why you had to feed me dinner, huh? So I didn't remind you of that guy?"

"Well, you're nothing like him. For starters, he was… much more diminutive."

Sam laughed. "You make it sound like you had an affair with a leprechaun."

"Jockeys aren't brawny, Sam."

He only laughed harder. "That's true. I suppose that causes trouble with wind resistance and things."

She rolled her eyes. "You are terrible. Obviously he had some appeal." Though, she had a feeling it wasn't entirely physical. Seeing as she had basically been seeking attention and approval and a thousand other things besides orgasms.

"Obviously. It was his breeches," Sam said.

"A good-looking man in breeches is a thing."

"I believe you."

"But a good-looking man in Wranglers is better." At least, that was her way of thinking right at the moment.

"Good to know."

"But you can see. Why I don't really want to advertise this. It has nothing to do with what you do or who you are or who I am. Well, I guess it is all to do with who I am. What people already think about me. I've been completely defined by a sex life I barely have. And that was… It was the smallest part of that betrayal. At least for me. I loved him. And he was just using me."

"I hope his life was hell after."

"No. His wife forgave him. He went on to compete in the Olympics. He won a silver medal."

"That's kind of a karmic letdown."

"You're telling me. Meanwhile, I've basically lived like

a nun and continued giving riding lessons here on the family ranch. I didn't go on to do any of the competing that I wanted to, because I couldn't throw a rock without hitting a judge who was going to be angry with me for my involvement with David."

"In my opinion," Sam said, his expression turning dark, focused, "people are far too concerned with who women sleep with and not near enough as concerned as they should be about whether or not the man does it well. Was he good?"

She felt her face heat. "Not like you."

"I don't care who you had sex with, how many times or who he was. What I do care is that I am the best you've ever had. I'm going to aim to make sure that's the case."

He reached across the table, grabbing hold of her hand. "I'm ready for dessert," he said.

"Me too," she said, pushing her plate back and moving to her feet. "Upstairs?"

He nodded once, the slow burn in his dark eyes searing through her. "Upstairs."

Chapter 7

"Well, it looks like everything is coming together for Dad's Christmas party," Sierra said brightly, looking down at the car seat next to her that contained a sleeping new-born. "Gage will be there, kind of a triumphant return, coming-out kind of thing."

Maddy's older brother shifted in his seat, his arms crossed over his broad chest. "You make me sound like a debutante having a coming-out ball."

"That would be a surprise," his girlfriend, Rebecca Bear, said, putting her hand over his.

"I didn't mean it that way," Sierra said, smiling, her slightly rounder post-childbirth cheeks making her look even younger than she usually did.

Maddy was having a difficult time concentrating. She had met her siblings early at The Grind, the most popular coffee shop in Copper Ridge, so that they could all get on the same page about the big West family soiree that would be thrown on Christmas Eve.

Maddy was ambivalent about it. Mostly she wanted to crawl back under the covers with Sam and burrow until winter passed. But they had agreed that it would go on only until Christmas. Which meant that not only was she dreading the party, it also marked the end of their blissful affair.

By the time Sam had left last night, it had been the next morning, just very early, the sun still inky black as he'd walked out of her house and to his truck.

She had wanted him to stay the entire night, and that was dangerous. She didn't need all that. Didn't need to be held by him, didn't need to wake up in his arms.

"Madison." The sound of her full name jerked her out of her fantasy. She looked up, to see that Colton had been addressing her.

"What?" she asked. "I zoned out for a minute. I haven't had all the caffeine I need yet." Mostly because she had barely slept. She had expected to go out like a light after Sam had left her, but that had not been the case. She had just sort of lay there feeling a little bit achy and lonely and wishing that she didn't.

"Just wondering how you were feeling about Jack coming. You know, now that the whole town knows that he's our half brother, it really is for the best if he comes. I've already talked to Dad about it, and he agrees."

"Great," she said, "and what about Mom?"

"I expect she'll go along with it. She always does. Anyway, Jack is a thirty-five-year-old sin. There's not much use holding it against him now."

"There never was," Maddy said, staring fixedly at her

disposable coffee cup, allowing the warm liquid inside to heat her fingertips. She felt like a hypocrite saying that. Mostly because there was something about Jack that was difficult for her.

Well, she knew what it was. The fact that he was evidence of an affair her father had had. The fact that her father was the sort of man who cheated on his wife.

That her father was the sort of man more able to identify with the man who had broken Maddy's heart than he was able to identify with Maddy herself.

But Jack had nothing to do with that. Not really. She knew that logically. He was a good man, married to a great woman, with an adorable baby she really *did* want in her life. It was just that sometimes it needled at her. Got under her skin.

"True enough," Colton said. If he noticed her unease, he certainly didn't betray that he did.

The idea of trying to survive through another West family party just about made her jump up from the coffee shop, run down Main Street and scamper under a rock. She just didn't know if she could do it. Stand there in a pretty dress trying to pretend that she was something the entire town knew she wasn't. Trying to pretend that she was anything other than a disappointment. That her whole family was anything other than tarnished.

Sam didn't feel that way. Not about her. Suddenly, she thought about standing there with him. Sam in a tux, warm and solid next to her...

She blinked, cutting off that line of thinking. There was no reason to be having those fantasies. What she and Sam had was not that. Whatever it was, it wasn't that.

"Then it's settled," Maddy said, a little bit too brightly. "Jack and his family will come to the party."

That sentence made another strange, hollow sensation echo through her. Jack would be there with his family. Sierra and Ace would be there together with their baby. Colton would be there with his wife, Lydia, and while they hadn't made it official yet, Gage and Rebecca were rarely anywhere without each other, and it was plain to anyone who had eyes that Rebecca had changed Gage in a profound way. That she was his support and he was hers.

It was just another way in which Maddy stood alone.

Wow, what a whiny, tragic thought. It wasn't like she wanted her siblings to have nothing. It wasn't like she wanted them to spend their lives alone. Of course she wanted them to have significant others. Maybe she would get around to having one too, eventually.

But it wouldn't be Sam. So she needed to stop having fantasies about him in that role. Naked fantasies. That was all she was allowed.

"Great," Sierra said, lifting up her coffee cup. "I'm going to go order a coffee for Ace and head back home. He's probably just now getting up. He worked closing at the bar last night and then got up to feed the baby. I owe him caffeine and my eternal devotion. But he will want me to lead with the caffeine." She waved and picked up the bucket seat, heading toward the counter.

"I have to go too," Colton said, leaning forward and kissing Maddy on the cheek. "See you later."

Gage nodded slowly, his dark gaze on Rebecca. She nodded, almost imperceptibly, and stood up. "I'm going to grab a refill," she said, making her way to the counter.

As soon as she was out of earshot, Gage turned his

focus to her, and Maddy knew that the refill was only a decoy.

"Are you okay?"

This question, coming from the brother she knew the least, the brother who had been out of her life for seventeen years before coming back into town almost two months ago, was strange. And yet in some ways it wasn't. She had felt, from the moment he had returned, that there was something similar in the two of them.

Something broken and strong that maybe the rest of them couldn't understand.

Since then, she had learned more about the circumstances behind his leaving. The accident that he had been involved in that had left Rebecca Bear scarred as a child. Much to Maddy's surprise, they now seemed to be in love.

Which, while she was happy for him, was also a little annoying. Rebecca was the woman he had damaged—however accidentally—and she could love him, while Maddy seemed to be some kind of remote island no one wanted to connect with.

If she took the Gage approach, she could throw hot coffee on the nearest handsome guy, wait a decade and a half and see if his feelings changed for her over time. However, she imagined that was somewhat unrealistic.

"I'm fine," she said brightly. "Always fine."

"Right. Except I'm used to you sounding dry with notes of sarcasm and today you've been overly peppy and sparkly like a Christmas angel, and I think we both know that isn't real."

"Well, the alternative is me complaining about how this time of year gets me a little bit down, and given the general mood around the table, that didn't seem to be the best idea."

"Right. Why don't you like this time of year?"

"I don't know, Gage. Think back to all the years you spent in solitude on the road. Then tell me how you felt about Christmas."

"At best, it didn't seem to matter much. At worst, it reminded me of when I was happy. When I was home with all of you. And when home felt like a happy place. That was the hardest part, Maddy. Being away and longing for a home I couldn't go back to. Because it didn't exist. Not really. After everything I found out about Dad, I knew it wouldn't ever feel the same."

Her throat tightened, emotion swamping her. She had always known that Gage was the one who would understand her. She had been right. Because no one had ever said quite so perfectly exactly what she felt inside, what she had felt ever since news of her dalliance with her dressage trainer had made its way back to Nathan West's ears.

"It's so strange that you put it that way," she said, "because that is exactly how it feels. I live at home. I never left. And I… I ache for something I can never have again. Even if it's just to see my parents in the way that I used to."

"You saw how it was with all of us sitting here," Gage said. "It's something that I never thought I would have. The fact that you've all been willing to forgive me, to let me back into your lives after I was gone for so long, changes the shape of things. We are the ones that can make it different. We can fix what happened with Jack— or move forward into fixing it. There's no reason you and I can't be fixed too, Maddy."

She nodded, her throat so tight she couldn't speak. She

stood, holding her coffee cup against her chest. "I am looking forward to seeing you at the Christmas party." Then she forced a smile and walked out of The Grind.

She took a deep breath of the freezing air, hoping that it might wash some of the stale feelings of sadness and grief right out of her body. Then she looked down Main Street, at all of the Christmas lights gilding the edges of the brick buildings like glimmering precious metal.

Christmas wreaths hung from every surface that would take them, velvet bows a crimson beacon against the intense green.

Copper Ridge at Christmas was beautiful, but walking around, she still felt a bit like a stranger, separate and somehow not a part of it all. Everyone here was so good. People like her and Gage had to leave when they got too bad. Except she hadn't left. She just hovered around the edges like a ghost, making inappropriate and sarcastic comments on demand so that no one would ever look at her too closely and see just what a mess she was.

She lowered her head, the wind whipping through her hair, over her cheeks, as she made her way down the street—the opposite direction of her car. She wasn't really sure what she was doing, only that she couldn't face heading back to the ranch right now. Not when she felt nostalgic for something that didn't exist anymore. When she felt raw from the conversation with Gage.

She kept going down Main, pausing at the front door of the Mercantile when she saw a display of Christmas candy sitting in the window. It made her smile to see it there, a sugary reminder of some old memory that wasn't tainted by reality.

She closed her eyes tight, and she remembered what it

was. Walking down the street with her father, who was always treated like he was a king then. She had been small, and it had been before Gage had left. Before she had ever disappointed anyone.

It was Christmastime, and carolers were milling around, and she had looked up and seen sugarplums and candy canes, little peppermint chocolates and other sweets in the window. He had taken her inside and allowed her to choose whatever she wanted.

A simple memory. A reminder of a time when things hadn't been quite so hard, or quite so real, between herself and Nathan West.

She found herself heading inside, in spite of the fact that the entire point of this walk had been to avoid memories. But then, she really wanted to avoid the memories that were at the ranch. This was different.

She opened the door, taking a deep breath of gingerbread and cloves upon entry. The narrow little store with exposed brick walls was packed with goodies. Cakes, cheeses and breads, imported and made locally.

Lane Jensen, the owner of the Mercantile, was standing toward the back of the store talking to somebody. Maddy didn't see another person right away, and then, when the broad figure came into view, her heart slammed against her breastbone.

When she realized it was Sam, she had to ask herself if she had been drawn down this way because of a sense of nostalgia or because something in her head sensed that he was around. That was silly. Of course she didn't *sense* his presence.

Though, given pheromones and all of that, maybe it wasn't too ridiculous. It certainly wasn't some kind of emotional crap. Not her heart recognizing where his was beating or some such nonsense.

For a split second she considered running the other direction. Before he saw her, before it got weird. But she hesitated, just for the space of a breath, and that was long enough for Sam to look past Lane, his eyes locking with hers.

She stood, frozen to the spot. "Hi," she said, knowing that she sounded awkward, knowing that she looked awkward.

She was unaccustomed to that. At least, these days. She had grown a tough outer shell, trained herself to never feel ashamed, to never feel embarrassed—not in a way that people would be able to see.

Because after her little scandal, she had always imagined that it was the only thing people thought about when they looked at her. Walking around, feeling like that, feeling like you had a scarlet *A* burned into your skin, it forced you to figure out a way to exist.

In her case it had meant cultivating a kind of brash persona. So, being caught like this, looking like a deer in the headlights—which was what she imagined she looked like right now, wide-eyed and trembling—it all felt a bit disorienting.

"Maddy," Sam said, "I wasn't expecting to see you here."

"That's because we didn't make any plans to meet here," she said. "I promise I didn't follow you." She looked over at Lane, who was studying them with great interest. "Not that I would. Because there's no reason for me to do that. Because you're the farrier for my horses. And that's it." She felt distinctly detached and light-headed, as though she might drift away on a cloud of embarrassment at a moment's notice.

"Right," he said. "Thank you, Lane," he said, turning his attention back to the other woman. "I can bring the installation down tomorrow." He tipped his hat, then moved away from Lane, making his way toward her.

"Hi, Lane," she said. Sam grabbed hold of her elbow and began to propel her out of the store. "Bye, Lane."

As soon as they were back out on the street, she rounded on him. "What was that? I thought we were trying to be discreet."

"Lane Jensen isn't a gossip. Anyway, you standing there turning the color of a beet wasn't exactly subtle."

"I am not a beet," she protested, stamping.

"A tiny tomato."

"Stop comparing me to vegetables."

"A tomato isn't a vegetable."

She let out a growl and began to walk away from him, heading back up Main Street and toward her car. "Wait," he said, his voice possessing some kind of unknowable power to actually make her obey.

She stopped, rooted to the cement. "What?"

"We live in the same town. We're going to have to figure out how to interact with each other."

"Or," she said, "we continue on with this very special brand of awkwardness."

"Would it be the worst thing in the world if people knew?"

"You know my past, and you can ask me that?" She looked around the street, trying to see if anybody was watching their little play. "I'm not going to talk to you about this on the town stage."

He closed the distance between them. "Fine. We don't have to have the discussion. And it doesn't matter to me either way. But you really think you should spend the rest of your life punishing yourself for a mistake that happened when you were seventeen? He took advantage of you—it isn't your fault. And apart from any of that, you don't deserve to be labeled by a bunch of people that don't even know you."

That wasn't even it. And as she stood there, staring him down, she realized that fully. It had nothing to do with what the town thought. Nothing to do with whether or not the town thought she was a scarlet woman, or if people still thought about her indiscretion, or if people blamed her or David. None of that mattered.

She realized that in a flash of blinding brilliance that shone brighter than the Christmas lights all around her. And that realization made her knees buckle, because it made her remember the conversation that had happened in her father's office. The conversation that had occurred right after one of David's students had discovered the affair between the two of them and begun spreading rumors.

Rumors that were true, regrettably.

Rumors that had made their way all the way back to Nathan West's home office.

"I can't talk about this right now," she said, brushing past him and striding down the sidewalk.

"You don't have to talk about it with me, not ever. But what's going to happen when this is over? You're going to go another ten years between lovers? Just break down and hold your breath and do it again when you can't take the celibacy anymore?"

"Stop it," she said, walking faster.

"Like I said, it doesn't matter to me…"

She whirled around. "You keep saying it doesn't matter to you, and then you keep pushing the issue. So I would say that it does matter to you. Whatever complex you have about not being good enough, this is digging at that. But it isn't my problem. Because it isn't about you. Nobody would care if they knew that we were sleeping together. I mean, they would talk about it, but they wouldn't care. But it makes it something more. And I just… I can't have more. Not more than this."

He shifted uncomfortably. "Well, neither can I. That was hardly an invitation for something deeper."

"Good. Because I don't have anything deeper to give."

The very idea made her feel like she was going into a free fall. The idea of trusting somebody again…

The betrayals she had dealt with back when she was seventeen had made it so that trusting another human being was almost unfathomable. When she had told Sam that the sex was the least of it, she had been telling the truth.

It had very little to do with her body, and everything to do with the battering her soul had taken.

"Neither do I."

"Then why are you… Why are you pushing me like this?"

He looked stunned by the question, his face frozen. "I just… I don't want to leave you broken."

Something inside her softened, cracked a little bit. "I'm not sure that you have a choice. It kind of is what it is, you know?"

"Maybe it doesn't have to be."

"Did you think you were going to fix me, Sam?"

"No," he said, his voice rough.

But she knew he was lying. "Don't put that on yourself. Two broken people can't fix each other."

She was certain in that moment that he was broken too, even though she wasn't quite sure how.

"We only have twelve days. Any kind of fixing was a bit ambitious anyway," he said.

"Eleven days," she reminded him. "I'll see you tonight?"

"Yeah. See you then."

And then she turned and walked away from Sam McCormack for all the town to see, as if he were just a casual acquaintance and nothing more. And she tried to ignore the ache in the center of her chest that didn't seem to go away, even after she got in the car and drove home.

Chapter 8

Seven days after beginning the affair with Maddy, she called and asked him if he could come down and check the shoes on one of the horses. It was the middle of the afternoon, so if it was her version of a booty call, he thought it was kind of an odd time. And since their entire relationship was a series of those, he didn't exactly see why she wouldn't be up front about it.

But when he showed up, she was waiting for him outside the stall.

"What are you up to?"

She lifted her shoulder. "I just wanted you to come and check on the horse."

"Something you couldn't check yourself?"

She looked slightly rueful. "Okay, maybe I could have checked it myself. But she really is walking a little bit funny, and I'm wondering if something is off."

She opened the stall door, clipped a lead rope to the

horse's harness and brought her out into the main part of the barn.

He looked at her, then pushed up the sleeves on his thermal shirt and knelt down in front of the large animal, drawing his hand slowly down her leg and lifting it gently. Then he did the same to the next before moving to her hindquarters and repeating the motion again.

He stole a glance up at Maddy, who was staring at him with rapt attention.

"What?"

"I like watching you work," she said. "I've always liked watching you work. That's why I used to come down here and give orders. Okay, honestly? I wanted to give myself permission to watch you and enjoy it." She swallowed hard. "You're right. I've been punishing myself. So, I thought I might indulge myself."

"I'm going to have to charge your dad for this visit," he said.

"He won't notice," she said. "Trust me."

"I don't believe that. Your father is a pretty well-known businessman." He straightened, petting the horse on its haunches. "Everything looks fine."

Maddy looked sheepish. "Great."

"Why don't you think your dad would notice?"

"A lot of stuff has come out over the past few months. You know he had a stroke three months ago or so, and while he's recovered pretty well since then, it changed things. I mean, it didn't change *him*. It's not like he miraculously became some soft, easy man. Though, I think he's maybe a little bit more in touch with his mortality. Not happily, mind you. I think he always saw himself as something of a god."

"Well," Sam said, "what man doesn't?" At least, until he was set firmly back down to earth and reminded of just how badly he could mess things up. How badly things could hurt.

"Yet another difference between men and women," Maddy said drily. "But after he had his stroke, the control of the finances went to my brother Gage. That was why he came back to town initially. He discovered that there was a lot of debt. I mean, I know you've heard about how many properties we've had to sell downtown."

Sam stuffed his hands in his pockets, lifting his shoulders. "Not really. But then, I don't exactly keep up on that kind of stuff. That's Chase's arena. Businesses and the real estate market. That's not me. I just screw around with metal."

"You downplay what you do," she returned. "From the art to the physical labor. I've watched you do it. I don't know why you do it, only that you do. You're always acting like your brother is smarter than you, but he can't do what you do either."

"Art was never particularly useful as far as my father was concerned," Sam said. "I imagine he would be pretty damned upset to see that it's the art that keeps the ranch afloat so nicely. He would have wanted us to do it the way our ancestors did. Making leatherwork and pounding nails. Of course, it was always hard for him to understand that mass production was inevitably going to win out against more expensive handmade things. Unless we targeted our products and people who could afford what we did. Which is what we did. What we've been successful with far beyond what we even imagined."

"Dads," she said, her voice soft. "They do get in your head, don't they?"

"I mean, my father didn't have gambling debts and a secret child, but he was kind of a difficult bastard. I still wish he wasn't dead." He laughed. "It would kind of be nice to have him wandering around the place shaking his head disapprovingly as I loaded up that art installation to take down to the Mercantile."

"I don't know, having your dad hanging around disapproving is kind of overrated." Suddenly, her face contorted with horror. "I'm sorry—I had no business saying something like that. It isn't fair. I shouldn't make light of your loss."

"It was a long time ago. And anyway, I do it all the time. I think it's the way the emotionally crippled deal with things." Anger. Laughter. It was all better than hurt.

"Yeah," she said, laughing uneasily. "That sounds about right."

"What exactly does your dad disapprove of, Madison?" he asked, reverting back to her full name. He kind of liked it, because nobody else called her that. And she had gone from looking like she wanted to claw his eyes out when he used it to responding. There was something that felt deep about that. Connected. He shouldn't care. If anything, it should entice him not to do it. But it didn't.

"Isn't it obvious?"

"No," he returned. "I've done a lot of work on this ranch over the years. You're always busy. You have students scheduled all day every day—except today, apparently—and it is a major part of both the reputation and the income of this facility. You've poured everything you have into reinforcing his legacy while letting your own take a backseat."

"Well, when you put it like that," she said, the smile on her lips obviously forced, "I am kind of amazing."

"What exactly does he disapprove of?"

"What do you think?"

"Does it all come back to that? Something you did when you were seventeen?" The hypocrisy of the outrage in his tone wasn't lost on him.

"I'm not sure," she said, the words biting. "I'm really not." She grabbed hold of the horse's lead rope, taking her back into the stall before clipping the rope and coming back out, shutting the door firmly.

"What do you mean by that?"

She growled, making her way out of the barn and walking down the paved path that led toward one of the covered arenas. "I don't know. Feel free to choose your own adventure with that one."

"Come on, Maddy," he said, closing the distance between them and lowering his voice. "I've tasted parts of you that most other people have never seen. A little bit of honesty isn't going to hurt you."

She whipped around, her eyes bright. "Maybe it isn't him. Maybe it's me. Maybe I'm the one that can't look at him the same way."

Maddy felt rage simmering over her skin like heat waves. She had not intended to have this conversation—not with Sam, not with anyone.

But now she had started, she didn't know if she could stop. "The night that he found out about my affair with David was the night I found out about Jack."

"So, it isn't a recent revelation to all of you?"

"No," she said. "Colton and Sierra didn't know. I'm sure

of that. But I found out that Gage did. I didn't know who it was, I should clarify. I just found out that he had another child." She looked away from Sam, trying to ignore the burning sensation in her stomach. Like there was molten lava rolling around in there. She associated that feeling with being called into her father's home office.

It had always given her anxiety, even before everything had happened with David. Even before she had ever seriously disappointed him.

Nathan West was exacting, and Maddy had wanted nothing more than to please him. That desire took up much more of her life than she had ever wanted it to. But then, she knew that was true in some way or another for all of her siblings. It was why Sierra had gone to school for business. Why Colton had taken over the construction company. It was even what had driven Gage to leave.

It was the reason Maddy had poured all of her focus into dressage. Because she had anticipated becoming great. Going to the Olympics. And she knew her father had anticipated that. Then she had ruined all of it.

But not as badly as he had ruined the relationship between the two of them.

"Like I told you, one of David's other students caught us together. Down at the barn where he gave his lessons. We were just kissing, but it was definitely enough. That girl told her father, who in turn went to mine as a courtesy."

Sam laughed, a hard, bitter sound. "A courtesy to who?"

"Not to me," Maddy said. "Or maybe it was. I don't know. It was so awful. The whole situation. I wish there had been a less painful way for it to end. But it had to

end, whether it ended that way or some other way, so…
so I guess that worked as well as anything."

"Except you had to deal with your father. And then rumors were spread anyway."

She looked away from Sam. "Well, the rumors I kind of blame on David. Because once his wife knew, there was really no reason for the whole world not to know. And I think it suited him to paint me in an unflattering light. He took a gamble. A gamble that the man in the situation would come out of it all just fine. It was not a bad gamble, it turned out."

"I guess not."

"Full house. Douche bag takes the pot."

She was avoiding the point of this conversation. Avoiding the truth of it. She didn't even know why she should tell him. She didn't know why anything. Except that she had never confided any of this to anyone before. She was close to her sister, and Sierra had shared almost everything about her relationship with Ace with Maddy, and here Maddy was keeping more secrets from her.

She had kept David from her. She had kept Sam from her too. And she had kept this all to herself, as well.

She knew why. In a blinding flash she knew why. She couldn't stand being rejected, not again. She had been rejected by her first love; she had been rejected by an entire community. She had been rejected by her father with a few cold dismissive words in his beautifully appointed office in her childhood home.

But maybe, just maybe, that was why she should confide in Sam. Because at the end of their affair it wouldn't matter. Because then they would go back to sniping at each other or not talking to each other at all.

Because he hadn't rejected her yet.

"When he called me into his office, I knew I was in trouble," she said, rubbing her hand over her forehead. "He never did that for good things. Ever. If there was something good to discuss, we would talk about it around the dinner table. Only bad things were ever talked about in his office with the door firmly closed. He talked to Gage like that. Right before he left town. So, I always knew it had to be bad."

She cleared her throat, looking out across the arena, through the gap in the trees and at the distant view of the misty waves beyond. It was so very gray, the clouds hanging low in the sky, touching the top of the angry, steel-colored sea.

"Anyway, I *knew*. As soon as I walked in, I knew. He looked grim. Like I've never seen him before. And he asked me what was going on with myself and David Smithson. Well, I knew there was no point in denying it. So I told him. He didn't yell. I wish he had. He said… He said the worst thing you could ever do was get caught. That a man like David spent years building up his reputation, not to have it undone by the temptation of some young girl." She blinked furiously. "He said that if a woman was going to present more temptation than a man could handle, the least she could do was keep it discreet."

"How could he say that to you? To his daughter? Look, my dad was a difficult son of a bitch, but if he'd had a daughter and some man had hurt her, he'd have ridden out on his meanest stallion with a pair of pliers to dole out the world's least sterile castration."

Maddy choked out a laugh that was mixed with a sob. "That's what I thought. It really was. I thought… I thought he would be angry, but one of the things that scared me most, at least initially, was the idea that he would take it out on David. And I still loved David then. But no. He was angry at me."

"I don't understand how that's possible."

"That was when he told me," she choked out. "Told me that he had mistresses, that it was just something men did, but that the world didn't run if the mistress didn't know her place, and if I was intent on lowering myself to be that sort of woman when I could have easily been a wife, that was none of his business. He told me a woman had had his child and never betrayed him." Her throat tightened, almost painfully, a tear sliding down her cheek. "Even he saw me as the villain. If my own father couldn't stand up for me, if even he thought it was my fault somehow, how was I ever supposed to stand up for myself when other people accused me of being a whore?"

"Maddy…"

"That's why," she said, the words thin, barely making their way through her constricted throat. "That's why it hurts so much. And that's why I'm not over it. There were two men involved in that who said they loved me. There was David, the man I had given my heart to, the man I had given my body to, who had lied to me from the very beginning, who threw me under the bus the moment he got the opportunity. And then there was my own father. My own father, who should have been on my side simply because I was born his. I loved them both. And they both let me down." She blinked, a mist rolling over her insides, matching the setting all around them. "How do you ever trust anyone after that? If it had only been David, I think I would have been over it a long time ago."

Sam was looking at her, regarding her with dark, intense eyes. He looked like he was about to say something, his chest shifting as he took in a breath that seemed to contain purpose. But then he said nothing. He simply closed the distance between them, tugging her into his arms, holding her against his chest, his large, warm hand moving between her shoulder blades in a soothing rhythm.

She hadn't rested on anyone in longer than she could remember. Hadn't been held like this in years. Her mother was too brittle to lean on. She would break beneath the weight of somebody else's sorrow. Her father had never offered a word of comfort to anyone. And she had gotten in the habit of pretending she was tough so that Colton and Sierra wouldn't worry about her. So that they wouldn't look too deeply at how damaged she was still from the events of the past.

So she put all her weight on him and total peace washed over her. She shouldn't indulge in this. She shouldn't allow herself this. It was dangerous. But she couldn't stop. And she didn't want to.

She squeezed her eyes shut, a few more tears falling down her cheeks, soaking into his shirt. If anybody knew that Madison West had wept all over a man in the broad light of day, they wouldn't believe it. But she didn't care. This wasn't about anyone else. It was just about her. About purging her soul of some of the poison that had taken up residence there ten years ago and never quite left.

About dealing with some of the heavy longing that existed inside her for a time and a place she could never return to. For a Christmas when she had walked down Main Street with her father and seen him as a hero.

But of course, when she was through crying, she felt

exposed. Horribly. Hideously, and she knew this was why she didn't make a habit out of confiding in people. Because now Sam McCormack knew too much about her. Knew more about her than maybe anybody else on earth. At least, he knew about parts of her that no one else did.

The tenderness. The insecurity. The parts that were on the verge of cracking open, crumbling the foundation of her and leaving nothing more than a dusty pile of Maddy behind.

She took a deep breath, hoping that the pressure would squeeze some of those shattering pieces of herself back together with the sheer force of it. Too bad it just made her aware of more places down deep that were compromised.

Still, she wiggled out of his grasp, needing a moment to get ahold of herself. Needing very much to not get caught being held by a strange man down at the arena by any of the staff or anyone in her family.

"Thank you," she said, her voice shaking. "I just… I didn't know how much I needed that."

"I didn't do anything."

"You listened. You didn't try to give me advice or tell me I was wrong. That's actually doing a lot. A lot more than most people are willing to do."

"So, do you want me to come back here tonight?"

"Actually," she said, grabbing hold of her hands, twisting them, trying to deal with the nervous energy that was rioting through her, "I was thinking maybe I could come out a little bit early. And I could see where you work."

She didn't know why she was doing this. She didn't know where she imagined it could possibly end or how it would be helpful to her in any way. To add more pieces of him to her heart, to her mind.

That's what it felt like she was trying to do. Like collecting shells on the seashore. Picking up all the shimmering pieces of Sam she possibly could and sticking them in her little pail, hoarding them. Making a collection.

For what? Maybe for when it was over.

Maybe that wasn't so bad.

She had pieces of David, whether she wanted them or not. And she'd entertained the idea that maybe she could sleep with someone and not do that. Not carry them forward with her.

But the reality of it was that she wasn't going to walk away from this affair and never think of Sam again. He was never going to be the farrier again. He would always be Sam. Why not leave herself with beautiful memories instead of terrible ones? Maybe this was what she needed to do.

"You want to see the forge?" he asked.

"Sure. That would be interesting. But also your studio. I'm curious about your art, and I realize that I don't really know anything about it. Seeing you in the Mercantile the other day talking to Lane…" She didn't know how to phrase what she was thinking without sounding a little bit crazy. Without sounding overly attached. So she just let the sentence trail off.

But she was curious. She was curious about him. About who he was when he wasn't here. About who he was as a whole person, without the blinders around him that she had put there. She had very purposefully gone out of her way to know nothing about him. And so he had always been Sam McCormack, grumpy guy who worked at her family ranch on occasion and who she often bantered with in the sharpest of senses.

But there was more to him. So much more. This man who had held her, this man who had listened, this man who seemed to know everyone in town and have decent relationships with them. Who created beautiful things that started in his mind and were then formed with his hands. She wanted to know him.

Yeah, she wouldn't be telling him any of that.

"Were you jealous? Because there is nothing between myself and Lane Jensen. First of all, anyone who wants anything to do with her has to go through Finn Donnelly, and I have no desire to step in the middle of *that* weird dynamic and his older-brother complex."

It struck her then that jealousy hadn't even been a component to what she had felt the other day. How strange. Considering everything she had been through with men, it seemed like maybe trust should be the issue here. But it wasn't. It never had been.

It had just been this moment of catching sight of him at a different angle. Like a different side to a prism that cast a different color on the wall and made her want to investigate further. To see how one person could contain so many different things.

A person who was so desperate to hide anything beyond that single dimension he seemed comfortable with.

Another thing she would definitely not say to him. She couldn't imagine the twenty shades of rainbow horror that would cross Sam's face if she compared him to a prism out loud.

"I was not," she said. "But it made me aware of the fact that you're kind of a big deal. And I haven't fully appreciated that."

"Of course you haven't," he said, his tone dry. "It interferes with your stable-boy fantasy."

She made a scoffing sound. "I do not have a stable-boy fantasy."

"Yes, you do. You like slumming it."

Those words called up heated memories out of the depths of her mind. Him whispering things in her ear. His rough hands skimming over her skin. She bit her lip. "I like nothing of the kind, Sam McCormack. Not with you, not with any man. Are you going to show me your pretty art or not?"

"Not if you call it pretty."

"You'll have to take your chances. I'm not putting a cap on my vocabulary for your comfort. Anyway, if you haven't noticed, unnerving people with what I may or may not say next is kind of my thing."

"I've noticed."

"You do it too," she said.

His lips tipped upward into a small smile. "Do I?"

She rolled her eyes. "Oh, don't pretend you don't know. You're way too smart for that. And you act like the word *smart* is possibly the world's most vile swear when it's applied to you. But you are. You can throw around accusations of slumming it all you want, but if we didn't connect mentally, and if I didn't respect you in some way, this wouldn't work."

"Our brains have nothing to do with this."

She lifted a finger. "A woman's largest sexual organ is her brain."

He chuckled, wrapping his arm around her waist and drawing her close. "Sure, Maddy. But we both know what the most important one is." He leaned in, whispering dirty things in her ear, and she laughed, pushing against his chest. "Okay," he said, finally. "I will let you come see my studio."

She fought against the trickle of warmth that ran through her, that rested deep in her stomach and spread out from there, making her feel a kind of languid satisfaction that she had no business feeling over something like this. "Then I guess I'll see you for the art show."

Chapter 9

Sam had no idea what in hell had possessed him to let Maddy come out to his property tonight. Chase and Anna were not going to let this go ignored. In fact, Anna was already starting to make comments about the fact that he hadn't been around for dinner recently. Which was why he was there tonight, eating as quickly as possible so he could get back out to his place on the property before Maddy arrived. He had given her directions to go on the road that would allow her to bypass the main house, which Chase and Anna inhabited.

"Sam." His sister-in-law's voice cut into his thoughts. "I thought you were going to join us for dinner tonight?"

"I'm here," he said.

"Your body is. Your brain isn't. And Chase worked very hard on this meal," Anna said.

Anna was a tractor mechanic, and formerly Chase's best friend in a platonic sense. All of that had come to an end a few months ago when they had realized there was a lot more between them than friendship.

Still, the marriage had not transformed Anna into a domestic goddess. Instead, it had forced Chase to figure out how to share a household with somebody. They were never going to have a traditional relationship, but it seemed to suit Chase just fine.

"It's very good, Chase," Sam said, keeping his tone dry.

"Thanks," Chase said, "I opened the jar of pasta sauce myself."

"Sadly, no one in this house is ever going to win a cooking competition," Anna said.

"You keep *me* from starving," Sam pointed out.

Though, in all honesty, he was a better cook than either of them. Still, it was an excuse to get together with his brother. And sometimes it felt like he needed excuses. So that he didn't have to think deeply about a feeling that was more driving than hunger pangs.

"Not recently," Chase remarked. "You haven't been around."

Sam let out a heavy sigh. "Yes, sometimes a man assumes that newlyweds want time alone without their crabby brother around."

"We always want you around," Anna said. Then she screwed up her face. "Okay, we don't *always* want you around. But for dinner, when we invite you, it's fine."

"Just no unexpected visits to the house," Chase said. "In the evening. Or anytime. And maybe also don't walk into Anna's shop without knocking after hours."

Sam grimaced. "I get the point. Anyway, I've just been busy. And I'm about to be busy again." He stood up, anticipation shooting through him. He had gone a long time without sex, and now sex with Maddy was about all he could think about. Five years of celibacy would do that to a man.

Made a man do stupid things, like invite the woman he was currently sleeping with to come to his place and to come see his art. Whatever the hell she thought that would entail. He was inclined to figure it out. Just so she would feel happy, so he could see her smile again.

So she would be in the mood to put out. And nothing more. Certainly no emotional reasoning behind that.

He couldn't do that. Not ever again.

"Okay," Anna said, "you're always cagey, Sam, I'll give you that. But you have to give me a hint about what's going on."

"No," Sam said, turning to go. "I really don't."

"Sculpture? A woman?"

Well, sadly, Anna was mostly on point with both. "Not your business."

"That's hilarious," Chase said, "coming from the man who meddled in our relationship."

"You jackasses needed meddling," Sam said. "You were going to let her go." Of the two of them, Chase was undoubtedly the better man. And Anna was one of the best, man or woman. When Sam had realized his brother was about to let Anna get away because of baggage from his past, Sam had had no choice but to play the older-brother card and give advice that he himself would never have taken.

But it was different for Chase. Sam wanted it to be different for Chase. He didn't want his younger brother living the same stripped-down existence he did.

"Well, maybe you need meddling too, jackass," Anna said.

Sam ignored his sister-in-law and continued on out of

the house, taking the steps on the porch two at a time, the frosted ground crunching beneath his boots as he walked across the field, taking the short route between the two houses.

He shoved his hands in his pockets, looking up, watching his breath float up into the dense sky, joining the mist there. It was already getting dark, the twilight hanging low around him, a deep blue ink spill that bled down over everything.

It reminded him of grief. A darkness that descended without warning, covering everything around it, changing it. Taking things that were familiar and twisting them into foreign objects and strangers.

That thought nibbled at the back of his mind. He couldn't let it go. It just hovered there as he made his way back to his place, trying to push its way to the front of his mind and form the obvious conclusion.

He resisted it. The way that he always did. Anytime he got inspiration that seemed related to these kinds of feelings. And then he would go out to his shop and start working on another Texas longhorn sculpture. Because that didn't mean anything and people would want to buy it.

Just as he approached his house, so did Maddy's car. She parked right next to his truck, and a strange feeling of domesticity overtook him. Two cars in the driveway. His and hers.

He pushed that aside too.

He watched her open the car door, her blond hair even paler in the advancing moonlight. She was wearing a hat, the shimmering curls spilling out from underneath it. She also had on a scarf and gloves. And there was something about her, looking soft and bundled up, and very much not like prickly, brittle Maddy, that made him want to pull her back into his arms like he had done earlier that day and hold her up against his chest.

Hold her until she quit shaking. Or until she started shaking for a different reason entirely.

"You made it," he said.

"You say that like you had some doubt that I would."

"Well, at the very least I thought you might change your mind."

"No such luck for you. I'm curious. And once my curiosity is piqued, I will have it satisfied."

"You're like a particularly meddlesome cat," he said.

"You're going to have to make up your mind, Sam," Maddy said, smiling broadly.

"About what?"

"Am I vegetable or mammal? You have now compared me to both."

"A tomato is a fruit."

"Whatever," she said, waving a gloved hand.

"Do you want to come out and see the sculptures or do you want to stand here arguing about whether or not you're animal, vegetable or mineral?"

Her smile only broadened. "Sculptures, please."

"Well, follow me. And it's a good thing you bundled up."

"This is how much I had to bundle to get in the car and drive over here. My heater is *not* broken. I didn't know that I was going to be wandering around out in the dark, in the cold."

He snorted. "You run cold?"

"I do."

"I hadn't noticed."

She lifted a shoulder, taking two steps to his every one, doing her best to keep up with him as he led them both across the expanse of frozen field. "Well, I'm usually very hot when you're around. Anyway, the combination of you and blankets is very warming."

"What happens when I leave?"

"I get cold," she returned.

Something about those words felt like a knife in the center of his chest. Damned if he knew why. At least, damned if he wanted to know why.

What he wanted was to figure out how to make it go away.

They continued on the rest of the walk in silence, and he increased his pace when the shop came into view. "Over here is where Chase and I work," he said, gesturing to the first building. "Anna's is on a different section of the property, one closer to the road so that it's easier for her customers to get in there, since they usually have heavy equipment being towed by heavier equipment. And this one is mine." He pointed to another outbuilding, one that had once been a separate machine shed.

"We remodeled it this past year. Expanded and made room for the new equipment. I have a feeling my dad would piss himself if he knew what this was being used for now," he continued, not quite able to keep the thought in his mind.

Maddy came up beside him, looping her arm through his. "Maybe. But I want to see it. And I promise you I won't…do *that*."

"Appreciated," he said, allowing her to keep hold of him while they walked inside.

He realized then that nobody other than Chase and

Anna had ever been in here. And he had never grandly showed it to either of them. They just popped in on occasion to let him know that lunch or dinner was ready or to ask if he was ever going to resurface.

He had never invited anyone here. Though, he supposed that Maddy had invited herself here. Either way, this was strange. It was exposing in a way he hadn't anticipated it being. Mostly because that required he admit that there was something of himself in his work. And he resisted that. Resisted it hard.

It had always been an uncomfortable fit for him. That he had this ability, this compulsion to create things, that could come only from inside him. Which was a little bit like opening up his chest and showing bits of it to the world. Which was the last thing on earth he ever wanted to do. He didn't like sharing himself with other people. Not at all.

Maddy turned a slow circle, her soft, pink mouth falling open. "Wow," she said. "Is this all of them?"

"No," he said, following her line of sight, looking at the various iron sculptures all around them. Most of them were to scale with whatever they were representing. Giant two-ton metal cows and horses, one with a cowboy upon its back, took up most of the space in the room.

Pieces that came from what he saw. From a place he loved. But not from inside him.

"What are these?"

"Works in progress, mostly. Almost all of them are close to being done. Which was why I was up at the cabin, remember? I'm trying to figure out what I'm going to do next. But I can always make more things like this. They sell. I can put them in places around town and tourists will always come in and buy them. People pay obscene amounts of money for stuff like this." He let out a long, slow breath. "I'm kind of mystified by it."

"You shouldn't be. It's amazing." She moved around the space, reaching out and brushing her fingertips over the back of one of the cows. "We have to get some for the ranch. They're perfect."

Something shifted in his chest, a question hovering on the tip of his tongue. But he held it back. He had been about to ask her if he should do something different. If he should follow that compulsion that had hit him on the walk back. Those ideas about grief. About loss.

Who the hell wanted to look at something like that? Anyway, he didn't want to show anyone that part of himself. And he sure as hell didn't deserve to profit off any of his losses.

He gritted his teeth. "Great."

"You sound like you think it's great," she said, her tone deeply insincere.

"I wasn't aware my enthusiasm was going to be graded."

She looked around, the shop light making her hair look even deeper gold than it normally did. She reached up, grabbing the knit hat on her head and flinging it onto the ground. He knew what she was doing. He wanted to stop her. Because this was his shop. His studio. It was personal in a way that nothing else was. She could sleep in his bed. She could go to his house, stay there all night, and it would never be the same as her getting naked here.

He was going to stop her.

But then she grabbed the zipper tab on her jacket and shrugged it off before taking hold of the hem of her top, yanking it over her head and sending it the same way as her outerwear.

Then Maddy was standing there, wearing nothing but a flimsy lace bra, the pale curve of her breasts rising and falling with every breath she took.

"Since it's clear how talented your hands are, particularly here…" she said, looking all wide-eyed and innocent. He loved that. The way she could look like this, then spew profanities with the best of them. The way she could make her eyes all dewy, then do something that would make even the most hardened cowboy blush. "I thought I might see if I could take advantage of the inspirational quality of the place."

Immediately, his blood ran hotter, faster, desire roaring in him like a beast. He wanted her. He wanted this. There was nowhere soft to take her, not here. Not in this place full of nails and iron, in this place that was hard and jagged just like his soul, that was more evidence of what he contained than anyone would ever know.

"The rest," he said, his voice as uncompromising as the sculpture all around them. "Take off the rest, Madison."

Her lashes fluttered as she looked down, undoing the snap on her jeans, then the zipper, maddeningly slowly. And of course, she did her best to look like she had no idea what she was doing to him.

She pushed her jeans down her hips, and all that was left covering her was those few pale scraps of lace. She was so soft. And everything around her was so hard.

It should make him want to protect her. Should make him want to get her out of here. Away from this place. Away from him. But it didn't. He was that much of a bastard.

He didn't take off any of his own clothes, because there

was something about the contrast that turned him on even more. Instead, he moved toward her, slowly, not bothering to hide his open appreciation for her curves.

He closed the distance between them, wrapping his hand around the back of her head, sifting his fingers through her hair before tightening his hold on her, tugging gently. She gasped, following his lead, tilting her face upward.

He leaned in, and he could tell that she was expecting a kiss. By the way her lips softened, by the way her eyes fluttered closed. Instead, he angled his head, pressing his lips to that tender skin on her neck. She shivered, the contact clearly an unexpected surprise. But not an unwelcome one.

He kept his fingers buried firmly in her hair, holding her steady as he shifted again, brushing his mouth over the line of her collarbone, following it all the way toward the center of her chest and down to the plush curves of her breasts.

He traced that feathery line there where lace met skin with the tip of his tongue, daring to delve briefly beneath the fabric, relishing the hitch in her breathing when he came close to her sensitized nipples.

He slid his hands up her arms, grabbed hold of the delicate bra straps and tugged them down, moving slowly, ever so slowly, bringing the cups down just beneath her breasts, exposing those dusky nipples to him.

"Beautiful," he said. "Prettier than anything in here."

"I didn't think you wanted the word *pretty* uttered in here," she said, breathless.

"About my work. About you… That's an entirely different situation. You are pretty. These are pretty." He leaned in, brushing his lips lightly over one tightened bud, relishing the sweet sound of pleasure that she made.

"Now who's a tease?" she asked, her voice labored.

"I haven't even started to tease you yet."

He slid his hands around her back, pressing his palms hard between her shoulder blades, lowering his head so that he could draw the center of her breast deep into his mouth. He sucked hard until she whimpered, until she squirmed against him, clearly looking for some kind of relief for the intense arousal that he was building inside her.

He looked up, really looked at her face, a deep, primitive sense of pleasure washing through him. That he was touching such a soft, beautiful woman. That he was allowing himself such an indulgence. That he was doing this to her.

He had forgotten. He had forgotten what it was like to really relish the fact that he possessed the power to make a woman feel good. Because he had reduced his hands to something else entirely. Hands that had failed him, that had failed Elizabeth.

Hands that could form iron into impossible shapes but couldn't be allowed to handle something this fragile.

But here he was with Madison. She was soft, and he wasn't breaking her. She was beautiful, and she was his.

Not yours. Never yours.

He tightened his hold on her, battling the unwelcome thoughts that were trying to crowd in, trying to take over this experience, this moment. When Madison was gone, he would go back to the austere existence he'd been living for the past five years. But right now, he had her, and he wasn't going to let anything damage that. Not now.

Instead of thinking, which was never a good thing, not

for him, he continued his exploration of her body. Lowering himself down to his knees in front of her, kissing her just beneath her breasts, and down lower, tracing a line across her soft stomach.

She was everything a woman should be. He was confident of that. Because she was the only woman he could remember. Right now, she was everything.

He moved his hands down her thighs, then back up again, pushing his fingertips beneath the waistband of her panties as he gripped her hips and leaned in, kissing her just beneath her belly button. She shook beneath him, a sweet little trembling that betrayed just how much she wanted him.

She wouldn't, if she knew. If she knew, she wouldn't want him. But she didn't know. And she never had to. There were only five days left. They would never have to talk about it. Ever. They would only ever have this. That was important. Because if they ever tried to have more, there would be nothing. She would run so far the other direction he would never see her again.

Or maybe she wouldn't. Maybe she would stick around. But that was even worse. Because of what he would have to do.

He flexed his fingers, the blunt tips digging into that soft skin at her hips. He growled, moving them around to cup her ass beneath the thin lace fabric on her panties. He squeezed her there too and she moaned, her obvious enjoyment of his hands all over her body sending a surge of pleasure through him.

He shifted, delving between her thighs, sliding his fingers through her slick folds, moving his fingers over her clit before drawing them back, pushing one finger inside her.

She gasped, grabbing his shoulders, pitching forward. He could feel her thigh muscles shaking as he pleasured her slowly, drawing his finger in and out of her body before adding a second. Her nails dug into his skin, clinging to him harder and harder as he continued tormenting her.

He looked up at her and allowed himself to get lost in this. In the feeling of her slick arousal beneath his hands, in the completely overwhelmed, helpless expression on her beautiful face. Her eyes were shut tight, and she was biting her lip, probably to keep herself from screaming. He decided he had a new goal.

He lowered his head, pressing his lips right to the center of her body, her lace panties holding the warmth of his breath as he slowly lapped at her through the thin fabric.

She swore, a short, harsh sound that verged on being a scream. But it wasn't enough. He teased her that way, his fingers deep inside her, his mouth on her, for as long as he could stand it.

Then he took his other hand, swept the panties aside and pushed his fingers in deep while he lapped at her bare skin, dragging his tongue through her folds, over that sensitized bundle of nerves.

And then she screamed.

Her internal muscles pulsed around him, her pleasure ramping his up two impossible degrees.

"I hope like *hell* you brought a condom," he said, his voice ragged, rough.

"I think I did," she said, her tone wavering. "Yes, I did. It's in my purse. Hurry."

"You want me to dig through your purse."

"I can't breathe. I can't move. If I do anything, I'm going to fall down. So I suggest you get the condom so that I don't permanently wound myself attempting to procure it."

"Your tongue seems fine," he said, moving away from her and going to grab the purse that she had discarded along with the rest of her clothes.

"So does yours," she muttered.

And he knew that what she was referring to had nothing to do with talking.

He found the condom easily enough, since it was obviously the last thing she had thrown into her bag. Then he stood, stripping his shirt off and his pants, adding to the pile of clothing that Maddy had already left on the studio floor.

Then he tore open the packet and took care of the protection. He looked around the room, searching for some surface that he could use. That they could use.

There was no way to lay her down, which he kind of regretted. Mostly because he always felt like she deserved a little bit more than the rough stuff that he doled out to her. Except she seemed to like it. So if it was what she wanted, she was about to get the full experience tonight.

He wrapped his arm around her waist, pulling her up against him, pressing their bodies together, her bare breasts pressing hard against his chest. He was so turned on, his arousal felt like a crowbar between them.

She didn't seem to mind.

He took hold of her chin, tilting her face up so she had to look at him. And then he leaned in, kissing her lightly, gently. It would be the last gentle thing he did all night.

He slid his hands along her body, moving them to grip

her hips. Then he turned her so that she was facing away from him. She gasped but followed the momentum as he propelled her forward, toward one of the iron figures—a horse—and placed his hand between her shoulder blades.

"Hold on to the horse, cowgirl," he said, his voice so rough it sounded like a stranger's.

"What?"

He pushed more firmly against her back, bending her forward slightly, and she lifted her hands, placing them over the back of the statue. "Just like that," he said.

Her back arched slightly, and he drew his fingertips down the line of her spine, all the way down to her butt. He squeezed her there, then slipped his hand to her hip.

"Spread your legs," he instructed.

She did, widening her stance, allowing him a good view and all access. He moved his hand back there, just for a second, testing her readiness. Then he positioned his arousal at the entrance to her body. He pushed into her, hard and deep, and she let out a low, slow sound of approval.

He braced himself, putting one hand on her shoulder, his thumb pressed firmly against the back of her neck, the other holding her hip as he began to move inside her.

He lost himself. In her, in the moment. In this soft, beautiful woman, all curves and round shapes in the middle of this hard, angular garden of iron.

The horse was hard in front of her; he was hard behind her. Only Maddy was soft.

Her voice was soft—the little gasps of pleasure that escaped her lips like balm for his soul. Her body was soft, her curves giving against him every time he thrust home.

When she began to rock back against him, her desperation clearly increasing along with his, he moved his hand from her hip to between her thighs. He stroked her in time with his thrusts, bringing her along with him, higher and higher until he thought they would both shatter. Until he thought they might shatter everything in this room. All of these unbreakable, unbending things.

She lowered her head, her body going stiff as her release broke over her, her body spasming around his, that evidence of her own loss of control stealing every ounce of his own.

He gave himself up to this. Up to her. And when his climax hit him, it was with the realization that it was somehow hers. That she owned this. Owned this moment. Owned his body.

That realization only made it more intense. Only made it more arousing.

His muscles shook as he poured himself into her. As he gave himself up to it totally, completely, in a way he had given himself up to nothing and no one for more than five years. Maybe ever.

In this moment, surrounded by all of these creations that had come out of him, he was exposed, undone. As though he had ripped his chest open completely and exposed his every secret to her, as though she could see everything, not just these creations, but the ugly, secret things that he kept contained inside his soul.

It was enough to make his knees buckle, and he had to reach out, pressing his palm against the rough surface of the iron horse to keep himself from falling to the ground and dragging Maddy with him.

The only sound in the room was their broken breathing, fractured and unsteady. He gathered her up against his body, one hand against her stomach, the other still on the back of the horse, keeping them upright.

He angled his head, buried his face in her neck, kissed her.

"Well," Maddy said, her voice unsteady, "that was amazing."

He couldn't respond. Because he couldn't say anything. His tongue wasn't working; his brain wasn't working. His voice had dried up like a desert. Instead, he released his grip on the horse, turned her to face him and claimed her mouth in a deep, hard kiss.

Chapter 10

Maybe it wasn't the best thing to make assumptions, but when they got back to Sam's house, that was exactly what Maddy did. She simply assumed that she would be invited inside because he wanted her to stay.

If her assumption was wrong, he didn't correct her.

She soaked in the details of his home, the simple, completely spare surroundings, and how it seemed to clash with his newfound wealth.

Except, in many ways it didn't, she supposed. Sam just didn't seem the type to go out and spend large. He was too…well, Sam.

The cabin was neat, well kept and small. Rustic and void of any kind of frills. Honestly, it was more rustic than the cabins they had stayed in up in the mountain.

It was just another piece that she could add to the Sam puzzle. He was such a strange man. So difficult to find the center of. To find the key to. He was one giant sheet of code and she was missing some essential bit that might help her make heads or tails of him.

He was rough; he was distant. He was caring and kinder in many ways than almost anyone else she had ever known. Certainly, he had listened to her in a way that no one else ever had before. Offering nothing and simply taking everything onto his shoulders, letting her feel whatever she did without telling her it was wrong.

That was valuable in a way that she hadn't realized it would be.

She wished that she could do the same for him. That she could figure out what the thing was that made Sam… Sam. That made him distant and difficult and a lot like a brick wall. But she knew there was more behind his aloofness. A potential for feeling, for emotion, that surpassed what he showed the world.

She didn't even bother to ask herself why she cared. She suspected she already knew.

Sam busied himself making a fire in the simple, old-fashioned fireplace in the living room. It was nothing like the massive, modern adorned piece that was in the West family living room. One with fake logs and a switch that turned it on. One with a mantel that boasted the various awards won by Nathan West's superior horses.

There was something about this that she liked. The lack of pretension. Though, she wondered if it reflected Sam any more honestly than her own home—decorated by her mother's interior designer—did her. She could see it, in a way. The fact that he was no-nonsense and a little bit spare.

And yet in other ways she couldn't.

His art pieces looked like they were ready to take a

breath and come to life any moment. The fact that such beautiful things came out of him made her think there had to be beautiful things in him. An appreciation for aesthetics. And yet none of that was in evidence here. Of course, it would be an appreciation for a hard aesthetic, since there was nothing soft about what he did.

Still, he wasn't quite this cold and empty either.

Neither of them spoke while he stoked the fire, and pretty soon the small space began to warm. Her whole body was still buzzing with the aftereffects of what had happened in his studio. But still, she wanted more.

She hadn't intended to seduce him in his studio; it had just happened. But she didn't regret it. She had brought a condom, just in case, so she supposed she couldn't claim total innocence. But still.

It had been a little bit reckless. The kind of thing a person could get caught doing. It was definitely not as discreet as she should have been. The thought made her smile. Made her feel like Sam was washing away some of the wounds of her past. That he was healing her in a way she hadn't imagined she could be.

She walked over to where he was, still kneeling down in front of the fireplace, and she placed her hands on his shoulders. She felt his muscles tighten beneath her touch. All of the tension that he carried in his shoulders. Why? Because he wanted her again and that bothered him? It wasn't because he didn't want her, she was convinced of that. There was no faking what was between them.

She let her fingertips drift down lower. Then she leaned in, pressing a kiss to his neck, as he was so fond of doing to her. As she was so fond of him doing.

"What are you doing?" he asked, his voice rumbling inside him.

"Honestly, if you have to ask, I'm not doing a very good job of it."

"Aren't you exhausted?"

"The way I see it, I have five days left with you. I could go five days without sleep if I needed to."

He reached up, grabbing hold of her wrist and turning, then pulling her down onto the floor, onto his lap. "Is that a challenge? Because I'm more than up to meeting that."

"If you want to take it as one, I suppose that's up to you."

She put her hands on his face, sliding her thumbs alongside the grooves next to his mouth. He wasn't that old. In his early to midthirties, she guessed. But he wore some serious cares on that handsome face of his, etched into his skin. She wondered what they were. It was easy to assume it was the death of his parents, and perhaps that was part of it. But there was more.

She'd had the impression earlier today that she'd only ever glimpsed a small part of him. That there were deep pieces of himself that he kept concealed from the world. And she had a feeling this was one of them. That he was a man who presented himself as simple, who lived in these simple surroundings, hard and spare, while he contained multitudes of feeling and complexity.

She also had a feeling he would rather die than admit that.

"All right," he said, "if you insist."

He leaned in, kissing her. It was slower and more luxurious than any of the kisses they had shared back in the studio. A little bit less frantic. A little bit less desperate.

Less driven toward its ultimate conclusion, much more about the journey.

She found herself being disrobed again, for the second time that day, and she really couldn't complain. Especially not when Sam joined her in a state of undress.

She pressed her hand against his chest, tracing the strongly delineated muscles, her eyes following the movement.

"I'm going to miss this," she said, not quite sure what possessed her to speak the words out loud. Because they went so much deeper than just appreciation for his body. So much deeper than just missing his beautiful chest or his perfect abs.

She wished that they didn't, but they did. She wished she were a little more confused by the things she did and said with him, like she had been earlier today. But somehow, between her pouring her heart out to him at the ranch today and making love with him in the studio, a few things had become a lot clearer.

His lips twitched, like he was considering making light of the statement. Saying something to defuse the tension between them. Instead, he wrapped his fingers around her wrist, holding her tight, pressing her palms flat against him so that she could feel his heart beating. Then he kissed her. Long, powerful. A claiming, a complete and total invasion of her soul.

She didn't even care.

Or maybe, more accurately, she did care. She cared all the way down, and what she couldn't bother with anymore was all the pretending that she didn't. That she cared about nothing and no one, that she existed on the Isle of Maddy. Where she was wholly self-sufficient.

She was pretty sure, in this moment, that she might need him. That she might need him in ways she hadn't needed another person in a very long time, if ever. When she had met David, she had been a teenager. She hadn't had any baggage; she hadn't run into any kind of resistance in the world. She was young, and she didn't know what giving her heart away might cost.

She knew now. She knew so much more. She had been hurt; she had been broken. And when she allowed herself to see that she needed someone, she could see too just how badly it could go.

When they parted, they were both breathing hard, and his dark eyes were watchful on hers. She felt like she could see further than she normally could. Past all of that strength that he wore with ease, down to the parts of him that were scarred, that had been wounded.

That were vulnerable.

Even Sam McCormack was vulnerable. What a revelation. Perhaps if he was, everyone was.

He lifted his hand, brushing up against her cheek, down to her chin, and then he pushed her hair back off her face, slowly letting his fingers sift through the strands. And he watched them slide through his fingers, just as she had watched her own hand as she'd touched his chest. She wondered what he was thinking. If he was thinking what she'd been. If he was attached to her in spite of himself.

Part of her hoped so. Part of her hoped not.

He leaned down, kissing her on the shoulder, the seemingly nonsexual contact affecting her intensely. Making her skin feel like it was on fire, making her heart feel like it might burst right out of her chest.

She found herself being propelled backward, but it felt

like slow motion, as he lowered her down onto the floor. Onto the carpet there in front of the fireplace.

She had the thought that this was definitely a perfect component for a winter affair. But then the thought made her sad. Because she wanted so much more than a winter affair with him. So much more than this desperate grab in front of the fire, knowing that they had only five days left with each other.

But then he was kissing her and she couldn't think anymore. She couldn't regret. She could only kiss him back.

His hands skimmed over her curves, her breasts, her waist, her hips, all the way down to her thighs, where he squeezed her tight, held on to her as though she were his lifeline. As though he were trying to memorize every curve, every dip and swell.

She closed her eyes, gave herself over to it, to the sensation of being known by Sam. The thought filled her, made her chest feel like it was expanding. He knew her. He really knew her. And he was still here. Still with her. He didn't judge her; he didn't find her disgusting.

He didn't treat her like she was breakable. He could still bend her over a horse statue in his studio, then be like this with her in front of the fire. Tender. Sweet.

Because she was a woman who wanted both things. And he seemed to know it.

He also seemed to be a man who might need both too.

Or maybe everybody did. But you didn't see it until you were with the person you wanted to be both of those things with.

"Hang on just a second," he said, suddenly, breaking into her sensual reverie. She had lost track of time. Lost track of everything except the feel of his hands on her skin.

He moved away from her, the loss of his body leaving her cold. But he returned a moment later, settling himself in between her thighs. "Condom," he said by way of explanation.

At least one of them had been thinking. She certainly hadn't been.

He joined their bodies together, entering her slowly, the sensation of fullness, of being joined to him, suddenly so profound that she wanted to weep with it. It always felt good. From the first time with him it had felt good. But this was different.

It was like whatever veil had been between them, whatever stack of issues had existed, had been driving them, was suddenly dropped. And there was nothing between them. When he looked at her, poised over her, deep inside her, she felt like he could see all the way down.

When he moved, she moved with him, meeting him thrust for thrust, pushing them both to the brink. And when she came, he came along with her, his rough gasp of pleasure in her ears ramping up her own release.

In the aftermath, skin to skin, she couldn't deny anymore what all these feelings were. She couldn't pretend that she didn't know.

She'd signed herself up for a twelve-day fling with a man she didn't even like, and only one week in she had gone and fallen in love with Sam McCormack.

"Sam." Maddy's voice broke into his sensual haze. He was lying on his back in front of the fireplace, feeling drained and like he had just had some kind of out-of-body experience. Except he had been firmly in his body and feeling everything, everything and then some.

"What?" he asked, his voice rusty.

"Why do you make farm animals?"

"What the hell kind of question is that?" he asked.

"A valid one," she said, moving nearer to him, putting her hand on his chest, tracing shapes there. "I mean, not that they aren't good."

"The horse seemed good enough for you a couple hours ago."

"It's good," she said, her tone irritated, because she obviously thought he was misunderstanding her on purpose.

Which she wasn't wrong about.

"Okay, but you don't think I should be making farm animals."

"No, I think it's fine that you make farm animals. I just think it's not actually you."

He shifted underneath her, trying to decide whether or not he should say anything. Or if he should sidestep the question. If it were anyone else, he would laugh. Play it off. Pretend like there was no answer. That there was nothing deeper in him than simply re-creating what he literally saw out in the fields in front of him.

And a lot of people would have bought that. His own brother probably would have, or at the very least, he wouldn't have pushed. But this was Maddy. Maddy, who had come apart in his arms in more than one way over the past week. Maddy, who perhaps saw deeper inside him than anyone else ever had.

Why not tell her? Why not? Because he could sense her getting closer to him. Could sense it like an invisible cord winding itself around the two of them, no matter that he was going to have to cut it in the end. Maybe it would be best to do it now.

"If I don't make what I see, I'll have to make what I feel," he said. "Nobody wants that."

"Why not?"

"Because the art has to sell," he said, his voice flat. Although, that was somewhat disingenuous. It wasn't that he didn't think he could sell darker pieces. In fact, he was sure that he could. "I don't do it for myself. I do it for Chase. I was perfectly content to keep it some kind of weird hobby that I messed around with after hours. Chase was the one who thought that I needed to pursue it full-time. Chase was the one who thought it was the way to save our business. And it started out doing kind of custom artistry for big houses. Gates and the detail work on stairs and decks and things. But then I started making bigger pieces and we started selling them. I say *we* because without Chase they would just sit in the shop."

"So you're just making what sells. That's the beginning and end of the story." Her blue eyes were too sharp, too insightful and far too close to the firelight for him to try to play at any games.

"I make what I want to let people see."

"What happened, Sam? And don't tell me nothing. You're talking to somebody who clung to one event in the past for as long as humanly possible. Who let it dictate her entire life. You're talking to the queen of residual issues here. Don't try to pretend that you don't have any. I know what it looks like." She took a deep breath. "I know what it looks like when somebody uses anger, spite and a whole bunch of unfriendliness to keep the world at a safe distance. I know, because I've spent the past ten years doing it. Nobody gets too close to the girl who says unpredictable things. The one who might come out and tell you that your dress does make you look fat and then turn around and say something crude about male anatomy. It's how you give yourself power in social situations. Act like you don't care about the rules that everyone else is a slave to." She laughed. "And why not? I already broke the rules. That's me. It's been me for a long time. And it isn't because I didn't know better. It's because I absolutely knew better. You're smart, Sam. The way that you walk around, the way you present yourself, even here, it's calculated."

Sam didn't think anyone had ever accused him of being calculated before. But it was true. Truer than most things that had been leveled at him. That he was grumpy, that he was antisocial. He was those things. But for a very specific reason.

And of course Madison would know. Of course she would see.

"I've never been comfortable sharing my life," Sam said. "I suppose that comes from having a father who was less than thrilled to have a son who was interested in art. In fact, I think my father considered it a moral failing of his. To have a son who wanted to use materials to create frivolous things. Things that had no use. To have a son who was more interested in that than honest labor. I learned to keep things to myself a long time ago. Which all sounds a whole lot like a sad, cliché story. Except it's not. It worked. I would have made a relationship with my dad work. But he died. So then it didn't matter anymore. But still, I just never… I never wanted to keep people up on what was happening with my life. I was kind of trained that way."

Hell, a lot of guys were that way, anyway. A lot of men didn't want to talk about what was happening in their day-to-day existence. Though most of them wouldn't have gone to the lengths that Sam did to keep everything separate.

"Most especially when Chase and I were neck-deep in trying to keep the business afloat, I didn't like him seeing that I was working on anything else. Anything at all." Sam took a deep breath. "That included any kind of relationships I might have. I didn't have a lot. But you know Chase never had a problem with people in town knowing that he was spreading it around. He never had a problem sleeping with the women here."

"No, he did not," Maddy said. "Never with me, to be clear."

"Considering I'm your first in a decade, I wasn't exactly that worried about it."

"Just making sure."

"I didn't like that. I didn't want my life to be part of this real-time small-town TV program. I preferred to find women out of town. When I was making deliveries, going to bigger ranches down the coast, that was when I would…"

"When you would find yourself a buckle bunny for the evening?"

"Yes," he said. "Except I met a woman I liked a lot. She was the daughter of one of the big ranchers down near Coos County. And I tried to keep things business oriented. We were actually doing business with her family. But I… I saw her out at a bar one night, and even though I knew she was too young, too nice of a girl for a guy like me… I slept with her. And a few times after. I was pretty obsessed with her, actually."

He was downplaying it. But what was the point of doing

anything else? Of admitting that for just a little while he'd thought he'd found something. Someone who wanted him. All of him. Someone who knew him.

The possibility of a future. Like the first hint of spring in the air after a long winter.

Maddy moved closer to him, looking up at him, and he decided to take a moment to enjoy that for a second. Because after this, she would probably never want to touch him again.

"Without warning, she cut me off. Completely. Didn't want to see me anymore. And since she was a few hours down the highway, that really meant not seeing her. I'd had to make an effort to work her into my life. Cutting her out of it was actually a lot easier."

"Sure," Maddy said, obviously not convinced.

"I got a phone call one night. Late. From the hospital. They told me to come down because Elizabeth was asking for me. They said it wasn't good."

"Oh, Sam," Maddy said, her tone tinged with sympathy.

He brush right past that. Continued on. "I white-knuckled it down there. Went as fast as I could. I didn't tell anyone I was going. When I got there, they wouldn't let me in. Because I wasn't family."

"But she wanted them to call you."

"It didn't matter." It was difficult for him to talk about that day. In fact, he never had. He could see it all playing out in his mind as he spoke the words. Could see the image of her father walking out of the double doors, looking harried, older than Sam had ever seen him look during any of their business dealings.

"I never got to see her," Sam said. "She died a few minutes after I got there."

"Sam, I'm so sorry…"

"No, don't misunderstand me. This isn't a story about me being angry because I lost a woman that I loved. I *didn't* love her. That's the worst part." He swallowed hard, trying to diffuse the pressure in his throat crushing down, making it hard to breathe. "I mean, maybe I could have. But that's not the same. You know who loved her? Her family. Her family loved her. I have never seen a man look so destroyed as I did that day. Looking at her father, who clearly wondered why in hell I was sitting down there in the emergency room. Why I had been called to come down. He didn't have to wonder long. Not when they told him exactly how his daughter died." Sam took a deep breath. "Elizabeth died of internal bleeding. Complications from an ectopic pregnancy."

Maddy's face paled, her lips looking waxen. "Did you…? You didn't know she was pregnant."

"No. Neither did anyone in her family. But I know it was mine. I know it was mine, and she didn't want me to know. And that was probably why she didn't tell me, why she broke things off with me. Nobody knew because she was ashamed. Because it was my baby. Because it was a man that she knew she couldn't have a future with. Nobody knew, so when she felt tired and lay down for a nap because she was bleeding and feeling discomfort, no one was there."

Silence settled around them, the house creaking beneath the weight of it.

"Did you ever find out why…why she called you then?"

"I don't know. Maybe she wanted me there to blame me. Maybe she just needed me. I'll never know. She was gone before I ever got to see her."

"That must have been…" Maddy let that sentence trail off. "That's horrible."

"It's nothing but horrible. It's everything horrible. I know why she got pregnant, Maddy. It's because… I was so careless with her. I had sex with her once without a condom. And I thought that it would be fine. Hell, I figured if something did happen, I'd be willing to marry her. All of that happened because I didn't think. Because I lost control. I don't deserve…"

"You can't blame yourself for a death that was some kind of freak medical event."

"Tell me you wouldn't blame yourself, Maddy. Tell me you wouldn't." He sat up, and Maddy sat up too. Then he gripped her shoulders, holding her steady, forcing her to meet his gaze. "You, who blame yourself for the affair with your dressage teacher even though you were an underage girl. You could tell me you don't. You could tell me that you were just hurt by the way everybody treated you, but I know it's more than that. You blame yourself. So don't you dare look at me with those wide blue eyes and tell me that I have no business blaming myself."

She blinked. "I… I don't blame myself. I don't. I mean, I'm not proud of what I did, but I'm not going to take all of the blame. Not for something I couldn't control. He lied to me. I was dumb, yes. I was naive. But dammit, Sam, my father should have had my back. My friends should have had my back. And my teacher should never have taken advantage of me."

He moved away from her then, pushing himself into a standing position and forking his fingers through his hair. She wasn't blaming him. It was supposed to push her away. She certainly wasn't supposed to look at him with sympathy. She was supposed to be appalled. Appalled that he had taken the chances he had with Elizabeth's body. Appalled at his lack of control.

It was the object lesson. The one that proved that he wasn't good enough for a woman like her. That he wasn't good enough for anyone.

"You don't blame yourself at all?"

"I don't know," she said. "It's kind of a loaded question. I could have made another decision. And because of that, I guess I share blame. But I'm not going to sit around feeling endless guilt. I'm hurt. I'm wounded. But that's not the same thing. Like I told you, the sex was the least of it. If it was all guilt, I would have found somebody a long time ago. I would have dealt with it. But it's more than that. I think it's more than that with you. Because you're not an idiot. You know full well that it isn't like you're the first man to have unprotected sex with a woman. You know full well you weren't in control of where an embryo implanted inside a woman. You couldn't have taken her to the hospital, because you didn't know she was pregnant. You didn't know she needed you. She sent you away. She made some choices here, and I don't really think it's her fault either, because how could she have known? But still. It isn't your fault."

He drew back, anger roaring through him. "I'm the one…"

"You're very dedicated to this. But that doesn't make it true."

"Her father thought it was my fault," he said. "That matters. I had to look at a man who was going to have to bury his daughter because of me."

"Maybe he felt that way," Maddy said. "I can understand that. People want to blame. I know. Because I've been put in that position. Where I was the one that people wanted to blame. Because I wasn't as well liked. Because I wasn't as important. I know that David's wife certainly wanted to blame me, because she wanted to make her marriage work, and if she blamed David, how would she do that? And without blame, your anger is aimless."

Those words hit hard, settled somewhere down deep inside him. And he knew that no matter what, no matter that he didn't want to think about them, no matter that he didn't want to believe them, they were going to stay with him. Truth had a funny way of doing that.

"I'm not looking for absolution, Maddy." He shook his head. "I was never looking for it."

"What are you looking for, then?"

He shrugged. "Nothing. I'm not looking for anything. I'm not looking for you to forgive me. I'm not looking to forgive myself."

"No," she said, "you're just looking to keep punishing yourself. To hold everything inside and keep it buried down deep. I don't think it's the rest of the world you're hiding yourself from. I think you're hiding from yourself."

"You think that you are qualified to talk about my issues? You. The woman who didn't have a lover for ten years because she's so mired in the past?"

"Do you think that's going to hurt my feelings? I know I'm messed up. I'm well aware. In fact, I would argue that it takes somebody as profoundly screwed up as I am to look at another person and see it. Maybe other people would look at you and see a man who is strong. A man who has it all laid out. A man who has iron control. But I see you for what you are. You're completely and totally bound up inside. And you're ready to crack apart. You can't go on like this."

"Watch me," he said.

"How long has it been?" she asked, her tone soft.

"Five years," he ground out.

"Well, it's only half the time I've been punishing myself, but it's pretty good. Where do you see it ending, Sam?"

"Well, you were part of it for me too."

He gritted his teeth, regretting introducing that revelation into the conversation.

"What do you mean?"

"I haven't been with a woman in five years. So I guess you could say you are part of me dealing with some of my issues."

Maddy looked like she'd been slapped. She did not, in any way, look complimented. "What does that mean? What does that mean?" She repeated the phrase twice, sounding more horrified, more frantic each time.

"It had to end at some point. The celibacy, I mean. And when you offered yourself, I wasn't in a position to say no."

"After all of your righteous indignation—the accusation that I was using you for sexual healing—it turns out you were using me for the same thing?" she asked.

"Why does that upset you so much?"

"Because…because you're still so completely wrapped up in it. Because you obviously don't have any intention to really be healed."

Unease settled in his chest. "What's me being healed to you, Maddy? What does that mean? I changed something, didn't I? Same as you."

"But…" Her tone became frantic. "I just… You aren't planning on letting it change you."

"What change are you talking about?" he pressed.

"I don't know," she said, her throat sounding constricted.

"Like hell, Madison. Don't give me that. If you've changed the rules in your head, that's hardly my fault."

She whirled around, lowering her head, burying her face in her hands. "You're so infuriating." She turned back to him, her cheeks crimson. "I don't know what either of us was thinking. That we were going to go into this and come out the other side without changing anything? We are idiots. We are idiots who didn't let another human being touch us for years. And somehow we thought we could come together and nothing would change? I mean, it was one thing when it was just me. I assumed that you went around having sex with women you didn't like all the time."

"Why would you think that?"

"Because you don't like anyone. So, that stands to reason. That you would sleep with women you don't like. I certainly didn't figure you didn't sleep with women at all. That's ridiculous. You're… *Look* at you. Of course you have sex. Who would assume that you didn't? Not me. That's who."

He gritted his teeth, wanting desperately to redirect the conversation. Because it was going into territory that would end badly for both of them. He wanted to leave the core of the energy arcing between them unspoken. He wanted to make sure that neither of them acknowledged it. He wanted to pretend he had no idea what she was thinking. No idea what she was about to say.

The problem was, he knew her. Better than he knew

anyone else, maybe. And it had all happened in a week. A week of talking, of being skin to skin. Of being real.

No wonder he had spent so many years avoiding exactly this. No wonder he had spent so long hiding everything that he was, everything that he wanted. Because the alternative was letting it hang out there, exposed and acting as some kind of all-access pass to anyone who bothered to take a look.

"Well, you assumed wrong. But it doesn't have to change anything. We have five more days, Maddy. Why does it have to be like this?"

"Honest?"

"Why do we have to fight with each other? We shouldn't. We don't have to. We don't have to continue this discussion. We are not going to come to any kind of understanding, whatever you might think. Whatever you think you're pushing for here…just don't."

"Are you going to walk away from this and just not change? Are you going to find another woman? Is that all this was? A chance for you to get your sexual mojo back? To prove that you could use a condom every time? Did you want me to sew you a little sexual merit badge for your new Boy Scout vest?" She let out a frustrated growl. "I don't want you to be a Boy Scout, Sam. I want you to be you."

Sam growled, advancing on her. She backed away from him until her shoulder blades hit the wall. Then he pressed his palms to the flat surface on either side of her face. "You don't want me to be me. Trust me. I don't know how to give the kinds of things you want."

"You don't want to," she said, the words soft, penetrating deeper than a shout ever could have.

"No, you don't want me to."

"Why is that so desperately important for you to make yourself believe?"

"Because it's true."

She let silence hang between them for a moment. "Why won't you let yourself feel this?"

"What?"

"*This* is why you do farm animals. That's what you said. And you said it was because nobody would want to see this. But that isn't true. Everybody feels grief, Sam. Everybody has lost. Plenty of people would want to see what you would make from this. Why is it that you can't do it?"

"You want me to go ahead and make a profit off my sins? Out of the way I hurt other people? You want me to make some kind of artistic homage to a father who never wanted me to do art in the first place? You want me to do a tribute to a woman whose death I contributed to."

"Yes. Because it's not about how anyone else feels. It's about how you feel."

He didn't know why this reached in and cut him so deeply. He didn't know why it bothered him so much. Mostly he didn't know why he was having this conversation with her at all. It didn't change anything. It didn't change him.

"No," she said, "that isn't what I think you should do. It's not about profiting off sins—real or perceived. It's about you dealing with all of these things. It's about you acknowledging that you have feelings."

He snorted. "I'm entitled to more grief than Elizabeth's parents? To any?"

"You lost somebody that you cared about. That matters. Of course it matters. You lost… I don't know. She was pregnant. It was your baby. Of course that matters. Of course you think about it."

"No," he said, the words as flat as everything inside him. "I don't. I don't think about that. Ever. I don't talk about it. I don't do anything with it."

"Except make sure you never make a piece of art that means anything to you. Except not sleep with anyone. Except punish yourself. Which you had such a clear vision of when you felt like I was doing it to myself but you seem to be completely blind to when it comes to you."

"All right. Let's examine your mistake, then, Maddy. Since you're so determined to draw a comparison between the two of us. Who's dead? Come on. Who died as a result of your youthful mistakes? No one. Until you make a mistake like that, something that's that irreversible, don't pretend you have any idea what I've been through. Don't pretend you have any idea of what I should feel."

He despised himself for even saying that. For saying he had been through something. He didn't deserve to walk around claiming that baggage. It was why he didn't like talking about it. It was why he didn't like thinking about it. Because Elizabeth's family members were the ones who had been left with a giant hole in their lives. Not him. Because they were the ones who had to deal with her loss around the dinner table, with thinking about her on her birthday and all of the holidays they didn't have her.

He didn't even know when her birthday was.

"Well, I care about you," Maddy said, her voice small. "Doesn't that count for anything?"

"No," he said, his voice rough. "Five more days, Maddy. That's it. That's all it can ever be."

He should end it now. He knew that. Beyond anything else, he knew that he should end it now. But if Maddy West had taught him anything, it was that he wasn't nearly as controlled as he wanted to be. At least, not where she was concerned. He could stand around and shout about it, self-flagellate all he wanted, but when push came to shove, he was going to make the selfish decision.

"Either you come to bed with me and we spend the rest of the night not talking, or you go home and we can forget the rest of this."

Maddy nodded mutely. He expected her to turn and walk out the door. Maybe not even pausing to collect her clothes, in spite of the cold weather. Instead, she surprised him. Instead, she took his hand, even knowing the kind of devastation it had caused, and she turned and led him up the stairs.

Chapter 11

Maddy hadn't slept at all. It wasn't typical for her and Sam to share a bed the entire night. But they had last night. After all that shouting and screaming and lovemaking, it hadn't seemed right to leave. And he hadn't asked her to.

She knew more about him now than she had before. In fact, she had a suspicion that she knew everything about him. Even if it wasn't all put together into a complete picture. It was there. And now, with the pale morning light filtering through the window, she was staring at him as though she could make it all form a cohesive image.

As if she could will herself to somehow understand what all of those little pieces meant. As if she could make herself see the big picture.

Sam couldn't even see it, of that she was certain. So she had no idea how she could expect herself to see it. Except that she wanted to. Except that she needed to. She didn't want to leave him alone with all of that. It was too much.

It was too much for any one man. He felt responsible for the death of that woman. Or at least, he was letting himself think he did.

Protecting himself. Protecting himself with pain.

It made a strange kind of sense to her, only because she was a professional at protecting herself. At insulating herself from whatever else might come her way. Yes, it was a solitary existence. Yes, it was lonely. But there was control within that. She had a feeling that Sam operated in much the same way.

She shifted, brushing his hair out of his face. He had meant to frighten her off. He had given her an out. And she knew that somehow he had imagined she would take it. She knew that he believed he was some kind of monster. At least, part of him believed it.

Because she could also tell that he had been genuinely surprised that she hadn't turned tail and run.

But she hadn't. And she wouldn't. Mostly because she was just too stubborn. She had spent the past ten years being stubborn. Burying who she was underneath a whole bunch of bad attitude and sharp words. Not letting anyone get close, even though she had a bunch of people around her who cared. She had chosen to focus on the people who didn't. The people who didn't care enough. While simultaneously deciding that the people who did care enough, who cared more than enough, somehow weren't as important.

Well, she was done with that. There were people in her life who loved her. Who loved her no matter what. And she had a feeling that Sam had the ability to be one of those people. She didn't want to abandon him to this. Not when he had—whether he would admit it or not—

been instrumental in digging her out of her self-imposed emotional prison.

"Good morning," she whispered, pressing her lips to his cheek.

As soon as she did that, a strange sense of foreboding stole over her. As though she knew that the next few moments were going to go badly. But maybe that was just her natural pessimism. The little beast she had built up to be the strongest and best-developed piece of her. Another defense.

Sam's eyes opened, and the shock that she glimpsed there absolutely did not bode well for the next few moments. She knew that. "I stayed the night," she said, in response to the unasked question she could see lurking on his face.

"I guess I fell asleep," he said, his voice husky.

"Clearly." She took a deep breath. Oh well. If it was all going to hell, it might as well go in style. "I want you to come to the family Christmas party with me."

It took only a few moments for her to decide that she was going to say those words. And that she was going to follow them up with everything that was brimming inside her. Feelings that she didn't feel like keeping hidden. Not anymore. Maybe it was selfish. But she didn't really care. She knew his stuff. He knew hers. The only excuse she had for not telling him how she felt was self-protection.

She knew where self-protection got her. Absolutely nowhere. Treading water in a stagnant pool of her own failings, never advancing any further on in her life. In her existence. It left her lonely. It left her without any real, true friends. She didn't want that. Not anymore. And if she had to allow herself to be wounded in the name of authenticity, in the name of trying again, then she would.

An easy decision to make before the injury occurred. But it was made nonetheless.

"Why?" Sam asked, rolling away from her, getting up out of bed.

She took that opportunity to drink in every detail of his perfect body. His powerful chest, his muscular thighs. Memorizing every little piece of him. More Sam for her collection. She had a feeling that eventually she would walk away from him with nothing but that collection. A little pail full of the shadows of what she used to have.

"Because I would like to have a date." She was stalling now.

"You want to make your dad mad? Is that what we're doing? A little bit of revenge for everything he put you through?"

"I would never use you that way, Sam. I hope you know me better than that."

"We don't know each other, Maddy. We don't. We've had a few conversations, and we've had some sex. But that doesn't mean knowing somebody. Not really."

"That just isn't true. Nobody else knows how I feel about what happened to me. Nobody. Nobody else knows about the conversation I had with my dad. And I would imagine that nobody knows about Elizabeth. Not the way that I do."

"We used each other as a confessional. That isn't the same."

"The funny thing is it did start that way. At least for me. Because what did it matter what you knew. We weren't going to have a relationship after. So I didn't have to worry about you judging me. I didn't have to worry about anything."

"And?"

"That was just what I told myself. It was what made it feel okay to do what I wanted to do. We lie to ourselves. We get really deep in it when we feel like we need protection. That was what I was doing. But the simple truth is I felt a connection with you from the beginning. It was why I was so terrible to you. Because it scared me."

"You should have kept on letting it scare you, baby girl."

Those words acted like a shot of rage that went straight to her stomach, then fired onto her head. "Why? Because it's the thing that allows you to maintain your cranky-loner mystique? That isn't you. I thought maybe you didn't feel anything. But now I think you feel everything. And it scares you. I'm the same way."

"I see where this is going, Maddy. Don't do it. Don't. I can tell you right now it isn't going to go the way you think it will."

"Oh, go ahead, Sam. Tell me what I think. Please. I'm dying to hear it."

"You think that because you've had some kind of transformation, some kind of deep realization, that I'm headed for the same. But it's bullshit. I'm sorry to be the one to tell you. Wishful thinking on a level I never wanted you to start thinking on. You knew the rules. You knew them from the beginning."

"Don't," she said, her throat tightening, her chest constricting. "Don't do this to us. Don't pretend it can stay the same thing it started out as. Because it isn't. And you know it."

"You're composing a really compelling story, Madison." The reversion back to her full name felt significant. "And we both know that's something you do. Make more out of sex than it was supposed to be."

She gritted her teeth, battling through. Because he wanted her to stop. He wanted this to intimidate, to hurt. He wanted it to stop her. But she wasn't going to let him win. Not at this. Not at his own self-destruction. "Jackass 101. Using somebody's deep pain against them. I thought you were above that, Sam."

"It turns out I'm not. You might want to pay attention to that."

"I'm paying attention. I want you to come with me to the Christmas party, Sam. Because I want it to be the beginning. I don't want it to be the end."

"Don't do this."

He bent down, beginning to collect his clothes, his focus on anything in the room but her. She took a deep breath, knowing that what happened next was going to shatter all of this.

"I need more. I need more than twelve days of Christmas. I want it every day. I want to wake up with you every morning and go to bed with you every night. I want to fight with you. I want to make love with you. I want to tell you my secrets. To show you every dark, hidden thing in me. The serious things and the silly things. Because I love you. It's that complicated and that simple. I love you and that means I'm willing to do this, no matter how it ends."

Sam tugged his pants on, did them up, then pulled his shirt over his head. "I told you not to do this, Maddy. But you're doing it anyway. And you know what that makes it? A suicide mission. You stand there, thinking you're being brave because you're telling the truth. But you know how it's going to end. You know that after you make this confession, you're not actually going to have to deal with the relationship with me, because I already told you it isn't happening. I wonder if you would have been so brave if you knew I might turn around and offer you forever."

His words hit her with the force of bullets. But for some reason, they didn't hurt. Not really. She could remember distinctly when David had broken things off with her. Saying that she had never been anything serious. That she had been only a little bit of tail on the side and he was of course going to have to stay with his wife. Because she was the center of his life. Of his career. Because she mattered, and Maddy didn't. That had hurt. It had hurt because it had been true.

Because David hadn't loved her. And it had been easy for him to break up with her because he had never intended on having more with her, and not a single part of him wanted more.

This was different. It was different because Sam was trying to hurt her out of desperation. Because Sam was lying. Or at the very least, was sidestepping. Because he didn't want to have the conversation.

Because he would have to lie to protect himself. Because he couldn't look her in the eye and tell her that he didn't love her, that she didn't matter.

But she wasn't certain he would let himself feel it. That was the gamble. She knew he felt it. She knew it. That deep down, Sam cared. She wasn't sure if he knew it. If he had allowed himself access to those feelings. Feelings that Sam seemed to think were a luxury, or a danger. Grief. Desire. Love.

"Go ahead and offer it. You won't. You won't, because you know I would actually say yes. You can try to make this about how damaged I am, but all of this is because of you."

"You have to be damaged to want somebody like me. You know what's in my past."

"Grief. Grief that you won't let yourself feel. Sadness you don't feel like you're allowed to have. That's what's in your past. Along with lost hope. Let's not pretend you blame yourself. You felt so comfortable calling me out, telling me that I was playing games. Well, guess what. That's what you're doing. You think if you don't want anything, if you don't need anything, you won't be hurt again. But you're just living in hurt and that isn't better."

"You have all this clarity about your own emotional situation, and you think that gives you a right to talk about mine?"

She threw the blankets off her and got out of bed. "Why not?" she asked, throwing her arms wide. She didn't care that she was naked. In fact, in many ways it seemed appropriate. That Sam had put clothes on, that he had felt the need to cover himself, and that she didn't even care anymore. She had no pride left. But this wasn't about pride.

"You think you have the right to talk about mine," she continued. "You think you're going to twist everything that I'm saying and eventually you'll find some little doubt inside me that will make me believe you're telling the truth. I've had enough of that. I've had enough of men telling me what I feel. Of them telling me what I should do. I'm not going to let you do it. You're better than that. At least, I thought you were."

"Maybe I'm not."

"Right now? I think you don't want to be. But I would love you through this too, Sam. You need to know that. You need to know that whatever you say right now, in this room, it's not going to change the way that I feel about you. You don't have that kind of power."

"That's pathetic. There's nothing I can say to make you not love me? Why don't you love yourself a little bit more than that, Madison," he said, his tone hard.

And regardless of what she had just said, that did hit something in her. Something vulnerable and scared. Something that was afraid she really hadn't learned how to be anything more than a pathetic creature, desperate for a man to show her affection.

"I love myself just enough to put myself out there and demand this," she said finally, her voice vibrating with conviction. "I love myself too much to slink off silently. I love myself too much not to fight for what I know we could have. If I didn't do this, if I didn't say this, it would only be for my pride. It would be so I could score points and feel like maybe I won. But in the end, if I walk away without having fought for you with everything I have in me, we will have both lost. I think you're worth that. I know you are. Why don't you think so?"

"Why do you?" he asked, his voice thin, brittle. "I don't think I've shown you any particular kindness or tenderness."

"Don't. Don't erase everything that's happened between us. Everything I told you. Everything you gave me."

"Keeping my mouth shut while I held a beautiful woman and let her talk? That's easy."

"I love you, Sam. That's all. I'm not going to stand here and have an argument. I'm not going to let you get in endless barbs while you try to make those words something less than true. I love you. I would really like it if you could tell me you loved me too."

"I don't." His words were flat in the room. And she knew they were all she would get from him. Right now, it was all he could say. And he believed it. He believed it down to his bones. That he didn't love her. That everything that had taken place between them over the past week meant nothing. Because he had to. Because behind that certainty, that flat, horrifying expression in his eyes, was fear.

Strong, beautiful Sam, who could bend iron to his will, couldn't overpower the fear that lived inside him. And she would never be able to do it for him.

"Okay," she said softly, beginning to gather her clothes. She didn't know how to do this. She didn't know what to do now. How to make a triumphant exit. So she decided she wouldn't. She decided to let the tears fall down her cheeks; she decided not to make a joke. She decided not to say anything flippant or amusing.

Because that was what the old Maddy would have done. She would have played it off. She would have tried to laugh. She wouldn't have let herself feel this, not all the way down. She wouldn't have let her heart feel bruised or tender. Wouldn't have let a wave of pain roll over her. Wouldn't have let herself feel it, not really.

And when she walked out of his house, sniffling, her shoulders shaking, and could no longer hold back the sob that was building in her chest by the time she reached her car, she didn't care. She didn't feel ashamed.

There was no shame in loving someone.

She opened the driver-side door and sat down. And

then the dam burst. She had loved so many people who had never loved her in return. Not the way she loved them. She had made herself hard because of it. She had put the shame on her own shoulders.

That somehow a seventeen-year-old girl should have known that her teacher was lying to her. That somehow a daughter whose father had walked her down Main Street and bought her sweets in a little shop should have known that her father's affection had its limits.

That a woman who had met a man who had finally reached deep inside her and moved all those defenses she had erected around her heart should have known that in the end he would break it.

No. It wasn't her. It wasn't the love that was bad. It was the pride. The shame. The fear. Those were the things that needed to be gotten rid of.

She took a deep, shaking breath. She blinked hard, forcing the rest of her tears to fall, and then she started the car.

She would be okay. Because she had found herself again. Had learned how to love again. Had found a deep certainty and confidence in herself that had been missing for so long.

But as she drove away, she still felt torn in two. Because while she had been made whole, she knew that she was leaving Sam behind, still as broken as she had found him.

Chapter 12

Sam thought he might be dying. But then, that could easily be alcohol poisoning. He had been drinking and going from his house into his studio for the past two days. And that was it. He hadn't talked to anyone. He had nothing to say. He had sent Maddy away, and while he was firmly convinced it was the only thing he could have done, it hurt like a son of a bitch.

It shouldn't. It had been necessary. He couldn't love her the way that she wanted him to. He couldn't. There was no way in hell. Not a man like him.

Her words started to crowd in on him unbidden, the exact opposite thing that he wanted to remember right now. About how there was no point blaming himself. About how that wasn't the real issue. He growled, grabbing hold of the hammer he'd been using and flinging it across the room. It landed in a pile of scrap metal, the sound satisfying, the lack of damage unsatisfying.

He had a fire burning hot, and the room was stifling. He stripped his shirt off, feeling like he couldn't catch his breath. He felt like he was losing his mind. But then, he wasn't a stranger to it. He had felt this way after his parents had died. Again after Elizabeth. There was so much inside him, and there was nowhere for it to go.

And just like those other times, he didn't deserve this pain. Not at all. He was the one who had hurt her. He was the one who couldn't stand up to that declaration of love. He didn't deserve this pain.

But no matter how deep he tried to push it down, no matter how he tried to pound it out with a hammer, it still remained. And his brain was blank. He couldn't even figure out how the hell he might fashion some of this material into another cow.

It was like the thing inside him that told him how to create things had left along with Maddy.

He looked over at the bottle of Jack Daniel's that was sitting on his workbench. And cursed when he saw that it was empty. He was going to have to get more. But he wasn't sure he had more in the house. Which meant leaving the house. Maybe going to Chase's place and seeing if there was anything to take. Between that and sobriety it was a difficult choice.

He looked around, looked at the horse that he had bent Maddy over just three days ago. Everything seemed dead now. Cold. Dark. Usually he felt the life in the things that he made. Something he would never tell anyone, because it sounded stupid. Because it exposed him.

But it was like Maddy had come in here and changed things. Taken everything with her when she left.

He walked over to the horse, braced his hands on the

back of it and leaned forward, giving into the wave of pain that crashed over him suddenly, uncontrollably.

"I thought I might find you in here."

Sam lifted his head at the sound of his brother's voice. "I'm busy."

"Right. Which is why there is nothing new in here, but it smells flammable."

"I had a drink."

"Or twelve," Chase said, sounding surprisingly sympathetic. "If you get too close to that forge, you're going to burst into flame."

"That might not be so bad."

"What's going on? You're always a grumpy bastard, but this is different. You don't usually disappear for days at a time. Actually, I can pick up a couple of times that you've done that in the past. You usually reemerge worse and even more impossible than you were before. So if that is what's happening here, I would appreciate a heads-up."

"It's nothing. Artistic temper tantrum."

"I don't believe that." Chase crossed his arms and leaned against the back wall of the studio, making it very clear that he intended to stay until Sam told him something.

Fine. The bastard could hang out all day for all he cared. It didn't mean he had to talk.

"Believe whatever you want," Sam said. "But it's not going to make hanging out here any more interesting. I can't figure out what to make next. Are you happy? I have no idea. I have no inspiration." Suddenly, everything in him boiled over. "And I hate that. I hate that it matters. I should just be able to think of something to do. Or not care if I don't want to do it. But somehow, I can't make it work if I don't care at least a little bit. I hate caring, Chase. I *hate* it."

He hated it for every damn thing. Every damn, fragile thing.

"I know," Chase said. "And I blame Dad for that. He didn't understand. That isn't your fault. And it's not your flaw that you care. Think about the way he was about ranching. It was ridiculous. Weather that didn't go his way would send him into some kind of emotional tailspin for weeks. And he felt the same way about iron that you do. It's just that he felt compelled to shape it into things that had a function. But he took pride in his work. And he was an artist with it—you know he was. If anything, I think he was shocked by what you could do. Maybe even a little bit jealous. And he didn't know what to do with it."

Sam resisted those words. And the truth in them. "It doesn't matter."

"It does. Because it's why you can't talk about what you do. It's why you don't take pride in it the way that you should. It's why you're sitting here downplaying the fact you're having some kind of art block when it's been pretty clear for a few months that you have been."

"It shouldn't be a thing."

Chase shrugged. "Maybe not. But the very thing that makes your work valuable is also what makes it difficult. You're not a machine."

Sam wished he was. More than anything, he wished that he was. So that he wouldn't care about a damn thing. So that he wouldn't care about Maddy.

Softness, curves, floated to the forefront of his mind. Darkness and grief. All the inspiration he could ever want. Except that he couldn't take it. It wasn't his. He didn't own it. None of it.

He was still trying to pull things out of his own soul,

and all he got was dry, hard work that looked downright ugly to him.

"I should be," he said, stubborn.

"This isn't about Dad, though. I don't even think it's about the art, though I think it's related. There was a woman, wasn't there?"

Sam snorted. "When?"

"Recently. Like the past week. Mostly I think so because I recognize that all-consuming obsession. Because I recognize this. Because you came and kicked my ass when I was in a very similar position just a year ago. And you know what you told me? With great authority, you told me that iron had to get hot to get shaped into something. You told me that I was in my fire, and I had to let it shape me into the man Anna needed me to be."

"Yeah, I guess I did tell you that," Sam said.

"Obviously I'm not privy to all the details of your personal life, Sam, which is your prerogative. But you're in here actively attempting to drink yourself to death. You say that you can't find any inspiration for your art. I would say that you're in a pretty damn bad situation. And maybe you need to pull yourself out of it. If that means grabbing hold of her—whoever she is—then do it."

Sam felt like the frustration inside him was about to overflow. "I can't. There's too much… There's too much. If you knew, Chase. If you knew everything about me, you wouldn't think I deserved it."

"Who deserves it?" Chase asked. "Does anybody? Do you honestly think I deserve Anna? I don't. But I love her. And I work every day to deserve her. It's a work in progress, let me tell you. But that's love. You just kind of keep working for it."

"There are too many other things in the way," Sam said, because he didn't know how else to articulate it. Without having a confessional, here in his studio, he didn't know how else to have this conversation.

"What things? What are you afraid of, Sam? Having a feeling? Is that what all this is about? The fact you want to protect yourself? The fact that it matters more to you that you get to keep your stoic expression and your who-gives-a-damn attitude intact?"

"It isn't that. It's never been that. But how—" He started again. "How was I supposed to grieve for Dad when you lost your mentor? How was I supposed to grieve for Mom when you were so young? It wasn't fair." And how the hell was he supposed to grieve for Elizabeth, for the child he didn't even know she had been carrying, when her own family was left with nothing.

"Of course you could grieve for them. They were your parents."

"Somebody has to be strong, Chase."

"And you thought I was weak? You think somehow grieving for my parents was weak?"

"Of course not. But… I was never the man that Dad wanted me to be. Now when he was alive. I didn't do what he wanted me to do. I didn't want the things that he wanted."

"Neither did I. And we both just about killed ourselves working this place the way that he wanted us to while it slowly sank into the ground. Then we had to do things on our terms. Because actually, we did know what we were talking about. And who we are, the gifts that we have, those mattered. If it wasn't for the fact that I have a business mind, if it wasn't for the fact that you could do the artwork, the ranch wouldn't be here. McCormack Ironworks wouldn't exist. And if Dad had lived, he would be proud of us. Because in the end we saved this place."

"I just don't… I had a girlfriend who died." He didn't know why he had spoken the words. He hadn't intended to. "She wasn't my girlfriend when she died. But she bled to death. At the hospital. She had been pregnant. And it was mine."

Chase cursed and fell back against the wall, bracing himself. "Seriously?"

"Yes. And I want… I want to do something with that feeling. But her family is devastated, Chase. They lost so much more than I did. And I don't know how… I don't know what to do with all of this. I don't know what to do with all of these feelings. I don't feel like I deserve them. I don't feel like I deserve the pain. Not in the way that I deserve to walk away from it unscathed. But I feel like it isn't mine. Like I'm taking something from them, or making something about me that just shouldn't be. But it's there all the same. And it follows me around. And Maddy loves me. She said she loves me. And I don't know how to take that either."

"Bullshit," Chase said, his voice rough. "That's not it."

"Don't tell me how it is, Chase, not when you don't know."

"Of course I know, Sam. Loss is hell. And I didn't lose half of what you did."

"It was just the possibility of something. Elizabeth. It wasn't… It was just…"

"Sam. You lost your parents. And a woman you were involved with who was carrying your baby. Of course you're screwed up. But walking around pretending you're just grumpy, pretending you don't want anything, that you don't care about anything, doesn't protect you from pain. It's just letting fear poison you from the inside."

Sam felt like he was staring down into an abyss that had no end. A yawning, bottomless cavern that was just full of need. All the need he had ever felt his entire life. The words ricocheted back at him, hit him like shrapnel, damaging, wounding. They were the truth. That it was what drove him, that it was what stopped him.

Fear.

That it was why he had spent so many years hiding.

And as blindingly clear as it was, it was also clear that Maddy was right about him. More right about him than he'd ever been about himself.

That confession made him think of Maddy too. Of the situation she was in with her father. Of those broken words she had spoken to him about how if her own father didn't think she was worth defending, who would? And he had sent her away, like he didn't think she was worth it either. Like he didn't think she was worth the pain or the risk.

Except he did. He thought she was worth defending. That she was worth loving. That she was worth everything.

Sam felt… Well, nothing on this earth had ever made him feel small before. But this did it. He felt scared. He felt weak. Mostly he felt a kind of overwhelming sadness for everything he'd lost. For all the words that were left unsaid. The years of grief that had built up.

It had never been about control. It had never been based in reality. Or about whether or not he deserved something. Not really. He was afraid of feeling. Of loss. More loss after years and years of it.

But his father had died without knowing. Without

knowing that even though things weren't always the best between them, Sam had loved him. Elizabeth had died without knowing Sam had cared.

Protecting himself meant hurting other people. And it damn well hurt him.

Maddy had been brave enough to show him. And he had rejected it. Utterly. Completely. She had been so brave, and he had remained shut down as he'd been for years.

She had removed any risk of rejection and still he had been afraid. He had been willing to lose her this time.

"Do you know why the art is hard?" he asked.

"Why?"

"Because. If I make what I really want to, then I actually have to feel it."

He hated saying it. Hated admitting it. But he knew, somehow, that this was essential to his soul. That if he was ever going to move on from this place, from this dry, drunken place that produced nothing but anguish, he had to start saying these things. He had to start committing to these things.

"I had a lot behind this idea that I wasn't good enough. That I didn't deserve to feel. Because…the alternative is feeling it. It's caring when it's easier to be mad at everything. Hoping for things when so much is already dead."

"What's the alternative?" Chase asked.

He looked around his studio. At all the lifeless things. Hard and sharp. Just like he was. The alternative was living without hope. The alternative was acting like he was dead too.

"This," he said finally. "And life without Maddy. I'd rather risk everything than live without her."

Chapter 13

Madison looked around the beautifully appointed room. The grand party facility at the ranch was decorated in evergreen boughs and white Christmas lights, the trays of glittering champagne moving by somehow adding to the motif. Sparkling. Pristine.

Maddy herself was dressed in a gown that could be described in much the same manner. A pale yellow that caught the lights and glimmered like sun on new-fallen snow.

However, it was a prime example of how appearances can be deceiving. She felt horrible. Much more like snow that had been mixed up with gravel. Gritty. Gray.

Hopefully no one was any the wiser. She was good at putting on a brave face. Good at pretending everything was fine. Something she had perfected over the years. Not just at these kinds of public events but at family events too.

Self-protection was her favorite accessory. It went with everything.

She looked outside, at the terrace, which was lit by a thatch of Christmas lights, heated by a few freestanding heaters. However, no one was out there. She took a deep breath, seeing her opportunity for escape. And she took it. She just needed a few minutes. A few minutes to feel a little bit less like her face would crack beneath the weight of her fake smile.

A few minutes to take a deep breath and not worry so much that it would turn into a sob.

She grabbed hold of a glass of champagne, then moved quickly to the door, slipping out into the chilly night air. She went over near one of the heaters, wrapping her arms around herself and simply standing for a moment, looking out into the inky blackness, looking at nothing. It felt good. It was a relief to her burning eyes. A relief to her scorched soul.

All of this feelings business was rough. She wasn't entirely certain she could recommend it.

"What's going on, Maddy?"

She turned around, trying to force a smile when she saw her brother Gage standing there.

"I just needed a little bit of quiet," she said, lifting her glass of champagne.

"Sure." He stuffed his hands in his pockets. "I'm not used to this kind of thing. I spent a lot of time on the road. In crappy hotels. Not a lot of time at these sorts of get-togethers."

"Regretting the whole return-of-the-prodigal-son thing? Because it's too late to unkill that fatted calf, young man. You're stuck."

He laughed. "No. I'm glad that I'm back. Because of you. Because of Colton, Sierra. Even Jack."

"Rebecca?"

"Of course." He took a deep breath, closing the distance between them. "So what's going on with you?"

"Nothing," she said, smiling.

"I have a feeling that everybody else usually buys that. Which is why you do it. But I don't. Is it Jack? Is it having him here?"

She thought about that. Seriously thought about it. "No," she said, truthful. "I'm glad. I'm so glad that we're starting to fix some of this. I spent a long time holding on to my anger. My anger at Dad. At the past. All of my pain. And Jack got caught up in that. Because of the circumstances. We are all very different people. And getting to this point... I feel like we took five different paths. But here we are. And it isn't for Dad. It's for us. I think that's good. I spent a lot of time doing things in response to him. In response to the pain that he caused me. I don't want to do that anymore. I don't want to act from a place of pain and fear anymore."

"That's quite a different stance. I mean, since last we talked at The Grind."

She tried to smile again, wandering over to one of the wooden pillars. "I guess some things happened." She pressed her palm against the cold surface, then her forehead. She took a deep breath. In and out, slowly, evenly.

"Are you okay?"

She shook her head. "Not really. But I will be."

"I know I missed your first big heartbreak. And I feel like I would have done that bastard some bodily harm. I have quite a bit of internalized rage built up. If you need me to hurt anyone… I will. Gladly."

She laughed. "I appreciate that. Really, I do. It's just that…it's a good thing this is happening. It's making me realize a lot of things. It's making me change a lot of things. I just wish it didn't hurt."

"You know…when Rebecca told me that she loved me, it scared the hell out of me. And I said some things that I shouldn't have said. That no one should ever say to anyone. I regretted it. But I was running scared, and I wanted to make sure she didn't come after me. I'm so glad that she forgave me when I realized what an idiot I was."

She lifted her head, turning to face him. "That sounds a lot like brotherly advice."

"It is. And maybe it's not relevant to your situation. I don't know. But what I do know is that we both have a tendency to hold on to pain. On to anger. If you get a chance to fix this, I hope you forgive the bastard. As long as he's worthy."

"How will I know he's worthy?" she asked, a bit of humor lacing her voice.

"Well, I'll have to vet him. At some point."

"Assuming he ever speaks to me again, I would be happy to arrange that."

Gage nodded. "If he's half as miserable as you are, trust me, he'll be coming after you pretty quick."

"And you think I should forgive him?"

"I think that men are a bunch of hardheaded dumb-asses. And some of us need more chances than others. And I thank God every day I got mine. With this family. With Rebecca. So it would be mean-spirited of me not to advocate for the same for another of my species."

"I'll keep that under advisement."

Gage turned to go. "Do that. But if he keeps being a dumbass, let me know. Because I'll get together a posse or something."

"Thank you," she said. "Hopefully the posse won't be necessary."

He shrugged, then walked back into the party. She felt fortified then. Because she knew she had people on her side. No matter what. She wasn't alone. And that felt good. Even when most everything felt bad.

She let out a long, slow breath and rested her forearms on the railing, leaning forward, staring out across the darkened field. If she closed her eyes, she could almost imagine that she could see straight out to the ocean in spite of the fact that it was dark.

She was starting to get cold, even with the artificial heat. But it was entirely possible the chill was coming from inside her. Side effects of heartbreak and all of that.

"Merry Christmas Eve."

She straightened, blinking, looking out into the darkness. Afraid to turn around. That voice was familiar. And it didn't belong to anyone in her family.

She turned slowly, her heart stalling when she saw Sam standing there. He was wearing a white shirt unbuttoned at the collar, a black jacket and a pair of black slacks. His hair was disheveled, and she was pretty sure she could see a bit of soot on his chest where the open shirt exposed his skin.

"What are you doing here?"

"I had to see you." He took a step closer to her. "Bad enough that I put this on."

"Where did you get it?"

"The secondhand store on Main."

"Wow." No matter what he had to say, the fact that Sam McCormack had shown up in a suit said a whole lot without him ever opening his mouth.

"It doesn't really fit. And I couldn't figure out how to tie the tie." And of course, he hadn't asked anyone for help. Sam never would. It just wasn't him.

"Well, then going without was definitely the right method."

"I have my moments of brilliance." He shook his head. "But the other day wasn't one of them."

Her heart felt as if it were in a free fall, her stomach clenching tight. "Really?"

"Yeah."

"I agree. I mean, unreservedly. But I am open to hearing about your version of why you didn't think you were brilliant. Just in case we have differing opinions on the event."

He cursed. "I'm not good at this." He took two steps toward her, then reached out, gripping her chin between his thumb and forefinger. "I hate this, in fact. I'm not good at talking about feelings. And I've spent a lot of years trying to bury them down deep. I would like to do it now. But I know there's no good ending to that. I know that I owe you more."

"Go on," she said, keeping her eyes on his, her voice trembling, betraying the depth of emotion she felt.

She had never seen Sam quite like this, on edge, like he might shatter completely at any moment. "I told you I thought I didn't deserve these feelings. And I believed it."

"I know you did," she said, the words broken. "I know that you never lied on purpose, Sam. I know."

"I don't deserve that. That certainty. I didn't do anything to earn it."

She shook her head. "Stop. We're not going to talk like that. About what we deserve. I don't know what I deserve. But I know what I want. I want you. And I don't care if I'm jumping the gun. I don't care if I didn't make you grovel enough. It's true. I do."

"Maddy…"

"This all comes because we tried to protect ourselves for too long. Because we buried everything down deep. I don't have any defenses anymore. I can't do it anymore. I couldn't even if I wanted to. Which you can see, because I'm basically throwing myself at you again."

"I've always been afraid there was something wrong with me." His dark eyes were intense, and she could tell that he was wishing he could turn to stone rather than finish what he was saying. But that he was determined. That he had put his foot on the path and he wasn't going to deviate from it. "Something wrong with what I felt. And I pushed it all down. I always have. I've been through stuff that would make a lot of people crazy. But if you keep shoving it on down, it never gets any better." He shook his head. "I've been holding on to grief. Holding on to anger. I didn't know what else to do with it. My feelings about my parents, my feelings about Elizabeth, the baby. It's complicated. It's a lot. And I think more than anything I just didn't want to deal with it. I had a lot of excuses, and they felt real. They even felt maybe a little bit noble?"

"I can see that. I can see it being preferable to grief."

"Just like you said, Maddy. You put all those defenses in front of it, and then nothing can hurt you, right?"

She nodded. "At least, that's been the way I've handled it for a long time."

"You run out. Of whatever it is you need to be a person. Whatever it is you need to contribute, to create. That's why I haven't been able to do anything new with my artwork." He rolled his eyes, shaking his head slightly. "It's hard for me to…"

"I know. You would rather die than talk about feelings. And talk about this. But I think you need to."

"I told myself it was wrong to make something for my dad. My mom. Because they didn't support my work. I told myself I didn't deserve to profit off Elizabeth's death in any way. But that was never the real issue. The real issue was not wanting to feel those things at all. I was walking across the field the other night, and I thought about grief. The way that it covers things, twists the world around you into something unrecognizable." He shook his head. "When you're in the thick of it, it's like walking in the dark. Even if you're in a place you've seen a thousand times by day, it all changes. And suddenly what seemed safe is now full of danger."

He took a sharp breath and continued. "You can't trust anymore. You can't trust everything will be okay, because you've seen that sometimes it isn't. That's what it's like to have lost people like I have. And I can think about a thousand pieces that I could create that would express that. But it would mean that I had to feel it. And it would mean I would have to show other people what I felt. I wanted… From the moment I laid my hands on you, Maddy, I wanted to turn you into something. A sculpture. A painting. But that would mean looking at how I felt about you too. And I didn't want to do that either."

Maddy lifted her hand, cupping Sam's cheek. "I understand why you work with iron, Sam. Because it's just like you. You're so strong. And you really don't want to bend. But if you would just bend...just a little bit, I think you could be something even more beautiful than you already are."

"I'll do more than bend. If I have to, to have you, I'll break first. But I've decided... I don't care about protecting myself. From loss, from pain...doesn't matter. I just care about you. And I know that I have to fix myself if I'm going to become the kind of man you deserve. I know I have to reach inside and figure all that emotional crap out. I can't just decide that I love you and never look at the rest of it. I have to do all of it. To love you the way that you deserve, I know I have to deal with all of it."

"Do you love me?"

He nodded slowly. "I do." He reached into his jacket pocket and took out a notebook. "I've been working on a new collection. Just sketches right now. Just plans." He handed her the notebook. "I want you to see it. I know you'll understand."

She took it from him, opening it with shaking hands, her heart thundering hard in her throat. She looked at the first page, at the dark twisted mass he had sketched there. Maybe it was a beast, or maybe it was just menacing angles—it was hard to tell. She imagined that was the point.

There was more. Broken figures, twisted metal. Until the very last page. Where the lines smoothed out into rounded curves, until the mood shifted dramatically and everything looked a whole lot more like hope.

"It's hard to get a sense of scale and everything in the drawings. This is just me kind of blocking it out."

"I understand," she whispered. "I understand perfectly." It started with grief, and it ended with love. Unimaginable pain that was transformed.

"I lost a lot of things, Maddy. I would hate for you to be one of them. Especially because you're the one thing I chose to lose. And I have regretted it every moment since. But this is me." He put his fingertip on the notebook. "That's me. I'm not the nicest guy. I'm not what anybody would call cheerful. Frankly, I'm a grumpy son of a bitch. It's hard for me to talk about what I'm feeling. Harder for me to show it, and I'm in the world's worst line of work for that. But if you'll let me, I'll be your grumpy son of a bitch. And I'll try. I'll try for you."

"Sam," she said, "I love you. I love you, and I don't need you to be anything more than you. I'm willing to accept the fact that getting to your feelings may always be a little bit of an excavation. But if you promise to work on it, I'll promise not to be too sensitive about it. And maybe we can meet somewhere in the middle. One person doesn't have to do all the changing. And I don't want you to anyway." She smiled, and this time it wasn't forced. "You had me at 'You're at the wrong door.'"

He chuckled. "I think you had me a lot sooner than that. I just didn't know it."

"So," she said, looking up at him, feeling like the sun was shining inside her, in spite of the chill outside, "you want to go play Yahtzee?"

"Only if you mean it euphemistically."

"Absolutely not. I expect you to take the time to woo me, Sam McCormack. And if that includes board games, that's just a burden you'll have to bear."

Sam smiled. A real smile. One that showed his heart,

his soul, and held nothing back. "I would gladly spend the rest of my life bearing your burdens, Madison West."

"On second thought," she said, "board games not required."

"Oh yeah? What do you need, then?"

"Nothing much at all. Just hold me, cowboy. That's enough for me."

* * * * *

Also by Naima Simone

Harlequin Desire

Ruthless Pride
Back in the Texan's Bed
Trust Fund Fiancé

Blackout Billionaires

The Billionaire's Bargain
Black Tie Billionaire
Blame It on the Billionaire

Billionaires of Boston

Vows in Name Only
Secrets of a One Night Stand

HQN

Rose Bend

Slow Dance at Rose Bend
The Road to Rose Bend
A Kiss to Remember
Christmas in Rose Bend

Visit her Author Profile page on Harlequin.com,
or naimasimone.com, for more titles!

BLACK TIE BILLIONAIRE

Naima Simone

To Gary. 143.

Chapter 1

She was beautiful.

Gideon Knight tuned out the man speaking to him as he studied the petite woman weaving a path through the crowded ballroom. Even wearing the white shirt, black bow tie and dark pants of the waitstaff, she stood out like the brightest jewel among the hundreds of guests at the Du Sable City Gala, the annual event of the Chicago social season, rendering those around her to mere cubic zirconia.

How was it that only *he* noticed the elegant length of her neck, the straight line of her back that tapered at the waist and flowed out in a gentle, sensual swell of hips? How did the other people in the room not ogle the particular way the light from the crystal chandeliers hit her bronze skin, causing it to gleam? How did they not stop and study the graceful stride that wouldn't have been out of place on the most exclusive catwalk?

Had he said beautiful? He meant exquisite.

And he hadn't even seen her face.

Yet.

"Excuse me." Gideon abruptly interrupted the prattling of the older gentleman, not bothering with a polite explanation for walking away.

The other man's surprised sputtering should've dredged up a semblance of regret, especially since Gideon's mother had hammered better manners into him. But just ten years ago this gentleman wouldn't have deigned to acknowledge Gideon's existence. Then he'd been just another penniless, dream-filled, University of Chicago business student. He hadn't been *the* Gideon Knight, cofounder and CEO of KayCee Corp, one of the hottest and most successful start-up companies to hit the market in the last five years. Now that he was a multibillionaire, this businessman, and people of his tax bracket and social sphere, damn near scraped their chins on the floor with all the bowing and kowtowing they directed Gideon's way.

Money and power had that peculiar effect.

Usually, he could dredge up more patience, but he despised events like this high society benefit gala. One thing he'd learned in his grueling battle to breach the inner sanctum zealously guarded by the obscenely wealthy one percent was that a good portion of business deals were landed at dinner tables, country club golf courses and social events like the Du Sable City Gala. So even though attending ranked only slightly higher than shopping with his sister or vacationing in one of Dante's nine levels of hell, he attended.

But for the first time that he could remember, he was distracted from networking. And again, for the first time, he welcomed the disruption.

He wound his way through the tuxedoed and gowned throng, pretending not to hear when his name was called, and uttering a "Pardon me" when more persistent individuals tried to halt him with a touch to his arm. Many articles written about him had mentioned his laser-sharp focus, and at this moment, it was trained on a certain server with black hair swept into a low knot at the back of her head, a body created for the sweetest sin and skin that had his fingertips itching with the need to touch... to caress.

That need—the unprecedented urgency of it—should've been a warning to proceed with caution. And if he'd paused, he might've analyzed why the impulse to approach her, to look into her face, raked at him like a tiger's sharp claws. He might've retreated, or placed distance between him and her. Discipline, control, focus—they were the daily refrains of his life, the blocks upon which he'd built his business, his success. That this unknown woman already threatened all three by just being in the room... Not even his ex-fiancée had stirred this kind of attraction in him. Which only underscored why he should walk away. It boded nothing good.

Yet he followed her with the determination of a predator stalking its unsuspecting prey.

How cliché, but damn, how true. Because every instinct in him growled to capture, cover, take...bite.

She would be his tonight.

As the strength and certainty of the thought echoed inside him, he neared her. Close enough to glimpse the delicate line of her jaw and the vulnerable nape of her neck. To inhale the heady, sensual musk that contained notes of roses, and warmer hints of cedarwood and amber...or maybe almond.

Tonight's mission would be to discover which one.

For yet another time this evening, he murmured, "Excuse me." But in this instance, he wasn't trying to escape someone. No, he wanted to snare her. Keep her.

At least for the next few hours.

Look at me. Turn around and look at me.

The plea rebounded off his skull, and the seconds seemed to slow as she shifted, lifting her head and meeting his gaze.

His gut clenched, desire slamming into him so hard he braced himself against the impact. But it still left him reeling. Left his body tense, hard.

A long fringe of black hair swept over her forehead and dark-rimmed glasses perched on her nose, but neither could hide the strong, regal lines of her face, the sharp cheekbones, the chocolate eyes or the lush siren's call of her mouth.

Damn, that mouth.

He dragged his fascinated gaze away from it with a strength that deserved a gold medal. But nothing, not even God Himself, could cleanse his mind of the acts those curves elicited. Acts that left him throbbing and greedy.

"Did you need a glass of champagne?" she asked, lowering her eyes to the tray she held.

No, keep your eyes on me.

The order rolled up his throat and hovered on his tongue, but he locked it down. Damn, with just a few words uttered in a silk-and-midnight voice, he'd devolved into a caveman.

Once more, a warning to walk away clanged inside

him, but—like moments earlier—he ignored it. Nothing else mattered at the moment. Nothing but having that sex-and-sin voice stroke his ears. Having those hands slip under his clothes to caress his skin. And those oval-shaped eyes fixed on him.

"What's your name?" He delivered a question of his own, answering hers by picking up a glass flute full of pale wine.

If he hadn't been studying her so closely, he might've missed the slight stiffening of her shoulders, the minute hesitation before, head still bowed, she said, "I need to continue…"

She shifted away from him, preparing to escape into the crowd.

"Wait." He lifted his arm, instinct guiding him to grasp her elbow to prevent her departure. But at the last moment, he lowered his arm back to his side.

As much as he wanted to discover how she felt under his hand, he refused to touch her without her permission. Rich assholes accosting the waitstaff was as old a story as a boss chasing his secretary around the desk. Even though his palm itched with the lack of contact, he slid his free hand into his front pocket.

The aborted motion seemed to grab her attention. She raised her head, a frown drawing her eyebrows together.

"Gideon Knight," he said, offering her his name. "You have my name. Can I have yours?"

Again, that beat of hesitation. Then, with a small shake of her head, she murmured, "Camille."

"Camille," he repeated, savoring it as if it were one of the rich chocolate desserts that would follow the dinner course. "It's a lovely name. And it fits you."

Her eyes widened, an emotion he would've labeled panic flaring in their depths before she lowered her lashes, hiding her gaze from him. Again. "Thank you, Mr. Knight. If—"

"Gideon," he corrected. "For you, it's Gideon."

Her full lips firmed into a line seconds before she met his stare with one glinting in anger. How insane did it make him that he found the signs of her temper captivating...and sexy as hell?

"No offense, *Mr. Knight*—"

"In my experience, when someone starts a sentence with 'no offense,' they intend to offend," he drawled.

Once more he saw that flicker of anger, and an exhilaration that was usually reserved for fierce business negotiations surged in his chest. The exhilaration meant he was engaging with a worthy opponent.

"I'm going out on a limb and assuming your ego can take the hit," she shot back. Then, as if she realized what she'd snapped—and who she'd snapped at—she winced, briefly squeezing her eyes shut. "I apologize—"

"Oh, don't disappoint me now by turning meek, Camille," he purred, arching an eyebrow.

In a distant corner of his mind, he marveled at who he'd become in this moment. Flirting, teasing, goddamn *purring*—they weren't him. His mouth either didn't know this information or didn't care. "I assure you, I can take it," he added.

Take whatever she wanted to give him, whether it was her gaze, her conversation or more. And God, he hungered for the *more*. Greedy bastard that he was, he'd claim whatever she chose to dole out.

"Mr. Knight," she began, defiance clipping his name,

"I don't know if approaching the staff and toying with them is one of your usual forms of entertainment. But since you've invited me not to be *meek*, let me tell you this might be a game to you, but the waitstaff aren't toys to alleviate your boredom. This is a livelihood for workers who depend on a paycheck and not getting fired for fraternizing with the guests."

Shock vibrated through him like a plucked chord on his favorite Martin D-45 acoustic guitar.

Shock and…delight.

Other than his mother and family, no one had the balls to speak to him like she had, much less reprimand him. Excitement—something he hadn't experienced in so long he couldn't remember the last occurrence—tripped and stumbled down his spine.

"I don't play games," he said. "They're a waste of time. Why be coy when being honest achieves the goal faster?"

"And what's your goal here, Mr. Knight?" she challenged, not hiding her sneer.

If she understood how his pulse jumped and his body throbbed every time she stated "Mr. Knight" with a haughtiness worthy of royalty, she would probably swear a vow of silence.

"Cop a feel in a dark hallway? A little slap and tickle in a broom closet?" she asked.

"I'm too old to cop a feel. And I don't 'slap and tickle' either, whatever that is. I fuck."

Her head jerked back at his blunt statement, her eyes widening behind the dark frames. Even with the din of chatter and laughter flowing around them, he caught her sharp gasp.

A voice sounding suspiciously like that of Gray

Chandler, his business partner and best friend—his only friend—hissed a curse at him. How many times had Gray warned him to temper his brusque, straightforward manner? Well, to be more accurate, his friend described Gideon as tactless. Pretty words weren't his forte; honesty was. Normally, he didn't regret his abruptness. Like he'd told her, he didn't indulge in games. But in this moment, he almost regretted it.

Especially if she walked away from him.

"Is that why you stopped me? To proposition me?" She dropped her gaze to the champagne glass in his hand, and with just that glance let him know she didn't buy his pretense of wanting the wine. He shrugged, setting it behind him on one of the high tables scattered around the ballroom.

"Why single me out?" she continued. "Because I'm so beautiful you couldn't help yourself?" she mocked. "Or because I'm a server, and you're a guest in a position of power? What happens if I say no? Will I suddenly find myself relieved of my job?"

Disgust and the first flicker of anger wormed its way through his veins. "Do I want to spend a night with you? Inside you? Yes," he stated, and again her eyes flared wide at his frankness before narrowing. "I told you, I don't lie. I don't play games. But if you decline, then no, you would still have a check and employment at the end of the evening. I don't need to blackmail women into my bed, Camille. Besides, a willing woman, a woman who wants my hands on her body, who pleads for what she knows I can give her, is far more arousing, more pleasurable. And any man worth his dick would value that over a woman who's coerced or forced into handing over something that should be offered or surrendered of her own free will."

She silently studied him, the fire fading from her stare, but something else flicked in those dark eyes. And that "something" had him easing a step closer, yet stopping short of invading her personal space.

"To answer your other question," he murmured. "Why did I single you out? Your first guess was correct. Because you are so beautiful I couldn't help following you around this over-the-top ballroom filled with people who possess more money than sense. The women here can't outshine you. They're like peacocks, spreading their plumage, desperate to be noticed, and here you are among them, like the moon. Bright, alone, above it all and eclipsing every one of them. What I don't understand is how no one else noticed before me. Why every man in this place isn't standing behind me in a line just for the chance to be near you."

Silence swelled around them like a bubble, muting the din of the gala. His words seemed to echo in the cocoon, and he marveled at them. Hadn't he sworn he didn't do pretty words? Yet it had been him talking about peacocks and moons.

What was she doing to him?

Even as the question echoed in his mind, her head tilted back and she stared at him, her lovely eyes darker...hotter. In that moment, he'd stand under a damn balcony and serenade her if she continued looking at him like that. He curled his fingers into his palm, reminding himself with the pain that he couldn't touch her. Still, the only sound that reached his ears was the quick, soft pants breaking on her pretty lips.

As ridiculous as it seemed, he swore each breath slid under his clothes, swept over his skin. He ached to have each moist puff dampen his shoulders, his chest as her fingernails twisted in his hair, dug into his muscles, clinging to him as he drove them both to the point of carnal madness.

The growl prowled up his throat and out of him before he could contain it.

"I—I need to go," she whispered, already shifting back and away from him. "I—" She didn't finish the thought, but turned and waded into the crowd, distancing herself from him.

He didn't follow; she hadn't said no, but she hadn't said yes, either. And though he'd caught the desire in her gaze—his stomach still ached from the gut punch of it—she had to come to him.

Or ask him to come for her.

Rooted where she'd left him, he tracked her movements.

Saw the moment she cleared the mass of people and strode in the direction of the double doors where more tray-bearing staff emerged and exited.

Saw when she paused, palm pressed to one of the panels.

Saw when she glanced over her shoulder in his direction.

Even across the distance of the ballroom, the electric shock of that look whipped through him, sizzled in his veins. Moments later, she disappeared from view. Didn't matter; his feet were already moving in her direction.

That glance, that look. It'd sealed her fate.

Sealed it for both of them.

Chapter 2

Shay Camille Neal pushed through the doors leading into the huge, industrial kitchen that wouldn't have been out of place in a Michelin-star restaurant. With a world-famous chef renowned for his temper as well as his magic with food, a sous chef and army of station and line cooks bustling around the stainless steel countertops and range stoves, the area hummed with activity.

Under ordinary circumstances, she would've been enthralled, attempting to soak up whatever knowledge she could from the professionals attending. But the current circumstances were as far from ordinary as chicken nuggets were from coq au vin.

First, as a member of one of the oldest, wealthiest and most influential families in Chicago, she usually attended the Du Sable City Gala as a guest, not a server. But when her best friend, Bridgette, called her earlier in the afternoon sounding like a foghorn had replaced her voice box,

Shay had agreed to take Bridgette's place as a member of the catering staff. Though her friend owned and ran a fledgling food truck business, she still helped mitigate expenses and pay her personal bills with jobs on the side. The position with this particular catering company was one of her regulars, and Bridgette couldn't afford to lose the gig.

Shay had planned on skipping the gala, anyway. Facing a night at home with another binge of *House of Cards* on Netflix versus actually working in the periphery of a famous chef, the choice had been a no-brainer. Besides, Bridgette had assured Shay that most of her duties as an assistant to the line cooks would keep her in the kitchen.

Still, she'd donned a wig, dark brown contacts and glasses, as well as Bridgette's uniform. Because while she'd decided to skip out on the social event of the season, her older brother, Trevor, and his fiancée, Madison Reus—Senator Julian Reus's only daughter—were attending. Trevor already didn't approve of Shay's friendship with Bridgette. If he caught Shay doing anything less-than-becoming of the Neal name, especially because of her best friend, he would lose it. And Shay was pretty certain he would consider prepping vegetables and serving champagne cardinal sins.

In her defense, though, when the catering supervisor shoved a tray of sparkly wine at her and ordered her to make the rounds of the ballroom, she couldn't exactly say no.

Still, everything should've been fine—would've been fine—if not for one Gideon Knight.

Smoky desire coiled in her belly. She set the almost empty tray on one of the stations and pressed a fist to her navel. Not that the futile gesture extinguished the glowing embers.

Swallowing a groan, she strode toward the back of the kitchen and the employee break room. Shutting the door behind her, she entered the bathroom and twisted the faucets, thrusting her palms under the gushing water. Her quick version of a cold shower. Shaking her head at her foolishness, she finished washing her hands, but afterward, instead of returning to the kitchen, she stood in front of the mirror, staring at her reflection. But it wasn't her image she saw.

It was Gideon Knight.

They're like peacocks, spreading their plumage, desperate to be noticed, and here you are among them, like the moon. Bright, alone, above it all and eclipsing every one of them.

She exhaled slowly, the words spoken in that all-things-secret-and-sinful voice echoing in her head. In her chest. And lower. With any other man, she would've waved off the compliment as insincere flattery that tended to roll off men's tongues when they came across the heiress to one of the largest financial management conglomerates in the country. The compliments meant nothing, like dandelion fluff on a breeze. No substance and changing with the wind.

But not with Gideon Knight.

There had been a ring of truth in the blunt observation. As if his description of her wasn't an opinion but fact. She'd just met him, but she couldn't shake the sense that he didn't dole out flowery compliments often. As he'd stated so flatly, he didn't play games.

She believed him. But it only deepened her confusion over why he'd approached her of all people. To most of the attendees in the ballroom, she'd been invisible, inconsequential. Just another staff member there to serve them.

But not to him.

Even in a room full of Chicago's wealthiest and most glamorous people, he stood out. In the way a sleek, silent shark would stand out in a pool of clown fish.

God, she was officially losing it. And she laid the blame squarely at the feet of Gideon Knight.

Because, really, how could any woman stare into those midnight eyes and not forget everything but how she could willingly drown in them, even as he submerged her in a pleasure as dark and stunning as his gaze?

As soon as the illicit thought entered her head an image of him crouched over her, all that midnight-black hair loose from its knot and flowing over his shoulders, tumbling around them, flashed through her mind. Her heart thumped against her chest, and she exhaled an unsteady breath, that flame of unwanted desire dancing low in her belly again. With a mental shove, she thrust the hot image out of her mind, but the vision of how he'd looked just moments ago, when she turned for one last glance, refused to be evicted as easily.

His tailor, whoever he or she was, must've been in love with Gideon because his tuxedo traced his powerful but lean frame. From the wide shoulders and chest that tapered to a slim waist and down to long, muscular legs, he was the picture of urbane elegance and wealth. Strength. Beauty.

Imperial.

The word leaped into her head, and though she wanted to scoff at the description, she couldn't. It fit. With the beautiful eyes, the sharp slant of cheekbones, the arrogant nose, the wide, sensual, almost cruel curve of his mouth and the rock-hard jut of his jaw, he reminded her of a long-ago king from a mysterious Asian country, standing on a wall, an unseen wind teasing his long black hair as he surveyed the land he ruled. Hard, shrewd, somehow removed from the masses.

He would've been completely intimidating if not for the incongruity of all that hair pulled into a knot at the back of his head. Someone so polished, so sophisticated, so rigid in his appearance wearing a...man bun.

It was the rebellious flouting of the unspoken, constricting rules that governed their social realm that had stirred a curiosity she couldn't erase. Even now.

You're being ridiculous.

Shaking her head, she emitted a sound of self-directed disgust and yanked a brown paper towel from the dispensary. She quickly dried her hands, tossed the now damp towel in the trash and strode from the bathroom. With at least another three hours of work ahead of her, she couldn't afford to remain hiding back here any longer. More prep work awaited her, as dinner hadn't even been served yet—

The door to the break room swung open, and she barely managed to stifle her startled gasp.

The tall, imposing figure of Gideon Knight filled the doorway.

Her heart lodged in her throat. What the hell was he doing back here? But only seconds passed before the answer whispered through her skull.

You.

Denial, swift and firm, rose within her. But it couldn't extinguish the kindling of desire and traitorous, *foolish* hope.

"What are you doing here?" she demanded, swiping her

already-dry palms down the sides of her pants. And when his gaze took in the nervous gesture, she cursed herself for betraying her agitation to this man.

"Looking for you."

Excitement fluttered in her before she could smother the reaction. Crossing her arms over her chest, she frowned. Fought the instinctive urge to retreat from the intense, sexual magnetism that seemed to pour off him and vibrate in the room.

"Well, I need to return to work." She pretended to glance down at the slim, gold-faced watch on her wrist. "So, if you'll excuse me..."

An emotion crossed his face, but was there and gone before she could decipher it. Probably irritation at being told no. "I wanted to apol—"

But the rest of his explanation snapped off as the room plummeted into darkness.

Chapter 3

A cry slipped out of Shay, panic clawing at her throat.

The deep, thick dark pressed down on her chest like a weight, cutting off her breath.

What was going on? What happened? Why…?

"Camille." The sound of that calm voice carrying an undercurrent of steel snapped her out of the dizzying fall into hysteria. Hands wrapped around both her upper arms, the grip firm, steadying. His voice and his touch grounded her, although her pulse continued to thud and echo in her head like a hammer. "Easy." One of his hands slid up her arm, over her shoulder and slipped around the back of her neck. Squeezed. "Stay with me. Breathe."

She closed her eyes, as if that could block out the utter lack of light. Still, she latched on to him—his voice, his fresh yet earthy scent of wind and sandalwood, the solid density of the forearms she'd at some point clutched. Seconds, minutes—hell, it felt like hours—passed while she focused on calming her racing heart, on breathing. And soon, the sense of being buried alive started to lift.

His hold on her arm and neck never eased.

As the initial bite of panic slowly unhinged its jaws, the weight of his touch—the security and comforting effect of it—penetrated her fear.

"—I'm sorry." Embarrassed, she heard a wobbly chuckle escape her. Belatedly, she loosened her grip on him and dropped her arms. "God, I don't… I'm not even afraid of the dark," she whispered.

"You have nothing to apologize for," he reassured her.

His hands abandoned her neck and arm, but one located and clasped her fingers. In the next instant, a pale blue glow appeared. A cell phone. The illumination barely pushed back the inky thickness surrounding them, but it highlighted his face, and relief weakened her knees. Only moments ago, she'd wanted to get as far away from him as possible. And now her eyes stung with gratefulness for his serene presence. For not being alone.

"I need to go see if I can find out what's going on. Here." Holding the cell out in front of him, he carefully guided her to the couch against the far wall. Still holding her hand, he lowered her to the cushion. "Will you be all right? I have to take my cell with me to try and either get a call or text out. I promise to return in a few minutes."

"Of course." She nodded, injecting a vein of steel into her voice. God, she was stronger than this. "I'll be fine here."

In the cell's minimal light, she caught his steady, measuring stare. "Good," he said after a few moments, returning her nod. "I'll be right back."

He disappeared, returning her to the dark. She focused

on maintaining even breathing, reminding herself she hadn't been catapulted into a deep pit where terrifying, malformed things lurked, eager for the chance to take a bite out of her. She really shouldn't have watched Stephen King's *It* last night…

"Camille."

She jerked her head up, and once more that rush of relief washed over her as Gideon and his beautiful light appeared in front of her again.

"Hey," she said, unable to prevent the emotion from flooding her voice. "Were you able to find out anything?" Please let it be something fixable and short-lived, like the owner of this mansion had forgotten to pay his power bill.

"Blackout," he explained, tone grim, and her heart plummeted toward her stomach. "I wasn't able to get a call out, but I was able to send and receive a couple of texts to a contact on the police force. It's citywide. They're advising people to remain where they are, which," he continued, his full lips flattening for a brief second, "won't be an issue with us. I overheard security speaking to the chef and his staff. The tech guru who owns this overcompensating monstrosity of a home installed a so-called cutting-edge security system. And with the blackout, it's malfunctioned. We're all locked in for the foreseeable future."

She expelled a pent-up breath, pinching the bridge of her nose. Where was Trevor? Were he and Madison okay? What about Bridgette? Sick and in the dark? More than ever, Shay cursed leaving her phone in her car. Bridgette had warned her that her supervisor frowned on the staff having cells on them, so she'd stashed hers in her glove compartment, but now…

"We're going to be fine, Camille," Gideon said, his rough silk voice dragging her away from her worried thoughts. "Most likely, the blackout will only last several hours, and hopefully the boy genius will have his system worked out by them," he finished drily.

In spite of the anxiety over her brother and friend that still inundated her, she snorted. "Boy genius?"

Gideon arched a black eyebrow. "Have you seen him? He can't be more than twenty-three. I swear, I can still smell the milk on his breath."

This time she snickered, belatedly palming her mouth to contain her amusement. "So you're what? The ripe old age of thirty? Thirty-three? And if you're here as a guest, then that means you must be at least wealthy or connected enough to have been invited. Which makes you what, Mr. Knight?" she asked, narrowing her eyes. "An idle man living off his family name and money? Or a successful businessman in his own right?"

She didn't know him, but he struck her as the latter. There was nothing about him that screamed idle. No, the sharklike intelligence that gleamed from his dark eyes belonged to a man who forged his own path, not one satisfied with walking the one others had paved for him.

He didn't immediately reply, but treated her to another of his intense gazes. He seemed to peer beneath skin and bone to the soul. To her secrets. With effort, she didn't shirk away from his scrutiny, instead notching her chin up and meeting his eyes without flinching.

Something glinted in his gaze, and the faint light from his phone tricked her into believing it might be admiration.

"I own and run a start-up that provides privately held

companies with their equity needs. I suppose you can say we've been successful."

The vague and carefully constructed answer didn't stop recognition from rocking her. Start-up? As in Kay-Cee Corp start-up? He couldn't possibly be *the* Gideon Knight, founder of the corporation that had taken the financial world by storm five years ago? If so, he was either exceedingly modest or being cagey with information.

Because KayCee Corp had been more than "successful." The electronic platform serviced major businesses, helping them track their shares with its top-of-the-line, unrivaled software. They'd recently announced their intentions to branch out and work with companies that were rolling out their initial public offerings. Though Trevor tried to keep Shay securely ensconced in the Social Development branch of RemingtonNeal Inc., their family business, she knew of KayCee Corp. Knew that Trevor desperately longed to acquire it.

Her wig, contacts and glasses concealed her true identity, but she still lifted her fingers to her cheek as if Gideon could see beneath the camouflage. Her throat tightened. Now would be a good time to come clean about who he sat with in the dark. But something held her back. Something, hell… She could identify it even without him searching her soul.

In that ballroom, Gideon Knight had gazed upon her with fascination, admiration…hunger. And he'd had no idea she was Shay Neal, heiress to a global financial empire. Not that she was an ugly duckling in a lake full of swans, but she bore no illusions. Her money, social status and connections were often just as much, if not more, of an allure than her appearance.

But not for him.

Even now, his dark stare roamed her face, lingering on her eyes before drifting over her cheekbones, her jaw, her mouth. Though it belied reason, she swore she could feel his gaze stroke over her skin. An illicit, mysterious, desire-stoking caress.

And here, in the isolated depths of this mansion, she wanted more.

Even if just for a little while.

The cloak of anonymity bestowed her with a gift of boldness—of freedom—she didn't ordinarily possess.

"I wonder what's going through your head right now?" he murmured, drawing her from her thoughts. "And would you honestly tell me?"

That would be a no. "Careful, Mr. Knight," she drawled, tone dry. "You're beginning to sound a little too Edward Cullen-ish for my comfort."

"Last time I checked, I didn't sparkle in the sunlight or age out at eighteen years old. Although I do admit to a little biting. And liking it."

A blast of heat barreled through her, warring with surprise over his recognition of her *Twilight* reference. Curling her fingers into her palms, she willed the searing desire to abate, but it continued to burn a path along her veins.

"Still blunt, I see," she said, and no way could he miss the hoarseness rasping her voice. "You weren't lying when you claimed not to play games."

"Am I making you uncomfortable, Camille?" he asked, his head cocking to the side. His eyes narrowed on her, as if searching out the answer for himself.

She should say yes. Should order him to keep his

straight-no-chaser compliments and need-stirring comments to himself.

Instead, she matched his head tilt. "And if I said you were?"

"Then I'd go out there in that kitchen and drag one of those chefs in here so you wouldn't be. Is that what you want?"

She shook her head, the denial almost immediate. "No," she said, although wisdom argued she should have him invite the whole crew into this small room. Protect her from herself. The self that couldn't help wondering if those stark angles softened with pleasure. Wondering if that hard-looking mouth became more pliable.

Wondering if that icy shield of control shattered under desire's flame?

A shiver danced over her skin. Waltzed along her nerve endings.

She was the moth dancing too close to those flames.

"What do you want?" he pressed, the deep timbre of his voice dipping lower.

He didn't move, didn't inch closer to her on the couch. But God, all that intensity crowded her, rubbed over her, slipped inside her. He wasn't a coy or playful man; he grasped the wealth of possibilities that question carried. And he offered her the choice of not addressing them... or taking all of them.

A lifetime of playing by the rules slowly unraveled beneath his heated stare. His question vibrated between them, a gauntlet thrown down. A red flag waved.

"Too many things to possibly number in the space of a blackout," she finally replied. Truth. And evasion. "But I'm fine with you here with me." She paused, and with her heart tapping an unsteady rhythm against her chest, added, "Only you."

A fierce approval and satisfaction flashed like diamonds in his eyes. "Good," he said, those same emotions reflected in the one word. "Because now we don't have to share this with anyone else." Reaching down, he picked up a plate and set it on the cushion between them. A grin curved her lips at the sight of the braised lamb, roasted vegetable medley and risotto piled on the fine china.

"Now, that's lovely," he murmured, his gaze not on the dinner but on her face.

She ducked her head, wishing the strands of the wig weren't tied back in a bun so they could hide the red stain creeping up her neck and flooding her face.

"You're certainly resourceful," she said, reaching for an asparagus tip. "Or sneaky."

His soft snort echoed between them. "I've been accused of both before. And both are just words. Whatever works to achieve my goal."

"Yes, I clearly remember your goal for this evening. You didn't mince words out there earlier. I guess you've achieved your aim. Spending the night with me."

Why had she brought up that conversation? What had possessed her to remind him of his claim to be with her—*inside* her? To see that glint of hunger again? To tempt him? God, she was flirting with danger. And doing so with a rashness that bordered on recklessness.

"Do you really want to dive into that discussion right now, Camille?" The question—a tease, a taunt—set her pulse off on a rapid tattoo.

Yes.

No.

"Not on an empty stomach," she whispered, retreating. From the faint quirk of his lips—the first hint of a smile she'd glimpsed on his austere face—he caught her withdrawal. "And you wouldn't happen to be hiding a bottle of wine over there, would you?"

The quirk deepened, and her heart stuttered. Actually skipped a couple beats at the beauty of that half smile. Jesus, he would be absolutely devastating if he ever truly let go. Her fingertips itched with the urge to trace those sensual lips. To curb the need, she brought her hands to her pants, intent on rubbing them down her thighs. But stopped herself, recalling they were damp from the food she'd just eaten.

"Take this." He reached inside his jacket and offered her a small white handkerchief.

Startled, she accepted it, again struck with how perceptive he seemed to be.

"Thank you," she murmured.

For the next half hour, they dined on the pilfered food, and as stellar and flavorful as the cuisine was, it didn't steal her attention like the man across from her. He...fascinated her. And after they finished, when he asked her if she would be fine with him turning off the phone's light to conserve the battery, she okayed it without hesitation.

Though he was basically a stranger to her, he emanated safety. Comfort. As if he would release all that barely leashed mercilessness on her behalf instead of against her. Maybe that made her fanciful, too. But in the dark, she could afford it.

Perhaps the blackness affected him in a similar fashion, because he opened up to her—well, as much as someone as controlled as Gideon Knight probably did. They spoke of mundane things. Hobbies. Worst dates. The best way to spend a perfect, lazy afternoon. All so simple, but she hung on every word. Enjoyed it. Enjoyed him.

Enjoyed the lack of sight that peeled away barriers.

Reveled in the desire that thrummed just below the surface like a drum keeping time, marching them forward to...what? She didn't know. And for the first time in longer than she could remember, she didn't weigh the effect of every word, the consequence of every action on the Neal family name.

Here, with him, she was just... Camille.

"We'll never see each other again once the lights come back on," she said. And it was true. They'd never see each other as Camille and Gideon, even if they happened to cross paths in the future. Because then, she would once more be Shay Neal of the Chicago Neals. "That almost makes me...sad," she confessed, then scoffed, shaking her head, though he couldn't see the gesture. "Ridiculous, right?"

"Why?" he asked. "Honesty is never silly. It's too rare to be ridiculous."

A twinge of guilt pinged inside her chest. She was being dishonest about the most basic thing—her identity. "Because fantasies are for teenage girls, not for grown women who know better."

"And what do you believe you know, Camille?"

She turned toward him, toward the temptation of his voice. "That if not for a citywide blackout, a man like you wouldn't be with me..." She paused. "Talking."

"I don't know if I should be more offended that you're belittling me or yourself with that statement." A whisper of sound and then fingers—questing, gentle, but so damn sure—stroked across her jaw, her temple, the strangely callused tips abrading her skin. What did a man like him do to earn that hardened skin that spoke of hard labor, not crunching numbers? "Yes, I do. It annoys me more that you would demean yourself. A woman like you," he murmured. "Beautiful. Intelligent. Bold. Confident. What man wouldn't want to spend time with you? Only one too blind or stupid to see who stands right before his eyes. Read any financial blog or journal, Camille. I'm not a stupid man."

She snorted, trying to mask the flame licking at her from the inside out. Cover the yearning his words caused deep within her. "How did you manage to compliment yourself and reprimand me at the same time?"

But he ignored her attempt to inject levity into the thick, pulsing atmosphere. No, instead, he swept another caress over her skin. This time, brushing a barely there touch to the curve of her bottom lip. She trembled. And God, he had to sense it, to feel it. Because he repeated it.

"I don't date," he informed her, and the frankness of the statement caught her off guard. Almost made her forget the long fingers still cradling her jaw.

Almost.

"Excuse me?" she breathed.

"I don't date," he repeated. "I know something, too, Camille. Relationships, commitments—they're lies we tell ourselves so we can justify using each other. Sex. Need. Passion—they're honest. The body can't lie. Lust is the great equalizer regardless of social status, race or tax bracket. So no, I rescind my earlier statement. If not for this blackout, it's very possible we wouldn't have passed these last couple of hours talking. But I don't care if we were in a ballroom or a boardroom, I would've noticed you. I would've wanted you. I would've done everything in my power to convince you to trust me with your body, your pleasure."

Oh damn.

She couldn't breathe. Couldn't move. Suspended by the hunger swamping her.

"Your turn, moonbeam," he said, his hand falling away from her face. And she immediately missed his touch, that firm grasp. Because he couldn't see her, she lifted her fingers to the skin that continued to tingle. "Tell me again what you know."

Moonbeam. The endearment reminded her of their conversation in the ballroom. Her brain argued that the word had nothing to do with love or sweetness and everything to do with hunger and darkness, and yet she jolted at the coiling in her lower belly.

"I know you're telling me you haven't changed your mind about wanting to spend the night with me. Inside me," she added, on a soft, almost hushed rush of breath.

"And have you changed yours?"

From the moment you called me your moon.

The truth reverberated against her skull, but she clenched her jaw, preventing it from escaping. Her defenses had started crumbling long before he'd come looking for her.

Did this make her a cliché? He wasn't the first man to profess he wanted her, but he was the first she longed to touch with a need that unnerved her. She'd never yearned for a man's hands on her body as much as she longed for Gideon Knight's big, elegant, long-fingered ones stroking over her breasts. Or gripping her hips, holding her steady for a deep, hot possession that had her sex spasming in anticipation...in preparation.

She exhaled a breath. Right, he still waited for her answer, and she suspected he wouldn't make a move, wouldn't feather another of those caresses over her until she gave it to him.

"Yes," she confessed, her heart thudding heavily against her rib cage.

"About what, Camille?" he pressed, relentless. "What have you decided? What do you want?"

He wasn't granting her a reprieve; he was making her say it. Making her lay herself bare.

Her sense of self-preservation launched a last-ditch effort to save her from who she'd become in the dark. Who she'd become in that ballroom. But desire crushed it, and she willingly surrendered to the irresistible lure of freedom…of him.

"You," she whispered. "I've decided on you."

She slid across the small space separating them and located his face. A soft groan rolled up her throat, and she didn't even try and trap it. Not when she curved her hand around the strong jut of his jaw, the faintest bristles of what would become a five o'clock shadow abrading her palm. Unable to stop, she stroked the pad of her thumb over the mouth she had been craving since she first noticed him.

Strong teeth sank into the flesh of her thumb, not hurting her but exerting enough pressure that she gasped. Then whimpered.

How had she gone twenty-five years without being aware that spot connected to her sex? That it would make her thighs clench on an ache so sweet, it maddened her?

Another gasp broke free of her, this one of surprise, as his fingers closed around her arms and abruptly dragged her to her feet. She swayed, but he didn't release her until she steadied. Then the sudden flare of light from his cell phone startled her again. After the dark, the pale glow seemed almost too bright. She blinked, glancing from the screen to the shadows it cast over Gideon's face.

"Why..." She waved toward the phone. "What about saving the battery?"

He shook his head, his features sharper, appearing to be hewn from flint. Except for those glittering, almost fevered eyes. *Oh wow...* Such intensity and...and greed there. It stirred her own hunger, stoking the fire inside her until she burned with it.

"I don't give a damn. I need to see you," he growled, shrugging out of his jacket and tossing it to the floor. Still controlled, but the movement carried an edge. And it thrilled her. "Take off your shirt, Camille. Show me what you've decided I can have."

With trembling fingers, she reached for the buttons of her white shirt. It required several attempts, but she managed to open it, and with his black gaze fixed on her, slipped it off. Warm air kissed her bared shoulders, the tops of her breasts and stomach.

A part of her argued that she should feel at least a modicum of modesty, and maybe Shay would. But not Camille.

As crazy as it seemed, here, with Gideon, she had become a different person. The flip side of the same coin. Normally reserved, bound by expectations and family. But now... uninhibited, free to indulge in her own selfish desires.

"Gorgeous," he rasped. "So fucking gorgeous. Come here." He beckoned.

His almost growled compliment stole more of her breath.

"Your turn," she ordered, remaining in place, although her fingers already prickled to stroke the skin and muscle hidden beneath the thin veneer of civility presented by his tuxedo. "Show me what you promised me I can take."

His fingers tightened around the edges of his shirt, and for a moment, she feared—hoped—he would just rip it off. But once more, that control reemerged, and he removed his cuff links, tossing them carelessly on top of his jacket. Then, button by button, he revealed himself to her.

She stared at the male animal before her. Miles and miles of smooth flesh stretched taut over tight muscle and tendon. Wide shoulders, a deep chest. Narrowed waist. A corrugated ladder of abs. A thin, silky line of hair started just above a shadowed navel and traveled below, disappearing into the waistband of his suit pants. And darker swirls and shapes she couldn't make out spread over the left side of his ribs, emphasizing the hint of wildness, of fierceness he couldn't quite conceal.

Perfection.

He was utter perfection.

This time, he didn't need to demand she come to him. Shay covered the distance on her own, arms already extended. With a hum of pleasure, she settled her palms on him, smoothed them up to his shoulders, pushing the shirt down his arms. Then she returned to her exploration. Scraping her nails over small, flat nipples, mapping the thin network of veins under his skin, following the path of hair that started midchest. Dragging her fingertips down the delineated ridge of muscles covering his stomach. Tracing the black lines of his tattoo, wishing she could aim more light on it so she could decipher its shape.

He stood still, letting her tour him without interference, though he fairly hummed with intensity, with barely leashed power.

"Are you finished yet?" he growled, and she tilted her head back to meet his hooded gaze, her fingers settling on the band of his pants.

"Not even close," she breathed. "Kiss me."

Someone with his extraordinary sense of restraint most likely didn't take or obey orders from anyone. But with a flash in those eyes, he gripped the bun at the back of her head and tugged. She gave only a brief thought to the security of the wig before her neck arched. The next breath she took was his.

Her groan was ragged and so needy it should've embarrassed her. Maybe it would tomorrow in the harsh light of day. But tonight, with his tongue twisting and tangling with hers, she couldn't care. Not when he tasted like everything delicious but forbidden—chocolate-flavored wine, New York cheesecake, impropriety and wickedness. Not when he nipped at her bottom lip, then sucked it, soothing and enhancing the sting before returning to devour her mouth. As if she, too, was something he knew he shouldn't have but couldn't resist.

He lifted his head, taking that lovely mouth with him, and she cried out in disappointment. But he shushed her with hard, stinging kisses to the corner of her lips, along the line of her jaw, down her chin and neck…over the tops of her breasts. In seconds, he stripped her of her bra, baring her to him. His big hands lifted, cupping her, molding her to him. To his pleasure. And hers.

She grasped his shoulders, clung to him, her ability to think, to move, to breathe a thing of the past as he lowered his head to her flesh. All she could do was stand there with increasingly wobbly knees and receive each lick, suckle and draw of those sensual lips and tongue. And enjoy them.

Unable not to touch the lure of his hair, she swept her

fingers over his head, tunneling them under the knot containing the midnight strands. Eager to see him undone, she briefly wrestled with the thick locks, freeing the tie restraining them. The rough silk fell over her wrists, cool and dense, sliding through her fingers.

"Oh," she whispered, at a loss for words as the strands tumbled around his sharp cheekbones and strong jaw. They should've softened his features—should have. Instead, they only emphasized the stark planes of his face and his visceral sexuality.

"God, you're beautiful." The praise exited her mouth without her permission, but she couldn't regret the words. Not when they were the truth.

Pulling his mouth away from her breasts, he dragged a hot, wet path up her chest, her throat, until he recaptured her mouth. This kiss was hotter, wilder, as if the tether on his control had frayed, and suddenly, her one purpose was to see it snap completely.

With a small whimper, she trailed her hand over his shoulder, chest and torso, not stopping until she cupped his rigid length through his pants.

Damn. She shivered, both need and feminine anxiety tumbling in her belly and lower. He more than filled her palm. Reflexively, she squeezed his erection. God, he was so thick, hard…big.

A rumble emanated from his chest, and his larger hand covered hers, pressing her closer, clasping him tighter. His hips bucked against her palm in demand, and she gladly obeyed. Even as his mouth ravaged hers, she stroked him, loving the growl that rolled out of him. Wanting more.

Impatient, Shay attacked the clasp of his pants, jerking them open and tugging down the zipper in a haste that would later strike her as unseemly. But right now, she didn't give a damn. Nothing mattered but his bare, pulsing flesh in her hand. Touching him.

But just as she reached for him, an implacable grip circled her wrist, stilling her frantic movements.

"Not yet, moonbeam." He lifted one of her arms and placed an openmouthed kiss to the center of her palm, the resulting feeling radiating straight to her damp, quivering sex. With a quick crush of his lips to hers, he swiftly divested her of her remaining clothes and shoes, leaving her trembling and naked before him, except for the decidedly *un*sexy plain, black panties.

A burst of self-consciousness flared inside her chest, and she fought not to edge backward, away from the weak glow of the cell phone's light. But as if he'd read her intentions, Gideon cupped her hip, preempting any movement she might've made to hide.

"When a man stands before beauty like yours, there's only one position he's supposed to be in," he murmured. Slowly, he lowered himself to his knees, tipping his head back to continue to meet her gaze. "You deserve to be worshipped." He swept his lips across her stomach. "And pleasured." Another sweep, but over the top of her sex. Heat coiled tight, and her core clenched at the tantalizing caress. "Give me permission to give you that."

It might've emerged as an order, but he wouldn't continue without her go-ahead. She somehow knew that.

"Yes," she breathed, tunneling her fingers through his hair. Holding on tight.

With a deliberate pace that had her internally screaming, he drew her underwear down her legs and helped her step free of them. Big, elegant hands brushed up her calves and thighs, and once more she wondered at the calluses adding a hint of roughness to the caress. But then she ceased thinking at all.

"Gideon," she cried out, fisting his hair, trying to pull him away or tug him closer—she didn't know. Couldn't decide. Not when pleasure unlike anything she'd ever experienced struck her with great bolts of lightning. Jesus, his lips, his tongue… They were voracious. Feasting on her, leaving no part of her unexplored, untouched. Long, luxurious swirls, decadent and wicked laps and sucks… He drove her insane with pleasure.

Just as he'd promised. Just as he'd assured her she deserved.

He spread her wider, hooking her leg over one of his wide shoulders, granting himself easier access. Like a ravenous beast, he growled against her sensitive, wet sex, and the vibration shoved her closer to the edge of release.

"You're so fucking sweet," he rasped, nuzzling her. "So fucking sweet and pure. A man could get addicted to you. But you have more to give me, don't you, baby? I'm a greedy bastard, and I want it all." He uttered the last words almost as if to himself, and with one palm molded to her behind, he dragged the other up the inside of her spread thighs.

Then he was filling her. Two fingers plunged inside her, and like a match struck to dry kindling, she sparked, flared, exploded into flames. Dimly, she caught his rough encouragement of "That's it, baby. That's it." She loosened a hand from his hair and clapped it over her lips, muffling her cries as she came against his mouth, her hips rolling and jerking.

Raw, dirty ecstasy, stripped to its barest essentials. That's who she'd become in this moment as he lapped up every evidence of her desire from her flesh, from the insides of her thighs.

"Please," she begged, weakly pushing his head away as he circled her with tender but relentless strokes. "I can't."

"That's nothing but a challenge to me, moonbeam," he rumbled, standing, his mouth damp. But when he lowered his head and took her lips in a torrid kiss that replicated how he'd just consumed her, she didn't back away from the flavor of herself on his lips and tongue. No, she opened wider to him, turned on so bright it ached.

Palming the back of her thighs, he hiked her in the air. On reflex she wound her legs around his waist. He crossed to the couch, and with each bump of her swollen, sensitive core against his stomach, that recently satiated heat flickered back to life, and she moaned with each caress.

Her back met the cushions, and Gideon towered over her, half his face cast in shadow. That obsidian gaze never left hers as he removed a thin wallet from his pants pocket and withdrew a condom. He tossed it down, next to her feet, and then she watched, enraptured, as he stripped off his clothes. Her breath snagged in her throat. *Jesus.* He'd been stunning in a perfectly tailored tuxedo. But naked, the trappings torn away, all that thick, midnight hair falling around his face and broad shoulders... He was *magnificent.* Long legs, powerful thighs... Good God, she'd felt him, but *seeing* him... Like the rest of him, his erection was proud, beautiful. Perfect.

As if of their own volition, her arms lifted, beckoning him to her. He tore open the foil square and sheathed himself then came to her, moving the cell phone to the floor next to them. His hard body covered hers, and a sigh escaped her at the contact. For a second, she couldn't smother the sense of never having felt so cherished, so protected.

"Ready, moonbeam?" he murmured, raising off her slightly. Grasping her hand in his, he brought it between their bodies. As he'd done earlier, he wrapped her fingers around his thick length. "Show me," he ordered, planting his palms on either side of her head, granting her control.

Even if she harbored the smallest seed of doubt about this illicit encounter in the dark—which she didn't—his gesture would've eradicated it. Her chest tightened, her heart thudding against her rib cage. But her hand was steady as she guided him to her entrance. Shifting her palm to his taut behind, she pushed as she lifted her hips, taking him inside. Fully. Widening her thighs, she didn't stop until he was buried within her.

She gasped, a ripple rocking her body. God, he was *everywhere*. Over her, around her, inside her. So deep inside her. The weight and length of him stretched her, burned her, and she flexed against him, her flesh struggling to accommodate the sweet invasion.

His eyes closed, and he bowed his head, pressing his forehead to hers, his breath pulsing over her lips. Tension vibrated through him, strained the muscles in his arms, stilled his large frame. Long moments later, he lifted his head, and the effort to hold back was etched onto his features.

"Gideon," she whispered, waiting until he lifted his ridiculously dense lashes to meet her eyes. "Let go."

As if those two words sliced through the last threads of his restraint, he groaned and lost it.

On the tail of another of those sexy snarls, he dragged his erection free, lighting up nerve endings like an airport runway, before snapping his hips and thrusting back inside her. Driving her breath from her lungs and a wail of pleasure from her throat.

Oh God. She wasn't going to survive this.

Pleasure inundated her as he plunged into her body. Over and over, relentlessly. He hooked an arm under her leg, tugging it higher and impossibly wider. With a choked cry, she wrapped her arms around his neck, holding on, a willing sacrifice to his possession. He rode her, wild and untethered, giving her no quarter. Not that she asked for any. She loved it. Every roll of his hips, every slap of flesh against flesh, every rake of his teeth over her shoulder.

In his arms, under his body, she transformed into a sexual creature who lived, breathed for him, for the ecstasy only he could give.

Electric pulses crackled down her back, sizzling at the base of her spine. Every thrust intensified the sensation. When he slid a hand between them and rubbed her, an avalanche of pleasure rushed toward her, burying her, stealing her consciousness. But not before Gideon stiffened above her, his deep, tortured groan echoing in her ear, rumbling against her chest.

"Camille," he whispered, and it sounded like a benediction, a prayer.

And as she tightened her arms around him before sinking under, she foolishly wished to be his answer.

Chapter 4

Gideon frowned, reaching out to shut off his alarm. Drowsiness still clung to him, a warm lassitude weighing down his muscles, and he wanted to savor it instead of drive it away. But that damn alarm.

"Damn it," he grumbled, but instead of hitting the digital clock on his bedside table, he slapped air. No table. No clock. Hell, no bed.

He sat up, groaning at the pull of muscle in his lower back. Tunneling his fingers through his hair, he dragged it back from his face, scanning the small room with a television, a long table against the far wall, a short row of gray metal lockers and the couch he was sprawled on.

The blackout.

Camille.

As if her name released a floodgate, the memories from the previous night poured forward. Serving Camille dinner. Talking with her. Kissing her. Being inside her.

In response, his body stirred, hardening as image after image of her twisting and arching beneath him, taking him, flashed across his mind's screen like an HD movie.

He whipped around, scanning the room with new eyes, searching for any sign of her. But only his clothes and the empty dinner plates littered the floor. No Camille.

Adrenaline streaked through his veins, and he snatched his pants from the floor, dragging them on. She couldn't have gotten far. Weak morning light trickled into the room through the high window, so it still had to be pretty early. And with the house still locked down...

No, not locked down. For the first time, the low drone of the small refrigerator in the far corner reached his ears. Power had returned, which meant the blackout had ended. Still, how much of a head start could she have? He had to find her.

Just as he swept his shirt off the floor a Queen song erupted into the stifling room. It'd been this that he'd initially mistaken for his alarm, but it was his mom's special ringtone. He strode the few steps required to recover the phone from beside the couch, arching his eyebrows in surprise that it still had power.

Only 3 percent, he noted, swiping a thumb across the screen.

"Hey, Mom," he said in greeting, fastening buttons as he spoke. "I have very little battery left, so I can't talk long. But I'm okay—"

"Gideon," she said, and her solemn tone cut him off. Anxiety and the first spike of fear speared his chest. He'd come to associate that particular note with one thing. And as she murmured, "It's Olivia," his guess proved correct.

Closing his eyes, he straightened his shoulders, bracing himself. "What happened?"

"She's in the hospital. I had to take her in last night." Her sigh echoed in his ear; the weariness and worry tore at him. "Gideon." She paused. "She saw the news about Trevor Neal's engagement."

A familiar anger awakened in his chest, stretching to life.

"I'm on my way."

Gideon exited his sister's private room on the behavioral health floor of Mercy Hospital & Medical Center, quietly shutting the door behind him.

Behavioral health. Fancy words for psychiatric ward.

Scrubbing a hand down his face, he strode through the hall to the waiting area where his mother and her parents perched on chairs. The three of them zeroed in on him as soon as he entered the small space with the connected seating and mounted television. God, it reeked of sadness and exhaustion. The same emotions etched in his mother's and grandparents' faces.

"How is she?" his mom asked, rising.

Frustration, grief and anger choked him, and for a moment he couldn't speak. Instead he gathered his mother in his arms and hugged her close. Ai Knight had been his rock—his family's rock—since his dad died when Gideon was nine years old. Though his grandparents were here now, that hadn't always been the case. When she'd married Gideon's father, they'd disowned her. As immigrants from Kaiping who'd settled in Canada in the 1960s, they'd wanted their only daughter to marry a Chinese man from the "Four Counties," not a Caucasian from Chicago. But

Ai had, and after she'd moved to the US with him, she and her parents hadn't spoken for almost ten years. But since then they'd reconciled, and his grandparents had even moved to Chicago to be closer to Ai and their grandchildren. Which Gideon was thankful for, since his father had been a foster child, and so his mother's parents were the only extended family he and his sister had.

"Gideon?" his mother prompted.

Sighing, he released her. God, he hated seeing her here in this room, the gravity of her daughter's illness weighing down her delicate but strong shoulders.

"Sleeping. They have her heavily sedated at the moment," he replied. Which wasn't much of an answer.

"How long will she be here?" his grandmother inquired, stretching her arm out and clasping her daughter's hand.

"I'm not sure, Po Po," he said, using the Taishanese term for maternal grandmother. His grandfather—his gung gung—remained silent, but settled a hand on his wife's thin knee. "The doctor said definitely the next seventy-two hours. Maybe more."

They remained there, silent but connected through physical touch. After several moments, he squeezed his mom's shoulder. "Can I talk to you out in the hall?"

She nodded, following him out of the waiting room—and out of earshot of his grandparents. They might be a tight family, but there were some things even they didn't know, and Gideon preferred to keep it that way when it came to his younger sister.

"What happened?" he demanded, softening the hard tone of his question by enfolding her hand in his.

"Since the announcement of Trevor's engagement, I've

tried my best to keep her protected from the news. Even going on her computer and phone and blocking those society sites. But I knew that was only prolonging the inevitable. And last night, she found out. I heard her sobbing all the way from downstairs, Gideon," she whispered, the dark eyes she'd bequeathed to him liquid with tears. "I ran to her room and found her curled up in a ball on the floor of her bedroom, crying uncontrollably. Unable to stop. I was afraid. So I called the ambulance."

He ground his teeth together, an ache flaring along his jaw as he struggled to imprison the blistering stream of curses that would not only offend his mother but would be pointless.

Nothing he said could ease his sister's anguish. And no amount of release could extinguish his hatred toward Trevor Neal, the bastard responsible for shattering the kind, loving, fragile woman who'd given him her heart. A heart Trevor had trampled, then tossed aside like trash.

It'd been a year ago, but to Olivia, Trevor's betrayal might as well as have been yesterday. She'd kept her love affair with the CEO of RemingtonNeal, Inc. from Gideon, because he and Trevor had no love lost between them; they'd been rivals and enemies for years. Gideon had never hidden his hatred toward the other man.

Which explained why Trevor had targeted her in the first place.

He'd romanced Olivia, manipulated her into falling in love with him, making promises of a future together. Then, out of the blue, he'd cruelly dumped her. But that hadn't been the worst of it. Olivia had been pregnant with his child. Trevor hadn't cared. He'd even ordered her to get an abortion, which she'd refused. But in the end, it hadn't mattered. She'd miscarried, and the loss had sunk her into a depression that had begun to lift only a couple months ago. Seeking to protect her from any further hurt, Gideon and his mother had kept the information about the engagement to themselves.

But now this had happened.

"I'm sorry." His mother interrupted his thoughts by cupping his cheek. "I know this has to be difficult for you, too. This whole engagement thing. How're you doing?"

He covered her hand with his and then pressed a kiss to her palm before lowering it. Schooling his features, he submerged the jagged knife of pain and humiliation beneath a sheet of ice. "I'm fine, Mom. I'm not the one who needs your worry today."

She didn't immediately reply, studying him. "I'm a mother. I have enough concern to spread around evenly," she said, and amusement whispered through him. "She was your fiancée, Gideon," she pointed out, as if he didn't know. "Cheating on you was hurtful enough, but this? And with him of all people?" She shook her head. "There's no way you can possibly be 'fine.'"

"Let it go, Mom," he murmured, sliding his hands into the front pockets of his pants and slightly turning away from her incisive gaze. "I have."

Lies.

He would never forget Madison Reus's betrayal. Or forgive it. Not when the man she'd cheated with had been Trevor.

The other man had made it his mission to bring Gideon down a peg. And this latest stunt—pursuing Madison, fucking her and now marrying her—had been a direct hit. Anger at his enemy and his ex swelled within him.

Both were selfish, narcissistic and uncaring of who they destroyed.

Especially Trevor.

Gideon had been unable to protect his sister from him the first time. And now she still suffered from his cruelty. It sickened Gideon that he'd failed her, despite the fact that he hadn't known until it was too late. As her older brother, the man in the family, he should've been there. Should've asked questions. Should've…

Damn it. He ruthlessly scrubbed his hands down his face.

Never again. Trevor Neal wouldn't get away unscathed this time.

He would pay. Pay for them all.

Chapter 5

Shay approached the dining room entrance, pausing just outside, preparing herself for the first meal of the day. It was breakfast; it shouldn't be an event worthy of deep-breathing techniques. But depending on her brother's mood, it could go either way—calm and pleasant or tap dancing on her last damn nerve. Sighing, she straightened her shoulders and entered.

"Good morning," she said to Trevor, pulling out her chair to his left. As soon as she lowered herself into it, Jana, their maid, appeared at her elbow and set a plate with steaming hot food in front of her. "Thank you, Jana." She smiled at the other woman.

Trevor glanced up from the tablet next to his plate. "You're running late this morning," he said in lieu of a greeting.

"A little bit of a restless night," she explained.

Several restless nights, actually. But she kept that bit of

information to herself, since there was no way she could tell her brother what—or rather *who*—had been interrupting her sleep lately.

"Are you okay?" His eyes, hazel like her own, narrowed on her face. "Feeling well?"

There were moments like this, when concern shone in his gaze, that made it hard to remember the increasingly cold and callous man her brother could be. Right now, he was the caring big brother from her childhood who'd affectionately teased her, who'd spent hours watching TV with her when she'd been sick with the flu and bored. That man had started to make rarer appearances over the last few years—since their father had fallen sick and died.

"I'm fine," she replied, cutting into her vegetable omelet. "What am I running late for?"

"The office. You have a meeting with the representative from the ASPCA. You can't afford to be late for that, not with the fund-raising gala for Grace Sanctuary just a few nights away. I'm counting on you to make this a success for not just RemingtonNeal but for Mom's memory," he reminded her.

No pressure. She swallowed the retort. Barely.

While she firmly believed Trevor had created her position and department specifically for her—vice president of Social Development—she did her best for it. Yes, it was an important job—anything bettering their city and the people living there was worthy—but it wasn't her passion. And it damn sure wasn't what she'd attended college and earned a BBA and MBA to do. She'd wanted to join her brother in running RemingtonNeal, but like their controlling, domineering father, he'd shot down that idea.

Usually, Trevor took no interest in her work unless a

photo op happened to be attached to it. But Grace Sanctuary belonged to their mother—it had been her pet project before she died, when Shay was eleven and Trevor sixteen. Their father had continued its legacy until he passed, and now they did. The foundation funded various shelters throughout the city, as well as paid veterinarian, adoption and fostering fees for families taking in the animals. The fund-raising gala was important, as the donations from the attendees encompassed a large portion of the budget.

Still, Shay had headed the committee for the gala the past three years, and the last thing she needed was Trevor breathing down her neck or trying to micro-manage.

"Everything is going smoothly, and the benefit will be a success like it always has been," she said.

"I know it will. After all, it's in your hands," Trevor praised softly. "I'm sorry if I'm being overbearing, Shay. And if I haven't said it before, thank you. Believe me, I would be a lot more of a pain in the ass if you weren't in charge. I trust you to make this gala the best yet."

Warmth spread through her chest, and she swallowed past the lump of emotion lodged in her throat. Here was the big brother she knew and loved. The one whose approval she valued because it meant so much to her.

"Thank you," she murmured. Then, clearing her throat, she asked, "How's Madison?"

His fiancée had been joining them for breakfast more often lately. Actually, spending more time at the house, period. As if she were already preparing to be mistress of the home.

"She's fine." He picked up his napkin and dabbed at his mouth. "Just so you're aware, I gave her a key. She's dropping by later with an interior designer. There're some things she wants to change in the living and dining rooms, as I do most of my entertaining in those two places. And since she'll soon be living here…" He shrugged. "I didn't think you'd mind, so I told her to go forward with it."

Irritation twinged inside Shay's chest. As usual, Trevor didn't consult her about anything, even when it had to do with her home. Yes, Madison would soon be moving in as his wife, but it'd been Shay's home for twenty-five years. Yet it hadn't occurred to him to ask her opinion, which didn't count for much with her older brother. Again, like their father.

The irony of it always struck her. Trevor and their father had had a…complicated relationship. He'd loved and revered Daniel Shay, constantly seeking his stingy approval, while at the same time, resenting his my-way-and-there's-no-such-thing-as-a-highway attitude when it came to running his company and his family. Especially when it came to raising his only son, who would one day inherit his financial kingdom. Yet, over the years, Trevor had become the reflection of their father. And the battle inside her—the warring factions of anger at his overbearing arrogance and protectiveness for the brother she loved—continued to wage.

But, as she was discovering, it was pointless to argue with Trevor regarding anything having to do with Madison Reus. Winning the hand of a senator's daughter had been a coup for him, and he spoiled her like a princess. And like royalty, Madison accepted it as her due.

That sounded catty even in her own head. *God.* Shay winced, sipping the coffee Jana had set before her.

Doesn't make it any less true, her inner bitch whispered.

"Of course not," she said evenly.

"Good." He nodded. "What're your plans for lunch? We could meet so you can give me an update on the benefit."

She shook her head. "I can't. I'm meeting Bridgette."

Trevor's mouth thinned into a flat, grim line.

Yes, she already got that he didn't like her friendship with the other woman. Bridgette's mother had worked for the Neal family when they were younger. Lonely, Shay had immediately bonded with the precocious, funny little girl who'd wanted a friend regardless of the difference in their families' tax brackets. Continuing that friendship had been one of Shay's very few rebellions against her father's and brother's edicts about being a Neal. She loved Bridgette like a sister, and Trevor's disapproval wouldn't make her give up her friend.

"Which reminds me," Shay continued, not giving him a chance to offer yet another opinion on her relationship with Bridgette. "I won't be able to make dinner tonight, either. I made other plans."

His gaze narrowed on her. "Dinner is with the senator, his wife and several of his friends."

"I'm aware, and I apologize for backing out at the last moment, but something came up that I can't reschedule."

She returned his stare, not offering an explanation about the "something" even though his eyes demanded one. The words actually shoved at the back of her throat, but she refused to soothe him, to cave just to keep the peace. Especially since he'd been the one to make the plans for this dinner without even checking to see if she was available. Sometimes her brother misinterpreted her silence for meekness. And sometimes she let his high-handedness go. But not when it mattered. And tonight mattered. To her.

"Shay," he murmured, leaning back in his chair, his mouth hardening even more. "I know I don't need to remind you how important the next few months are to me, to our family and, therefore, to RemingtonNeal. This wedding isn't just gearing up to be the social event of next year, but it's also only months before Senator Reus's campaign kicks off. We can't afford to have anything go wrong. We're Neals, with a name and reputation above reproach. Don't do anything to taint either."

Anger at his thinly veiled admonishment surged within her, and she fought down the barrage of words blistering her throat. The same throat that constricted as the noose of the Neal name tightened, suffocating her. She'd always been the dutiful daughter, the proper socialite and, except for in her head, had done it all without complaint. But lately, the constraints were chafing, leaving her raw and irritated. In emotional pain.

Well, you haven't been that *proper.*

The same snarky voice that had taunted her about Madison mocked her again, this time following it up with a parade of vivid, explicit images of the night she'd spent with Gideon Knight. Her belly clenched, a dark swirl of desire eddying far south of her navel. Flashes of those lust-drenched hours burst in her head like fireworks across a dark July night. Gideon kneeling before her, lips glistening with the evidence of the desire he'd coaxed out of her with that same talented mouth. Gideon leaning over her, midnight hair tumbling around them, his big body moving over hers...in hers.

Gideon sleeping as she quietly dressed in the murky

morning light, the sharp angles and planes of his face not softened by slumber.

Heat rushed up her chest and throat and poured into her face. She ducked her head over her plate, concealing the flush that surely stained her cheekbones.

"Shay?"

She jerked her head up, freeing herself from thoughts of Gideon. Inhaling, she refocused on their conversation. "No, I don't need to be reminded. And missing one dinner isn't going to mar the Neal name or threaten the senator's campaign," she replied. Ignoring the narrowing of his eyes, she pushed her chair back and stood. "I need to get to the office. I'll see you later."

Leaning over, she brushed a kiss across his cheek, then left the room before he could attempt to dig into her reasons for not complying with his plans. As soon as she stepped over the threshold, she heaved a sigh. The tension that seemed to be more of a common occurrence when she was with Trevor eased from her shoulders.

Shoulders that were aching from carrying the heavy burden of her brother's expectations.

Chapter 6

Shay smiled up at her server as she accepted the black folder containing the check for the meal she'd just finished. Well, a little more than a meal. Her smile widened at the warm glow of satisfaction radiating inside her chest. A business meeting with the two women who had just left the restaurant, and one that had gone extremely well.

This had been her reason for ducking out on dinner with Trevor, Madison and her family. As much as Shay's job at RemingtonNeal bored the hell out of her, she was grateful for it. Without the six-figure salary, she wouldn't be able to finance her own secret company—an investment firm that funded innovative, promising start-ups— start-ups founded by women.

Shay made it possible for women to achieve their dreams, and with a percentage of the profits, she was able to continue growing her own business. Leida Investments— named after her mother—was hers alone, without any connection to her family. Even the incorporation documents weren't in her name. The anonymity—and the NDA she had all her clients sign—allowed her the freedom to use the degrees she'd earned without anyone trying to pigeonhole her. Yes, enduring the time she put in at her brother's company was well worth it when she could be her own boss.

If Trevor discovered her secret, he would do more than disapprove of it; he would sabotage it. As archaic as it sounded, he possessed firm ideas about her role in the family and the business. He might have created a lip service position for her at RemingtonNeal, but he intended for her to be a replica of their mother—wife, mother, philanthropist, socialite and the perfect hostess. The philanthropist part wasn't bad, but the rest of it? She mentally shuddered.

Tonight was a reminder of why she went to such measures to maintain her subterfuge. The excitement and joy that had lit Jennifer Ridland's and Marcia Brennan's faces as Shay slid an investment contract across the table had reinforced for her why her company must continue to thrive without any interference from her brother. The two women could revolutionize the travel industry, and she wanted to be the one who helped them do it.

Oh yes, this was well worth missing out on Trevor's dinner.

"Good evening, Ms. Neal. Do you mind if I join you?"

That voice. Shock blasted through her, and under it wound a current of something darker, sultrier. Her voice and breath crowded into her throat like an angry mob, strangling her for a long, panicked moment.

Even when Gideon Knight slid into the chair across from her, she remained speechless, frozen. It was as if her thoughts of him earlier that morning had conjured him. The bottomless onyx eyes no longer glittered with lust, but they held the same piercing intensity. It had her wavering between ducking her head and allowing him to pilfer her darkest secrets. The angular but beautiful face with its sharp angles and unsmiling, sinfully full lips... The tall, powerful body that seemed to dwarf the chair and table...

A shiver shuddered through her body, and she prayed he didn't notice. *What are you doing here?* almost tumbled from her lips before she hauled the words back. But recognition didn't shine in his eyes. Then, why would it? He'd spent a hot, sex-drenched night during a blackout with Camille, a member of the waitstaff. Across from him sat Shay Neal, composed heiress with long, dark brown hair instead of a wig, no glasses, hazel eyes instead of brown contacts and an eggplant-colored, long-sleeved cocktail dress instead of a uniform.

She bore no resemblance to the woman he'd known. Touched. Brought such immense pleasure.

"I'm afraid I'm just finishing up dinner, Mr..." She trailed off. God, she felt like such a hypocrite, a liar. Intentional deception wasn't her. But she couldn't confess how they knew one another, either. One, she'd lied to him about her identity. Two, if he discovered that she and Camille were the same person, he could use that to embarrass her family. If Trevor found out... She mentally shook her head. No, not an option.

"Gideon Knight," he said, setting a brown folder on the table. "And I promise not to take up too much of your time. But I believe you will want to hear what I have to say."

Though every instinct for self-preservation inside her screamed to run and run *now*, she remained seated. His almost emotionless tone didn't conceal the faint warning in his words.

And then there was the part of her—the part she struggled not to acknowledge—that trembled with desire from just being near Gideon. If she could just erase that night from her head…

"I'm sorry, Mr. Knight, but I don't know you." Not a lie. Biblical knowledge didn't equate *knowing* someone. "Therefore, I don't believe there is anything we need to speak about. So if you'll excuse me…"

She set her napkin on the table and started to rise from her chair. Yes, she was being rude, but desperation trumped manners. She needed to get away from him before she did something foolish. Such as beg him for a repeat of a night that never should've happened.

"I know your secret, Ms. Neal."

Shay froze. Except for her heart. It pounded against her sternum like an anvil against steel. Hard. Deafening.

Slowly, she lowered herself to her seat, forcing her expression into one of calm disinterest. Hiding the fear that coursed through her like a rushing current.

He knew about the night of the blackout? What had she done to betray her identity? Oh God. *What did he intend to do with the information?*

"I'm afraid I have no idea what you're talking about," she replied.

His aloof, shuttered demeanor didn't alter as he cocked his head and studied her. "Is your brother aware of where you are tonight? Does he know about the meeting you concluded just minutes ago?"

Wait. What? "I'm sorry?" she asked.

"Does he know about Leida Investments?" he clarified, leaning back in his chair. "I must admit, I can't imagine Trevor Neal supporting his sister running a company that is outside of RemingtonNeal. More specifically, out from under his control."

Equal parts relief and unease swirled in her belly. Relief because he still hadn't equated her with Camille. But unease because how did he know about her business? Better question, why did he care?

"Forgive me for not seeing how it's any of your concern," she answered, ice in her voice.

"Forgiveness. Oh, we're so far past that," he murmured, and as she frowned at the cryptic words, he slid the brown folder across the table toward her.

That sense of unease morphed into dread as she stared at the banded file. She lifted her hand, but at the last moment, she froze, her fingers hovering above it as if it were a scorpion, ready to strike and poison her with its venom.

Yet she grasped it, then opened it.

Minutes later, her heart thudded against her chest wall like a hammer against stone. The pounding clang in her head deafened her. God, she wished it would blind her to what she was reading.

Report after report detailing shady business deals involving her brother, and even some with his future father-in-law, Senator Reus. Bribery for product placement, undercutting bidding contracts, predatory practices, procuring illegal campaign contributions on behalf of the senator. And these were just some of the accusations leveled against Trevor and RemingtonNeal.

"Why are you showing me these…these lies?" She dropped the stack back on the table as if it singed her fingertips. If it didn't betray weakness, she would've shoved her chair back from the table just to place more space between that file and her.

"Lies?" He arched a black eyebrow, the corner of his mouth lifting in the faintest of sneers. "Facts, Ms. Neal. Your determination to believe they're false doesn't make it so."

"And your determination to believe they're true doesn't make it so," she snapped, throwing his words back at him. "I don't know you, and I damn sure don't know the people who gathered this defamatory conjecture." She flicked a corner of the folder. "Let's face it, Mr. Knight. If any of this was provable in court, you wouldn't be sitting here across from me at a restaurant table. You would be meeting with the DA or SEC."

"That's where you're wrong," he said, cruel satisfaction glinting in his eyes. "It's amazing how the court of public opinion will try and convict someone much swifter than a court of law."

Her stomach rolled, bile churning before racing for the back of her throat. She hated to admit it, but he was right. Good God, if *any* of this information leaked, it would destroy Trevor's reputation, his engagement, and irreparably harm the family company. It wouldn't matter if the claims couldn't be proved; the speculation alone would be detrimental and the damage irreversible. Since their father died, Trevor's one goal—no, his obsession—had been to enlarge RemingtonNeal, to make it even more successful and powerful than what their father had done. None of that would be possible if even an iota of the data in this dossier was true.

Not that she believed it. She *couldn't.* Yes, Trevor could be merciless and cut-throat. She'd increasingly seen more and more evidence of this, personally and professionally, in the last few years. And it worried her. The glimpses of the brother she'd revered and adored as a child and teen were becoming further and further apart.

But it was those glimpses that gave her hope. That reminded her that underneath the often cold demeanor existed a good man. A man incapable of the things noted in that defaming file.

And bottom line… She loved him.

Love and loyalty demanded she believe in him.

"What do you want?" she asked, forcing a calm into her voice that was a farce. Questions, thoughts and *fear* whipped through her in a chaotic gale.

The man who'd fed her and provided her protection and light in a blackout didn't sit across from her. No, this wasn't the man who'd introduced her to such pleasure she still felt the echo of it weeks later. This man… He was a stranger. A cold, calculating, beautiful stranger.

"You."

The blunt announcement doused her in a frigid blast, stunning her.

"Excuse me?" she rasped.

He couldn't mean…?

No. No way.

He didn't want her. He had to mean something else.

But God, her body was having one hell of a time getting the message. *You.* Heat prickled at the base of her spine, and desire wound through her veins like a molten stream. A barrage of memories assaulted her—the sound of his ragged breath in her ear as he thrust into her body, all that dark, thick hair tumbling around his lust-tautened face, his whispered "moonbeam" as he stroked her damn skin… Her breath evaporated in her lungs, and she struggled to keep any hint of arousal from her face.

"I want you." He leaned forward, his midnight gaze pinning her to her chair. "More specifically, I want you to be in love with me."

The images in her head splintered like glass, dousing the passion-kindled flames inside her. She gaped at him. Couldn't help it. After all, it wasn't every day that she sat across from a lunatic.

"Are you crazy?" she demanded, clutching the edge of the table as if it were the only thing keeping her from leaping out of her chair. "I don't even *like* you. And we've never met," she continued, ignoring the memory of skin pressed to damp skin that flashed across her mind's eye. "How could you believe you love me?"

He flicked a hand, the gesture impatient, dismissive. "Of course I don't love you. And I don't need your affection or professions of an emotion that is nothing but an excuse for fools and liars to behave badly."

Shay shook her head, confused. "But you just said—"

"Pretend," he interrupted. "You're going to pretend to be deeply enamored with me, and our whirlwind relationship will be as fake as that sentiment."

"You *are* crazy," she breathed. "That's ridiculous. Why would you even propose something like that?"

"Why?" he repeated, that damn eyebrow arching again. "Your brother."

She barked out a harsh crack of laughter. "My brother? Do you really think Trevor cares if I'm in a relationship with you?" Hell, he might be happy. Yes, he and Gideon were business rivals, and Trevor had been trying to acquire the other man's company for years, but her brother would probably consider it a coup for his sister to date such a successful and wealthy man.

But for the first time since sitting down across from her, Gideon smiled. The curling of his sensual lips was slow, deliberate…and menacing. "Oh yes. Your brother will care. And he'll understand."

"Another enigmatic message, Mr. Knight?" She waved a hand, frustrated. "I'm too old for games. Whatever your play is here, make it plain."

"I'll make this very plain, Shay," he said, using her given name even though she hadn't granted him permission to do so. His voice, as dark and sinful as his eyes, caressed her name like a long, luxurious stroke. It was damn near indecent.

"You can pretend to be my significant other, and convince your brother that you are mine. Or..." a steely edge that was both lethally sharp and smooth entered his voice "... I can let the truth about Leida Investments drop into your brother's lap. Imagine his fury when he realizes the secrets his sister has been keeping. And then, while that little bomb detonates, I will release the information in that file to not just the SEC but to every news outlet and journalist I have access to. And believe me, the list is long. As would be the jail sentences your brother and his precious senator would face for everything they've been up to. What effect do you think the meltdown of your family name and company will have? How many people will want to accept funds from a woman associated with a man whose name will be synonymous with financial scandal and fraud? Even the desperate will think twice about that. So both of you would be ruined, if everything in that dossier leaks. That leaves us at an impasse, Shay."

He paused, and the import of his words—no, his *threat*—sank into her like the realization of a floundering person being swallowed by quicksand.

Slow but no escape.

"And the choice is yours."

Chapter 7

Gideon inhaled as he entered his mother's Lincoln Park home, and the sense of calm that always settled on him when he was with his family wrapped around him like a warm embrace.

Though his mother and sister had lived in the six-bed-room, seven-bathroom home for only four years, it was home because they were there. It was as much his sanc-tuary as his own downtown Chicago condominium. As the sound of his mother and Pat Benatar singing about love being a battlefield on her ever-present radio reached him, he shook his head, amending his thought. No, it was *more* of a haven for him.

Because family was *everything*.

Striding past the formal living and dining rooms with their soaring twelve-foot ceilings, and the sweeping, curv-ing staircase, he headed toward the rear of the house. His mother might have initially balked at him purchasing this home for her and Olivia in one of Chicago's wealthiest neighborhoods, but there'd never been any doubt about how much she adored the airy, state-of-the-art kitchen. With its wall of windows, restaurant-style ranges and cooktops, top-of-the-line appliances, large marble island and butcher block and dual workhorse sinks, Ai had instantly fallen in love. And it was in this room that he usually found her.

Like now.

Ai stood at the stove, still clothed in her professor outfit—elegant gray pantsuit with crimson blouse and hair in a loose bun at the nape of her neck—and barefoot. Her slim body swayed back and forth to the eighties' rock anthem, and Gideon stifled a snort as she perfectly executed an arm-and-hip dance move he recognized from the classic MTV video.

He gave her a slow clap.

She whirled around with a gasp, brandishing a tea strainer like a club. "*Gideon*," she scolded, splaying the fingers of her free hand over her chest. "Are you trying to give me a heart attack?" She replaced the strainer in the waiting cup of steaming water and shot him a look over her shoulder. "I warn you, if I go, all of my money has been left to your grandmother's Maltese puppy."

Chuckling, he crossed the room and pulled his mother into a hug. Her familiar scent of gardenias greeted him like a childhood friend. Only with his family could he be Gideon Jian Knight, the oldest son of Ai Knight, former cafeteria worker who busted her ass to provide for her children and earn her PhD in educational studies at the same time. With them, he could lower the guards he'd erected between him and the rest of the world, especially those who greedily grasped for money, connections, time or sex from Gideon Knight, CEO of KayCee Corp.

He jealously guarded his moments with his family.

Zealously protected *them*.

"That's fine," he assured her, with a quick kiss to her forehead. "I have the very best legal department, and they would be capable of breaking that will." He smiled as she swatted at him. But then he noted the two cups on the gleaming countertop, and his amusement faded. "How is she?" he murmured.

The light in his mother's eyes dimmed. "Better," she answered. She sighed, turning back to preparing the hot tea. "She's still sleeping more than I like and hasn't left the house since coming home from the hospital a week and a half ago. But...better." She checked the strainer in the second cup. "I was just about to take this up and sit with her for a while."

"I can do that, Mom. You obviously just arrived home." She didn't have to continue to work as a social sciences and history professor at the University of Chicago. He was more than willing to provide for her, as she'd done for him and Olivia. But Ai Knight wouldn't hear of it, and Gideon was proud to have one of the most loved professors at U of C as his mother. "Go upstairs, relax and I'll take care of Livvie."

"Thank you." She turned, smiling softly and extending her hands toward him. He enfolded hers in his, squeezing them. "But no, I want to spend some time with her before I grade papers. Although she always loves to hear you play. Maybe you could bring your guitar by sometime this week."

"I'll do that," he agreed.

His mother had been responsible for him first picking up the instrument. She'd found a battered acoustic Fender at a garage sale, and from the second he'd held it, he'd been enamored. Though extra money had been almost nonexistent during his childhood, she'd still found a way to pay for lessons. No one outside the family had ever heard him play, because it was for him. His peace. His way to lose himself and get away from the stresses of running a multimillion-dollar tech company.

Ai cupped his cheek, giving it an affectionate pat before lowering her arm. "Now, not that I don't enjoy you dropping by, but is everything okay?"

"Yes. There's something I do need to speak with you about, though." He propped a hip against the island and crossed his arms over his chest.

She studied him, then nodded, copying his pose. "Okay. What's going on?"

"I had a…business meeting last night," he said. "With Shay Neal. Trevor Neal's sister."

Surprise widened his mother's eyes. "I didn't even know he had a sister," she whispered, then shook her head. "Why, Gideon? What could you possibly have to discuss with her?"

"Our common interest," he said. "Her brother."

"Gideon," she murmured, tilting her head to the side. "What did you do?"

Meeting his mother's gaze, he relayed his conversation with Shay, including his revelation of all he'd dug up on Trevor, the ultimatum he'd delivered and her refusal to give him an answer.

"What are you thinking, son?" she asked, worry crowding her gaze. "She's innocent in all this."

Innocent. His fingers curled around his biceps, tightening even as blood pumped hot and fast through his body. *Innocent* was one word he wouldn't have associated with Shay Neal.

He'd done his homework on her before ambushing her at the restaurant. Twenty-five years old. Graduated with honors from Loyola University's Quinlan School of Business with a bachelor's in finance and entrepreneurship and a master of business administration. A member of Women in Business and International Business Society. Currently worked as vice president of the Social Development department at RemingtonNeal. And from what he could tell, the position was nothing but a fancy term for event coordinator, and definitely underutilized the education she'd received. All this information could be found on her social network platforms or the company's website.

Only a deeper dive below the surface uncovered her ownership of Leida Investments. The degrees and obvious intelligence had made her interesting. But this—the company she owned in secrecy—fascinated him. This society princess who organized brunches and galas was a mystery wrapped in an enigma. And anything he couldn't dissect and analyze he mistrusted. Tack onto that her last name, and he wouldn't dare to blink around her, vigilant of the knife that might slide into his back in that flick of time.

Still…nothing, not his caution, his preparation or even the pictures included in his private investigator's file, could've prepared him for the impact of Shay Neal face-to-face.

His grandmother owned an antique locket that she'd brought with her from China. Inside was a black-and-white picture of her older sister, who'd died in childbirth. In the image, his great-aunt had been composed, stoic. But in her lovely features—in her eyes—there glimmered emotion, vitality. *Life*. It emanated through the aloof expression like dawn breaking through the last, clinging shadows of night.

And staring at Shay Neal had been like gazing upon that faded photo. Yes, she was gorgeous. No one could deny she was beautiful—the refined bone structure with high, proud cheekbones, the patrician nose with its flared nostrils, or the full curves of a mouth that belonged on a pin-up model and not a demure socialite. And he couldn't deny that just for a moment, his wayward, rebellious mind had wondered if her gleaming golden brown skin was as butter-soft as it appeared.

But it'd been none of those features that had drawn him. Fueled an insane impulse to drag his chair closer and discover what scent rose from the corner where neck and shoulder met. Had his fingers itching to pluck the strings of his guitar and find the melody that would encapsulate her.

No, it was the intelligence, the spark, the *fire* in those arresting hazel eyes.

It made him mistrust her even more.

And then there was the niggling sense of familiarity that had hit him the moment he'd sat down at her table. As if they'd met before… But like he'd done last night, he dismissed the feeling. If he'd ever met Shay Neal, no way in hell he wouldn't remember.

"She's a Neal, Mom," he said, shoving thoughts of her—of the unsettling effect she had on him—away. "She doesn't have clean hands."

"That's probably the same logic Trevor employed when

he went after your sister," she pointed out, and the words struck him in the chest, burrowing into his heart.

"I'm nothing like him," he ground out, lowering his arms and curling his fingers around the edge of the marble top. "He stalked Livvie, lied to her, used her, then tossed her aside like yesterday's trash. I've been completely upfront with Shay, laying my intentions out and offering her a choice. Trevor stole Livvie's choice from her." He broke off, tipping his head back and deliberately cooling his rising temper. "You might not agree with my methods, and I'm sorry for that. But I didn't do anything when he damn near broke my sister, because you both asked me not to. I can't let it go this time. I'm not going to allow Trevor Neal to continue mistreating women. By the time I'm finished with him, he will have nothing left, and no woman will fall victim to him again."

It was the guilt that drove him.

Because it was his fault Trevor had sought out Olivia in the first place. If not for their mutual hatred and ongoing feud, she would've been safe.

"Gideon." His mother shifted forward, once more cupping his cheek. "You're right. I don't agree with your methods. I believe they will more than likely backfire, and not only will an innocent woman be hurt, but you will, too, son. If you have a conscience—which I know you do—there's no way you can't be affected by this path. And I wish you would end it now before this goes too far." She sighed, her gaze searching his. "But I also know you. And from the moment you refused to be born on your due date, I figured out you're stubborn. I'm not going to change your mind, I get that. So just…please. Be careful."

"Don't worry about me. I have everything under control," he assured her, hugging her close.

She didn't reply, instead squeezed him tighter.

He hated disappointing her, but nothing, *nothing* could dissuade him from his plans. Not her disapproval. Not Shay's reluctance and refusal to give him a decision.

He had one purpose. To bring down Trevor Neal.

And hell couldn't stop him from accomplishing it.

Chapter 8

"Trevor, the gala is a wonderful success. You should be proud. I'm certain your parents would be," Senator Julian Reus praised, pumping his future son-in-law's hand.

I don't know how you can say that, since you never met either of them.

Shay mentally winced over the snarky comment echoing in her head. God, she really wanted to like the influential man who would soon be part of her family. But he was such a...politician. Charming. Affable.

And phony.

Good thing she never voted for him.

"Thank you, sir." Trevor smiled, then slid an arm around Shay's shoulders. "I wish I could take the credit, but it belongs to Shay. She's the reason we've already surpassed the donations from last year."

Pride glowed like an ember in her chest, and for the first time that evening, a genuine smile curled her lips.

"Thank you, Trev," she said, wrapping an arm around his waist and briefly squeezing.

"Next year, it'll be even more of a success, with Madison by your side. I'm sure she will be more than happy to step in and help organize this special event." Senator Reus announced his daughter's involvement in Grace Sanctuary as a foregone conclusion.

"Of course I will, Daddy," Madison agreed, tilting her head back expectantly, and Trevor obliged her with a soft, quick kiss on the lips. "Shay and I will make a wonderful team."

Madison turned that wide smile to Shay, and even though all the warmth that had filled her faded away, Shay returned it with one of her own.

Trevor's fiancée had been nothing but cordial to Shay, but again, there was something not quite genuine about her. Madison reminded Shay of the ice sculpture in the lobby outside the ballroom. Beautiful but cold. To stand too close would send a shiver through the body.

"Let's get through tonight first before thinking about next year," Shay said, not committing to anything. Trevor stiffened beside her, but she ignored the telltale sign of his irritation. Her mind jumped to that dark brown file Gideon Knight had slid across the table. She thought about how her brother donated significant funds to the senator's campaign. And she couldn't help but wonder if some of that money came from their mother's organization.

Stop it.

The sharp order ricocheted off her skull. Damn Gideon Knight. She hated that he'd infiltrated her head, and she couldn't evict him. Not his damn dossier or the man himself. It'd been four days since that meeting—no, ambush.

Four days since she was supposed to give him her decision about his preposterous ultimatum.

Four nights of heated fantasies that left her twisting and aching in her bed.

What kind of sister did it make her that she woke up shaking and hungry for the man who blackmailed her? Who threatened her brother's livelihood and freedom?

A sad excuse for one.

Smothering a sigh, she excused herself from their small group on the pretense of checking with the catering staff, and headed across the room. She'd taken only a dozen steps before tingles jangled up her bare arms and culminated at the nape of her neck.

She sucked in a breath and immediately scanned the crowded ballroom for the source of the unsettling, *exciting* feeling.

There. No...*there*.

Gideon Knight.

The unexpected sight of him glued her feet to the floor. *Unexpected? Really?*

Okay, maybe not. As soon as that prickle had sizzled over her skin, a part of her had instinctively known who'd caused it. Only one man had ever had that kind of effect on her.

She stared at him, trapped in an instant of déjà vu. Seeing him in his black tuxedo, she was swept back to the first night they'd met. Once more he seemed like the imposing but regal warlord surveying his subjects, his armor traded for perfectly tailored formal wear, his hair emphasizing the stark but gorgeous lines of his face. The distance of the ballroom separated them, but she somehow sensed those black eyes on her, just like then.

Just like then, she fought the dual urges of fight or flight.

And by fight she meant the warring of their mouths and bodies for dominance.

Damn.

She balled her fist, forcing her feet to maintain a steady, unhurried pace forward. Even as her heart pounded a relentless rhythm against her sternum.

"How did you get in here?" she gritted out.

Conscious of any gazes that might be leveled on them, she kept her polite, social mask in place, when in truth she wanted to glare daggers at him.

His aloof expression didn't change...except for the arch of that damnable dark eyebrow. "I expect like everyone else. The front entrance. And paying the seven-thousand-dollar-a-plate fee."

"That's not possible," she snapped. "I looked over and approved the final guest list myself. Neither you nor your company's name was on it."

"Then you missed it. Maybe other matters distracted you," he added. A beat of charged silence vibrated between them. No need to name the "other matters." They both were well aware of what he referred to.

"Is that why you're here?" she demanded, and in spite of her resolve, her voice dropped to a heated whisper. "To pressure me for an answer?"

"It's been four days, Shay," he replied, and in that moment, she resented his carefully modulated composure.

The rash and admittedly foolish urge—no, *need*—to shatter his control swelled within her. She wanted the man from the blackout, the one who stared at her with flames of desire burning in his onyx eyes as he drove them both to impossible pleasure.

"I've given your four days longer than I'd usually grant anyone else."

"Well, I'm flattered."

"You should be."

She clenched her teeth so hard an ache rose along her jaw. "The answer is n—"

"Is this man bothering you, Shay?" Trevor appeared at her elbow, and both the venom in his question and his sudden, hard grasp elicited a gasp from her.

Gideon's gaze dropped to her arm, and anger narrowed his eyes.

"Get your hand off of her," he ordered. The volume of his voice didn't rise, but only a simpleton could miss the warning. "You're hurting her."

Scowling, Trevor glanced down at his fingers pinching her arm, then jerked his hand away. He lifted his regard to her face, and she glimpsed disgust, but also regret. She dipped her chin in a silent acknowledgment of his equally silent apology.

Turning back to Gideon, he snarled, "What are you doing here? You weren't invited. Leave. Now."

"I'm afraid that's not going to happen," Gideon said, with no hint of remorse. If anything, satisfaction rang loud and clear in those words. "I paid to attend just like everyone else here, and made a hefty donation on top of that. I'm staying."

"You can have your money back. We don't need it," Trevor spat, nearly trembling with rage as he edged closer to Gideon. "We both know why you're here. You lost. Get over it. It's not like it's the first time, and it damn sure won't be the last."

Fear spiked inside Shay's chest. *Good God.* She'd never seen her brother this angry. His reaction to Gideon's presence had to be more than a business rivalry. This was... personal.

"Trevor," she quietly pleaded, gently but firmly grasping his arm. "Please."

Gideon shifted his attention from her brother to her. And the same fury that twisted her brother's face lit his eyes like a glittering night sky. But as he studied her, some of the anger dimmed.

He retreated a step, his gaze still pinned on her.

Shock pummeled the breath from her lungs. Had he backed away...for her?

No. That was impossible. He didn't give a damn about her or her feelings.

Still...

"Have a nice evening. Both of you," he said, though his regard never wavered from her. "It was wonderful seeing you again, Shay," he murmured, then turned and headed farther into the room, not toward the exit as Trevor had demanded.

"What was he talking about, 'seeing you again'?" Trevor hissed as soon as Gideon was out of earshot. "When did you meet him?"

With Herculean effort, she tore her gaze from Gideon and met her brother's glare. Hurt and hints of betrayal lurked there. And guilt pricked her. For what, though? She'd done nothing wrong.

"A few nights ago when I had dinner with friends. He was at the same restaurant." She delivered the half-truth with aplomb. *God, when did I become such an accomplished liar?* "He just introduced himself, that was all. What in the world was that all about, Trevor?"

"Nothing," he snapped. Then, sighing, he dragged a hand over his closely cropped hair. "I'm sorry. I didn't mean to bark at you. Just…stay away from him, Shay. I don't want you to have anything to do with him. Do you understand?"

"I'm not a child, Trevor," she murmured, meeting his fierce stare. "And this isn't the proper place for this discussion, either. We have guests."

With that reminder, she turned and strode away from him and the disturbing scene that had just unfolded.

Oh yes, there was bad blood between him and Gideon. Now more than ever, she felt like a pawn in whatever twisted game the two of them were engaged in. And she hated it.

As the evening progressed, she couldn't uproot the bitterness. Maintaining her not-a-care-in-the-world socialite persona became a weightier burden, and by the time dinner was being cleared away, she was bone-deep exhausted. Peeking at the slim, gold watch on her wrist, she thanked God she had only about an hour more to do her hostess duty before she could escape.

"I noticed you talking to Gideon Knight earlier," Madison said, her tone low enough that Trevor, who was engrossed in conversation with Senator Reus, didn't overhear.

Surprised that she knew of him, Shay nodded. "Yes."

"Do you know him well?" she asked, and unease niggled at Shay. The air of nonchalance in Madison's seemingly innocent question seemed forced.

"Not really," Shay replied cautiously. "Though Trevor seems to."

"Oh, you don't know, do you?" Madison studied her, a gleam in her dark brown eyes. "Trevor didn't tell you?" she prodded before Shay could answer. "Gideon and I were…close before I met your brother."

"Close," Shay repeated, though the twisting in her stomach interpreted the coy choice of phrasing.

"Engaged, actually," Madison confessed, and this time, there was no mistaking the cat-that-ate-the-whole-damn-flock-of-canaries smile that curved her mouth. "We were engaged for a year before we ended our relationship. He wasn't happy about it." She chuckled, apparently amused at her understatement.

We both know why you're here. You lost. Get over it. It's not like it's the first time, and it damn sure won't be the last.

Trevor's accusation echoed in her head, and it now made sickening sense. As did Gideon's reason about why he'd proposed his ridiculous plan, that night at the restaurant.

Your brother, he'd said. All of this—hatred, blackmail, rivalry—was over a woman.

Her belly lurched, and she fisted her fingers, willing the coq au vin she'd just eaten not to make a reappearance.

"If I may have your attention, please?" Senator Reus stood, his booming politician's voice carrying through the ballroom and silencing the after-dinner chatter.

"Thank you. Now I know this evening is about Grace Sanctuary, and I speak on behalf of both the Reus and Neal families when I thank you for your generosity in both spirit and donations." Applause rose, and Julian Reus basked in it, his smile benevolent. No, the evening wasn't about him, but somehow, he'd managed to make it all about him.

"I'd just like to take this moment to recognize this wonderful charity, as well as Trevor Neal, who has spearheaded it since the passing of his dear parents. I'm so proud that I will be able to call him son in the very near future, as he and my beautiful daughter, Madison, embark on a journey together as man and wife. Trevor…" he accepted a glass of champagne from a waiter who suddenly appeared at his elbow, and lifted it high "…congratulations to you and my daughter. You are the son I wasn't blessed with, but am so fortunate to now have."

Around them, people hoisted their own wineglasses and echoed "To Trevor," as her brother stood and clasped the senator's hand, his huge grin so blinding, Shay had to glance away. The sight of him soaking up the senator's validation like water on parched earth caused pain to shudder through her.

Their father would've never praised him so publicly— or privately. Lincoln Neal had been a hard man, huge on demands and criticism, and stingy with compliments. She, more than anyone, understood how Trevor had craved his approval. And it'd been their father's refusal to give it that had changed Trevor. Their father had been dead for five years, and Trevor still drove himself to be the best… to be better than their father. This high regard from such an important man had to be like Christmas to Trevor. A thousand of them packed into one short toast.

Oh God. She dipped her head so no one could glimpse the sting of tears in her eyes.

She was going to cave to Gideon's ultimatum.

Family. Loyalty.

Those were the tenets that had been drilled into them from childhood. Definitely by their father, and even in one of the last conversations she'd had with her mother before she died. She'd stressed that Shay and Trevor always take care of one another.

Family loyalty wouldn't allow her to let Trevor lose everything. The family name. His company. His fiancée. His future father-in-law. There was no one left to protect him, except her. And until she could verify the truth of the information Gideon held—and she still doubted the veracity of it, especially given what she'd learned from Madison—she couldn't permit her brother to be ruined. Not when the kind but wounded boy she remembered still existed inside him.

He was her brother.

And to keep that happiness shining on her brother's face, she would make a deal with the devil.

And Gideon Knight was close enough.

It wasn't difficult to locate him in the crowded room. The entire evening she'd been aware of his presence, and when she glanced over her shoulder to the table several feet away, their gazes immediately locked. As if he'd only been waiting for her to look his way.

She gave him a small nod, and he returned it.

Exhaling, she turned her attention to the glass of red wine she'd barely touched throughout dinner. Now it, and about four more, seemed like a fabulous idea.

She would need all the courage she could get.

Chapter 9

"When I agreed to meet you, I assumed we would go to another restaurant, not your home."

Gideon stepped down into the recessed living room of his downtown Chicago penthouse and slipped his hands into the pockets of his tuxedo pants. Shay hovered at the top of the two steps leading into the room.

He surveyed his home, attempting to view it through her eyes. The dual-level, four-bedroom, three-bath condominium was the epitome of luxury with its airy, open-floor plan, floor-to-ceiling windows, game and media rooms, indoor and outdoor kitchens and private rooftop lounge that boasted its own fireplace. But it'd been the stunning views of the Chicago River and Chicago skyline from every room that had sold him. It was like being a part of the elements while protected from them.

He'd left most of the simple, elegant decor to his interior designer, but scattered among the gray, white and black color scheme were pieces of him, if Shay cared to look close enough. Next to the god-awful piece of metallic abstract art on the fireplace mantel that he'd never gotten around to tossing stood a framed photo of him with his family, including his grandparents, at last year's Mid-Autumn Festival in Chinatown.

On top of the white baby grand piano where his sister sometimes plucked out "Mary Had a Little Lamb" sat the guitar pick he'd forgotten to put away the night before.

Peeking from between the couch pillows was the ear of a pair of Bluetooth headphones that he used to listen to music with while working from home.

Yes, if she paid attention, she might glimpse those hints into him. And part of him tensed with the need to go through the room and remove those clues from her sight. But the other half... That half wanted her to spy them, to ask questions. Which was bullshit, since their arrangement didn't require that kind of intimacy.

He shouldn't hunger for that—especially not from her. Not just sister to his enemy, but another beautiful woman who didn't want the real him. The last time he'd allowed a woman to enter into the space reserved for family, she'd betrayed that trust. Had left him so disillusioned, he'd vowed to never be that foolhardy, that reckless, again.

Only family could be trusted. Only family deserved his loyalty...his love.

Definitely not Trevor Neal's sister.

"This kind of conversation deserves more privacy than a crowded restaurant," he said, finally addressing her complaint. "Would you like a drink? Wine? Champagne? Water?"

"Champagne?" she scoffed, stepping down into the

living room. "I guess this would be a victory celebration for you. But no. I'll take a Scotch. This situation calls for something strong that tastes worse than the deal I'm about to swallow."

Her acerbic retort had an inappropriate spurt of amusement curling in his chest. He squelched it, turning to fix her a finger of Scotch and a bourbon for him. Moments later, he handed the tumbler to her and silently watched as she sipped the potent liquor. Not even a flinch. His admiration grew.

When she lifted those beautiful hazel eyes to him, that niggling sense of familiarity tugged at him again. He cocked his head to the side, studying her. What was it…?

"Can we get this started, please?" she asked, setting the glass on the small table flanking the sofa. She rubbed her bare arms, and the sign of nerves pricked a conscience he'd believed to be impervious. "I'm sure you've already guessed that I'm going to agree to your ridiculous plan. Or let's just call it what it is. Extortion."

"You have a choice, Shay," he reminded her, sipping his bourbon.

"Yes," she agreed, bitterness coating the word. "Sacrifice myself or my brother to the beast. That's a hell of a choice."

He shrugged. "But one, nonetheless."

"You're not really this cold and unfeeling. I know you're not," she whispered, her green-and-amber gaze roaming his face as if trying to peer beneath the mask he chose to let her see.

Unbidden, the night of the blackout wavered in his mind. No. Those dark, hungry hours had proved he wasn't cold or unfeeling. For a rare instant, he'd lost the control he was much lauded for. But those circumstances had been extreme, and she wasn't a hardworking, passionate and fiery server named Camille. That woman had disappeared without a trace, filling in for another member of the waitstaff, and not leaving behind a hint of her identity. She'd seen the man he rarely let anyone see.

One Shay would never witness.

"If you need to make up an idea of who I am in order to fulfill the pretense of falling in love with me, then go ahead. Whatever will allow you to deliver an award-winning performance for your brother and everyone else watching."

"Everyone else being Madison Reus."

The accusation punched him in the chest, and he braced himself against the impact. By sheer will he forced himself not to react. But inside…inside he snarled at the mention of *her*. The woman who'd taught him that love could be bought by the highest bidder. Who'd knowingly betrayed him with the one man he hated. Who'd shown him that placing his heart and trust in a person outside of family was a costly mistake—to his bank account and to his soul.

He would never repeat that particular mistake.

"You must have loved her very much to go to such lengths for your revenge," Shay continued when he remained silent. "That's what this is all about, right? How dare my brother date the woman you were once engaged to? You're punishing both of them by flaunting me in their faces?"

He caught the threads of hurt beneath that calm tone. And in spite of his resolve to maintain his distance, both emotionally and physically, he shifted forward. She didn't retreat, but instead tilted her head back to meet his gaze. Courageous. He hadn't been expecting that from her.

Just like he hadn't been expecting this inconvenient attraction. Even now, her scent—the fresh, wild lushness of rain right before a storm and roses in bloom—called to him like a siren's lure, urging him closer, until his hard, solid planes pressed against her soft, sensual curves.

Though all common sense railed at him not to touch, he ignored it and reached for the thick strands of hair that fell in a sleek glide behind her shoulders. Pinching a lock between his fingers, he lifted it, indulged himself and brushed it over his lips.

Never breaking his stare, he murmured, "You don't know what you're talking about."

He heard the slight catch of her breath. Noticed the erratic beat of her pulse at the base of her neck. From nerves? Desire? The hardening of his body telegraphed which one it voted for.

Step back. Remember the plan. Stick to the plan.

But he stayed. Playing with sin-wrapped-in-bronzed-skin fire.

"No?" she breathed, the corner of her mouth lifting in a sardonic smile. "Is this the part where I just blindly trust what you say because my lying eyes and lil' ol' brain can't possibly grasp the intricacies involved here?" She scoffed, jerking her head back, and he released her. "Please. I'm patted on the head and patronized every day, so forgive me if I call bullshit."

She turned away from him, and he ground his teeth together, his fingers curling into his palms to battle the urge to grab her and bring her back against him. She didn't understand. This wasn't about Madison; it was about another woman—his sister. And that bastard who'd abused her heart and shattered her mental state.

An eye for an eye. A sister for a sister.

But he couldn't admit any of that to her. Not when she would no doubt run back and tell Trevor everything.

"You're forgetting I know the secret about your job. And I don't mean that joke of a title at RemingtonNeal. I would be a fool to underestimate you, Shay."

She pivoted and something flashed in her hazel eyes, but before he could decipher it, she briefly closed them and pinched the bridge of her nose.

"Can we just get this over with?" she asked, weariness coating her voice. "Tell me what you need from me so you won't burn my brother's world to the ground."

"Like I told you at the restaurant. You and I will pretend to be a couple. A real couple, Shay. Which means convincing everyone that we're hopelessly in love." He couldn't prevent the bitter smile from curving his mouth. "I read that you took several drama classes in college. Time to dust off those old skills and bring them out of retirement. I'll require you to attend several events and dinners with me, and the same for you. The first time you try to twist out of this arrangement, it's off, and your brother's dirty dealings become public."

This time he clearly interpreted the emotion turning her gaze more green than brown. Anger. "Don't worry about me. I'll hold up my end of the bargain. But I won't carry this lie on indefinitely. You have a time limit of six months. That's all I'll agree to."

Six months would be more than enough time to carry out all he had planned. "Fine."

"And at the conclusion, you promise to destroy the report and all copies of it."

He nodded again, although he had no intention of doing that. Only a fool would reveal his hand. Did he feel a twinge of guilt for deceiving her? Yes, it didn't sit well. But he'd meant what he'd told his mother. His number one goal was to prevent Trevor from ever hurting another woman as he'd hurt Olivia. This arrangement with Shay was only one part of his plan.

"Okay, then." Shay inhaled a breath and tilted her chin up at a haughty angle, every inch the socialite. "One more thing. I'm not a whore. We might have to pretend affection for each other, but I won't have sex with you."

Irritation flashed inside him, and he took a step toward her before he drew to an abrupt halt. "I can promise you that when I take a woman to my bed, she wants to be there. I don't give a damn about love, because there's something much more honest—fucking. There are no lies when a woman is coming for me, and I don't want one in my bed who doesn't want to be there. If she can't give me the truth of her pleasure, then I don't want her under me. And any man who's satisfied with just getting a woman between the sheets, without giving a damn about her desire to be there, isn't a man."

Silence plummeted into the room, and that sense of déjà vu hit him again. He'd said something similar to Camille weeks ago when she'd accused him of using his position of power to screw her. He shook his head. He had to stop thinking about her. He couldn't afford to show any weakness or distraction around Shay.

"But you need to understand one thing, Shay, and come to terms with it." He moved forward again, lowering his head so their mouths were inches apart. So close he glimpsed the golden striations in her eyes and inhaled the heady scent of Scotch on her breath. "I'm not the other men you might have had dancing to your tune. For the next six months, you're mine. And while you might not be in my bed," he murmured, brushing the back of his finger over a sculpted cheekbone, "you'll act like you are. Which means you'll pretend to desire my touch, my hands on you. You'll behave as if you crave what I, and only I, can give you. Pleasure. Passion. A hunger so deep you don't know how you ever existed without me to take care of it for you. So, moonbeam, even if you loathe me, those beautiful eyes better convince everyone that I'm yours. And *you're mine*."

She wrenched away from him, stumbling backward, her panting audible testimony to the arousal that stained her cheeks and glinted in her eyes.

Fuck.

Need gripped his stomach, grinding and squeezing like a vise. He'd overplayed his hand. His aim had been to teach her a lesson, and he'd ended up the student with his knuckles rapped.

"Don't call me that," she ordered hoarsely. He frowned, at first not grasping what she meant. Then it hit him. Moonbeam.

Where had that come from? Why had he called her *that* name?

"Pet names, like we're something we're clearly not, aren't part of this, either." She tugged her shoulders back, and that delicate but stubborn chin went up again. "And for the record. I belong to *me*. Not my brother. Not RemingtonNeal. And definitely *not you*."

Shay spun around. Snatching up her coat, which he'd laid over the back of the foyer chair when they'd entered the penthouse, she strode out of his home.

He stood there, staring at the closed door, and a small smile played on his lips.

Whether she realized it or not, she'd just issued a challenge.

Accepted.

And he more than looked forward to winning.

Chapter 10

Shay grimaced at the vibration of her cell phone in her back pocket as she served up an order of green papaya salad and tom yum to another hungry customer standing outside Bridgette's food truck. Her best friend's delicious Thai cuisine made hers one of the more popular trucks stationed at Hyde Park during the lunch hour.

Bridgette was a wonderful chef, and when she'd proposed starting a food truck business, Shay had insisted on investing. The love of food and cooking were just a couple things the two of them bonded over. And because they were such good friends, when Bridgette had called this morning, frantic because she'd been down a person, Shay had been more than willing to jump in and help. It hadn't been the first time she'd volunteered, and if Bridgette needed her, it wouldn't be the last. Just another reason Trevor resented her "lowbrow" relationship with Bridgette.

Good thing that she'd never told him about cooking and serving on her food truck.

Another insistent buzz of her cell, and she sighed. She knew who was calling her.

Gideon.

He'd left a message about joining him for lunch about a half hour after Bridgette's panicked call. She'd shot a text off to him, letting him know meeting wouldn't be possible. But had he accepted that? Hell no. Well, that fell under the category of His Problem.

Yes, she'd agreed to attend events with him, but she'd also meant it when she told him he didn't own her. She was more than willing to accompany him to dinners, lunches, parties, whatever. But she also needed notice, and not just a couple hours. She had a life and refused to hand it over to him.

She was already an indentured servant to the Neal name and reputation. He wouldn't become another master.

You're mine.

Those two words had played over and over in her head like a rabid hamster in a wheel. It'd been two days since she'd left his penthouse, and she hadn't been able to erase the declaration from her mind.

Or deny the spark of desire that had erupted into a conflagration inside her. Her thighs had clenched at the dark, sensual note so dominant in his voice. And in that moment, she swore she could feel the heavy, thrilling possession of his body taking hers, filling hers.

Claiming hers.

God, it wasn't fair. Not the words he uttered to her. Not the out-of-control reaction of her body to his.

She didn't have to pretend to know his touch. No, she had intimate knowledge of it.

Which was why she'd reacted so strongly—and unwisely—to the "moonbeam" he'd so carelessly tossed at her. That endearment had been special to her, meant for her alone. But it hadn't been. God only knew how many women he'd said it to.

She wasn't special.

And damn, that had hurt. More than it should've.

Another buzz, and she gritted her teeth. Probably a threatening message this time. The tenacity that had made him so successful as a businessman was working the hell out of her nerves.

Six months. She just had to hold on for six months. Then she would be free. From both this "agreement" with Gideon and from under the yoke of the Neal name.

Gideon didn't know the significance of her time limit. In that time, she would turn twenty-six and be in control of the trust funds from her mother and maternal grandmother. With that came financial independence. She wouldn't need her paychecks from RemingtonNeal to help finance Leida Investments. With the money from her trust funds, she would have more than enough capital, and while she wouldn't totally be able to escape the assumptions because of her last name, she would no longer be under the restrictions and expectations of her brother and her family reputation.

From birth, she'd been under a man's thumb: her father's, her brother's and now Gideon's.

In just six months, she would be liberated from them all.

"Here you go, babe." Bridgette handed her an order of

pad thai, disrupting her thoughts of emancipation. "That's number 66."

"Thanks." Shay accepted it, bagged it and carried it to the window. "Here you go." She passed the food to the customer with a smile and turned to the next person in line. "Hi, how can I—"

Oh hell.

Gideon.

Her eyes widened as she stared at his cold, harsh expression. "What are you doing here?" she asked, and in spite of the "you don't own me" speech she'd just delivered to herself, apprehension quivered through her at the anger glittering in his gaze.

"Wasting my time hunting you down, apparently," he ground out. "You're already reneging on our arrangement, and it hasn't even been two days. I warned you about thinking I would dance—"

"Hey, man, order and move on. Some of us have to get back to work," someone yelled from in back of Gideon. And when several more grumbles of agreement followed, Gideon whipped his head around. Immediately, the mumbling ceased.

Good Lord. That was some superpower.

He returned his attention to her and in spite of his glare, she hiked her chin up. "I'm helping a friend out. She needed me today."

His gaze narrowed further, and he growled, "Open the door."

Before she could reply, he stalked off and disappeared. But seconds later, a hard rap at the side door echoed in the truck. From the grill, Bridgette tossed her a "what the hell?" look, and, bemused, Shay shrugged and unlocked it.

The door jerked open, and Gideon strode through it. His big body and intense presence seemed to shrink the interior to that of a toy truck.

Bridgette stared at him, openmouthed and struck silent. Which wasn't an easy feat. With sharp movements, he jerked off his coat and suit jacket and hung them on a wall hook. Then he rolled his sleeves up to his elbows and pinned both her and Bridgette with that dark glare.

"Well?" he snapped. "Where do you need me?"

Need him? What was happening?

Bridgette recovered first. "Can you cook?" At his abrupt nod, she handed him a knife. "You get an order of cashew chicken going, and I'll get the green curry."

Without a word, he crossed to the sink, washed his hands, then accepted the utensil and started chopping fresh vegetables and chicken like a pro. Bridgette again shot her a look, but Shay shrugged, still stunned and confused.

"You have customers waiting," Gideon reminded her, without turning around.

Now the man had eyes on the back of his head as well as cooking skills?

Again...*what the hell?*

Shaking her head, she returned to the window and the ever-growing line outside. For the next couple hours, the three of them worked like a well-oiled machine. Shay still couldn't quite grasp that Gideon Knight was there in the cramped quarters of a food truck, cooking Thai entrées like a professional.

She tried to imagine Trevor jumping in and helping out and couldn't. The image refused to solidify, because her brother would never have done it. Not many men of her acquaintance would've bothered getting their hands dirty. But then again, two hours ago she wouldn't have been able to picture Gideon getting his hands dirty, either. And especially not for her.

As Bridgette closed the serving window and hung the Closed sign, questions crowded into Shay's head. But before she could ask them, he turned, tugging down his sleeves and rebuttoning the cuffs.

"I'll be by to pick you up at seven tonight for a dinner party. This time, be there and ready," Gideon ordered, thrusting his arms into his jacket, then his coat, his tone warning her not to argue. And for once, she heeded it. "And don't keep me waiting."

With a brisk nod at Bridgette, he stalked out the door, leaving a weighty silence behind.

Bridgette was the first to break it.

"What in the hell just happened?" she yelled, voicing the same question that had been plaguing Shay since Gideon's sudden appearance.

And her answer was the same.

Damned if she knew.

Hours later, Shay stood in the foyer and stared at the front door as the ring of the doorbell echoed through her house.

Seven o'clock. Right on the dot.

Her pulse raced, and the roar of it filled her head, deafening her. Nerves. They waged war inside her, turning her belly into a churned-up battlefield. Any sane woman would be anxious about entering a charade and perpetrating a fraud on everyone she knew and cared about.

But she would be lying to herself if she attributed the

lion's share of the nerves to their arrangement. No, that honor belonged to the man himself.

Who was Gideon Knight?

The attentive, protective and devastatingly sensual stranger from the night of the blackout? The aloof billionaire and brilliant CEO of a global tech company? The ruthless, revenge-driven ex-fiancé? The man who barged into a food truck, rolled up his sleeves and selflessly helped serve the Chicago masses?

Which one was real? And why did they all fascinate her?

Exhaling a breath, she rubbed her damp palms down her thighs. No fascination. Or curiosity. Both were hazardous and would only lead to a slippery, dangerous slope. One where she could convince herself that the tender, generous man was the true one, and the one who held her brother's future over her head was the aberration.

What had been one of her mother's favorite sayings? "When someone shows you who they are, believe them." Well, Gideon had shown her he would go to any lengths, no matter how merciless, to achieve what he wanted. Even if it meant using and hurting other people in the process. She needed to believe this truth.

And accept it.

The doorbell rang again, and it unglued her feet, propelling her forward. She unlocked and opened the door, revealing her date for the evening. No, correction—the man she was madly in love with for the next six months.

Gideon stared down at her, his black eyes slowly traversing the curls and waves she'd opted for tonight, down the black cocktail dress with its sheer side cutouts and sleeves, to the stilettos that added four inches to her height.

When his eyes met hers again, she barely caught herself before taking a step back from the heat there. It practically seared her skin.

Hazardous. Dangerous. She silently chanted the warnings to herself like a mantra.

He would set fire to her life and leave her covered in ashes.

"Seven o'clock," she rasped, before clearing her throat of the arousal thickening it. "Just as you requested."

"You're beautiful."

Struck speechless, she could only stare at him. His expression hadn't changed from the cool, distant mask, but those eyes, and now his voice... If his gaze made her tremble, the low, sensual throb in that dark velvet voice had her squeezing her thighs against the ache deep inside her.

"Where's your coat?" he asked, glancing past her into the house.

"I have it."

Get it together, she silently ordered herself as she briefly returned inside to grab her coat off the stand.

"Here. Let me." He stepped inside the foyer and took the cape from her, holding it up while she slipped into it.

Fastening it, she turned back to him, and her voice did another vanishing act when he offered her a crooked elbow. Her breathing shallow, she hesitated, then slid her arm through his and let him guide her out of the house and to his waiting Town Car. A driver stood at the rear door, but Gideon waved him away and opened the door for her himself.

God, she was too old for Cinderella-like fairy tales. If she'd ever had stars in her eyes, they'd been dimmed a long time ago. But here, sitting with Gideon Knight in the back of a car that was more elegant and luxurious than any limousine she'd ridden in, with the heat from his body and his earthy sandalwood scent invading her senses, she could almost understand why Cinderella had lost a beautiful shoe over a man.

"I didn't have a chance to tell you earlier, but...thank you. For stepping in and helping Bridgette this afternoon." She glanced at his sharply hewn profile. "How do you know how to cook? I wouldn't have expected it of...a man like you."

He turned to her, and even in the shadowed interior, his dark eyes gleamed. Dim light from the streetlamps passed over his face, highlighting then hiding his too-handsome features. She fought the urge to stroke her fingertips over those planes and angles, over the full curves of his mouth. Free those thick, silken strands and tangle her fingers in them...

"A man like me?" he repeated, the sardonic note relaying that he understood exactly what she meant. "I hate to tarnish your image of me, Shay, but my beginnings aren't as rarefied as yours and your brother's. My grandparents immigrated from China with nothing more than they could carry, and both of my parents worked barely above minimum-wage jobs when I was a kid. When my father died, Mom often worked two jobs to provide for us. And as soon as I was old enough, I took any kind of employment I could to help her. One of those happened to be as a short-order cook. If you ever need your yard landscaped or your gutters cleaned, I can do those, too."

Shame sidled through her in a slick, oily glide. She'd unknowingly spoken from a lofty place of privilege, but her ignorance didn't excuse it. True, she didn't subscribe to the idle lives some of those in high society did—she believed in working hard and making a difference in the world—but she couldn't deny that she didn't know what it was to go without. To go to bed exhausted from menial labor or worried about how the next bill would be paid.

Gideon's mother, and even Gideon, obviously did.

"I'm sorry," she murmured. "I spoke out of turn." She paused, debated whether to say anything else, but ended up whispering, "Your mother must be proud of you."

He studied her for several silent, heavy moments. "She is. But then again, she would've been proud of me if I'd decided to remain a short-order cook in a fast-food restaurant."

Shay digested that, turned it over and analyzed it again. Could she say the same for her parents? *No.* Her father would've easily disowned her. And as much as Shay adored her mother, Leida Neal wouldn't have been proud of or happy for her daughter if she had been anything less than what her name demanded—respectable, wealthy, connected and married to a man who fit those same qualifications.

The certainty in that knowledge saddened her. Did Gideon realize how fortunate he was?

"She sounds lovely," Shay said, ready to drop the unsettling subject. But then, because her mouth apparently had no allegiance to her, she blurted out, "I'm sorry about your father."

Another heartbeat of weighty silence.

"It was a long time ago."

"My mother died fourteen years ago. And I still miss her every day," she admitted softly.

Slowly, he nodded. "I remember," he finally said, sur-

prising her. "Your brother and I went to high school together, and later attended the same college. But I recall
when your mother died. The principal came for him in
the middle of class and took him out."

"I didn't know you and Trevor went to school together."
Shock whistled through her. "He never mentioned knowing you." Not that he mentioned Gideon at all unless it
regarded acquiring his tech company. Or more recently,
not unless a blue streak of unflattering adjectives followed his name.

His sensual mouth curved into a hard, faintly cruel smile.
"Your brother and I have a long history. He was decent
until that day. I was a scholarship student at an elite, private prep school. That already made me a target for most
students there. But your brother wasn't one of them. Until
after your mother died. Then he became one of the worst.
That he and I were often head-to-head competitors in academics and athletics didn't help matters. Neither did the
fact that I didn't take his or any of the other assholes' shit."

"He changed after Mother passed," Shay murmured,
the dagger of pain stabbing her chest all too familiar when
she thought about the boy who'd become a hardened man.
"She was the…buffer between him and my father. My
dad…" Shay shook her head, turning to stare at the passing scenery outside the car window, but seeing Lincoln
Neal's disapproving, stern frown that was often directed
at his children. But more so at his first-born child. "He
was demanding, exacting and nearly impossible to please.
And Trevor desperately wanted to please him. Which became impossible after our father died. Yet, even now…"
Again she trailed off, feeling as if she betrayed her brother
by revealing even that much.

"That doesn't excuse his behavior," Gideon replied, ice coating his voice.

"No," she agreed, more to herself than him. "But no one is created in a bubble. And no one is all bad or all good. Sometimes it helps to understand why people behave the way they do. And it helps us give them compassion and mercy."

Strong, firm fingers gripped her chin and turned her to face him. Gideon's touch reverberated through her, echoing in the taut tips of her breasts, low in her belly, and in the pulsing flesh between her thighs. He'd clutched her like this the night of the blackout, holding her in place, so he could watch her as she came. Now, like then, she couldn't tear her gaze away from his. Like then, her lips parted, but now, she swallowed down the whimper that clawed at the back of her throat.

"Your brother doesn't deserve compassion or mercy, Shay. So don't try to convince me differently with sad stories of his childhood." He swept the pad of his thumb over her bottom lip, and this time she lost the battle and released that small sound of need. His eyes narrowed on her mouth, then after several moments, lifted to meet hers. "Why does it feel like I've—" He frowned, but didn't remove his hand.

"Why does it feel like you've what?" she breathed, dread filtering into the desire. He'd heard her plead for him, for his touch, many times during the night they'd spent together. Had the sound she'd released just now triggered his memory?

God, in hindsight, she should've been up front with him about her identity from the beginning. If she came clean now, he would only see her as a liar.

Maybe because you're lying by omission?

Shame crept in, mingling with the dread. She hated deception of any kind, and this didn't sit well with her. At all. But self-preservation trumped her conscience at this point. Her reasons for initially remaining quiet still stood. She didn't trust Gideon. Didn't know what he would do with the information that Shay Neal had masqueraded as waitstaff at one of the biggest social events of the year and then slept with him under false pretenses. Would he use it as another source of ammo in this war he waged with her brother, leaving her reputation and her company as casualties?

Possibly.

No, she couldn't afford to find out.

"Nothing." He dropped his hand from her face, his customary impassive expression falling firmly back in place. Turning from her, he picked up a small, rectangular box from the seat beside him. "Here. I have something for you."

She glanced down at the gift, then back up at him. After several moments, she returned her attention to the box and, with slightly trembling fingers, removed the lid. And gasped.

Delicate ruby-and-gold bangles nestled on black velvet. Tiny diamonds rimmed the bracelets, making the jewelry glitter in the dark.

They were beautiful. Just…beautiful.

"There're eight of them," he said, picking up the bangles when she didn't make a move toward them. "In Chinese culture, eight is a lucky number. Red is also lucky."

Gently grasping her hand, he slid the jewelry onto her wrist.

"Thank you," she whispered. In the past, she'd received earrings, necklaces and rings from men who hoped to win her over—or rather win over the Neal heiress. But none of them had been bought with thought or meaning. None of them had been for *her*, Shay. Whether he'd intended it or not, Gideon had given her a piece of himself, of his heritage. And for that alone, she'd accept. "They're gorgeous."

"You're welcome," he murmured, his fingers brushing over the tender skin on the inside of her wrist before withdrawing. For a moment, she caught a flicker of emotion in his eyes before he shut her out once again.

She felt the echo deep inside her.

And for some inexplicable reason—a reason she refused to explore—it hurt.

A charade, she reminded herself. They were both playing their parts, and gifts to his fake girlfriend were part of those roles.

As long as she kept that truth forefront in her mind, she wouldn't get caught up in the beautiful enigma that was Gideon Knight.

Chapter 11

"I feel like a zoo animal in a cage," Shay muttered, lifting a glass of white wine to her lips. "They could at least be subtler about the staring."

Gideon arched an eyebrow, scanning the large formal living room. Several pairs of eyes met, then slid away from his, caught ogling the newest couple in their midst. Satisfaction whispered through him. He'd accepted this particular dinner party invitation because of who would be in attendance. Not just business associates, but members of the social circle Shay was intricately a part of. Talk of their appearance together would rush through Chicago's society elite like a brush fire.

"They're wondering why you're with the beast," he said.

"Probably."

He snorted at her quick agreement, earning a dazzling smile from her. He had to hand it to her—Shay was a brilliant actress. As soon as they'd crossed the threshold into Janet and Donald's mansion, she'd immediately charmed his client and her husband. And though he knew the truth behind their arrangement, even he could almost believe Shay was smitten with him. Small, but intimate touches to his arm and chest. Gentle teasing. Special smiles. Yes, she deserved an award for her performance.

And as their hosts approached them, and she slid her arm through his, her soft breast pressing into side, he ordered his dick to stand down for about the fifty-fifth time…in two hours.

If he was a better man, he would insert some distance between them, not enjoy the sensual lure of her scent. Or savor each time he settled a palm at the small of her back—a back covered only by the same sheer material that "covered" her shoulders and arms. She was sex and class in this dress that skimmed every delicious curve.

Damn if the heat from her didn't seep into his palm and ignite every greedy need to stroke her skin, sift his fingers through the thick, dark strands of her hair…claim her saint-and-sinner body for his own.

The only woman to have stirred this unprecedented reaction in him had been Camille. It unsettled him. The mysterious waitress was no longer in his life. But Shay… Everything about her tested his control, his reason, his plans.

How he kept touching her when every rule of logic demanded he keep all displays of affection public to cement the facade of a happy, in-love couple. How she challenged him with those flashes of temper when no one except his best friend and business partner dared. How she surprised him with things like working in a food truck. How he couldn't jettison the sense that there was something familiar about her...

And then there was his jewelry on her wrist. The gold and rubies gleamed against her skin like sunlight and fire. And that fierce surge of possessiveness that had blindsided him in the car swelled within him again. He braced himself against it.

This wasn't the first time he'd bought a woman jewelry. Hell, the amount he'd bought Madison could have filled a store and still left enough diamonds to pay for a small city. He'd gone into the store this time intending to purchase a necklace or earrings, something that screamed wealth. But none of the pieces had felt...right. So he'd left, and instead had driven to a smaller jeweler. One where he'd bought his grandmother's birthday gift. And the bangles had been there, waiting. He hadn't intended to purchase something so personal to him, so... intimate, for what should've been just a flashy statement of ownership, with the sole purpose of making others take note. But he had. And unlike almost everything in his life, he didn't analyze it, instead going on impulse.

Because in that moment, as he'd handed his credit card over the counter, his need to see Shay wearing the pieces he'd personally chosen far outweighed caution.

And that need hadn't abated.

As he slid his hand up her spine and cupped the nape of her neck, the need deepened, sharpened.

"I should be annoyed with both of you," Janet Creighton said, her smile erasing the reproach from her words. Leaning forward, she dropped her voice to a conspiratorial whisper. "But the two of you outing yourselves as a couple tonight has made my little dinner party the social event of the season."

Shay smiled, glancing up at Gideon, and the warmth reflected in the gold-and-green depths of her eyes had his breath stumbling in his throat. "I told Gideon he should at least give you some warning of who his plus one would be, but…" She tipped her head to the side and murmured, "The rumors are true about that stubborn nature of his."

"I find myself giving in to you way too often, though. My reputation might not survive it," he replied, squeezing her neck and bringing her closer, brushing his lips over the side of her head.

Her fingernails bit into his arm, and he barely managed to fight back a groan. The tiny prick of pain echoed lower in his body, and he locked his jaw against asking her to do it again. But harder.

"You shouldn't let me know I'm a weakness," she teased, but only he caught the undercurrent of faint sarcasm. "I might be tempted to take advantage."

"I might be tempted to let you," he rejoined softly.

Silence thrummed between them, taut and tension-filled. Their gazes clashed, tangled, locked. The pretense seemed all too real. As did the desire that flared inside him, the excitement that flashed through him, as bright and hot as a bolt of lightning. What would she do if he lowered his head and took her soft mouth? Would she jerk away from him? Or would she use their act as an excuse to surrender, to let him taste her?

"Well, damn." Janet's awed, but amused whisper infiltrated the haze of arousal that had clouded him and his judgment. *Damn it,* he silently swore, returning his attention to his client. This was a facade, an act. One he'd set in motion. He couldn't afford to forget that. "Honey, I need you to take notes."

Beside Janet, her husband snorted lightly. "We've been married thirty-two years. My hand is cramped."

Shay's laughter drew more gazes in their direction, and Gideon smiled, both at the other couple and the pure delight in Shay's amusement.

"Dinner is almost ready," Janet said, shaking her head and throwing Donald a mock-irritated glance. "Let's go, you."

"That went well," Shay murmured, as soon as they were out of earshot. She slowly released his arm. "You can let go of me now."

Instead of obeying, he turned into her body, his hold on her drawing her closer until her breasts brushed his chest. He caught her sharp gasp, felt the puff against the base of his throat. Tiny flickers danced under his skin at that spot.

She stiffened, and he softly tsked, lowering his voice so it carried only as far as her ears. "You're supposed to enjoy my touch, Shay. Want more of it. But definitely not shy away from it." When she lifted her hands and settled them at his waist under his jacket, her fingernails digging into his skin through his shirt, he didn't hold back his low rumble of hunger. "I think you're intending to punish me, moonbeam," he growled above her mouth, pinching her chin with his free hand and tilting her head back. "But I don't mind a bit of pain with my pleasure. Would you sink those claws in deeper if I asked nicely?"

He expected her to wrench away from him; his muscles tightened in anticipation of controlling the reaction he purposefully coaxed from her.

But she sank her nails harder into his flesh, and the

stings were a precursor of how she would scratch and grip him if they were stretched out on his bed. He tried to swallow his groan, but some sound escaped against his will. And the molten gold in her eyes almost eclipsed the brown and green.

She'd played him. Turned the tables so completely he ground his teeth together, imprisoning the words that would reveal she'd knocked him on his ass. Those words being *more, harder, please...*

"Gideon," she whispered.

"Well, don't you two look cozy," a new, all-too-familiar and despised voice drawled from behind them.

Gideon released Shay, shifting to her side and slipping an arm around her waist. He faced Madison and Julian Reus, careful to compose his features so they betrayed none of the disgust and hatred that burned in his chest for her, or the disdain he harbored for her father.

Underneath those emotions, satisfaction hummed through his veins. *Good.* He'd been waiting for their arrival. He'd expected Trevor to be with them, but since he wasn't glued to Madison's side, the other man must not be in attendance. That was a disappointment, but Gideon's cheating ex and her equally deceptive father were good enough.

He switched his attention to Madison. It stunned him that he'd once missed the avaricious, calculating gleam in her brown eyes. Given her long dark hair, sensuous features and curvaceous body, he couldn't deny her beauty, but it was hard, like a lacquer that distracted from the coldness beneath.

Love had truly been blind. No. It'd made him dumb and deaf, too.

"I must admit, when we heard the rumors of you being here with Gideon, Shay, we didn't believe it at first," Julian said, his tone as amicable as any good politician's. But his eyes blazed, yelling the things one would never want heard on an open lapel mic. "Your brother didn't mention you were attending tonight. Or that you were…" he paused deliberately "…seeing someone new. I'm sure he'll be interested to discover this turn of events."

If the senator had expected Shay to quail under his not-so-subtle condemnation, he'd sadly underestimated her. "Trevor is a wonderful brother, but he's just that—my brother. And I don't require his approval for who I choose to spend time with. Just as he didn't ask for mine with Madison." Shay smiled, and it could've cut glass. "Although I would've gladly offered it."

Julian blinked, his mouth hardening at the corners. "Your brother and I have much in common. We both admire honesty—and loyalty."

"You don't really want to go there, do you, Julian?" Gideon interjected, arching an eyebrow. He forced his voice to remain even, bored, but injected a thread of steel through it. He'd be damned if he'd let the man intimidate Shay or belittle her with his condescending bullshit. Especially not in front of him. "I'd be willing to discuss both with you. At length."

"Let's go, Daddy." Madison chuckled, the sound strained, her lovely features tight. Like her father's, her gaze ordered Gideon to do unnatural things with his own anatomy. "There are more people we need to speak with."

Shay waited until her soon-to-be sister-in-law and her father were out of earshot, then sighed. "God. This evening just became infinitely longer."

"I beg to disagree." He settled a hand on the small of her back again, guiding her forward. "The fun has just begun."

Shay breathed deeply as she washed her hands in the Creightons' bathroom. This moment alone, without the narrow-eyed glares from both Madison and the senator, or the microscopic attention of the other guests, was a mercy.

She hated being the subject of all that speculation. They'd reminded her of vultures, waiting to see who'd get their pick of carrion. Gideon seemed unfazed. But all those sidelong, greedy glances and not-so-quiet whispers... They'd crawled over her like ants attacking a picnic. By the time dinner concluded, she'd nearly raced to the bathroom. To be free. If only for a few moments.

"Can't stay in here forever," she said to her reflection.

That was the first sign of losing it, right? Talking to oneself. She smiled, shaking her head as she headed toward the restroom door. Her mother used to do the same, mumble to herself as she puttered around the kitchen when Dad wasn't there to catch her. God, Shay missed her. Missed her hugs, her quiet assurances, her confidence in Shay.

Well, one thing Leida Neal would've reprimanded her about was hiding like a coward in the bathroom during a dinner party. Snorting lightly, Shay exited the powder room...and nearly collided with Madison.

Damn.

"Hi, Madison." She greeted her brother's fiancée with a smile. "I'm sorry if you had to wait. The bathroom's all yours."

She shifted to the side, prepared to walk around the

other woman, but the futile hope of avoiding a confrontation died a quick death when Madison stepped to the side as well, blocking Shay's escape. Madison smiled in turn, but it didn't reach her chilly brown eyes.

"No hurry, Shay. I was hoping to catch you alone for a few moments," she purred. "We have so much to catch up on, seeing as we apparently have more in common than I thought."

"I'm assuming you're referring to Gideon," Shay said, resigning herself to this conversation. It wasn't one she could've circumvented, but she hadn't anticipated having it outside of the guest restroom.

"You're a cool one, aren't you, Shay?" Madison asked, slowly shaking her head. "The other night you never mentioned you knew him. And when I told you about our past, you pretended to be dumb. It seems I underestimated you. I won't repeat the mistake."

Anger flickered to life, crackling like dry wood set ablaze. "I didn't pretend to be dumb, as you put it. Discussing my private life while you were at the table with my brother, your fiancé, didn't strike me as appropriate. And like I told your father, I don't need approval for my relationships," she said, working to keep the bite of rising irritation from her tone. After all, this was her future sister-in-law. Even if more and more she was beginning to question the wisdom of Trevor's choice. "Now, if I'd known you were attending this dinner party, I would've informed you so you weren't taken by surprise. But I wasn't aware."

Several silent moments passed, and a fury-filled tension thickened between them.

"Your brother always brags about how smart you are."

Madison tsked softly. "Shay earned this degree. Shay graduated with honors from this program. So intelligent. And yet, when it comes to men, you're so naive." Her expression softened with a sympathy that was as false as her lashes. "What are the odds that *my ex* would turn around and fall for *my new fiancé's sister*? A little too coincidental, don't you think?" She chuckled, the sound taunting. "It's almost pathetic in its transparency. He's using you, Shay. Gideon still wants me, and you're caught up in his little plan to make me jealous."

Pain, serrated and ugly, slashed at her, the truth of Madison's words the razor-sharp knife. Why did it hurt? She'd gone into this charade knowing the reason behind it. Gideon hadn't tried to deny it. But reason had no place when humiliation and pain pumped out of her with every heartbeat.

Forcing her lips to move and her arm to lift, she waved away Madison's barb-tipped claims as if they were petty annoyances. "I don't see how any of this is your business, Madison. What is between Gideon and me is just that. *Between us*. Now if you'll excuse me…"

She moved forward again. If Madison chose to get in the way, this time she'd find her ass meeting the floor. Thankfully, Madison didn't try to block her, and Shay headed toward the dining room with a smothered sigh of relief.

"Ask him who broke it off with whom. He hasn't let go of me. If I wanted him back, Shay, he would be mine."

Madison's parting shot struck true. By sheer force of will, Shay kept walking.

But it was with a limp.

Chapter 12

"You ambushed me. Again."

Gideon turned from his silent—okay, brooding—study of the scenery passing by the car window to look at Shay. She'd been quiet since they'd left the Creightons' mansion ten minutes earlier. No, she'd been distant since returning to the dining room after dinner.

And Madison had followed a couple minutes behind her, wearing a sly grin. Personal experience had taught him his ex could be a malicious bitch. Had she said something to Shay? Had Madison hurt her? A wave of protectiveness had surged inside him, and he'd just managed to check the impulse to drag Shay onto his lap and demand answers. To ease the tension that had strung her shoulders tight. To assure her that if Madison had sharpened that dagger she called a tongue against Shay, he would fix it.

Instead, he'd remained sitting beside her at the table, continuing the charade until they could politely leave.

Disgust ate at him like a caustic acid. Disgust with himself. He'd led her into the lion's den and hadn't shielded her.

Every war has casualties.

He mentally repeated the reminder like a mantra. He'd been aware when he'd included Shay as part of his plans that she might be wounded, but the end justified the means. He intentionally conjured an image of his sister lying on that hospital bed, black hair limp, skin pale as she stared listlessly out the window. Oh yes. The end justified the means. *Olivia*—her suffering, her brokenness, her loss—justified it.

"Am I supposed to know what that cryptic comment means, Shay?" he asked. "Because I can assure you, I don't."

She didn't flinch from his flat, indifferent tone or the dismissal in his question. "You knew Madison and the senator would be there tonight."

Gideon stared at her, not even debating whether to give her the truth or not. "Of course I did. Janet and Donald are business associates of Julian's."

"You didn't think to warn me?" She shook her head. "What if Trevor had been there?"

"And?" he asked, anger igniting inside him. "I hoped he would be. But it doesn't matter. Maybe him hearing about his sister dating his enemy from his future father-in-law or his fiancée might work out better than I intended."

"Do you care that your schemes and plans are hurting people?" she whispered.

The disappointment in her voice, as if he'd somehow let her down, raked over his skin. Burrowed beneath it. He hated it.

Dipping his head, he leaned closer until only inches separated them. So close her breath ghosted over his lips. "Your brother?" He paused. "No."

"All this for her," she breathed, her gold-and-green eyes roaming his face. Summer on the verge of autumn. That's what they reminded him of. Shaking his head as if he could physically rid himself of the sentimental thought, he leaned away from her, turning back to the window.

"Madison was right."

He stiffened, his suspicions confirmed.

Slowly, he straightened and shifted on the seat, meeting her gaze again.

"What did she say to you?" he growled.

"Nothing I didn't already know," she replied, her full bottom lip trembling before she seemed to catch the betraying sign. Her teeth sank into the sensual curve.

"What did she say to you, Shay?" he repeated, grounding out the question between clenched teeth.

"That you were using me to get back at her and Trevor. That she could have you back if she wanted. She…" Shay paused, and something flickered in her eyes. "She told me to ask you who broke up with whom. From that, I'm assuming she left you."

He didn't answer. Couldn't.

What did it matter if Shay knew the dirty details? Of how he'd walked in on her brother in Madison's bed. How the woman he'd believed he would spend the rest of his life with had told him she'd upgraded with Trevor.

None of it mattered now. Yet he couldn't shove the words past his throat.

Shay shook her head, chuckling softly. Except the sound contained no humor. "So is that your master plan?

Was the file on my brother your way of ensuring I cooperated while you plotted to steal back your ex? That would show Trevor who the better man was, right? Teach him—"

"You don't know what you're talking about."

"That's another thing Madison accused me of being. Dumb. But I'm not. You're fighting over her like she's some ball you lost on the playground. And in the end, I'll look like the idiot she called me. But that doesn't matter to you, does it? Not as long as you win."

Her accusation struck too close to the doubts that had pricked at his conscience only moments before. That only stirred his anger.

He didn't give a damn if she knew the truth.

"Win?" He arched an eyebrow, not bothering to prevent his sneer. "Win what, exactly? A relationship based on lies and greed? A woman who would jump to the next dick as long as he was willing to pay handsomely for the privilege? Tell me, Shay, doesn't that sound like a terrible grand prize?"

She gaped at him, no doubt stunned by the ferocity of his reply. "What do you mean?" she asked, her gaze roaming his face, as if searching for the truth. As if she actually wanted the truth. "Do you mean she—"

"Cheated on me? Oh yes." He nodded, and the smile on his mouth felt savage. "We'd been together a year and a half, engaged to be married. Gorgeous, fun, witty, exciting—I didn't care who her father was or about her family name. All I wanted was her. And all she wanted was what I could give her. At least, until she found someone else who could give her more. Care to guess who that someone was?"

Her lips formed her brother's name, but no sound came out.

"Yes, Trevor. I came home early from a business trip and stopped by her place. I had the key, so I went in and found them together. In the bed I'd just made love to her in two days earlier. It hadn't been the first time they'd been together. The next day, when giving me back my ring, Madison informed me that it'd been going on for some time—six months. According to her, I might be rich, but Trevor had prestige, connections and a family name. She'd upgraded."

Shay's chin jerked up as if he'd delivered a verbal punch to her jaw. Sorrow flashed in her eyes, and for a second, he resented her for it. He didn't want her pity; he wanted her to understand the kind of bastard she called brother.

"Your brother did it on purpose, Shay," he pressed. Just as he'd used Gideon's sister to get to him. "He went after Madison because she was my fiancée, and faithless bitch that she is, she had no problem sleeping with a man she knew I hated. She not only betrayed me with her body, but with her loyalty, her heart. So I don't need to prove to Trevor who the better man is. Because, Shay, your brother isn't a real one."

"Gideon," she whispered.

"No." He slashed a hand down between them, done with the topic. Done with laying out his stupidity before her. "And to address the second part of that statement, you're not dumb. Far from it. But you are blind." He narrowed his eyes on her. "Why are you so quick to believe the manipulative claims of a jealous woman?"

She blinked. "What do you mean?" She frowned. "Madison's not—"

"Jealous," he interrupted again. "Why is that so hard to accept?" He didn't wait for her to answer, but continued. "And this doesn't have anything to do with me. You're everything she wants to be. Respected. Admired not just for your beauty but for who you are—successful, brilliant, esteemed. She, like me, like Julian, watched as you charmed everyone around you tonight, and as they damn near competed to have a moment of your time. And that has nothing to do with your last name. That's all you. I'm the toy in this scenario, moonbeam," he murmured. The thought of being her plaything roughened his voice, tightened his gut. "And she wants me only because you—a woman she could never be—has me."

If he hadn't been watching her so closely, he might've missed her flinch before she controlled it. "Why are you calling me that?" she rasped.

"The other women there tonight… They were like the sun—bright, obvious. Trying so hard to be noticed. But you, Shay, you don't have to try to grab someone's attention. Like the moon, you're distant, cool and beautiful. Men can't help but notice you. Be drawn to you, ready to beg for some of your light rather than be lost and alone in the dark."

Only the harsh grating of their breaths filled the back of the car. Part of him demanded he rescind those too-revealing words. But the other part—the greedy, desperate part—refused to, instead waiting to see what she would do with them.

"What game are you playing now, Gideon?" she whispered, her eyes wide…vulnerable. "I don't know how to play this one."

"Then set the rules," he said, just as softly. Unable not

to touch her any longer, he cupped her deceptively delicate jaw, stroked the pad of his thumb over the elegant jut of her cheekbone. "Set the rules, and I'll follow them."

It was a dangerous allowance. In this "relationship" the balance of power couldn't shift; he couldn't hand her a weapon to use against him. Not when revenge for his sister's pain, his family's torment hung in the balance. But that knowledge didn't stop him from shifting closer to her, from tipping her head back and brushing a caress over her parted lips. From staring down into those beautiful eyes and letting her see the desire that hurtled through his veins.

"Just one. Make…" She paused, briefly closed her eyes, but then her lashes lifted. "Make me forget."

"Forget what, moonbeam?"

The answer was already yes. He'd surrender anything to her if she'd permit him to continue touching her.

But that same hunger to brand her vied with the need to conquer what haunted her. He'd never considered himself some knight facing dragons, not for anyone, but for Shay, he'd forgo the armor and charge into the fire.

One hand rose to his wrist, the slender fingers wrapping around and hanging on to him. The other slipped inside his jacket and settled on his chest before sliding up to his neck, her thumb resting on his pulse.

"Forget that you're trying to destroy my brother, my world," she whispered. "Forget that you're going to break me. And I'm going to let you."

A vise gripped his chest and tightened until the barest of breaths passed through his lungs. If he was a good man, he would release her, promise not to touch her again. Walk away from this whole plan that already ensnared her like barbed wire. She was right; he would probably end up hurting her, and if he had a conscience, he would warn her to protect herself from him.

But he'd never claimed to be good.

Still, he could do what she asked. He could make her forget.

"Kiss me," he ordered in a low rumble. "Take what you want—what you need from me. And, moonbeam?" He lowered his head, pushing his thumb past the seam of her lips and into her mouth. Moist heat bathed the tip. "Don't be gentle," he growled.

She studied him, and as he watched her in turn, desire eclipsed the vulnerability that lingered in her gaze. He felt her teeth first, and the tiny sting arrowed straight to his lower body.

"Don't be gentle," he repeated, harder.

Her eyes still on him, she moved the hand on his neck so her fingers encircled the front. She squeezed just as her lips closed around his thumb, and she bit him.

"Fuck," he groaned, the sting arcing through him like a sizzling bolt of electricity. "Baby." Her gaze darted to the side, toward the front of the car and his driver. "The divide is soundproof," he assured her, pulling his thumb free and rubbing the dampness over her bottom lip. Before repaying her with a nip of his own.

Another moan clawed free of him. Damn, he'd been aching—literally *aching*—to get his mouth on her. To taste her. Reaching for the console in front of the seat, he lifted the hood and hit a button, and another panel, this one smoke-tinted, slid across, concealing them.

"Are you good?" he asked. His dick throbbed, and he gritted his teeth.

He could wait until they reached their destination, but fuck if he *or* his dick wanted to. He needed to be inside her. From the moment he'd sat down across from her in that restaurant, he'd craved this. No, damn that. Longer. From the second he'd opened his private investigator's file and laid eyes on her picture. Even as he'd spun his plans of revenge, he'd envisioned those hazel eyes gleaming with the arousal he'd stirred. Pictured her sweet body bowing and twisting for him. Wondered if she would take him slow and easy, or hard and wild. God, he'd almost driven himself insane wondering that.

She nodded, but he shook his head. "Tell me, moonbeam. You good?"

"Yes," she breathed, giving his neck one last squeeze. She removed her hand, replacing it with her mouth, trailing a path up his throat, over his chin until she hovered over his lips. "I've set the rules," she reminded him, kneeling on the seat so she rose over him. "Now follow them like you promised."

She crushed her mouth to his.

The kiss wasn't patient, wasn't tentative. Her tongue thrust forward, parried with his, tangling and dueling. She took him as if she knew exactly what he liked, what he needed. It was…familiar. Something—a thought, a warning, maybe—tickled the back of his skull, but as she sucked on his tongue, drawing on him as if he were everything she needed to survive, that inkling winked out. Nothing mattered but the intoxicating, addictive taste of her. And in that instant, the question that had plagued him since he first gazed on her picture was answered: Shay would be hard and wild in bed. Or in the back of a Town Car.

"I want to…" She didn't finish her request, but reached behind him, removing the band holding back his hair.

The strands loosened, and her heavy sigh differed from the ones she'd been emitting during their kiss. This one? It matched the delight that softened her beautiful features as she drew his hair forward and up to her face. Tangling her fingers in the strands, she tugged on them, and the prickle across his scalp tripped down his spine, crackled at the base. He clutched her hips, digging his fingertips into the soft flesh.

"Beautiful," she whispered.

Only one other woman had ever called him that, and with that same note of awe coating the compliment. It'd shaken him then, and it did now. Once more that niggling sense of…something…teased him. But he shoved it away. Now, with his hands on Shay, with her storm-whipped rain and fresh roses scent embracing him, there wasn't room for thoughts of another woman. Especially one that was a ghost. Shay was sensual, golden-bronze flesh-and-bone. She was hot, pounding blood coursing through him. She was his insanity, his hunger brought to vivid life.

She was *here*.

For him.

With a growl, he skated his palms up the sides of her torso, and the zipper of her dress abraded his skin. Desperate to discover if his imagination matched reality, he impatiently tugged it down and wasted no time in pushing the material over her shoulders and down her arms. She obliged him, freeing his hair and joining him in getting rid of the clothing.

"No." The word escaped him before he could trap it.

"No?" she repeated, and he caught the hint of insecurity that crept into her voice. She started to lift her arms toward her torso, but he latched on to her wrists, lowering her arms back down before she could cross them.

"My imagination doesn't match reality. Doesn't even fucking compete." He cupped a breast and hissed at the delicious weight of her flesh filling his palm. Warm, soft, perfect. Reverently, he whisked his thumb over the nipple, watching in fascination as it beaded. No, she wasn't the first woman he'd touched like this, but none had been *her*. He tore his gaze from his hand on her to meet her eyes. "Nothing or no one could fucking compete."

Her lips parted, but no words emerged. Good. He was saying enough for both of them, and he needed to stop that before he took them somewhere they had no place being. Bending his head, he sucked a tip deep, flicking his tongue against her flesh before drawing hard. Shay shuddered, her hands cradling his head, holding him to her with a strength that telegraphed her passion. That and the nails pricking his scalp.

Switching breasts, he treated the other to the same devotion. She writhed against him, as if seeking to get closer. Cooperating, he fisted the hem of her dress and shoved it up her thighs. With a whimper, she straddled him, dropping down and pressing them sex to sex.

He growled around her flesh, suckling harder. And she rewarded his attention with a dirty grind of her hips that had him throwing his head back against the seat, eyes squeezed closed. Her panties and his pants and underwear separated them, but none of those inconsequential details mattered. Not when her hot, wet heat rode him. Not when each drag of her flesh over his cock shredded his control.

"Give me your mouth again," he ordered, in a voice so guttural he barely understood himself.

But she must've translated it, because she gave him what he asked for, her hips still working over him. She didn't stop, and the thrust of her tongue and pull of her lips mimicked each stroke below. Even as she yanked his jacket open and attacked his shirt, damn near ripping buttons loose to get her hands on his bare chest, she didn't lose him.

They groaned into each other when she touched him. Those slender, clever hands swept down his chest, lingering over his tattoos, tracing the ink with almost worshipful strokes.

"How is it possible that you just get more beautiful?" she whispered. He parted his lips to tell her she was the stunning one, not him, but she ripped away his ability to talk by brushing her fingertips over his nipples, rubbing them. His hips bucked into her. Live wires connected from her touch to the tip of his dick. He swelled, throbbing, *hurting*.

"I need to be inside you," he rasped against her mouth. He abandoned her breasts and burrowed his fingers in her hair, gripping it, holding her still so he could stare into those slumberous eyes. "Are you going to let me?"

"Yes," she breathed, trailing a route of fire over his clenched abs to the band of his pants.

"Are you going to take me like this?" he pressed, thrusting upward so she fully understood what he meant. "Take me like you own me?"

"Yes."

Almost too rough, he released her, reaching into his inner jacket pocket for his wallet. Quickly withdrawing a condom, he tossed the billfold to the floor. Within moments, he had his pants opened, his erection freed. Her swift intake of breath preceded the hot, tight clasp of her fist around him by seconds. His back bowed under the whip of pleasure, and his free hand wrapped around hers, so they pumped his flesh together. For several torturous and blissful moments, they stroked him, pushing closer to an ending that wouldn't include him balls-deep inside her.

"Enough," he muttered, and, removing their hands, tore open the small foil package and slid the protection over him. Above him, she fumbled under her dress, trying to push black lace panties down her hips. "Fuck that," he growled.

Shoving her dress higher until it encircled her waist like a band, he fisted the front of her underwear and jerked it to the side. For a couple seconds, he savored the vision of her bare, glistening sex and the erotic beauty of her silken thigh-high stockings against silkier skin. But then the lure of that feminine flesh proved too enticing, too much.

He slid his finger through the dark cleft, moaning at the wetness coating his skin. The sound dragged from her echoed his, and her head tipped back, shuddering when he circled her, applying minute pressure. Just enough to have her shaking like a leaf, but not enough to catapult her over the edge. That honor belonged to his dick.

Hands grasping his shoulders, she eased down his length, and though the drugging pleasure had his eyes nearly closing to savor the tight, smooth fit of her sex, he kept his attention on her. Because nothing—not the rippling clasp of her body, the quiver of her thighs, the sight of her taking him—could compare with the slight widening and darkening of those beautiful eyes. Those eyes conveyed how much she craved him, needed him.

Those eyes gave him all of her.

And greedy bastard that he was, he wanted it all.

Except for the very fine tremble of his tautly controlled muscles, he held completely still. Allowing her to claim him at her own pace. Even if each interminable second she took to inch down threatened to send him careening into insanity or orgasm—whichever came first. Finally, she sat on his thighs, and he was fully embedded inside her. And still he wouldn't free her from his gaze. Not when, in this moment, surrounded by her sweet flesh, everything clicked into place. He finally knew this gaze.

Knew *her*.

"Fuck me, moonbeam," he whispered. "And don't look away from me."

Sliding her hands over his shoulders and into his hair, she grabbed fistfuls of the strands and glided up his length. Air kissed his tip before she sank onto him again, swallowing him in the firmest, but softest heat. Again. And again. She released him, took him. Eased off him, claimed him.

She rode him, rising and falling over him, driving them both toward the rapidly crumbling edge of release. Her cries mixed with the litany of his own and still she continued to look at him. Letting him see what he did to her. Gifting him with that. Electric pulses zipped up and down his spine, crackling in the balls of his feet. He couldn't hold back much longer. He wasn't going to last.

He loosened a hand from her hair and tucked it between their undulating bodies and slicked it over the top of her sex. Once, twice. A third and a pinch.

She flew apart with a scream, stiffening, her sex gripping him, milking him. Daring him to dive into the abyss with her. Grabbing her hips, he slammed into her, plunging so deep he almost doubted he would ever find his way out of her.

She fucking leveled him.

Her arms closed around his shoulders, cradling him as he bowed his head, groaning out his release into her neck. He inhaled her thick, heady scent as his body calmed and his breathing evened. His senses gradually winked back online after pleasure short-circuited them.

Silence filled the interior of the car. Carefully, he withdrew from her, disposing of the condom and righting their clothes. Shay didn't look at him, paying undue attention to pulling down her dress and settling it around her thighs.

"Are you okay?" he asked, his voice seeming overly loud even to his own ears.

"Yes," she said, still not glancing in his direction.

Camille.

The name shivered on his tongue. He almost said it aloud just to see if she would respond. If her reaction would give her away. But he swallowed the name of the woman who'd haunted his thoughts since the night of the blackout.

The woman who was one and the same as Shay Neal.

It explained the nagging sense of familiarity. The feeling that they'd met before. Sinking into her body had sealed the knowledge for him. How had Shay thought she could continue to fool him once he was deep inside her? How could she believe he would ever forget the too-tight and utterly perfect fit of her?

She'd lied to him. All this time, she'd recognized him—how could she not?—but she'd kept the secret of her identity from him.

Why?

Several reasons entered his mind—embarrassment, protecting her reputation—but one kept blaring in his head, gaining validity.

Had meeting him at the Du Sable City Gala been a setup? Not the blackout, of course, but had she gone to the gala with a plan to meet him? To get close to him? Yes, he'd approached her, but what would've happened if he hadn't? Would she have found a way to get close to him? Found a way to get him to talk to her, to reveal information?

Had Trevor sent her to the gala with that purpose?

Minutes ago, Gideon would've said no. But with the haze of pleasure quickly evaporating and leaving him with a clearer mind, he couldn't know for sure. First and foremost, Shay was a Neal and her loyalty belonged to her brother. Hadn't she been willing to surrender to blackmail and sleep with the enemy—literally, now—to save Trevor? Gideon couldn't see her going so far as to fuck him in that dark break room for her brother. As she'd defiantly told him before, she didn't whore herself out for anyone. But…doing a little subterfuge on Trevor's behalf? Maybe that wasn't out of the question…

He studied her proud profile, waiting to see if she would tell him the truth now, after she'd allowed him back inside her body. Maybe she'd explain her reasons for deceiving him.

But she didn't.

Her silence was a punch-in-the-gut reminder of who she was—who they were to each other. She said she wanted to forget. But they never could. Especially when forgetting for even a moment meant letting his guard down and the enemy in.

And that's who she was.

The enemy.

Chapter 13

Shay shrugged into her suit jacket, studying herself in her room's cheval mirror. The slim fit of the gray, pin-striped jacket and pencil skirt were flattering, emphasizing the curves of her waist and hips. The cream blouse with the throat-to-waist ruffle lent it a feminine flair. She'd gathered her hair into a loose bun and fastened a pair of her mother's favorite diamond studs to her ears. The whole look was professional, fashionable…

And armor.

Yes, she needed it today. Hopefully, no one looking at her would guess that the previous night she'd had hot, wild sex in the back seat of a car.

God. She closed her eyes, pinching the bridge of her nose. What had she been thinking? But that was just it. She hadn't been.

Groaning, she turned from the mirror. It would've been so easy to stay in bed today and burrow under the covers. Just pretend last night hadn't happened. After all, that was her forte lately. Pretend to be in a relationship. Pretend to be in love with Gideon Knight. Pretend she hadn't just thrown all common sense and family loyalty out the window and screwed the man who was blackmailing her.

Regret weighed down her chest, so she couldn't inhale without feeling its bulk. Not regret about the sex. It had been as cataclysmic as the first time, and though it'd been foolish to give in to him, she didn't have remorse over experiencing passion.

No, it was what happened after that earned her regret. For a time, she'd forgotten that Gideon hated everything and everyone associated with the Neal name. That he planned on taking down her brother if she didn't capitulate to blackmail. That they stood on opposite sides of a Hatfield-and-McCoy-esque feud.

But as soon as the pleasure ebbed from her body, he'd returned to his aloof, distant self. She'd practically felt the wall slamming up between them. He'd been gentle when he'd shifted her off his lap and adjusted her dress, but unlike the hands that had cupped her breasts, tangled in her hair and stroked between her legs, his touch had been cold, almost clinical.

Other than asking if she was okay and wishing her good-night when he'd dropped her off at home, he hadn't spoken. And she'd never felt so vulnerable, so…alone. Not even after the night of the blackout.

And to think she'd been so close to telling him she was Camille. That would've gone over well. Not.

Well, lesson learned. Last night was a mistake she wouldn't repeat. She refused to let herself be vulnerable to him again. Get through the next six months. That was her goal. Protect Trevor from Gideon, come into her trust fund, then leave RemingtonNeal to concentrate on her own business.

The days of being under the thumb of the men in her life would come to an end.

To achieve the dream of independence, she could endure six more months of Gideon Knight.

With a sigh, she glanced at the clock on her bedside table. Well, no time for breakfast, and she could grab coffee at the office. If traffic cooperated, she would just make her nine o'clock meeting with the event planners for RemingtonNeal's huge annual holiday party.

Grabbing her coat and purse, she descended the steps, her mind already locked on the multiplying items on her to-do list today.

"Shay."

She halted at the front door, shooting Trevor a hurried smile as she set her purse on the foyer table to slip into her coat.

"Morning, Trevor. I'm sorry I don't have time for breakfast. I have a—"

"You'll need to make the time. I need to talk with you immediately. And it's too important to put off. I'll meet you in the study." He didn't wait for her agreement, but pivoted on his heel and strode toward the rear of the house.

Bemused, she stared after him. Removing her arm from her coat sleeve, she tossed the garment over her purse and followed her brother.

"Shut the door, please," he said, when she entered the room he considered his domain. As their father had done before him.

Trevor hadn't changed much in the room. Except for

the dark chocolate office chair that sat behind the massive oak-and-glass desk, everything else was the same. The tall bookshelves that lined two of the walls, the heavy floor-to-ceiling drapes, the two armchairs flanking the big fireplace. She'd hated being called into this room when her father had been alive; it'd meant she'd somehow screwed up. And she didn't like it any better now with her brother.

"What's going on, Trevor?" she asked, crossing her arms over her chest. Another thing she hated. Feeling defensive.

"Why did I have to find out about you and Gideon Knight from Madison and her father?" he snapped, stalking around his desk. "Do you know how humiliating that was for me, receiving that phone call?"

Of course. How could she have forgotten about Madison and the senator?

Gideon, that's how. Gideon and sex in the back seat of his car.

"I'm sorry, Trevor," she said, truly remorseful. She'd fully intended to tell him about her and Gideon's "relationship" when she arrived home last night, but it'd slipped her mind. "I wanted you to hear about us from me first."

"Us?" he sneered, his hands closing on the back of the chair several feet from her. "There shouldn't even be an *us*. I told you to stay away from him," he reminded her with a narrowed glare. "Do you remember? It was when you told me you barely knew him and there was nothing going on between you two."

"Like I told Madison last night, the fund-raiser wasn't the place to discuss my personal life. Especially when you didn't try to hide your hostility toward him. I've been seeing Gideon for a while now, but because of who we are, we decided not to make our relationship public until we knew we were serious about it." Great. Now she was lying about her lie. "But like I also told the senator, I don't need to run my relationships by you for permission. I did intend to give you the *courtesy* of telling you about Gideon last night. So again, I apologize if you were embarrassed discovering it from someone else."

"Where's your loyalty, Shay?" he hissed. "Your duty to family first?"

Pain struck her like a fiery dart to the breast. It spread through her until she vibrated with it. Reason whispered that he didn't know all she sacrificed—was still sacrificing—for him. But it didn't halt the hurt from his condemnation, his disgust.

"My loyalty is always to this family," she whispered. "Who I'm seeing socially should have nothing to do with you or my love for you."

"It does if you're screwing a man I hate. Have always hated," he snarled.

"Why?" she asked, lowering her arms and risking a step forward, closer to him. "Tell me why. Gideon told me you went to school together."

That hadn't been all he'd said, but even as shameful and horrible as her brother bullying him was, surely there had to be more to the story. Especially on Trevor's end. Yes, he was a snob, but she'd never seen him actively hate someone just because they came from humble beginnings.

"Yes, we went to school together, and he didn't know his place back then, either."

"Didn't know his place," she repeated slowly, not believing that he'd uttered those ugly, bigoted words. Yes, they were fortunate enough to be in that elevated percentage of wealthy Americans. But they were still black. They still endured racists who gave them the "you're not our kind, dear" looks when they dared enter some establishments. How dare *he*...

"Why? Because he's Chinese-American?" she rasped.

"No." He slashed a hand through the air. "I don't give a damn about that." The vise squeezing her chest eased a little, and relief coursed through her. "After Mom died, all I had left was Dad."

Oh God. "Trevor," she said, moving forward, holding a hand out toward him.

"No," he repeated, coupling it with another hand slash. "I know you were there, but she was something different to me than to you. She was the shield, the...insulation between him and me. When she died, she left me exposed to him. To his expectations, his impossibly high standards, his disapproval. I didn't get time to grieve for her because I had Dad riding my ass, wanting to make a real Neal man out of me without my mother's babying. His words," he added, his tone as caustic as acid.

"I know," Shay murmured. "I saw how hard he was on you. But, Trevor?" She lifted her hands, palms up. "What did that have to do with Gideon? Dad didn't know Gideon."

"But he did," Trevor snarled. "Who do you think funded the scholarship that enabled Gideon to attend the prep school? One of RemingtonNeal's charities. And Dad never let me forget it. Sports, academics, even the damn debate team—Gideon and I were always head-to-head in everything, and when he beat me, Dad was always right there to remind me that a poor scholarship kid was better than me. That maybe he should hire him to run the family company because he was smarter, stronger, quicker, more clever. He constantly compared us, and it didn't end with high school, but continued in college and beyond, even following Gideon's career after he graduated. The one thing I'm grateful for is that he's not alive today to see you with him. He probably would claim him as his son, give him RemingtonNeal."

Shock pummeled her. She'd had no clue. But now his animosity toward Gideon made sense, because she knew her father. Knew how denigrating and belittling and cruel he could be. Especially toward Trevor. Lincoln Neal probably didn't even like Gideon, but using him as an emotional weapon against his son sounded like something he would do.

And Trevor... God, if her brother didn't let go of his bitterness, he would live trying to prove to their dead father that he was better than a man he might have counted as a friend once upon a time.

"Do you understand why you can't be with him, Shay? That man has been the source of my pain and unhappiness for over a decade. I won't allow him in my home or to eat at my table, much less date my sister." He shook his head. "End it."

I can't.

The words bounced off her skull, pounded in her chest. To call off her relationship with Gideon would be to destroy her brother. But even in an alternate universe where she and Gideon had met under normal circumstances without blackmail and revenge, she still wouldn't have broken up with him based on what her brother had shared. Trevor's antagonism for Gideon wasn't his fault—it was their father's. But with Lincoln Neal gone, Trevor had transferred all his resentment and pain to the one who was still alive.

"No, I won't end it with Gideon," she said. Sighing, she moved across the small distance separating them and covered his hand. "Trevor, I—"

He jerked away from her, taking several steps back and glaring at her. A muscle ticked along his clenched jaw. "You won't break this *thing* off with him?"

"No, Trevor, I won't." *I'm doing this for you*, she silently screamed. But the words remained trapped in her throat.

"I didn't want to do this, but you've left me with no other choice. Leida Investments, Shay."

For the second time in the space of minutes, shock robbed her of speech. Icy fingers of astonishment and dread trailed down her spine.

Trevor cocked his head to the side. "You believed I didn't know about your little company all this time? Nothing gets by me. And as long as you were discreet, I didn't see the harm in letting you dabble in business. It didn't interfere with your responsibilities to this family. But now, your actions are jeopardizing us. If you don't end it with Gideon, I'll ruin every business that has received money from you. And with my name and reputation, you know I could do it with just a whisper. Now, while you take some time to make your decision about who you're giving your loyalty to, I'm going to insist you step back from your job at RemingtonNeal. I've already asked Madison to take over some of your duties for the next few weeks. Consider it a leave of absence while you choose between a man you barely know and your family."

With that parting shot, he exited the room, not pausing

to spare her a glance. Not even bothering to glimpse the devastation he'd left behind.

Not only had he dismissed her easily, replacing her with his fiancée, but he'd threatened her company, as well as the hard work and livelihoods of those she'd invested in.

He would cavalierly ruin others' lives to bring her to heel.

Forcing her feet to move, she left the study and retraced her steps to her room. There, she removed her suit and went to her closet for her suitcases. Forty minutes later, she once more descended the stairs, not knowing when she would return.

She couldn't stay here any longer.

Not when she wasn't sure who she was selling her soul to protect.

Chapter 14

Gideon pulled up in front of the small brick house in the Humboldt Park neighborhood. With its white trim, meticulously manicured front lawn and currently empty flower boxes, the home was cute and obviously well taken care of.

But Shay still had no business being here.

Not when she had a home.

So why had she sent him a text informing him he'd need to pick her up here tonight, as she would be living in this place for the foreseeable future?

What the hell was going on?

The questions had burned in his head, then twisted his gut into knots. The need for answers had propelled him out of his mother's house, where he'd been visiting her and Olivia. He hadn't bothered replying to Shay's text but had entered the address in his GPS and driven directly there.

He shut off his car and walked up the tidy sidewalk to the postage-stamp-size porch. Maybe she'd heard him arrive, because before he could knock on the storm door, Shay appeared in the entrance, wrapped in a cashmere shawl and evening gown. She joined him on the porch, scanning his attire, her gaze running over his peacoat, down his black jeans to his boots, then back up.

"You're going to the ballet dressed like that?" she asked, frowning.

"No," he answered shortly. "Come on."

He'd offered her his hand before considering the gesture. They weren't in public, so the display of affection wasn't necessary. But when she wrapped her fingers around his, he only tightened his hold. And didn't think about why he did it.

Moments later, with her safe in the passenger's seat, the full skirt of her gown tucked around her legs, he started the car and drove away.

"What's going on, Shay?" he asked. "Whose house is that?"

"My best friend, Bridgette. You met her that day in the food truck," she replied, keeping her gaze straight ahead.

Impatient, Gideon pressed, "And? Why are you staying with her—how did you put it—for the foreseeable future?"

She sighed, and he steeled himself against the punch of that tired sound. "Because I left home. And I don't know when, or if, I'll return."

Surprise winged through him, and quick on its heels was fury. Cold, bright fury. "Did you leave or did Trevor kick you out?"

Another sigh, and when he glanced over at her she shook her head. "I left. We…had a disagreement, and I thought it best if I gave us both space."

"You're trying to make me drag it out of you, aren't you?" he growled.

"I'm not trying to make you do anything," she said, every inch of the society princess in that reply. "What's more, I don't *want* you to."

His fingers curled around the steering wheel, his hold so tight the leather creaked. Part of him longed to jerk the car over three lanes to the side of the road and demand she confess everything to him, because he knew there was more to the story. And from those sighs and the tension in her slender frame, he sensed the "disagreement" with Trevor hadn't been pretty. It'd hurt her. And for that Gideon wished he could strangle the man.

But the other part... That part longed to pull over, too, but for a different reason. It wanted to park, release her seat belt and tug her onto his lap so he could hold her. Comfort her. Murmur into her ear that everything would be all right, that *she* would be all right.

Which was ridiculous. If there was a woman who didn't need comforting—didn't need *him*—it was Shay Neal.

Quiet settled in the car like a third passenger as he drove to his home. It wasn't until he pulled into the underground parking garage that she stirred.

"I can wait here or in the lobby while you change if you're not going to be long. The ballet starts in about thirty minutes," she said, straightening in the passenger's seat.

"Don't be ridiculous," he snapped, her obvious reluctance to be alone with him irritating him. Did she expect him to jump her? "I promise to keep my hands and dick to myself. Now can you please get out of the damn car?"

He didn't wait for her answer, but shoved the door open. But he still caught her grumbled, "Speaking of dicks..."

In spite of the anger and frustration churning in his chest, he couldn't suppress the quirk of his mouth. This woman gave as good as she got.

Minutes later, they entered his penthouse, and as he took her wrap to hang up, lust joined the cluster of emotions he was feeling. While the champagne-colored skirt of her dress flowed around her legs, the top clung to her shoulders, arms and torso—except for the deep V that dipped between her breasts and even lower in back. He briefly closed his eyes, turning away from the alluring sight of her. Immediately, images of the night in his Town Car skated over the back of his lids like a movie trailer. Him, cupping those breasts, drawing them into his mouth...

Cursing under his breath, he jerked open the closet door and, with more force than necessary, hung up her shawl and his coat.

How could she flaunt sex and sophistication at the same time?

"Would you like a glass of wine? Scotch?" he asked, stalking into the living room and toward the bar.

"Do we have time for that? If you don't hurry and dress, we're going to be late," she reminded him, following him, but halting on the top of the steps that led into the living room.

He removed the top of a crystal decanter and poured himself a finger of bourbon. Only after he'd downed a sip did he turn and face her. Staring at her golden skin and the inner curves of her breasts, he took another. He needed the fortification.

"We're not going to the ballet," he informed her.

She frowned. "What? Why not?" She stepped down into the room. "And why didn't you tell me you changed your mind at Bridgette's house?"

"Why?" he repeated, lifting the tumbler to his lips and staring at her over the rim as he sipped. "Because even though you won't admit it, you're hurting. Something more than a 'disagreement' had to have occurred to make you leave the only family you have left, as well as the only home you've known. I'm a self-confessed asshole, Shay, but even I wouldn't make you attend a social event and fake a happiness you're far from feeling. Especially when your brother might be in attendance." He swirled the amber liquor in his glass and arched an eyebrow. "And as for why I didn't tell you when I picked you up, that's simple. You wouldn't have come with me if I had. The last thing you need right now is to be alone. And since I know your friend supplements her food truck income with a part-time job, you would've been very much alone tonight. So that leaves me."

Her frown deepened. "It's a little creepy how you know so much about me and everyone I'm close to."

He shrugged, taking another taste of the bourbon. "Before going into battle, it's wise to be prepared and know everything you can about your enemy."

"Enemy," she breathed, then scoffed. "You just proved my point. We're not friends—far from it. So why do you care how I spend my night? I'm not your responsibility," she said softly.

"No," he agreed just as softly. "We're not friends. But can we call a truce and resume hostilities tomorrow?" He risked drawing nearer to her. "You're right, you're not my responsibility. But I am responsible. The argument was about me, wasn't it?" When she didn't reply, he gently pressed, "Shay?"

"Yes," she reluctantly admitted.

"Let me guess," he said, his anger rekindling. "Trevor wanted you to break it off with me and you refused."

"Correct again." She notched her chin up at a defiant angle, but he caught the slight tremble of her bottom lip. "But if I'd given in to his demand, then it would've meant destroying everything he cares about, destroying him. Still, it's not like I could share that with him. Instead, he threatened to dismantle my company, starting with ruining all the businesses I've invested in. Oh, and he fired me—or placed me on a temporary leave of absence. So those are my choices. End our relationship and destroy everything my brother loves. Or continue upholding our bargain and lose the company I love."

Fury blasted through him, and for a moment a red haze dropped over his vision. Trevor had threatened his own sister? Gideon grasped the tumbler so tightly the beveled edges dug into his flesh. He pictured that thick, brown file in his office safe, and had no regrets about his intentions to expose Trevor. A man like him deserved the hell Gideon planned to rain down on him.

"I won't let him do that," Gideon promised. Soon enough her brother would be too busy trying to pick up the flaming pieces of his life to worry about harming her company.

"It's not your concern." She waved a hand, dismissing his vow and the topic. "And you mentioned a truce? I accept." Moving forward, she extended her arm. "Should we shake on it?"

Gideon glanced down at her open palm before lifting his gaze to meet her eyes. Though his mind ordered him not to touch her, he wrapped his hand around hers. For several long moments, they stared at each other. An electric shock ran through him at lightning speed and jolted his body to attention. It would be an impossibility to be skin-to-skin with her and not respond. But he didn't pull her closer, didn't try to seduce with his words.

Space and sanctuary, that's what he'd promised her.

"Are you hungry?" he asked, lowering his arm to his side. "I can order in anything you'd like."

"I…" She hesitated, shrugged a shoulder and started again. "I can cook if you have something in the kitchen."

Since meeting Shay, he'd been surprised so many times, he should really stop being taken aback by her. But once more, she'd done the unexpected.

"You can cook?" Dubious, he scanned her beautiful hair, gown and shoes. "In that?"

She snorted. "You're not starting off this truce thing well. And yes, I can cook." If he hadn't been watching her so closely, he might've missed the flash of insecurity that was there and gone in an instant. "Show me to the kitchen? That is, if you don't mind me…?"

"No, this I have to see for myself," he assured her, and strode past her toward the room he rarely used. His housekeeper often prepared dinners for him that she left warming in the stove. So the pantry and refrigerator should both be stocked. "I'll even supply you with clothes so you don't get anything on your dress. See how accommodating I am?"

"Until tomorrow," she added from behind him.

"Until tomorrow," he agreed.

"I wouldn't have believed it if I hadn't tasted it for myself," Gideon exclaimed with wonder, staring down at his empty plate.

Shay shook her head, smothering a smile, although her cheeks hurt with the effort. Forking the last of the chicken carbonara to her mouth, she tried not to blush under his admiring scrutiny. She was twenty-five and an heiress—needless to say, she was used to compliments. But coming from this man... She returned her gaze to her plate, not wanting to analyze why it was different.

"Can I say something without breaking the tenuous bonds of our truce?" he asked, cocking his head to the side.

She wanted to duck her head and avoid his piercing contemplation. It cut deep. Exposing her. Even with the distance of the breakfast bar separating them, she had the sudden urge to lean back, insert more space between them.

But she remained seated and met his gaze. "Sure."

"I would've never pegged you for someone who enjoyed getting their hands dirty in a kitchen. I know you helped your friend out that day in the food truck, but I thought that was a fluke. What you did in there—" he dipped his head in the direction of the kitchen "—was skill. And spoke of someone who really enjoyed it. You're a walking contradiction."

"So your all-knowing file didn't include that information?" she mocked. Picking up her wineglass, she sipped the moscato, silently debating how much to tell him. Then, before she could make up her mind, her mouth was moving. "My mother loved to cook. We had a personal chef, but when Dad wasn't home, she'd commandeer the kitchen and cook for all of us. She would let me help, and some of my happiest memories are of the two of us preparing a pot of gumbo or baking a quiche. I learned to cook from her, but I also inherited my love of it from her."

God, where had all that come from? Embarrassment rose in her, swift and hot.

"Anyway, now your dossier is complete," she added flippantly. "I'll clean up."

She rose from her chair and, grabbing both their plates, circled the bar and headed toward the sink. As she set the dishes in it, a long-fingered hand settled over hers, stilling her movements.

"She would've been proud of you," Gideon murmured in her ear. Heat from his body pressed into her side, her shoulder. "Now, go relax. You did all the work, the least I can do is clean up."

Her first instinct with Gideon was always to defy his orders. She wasn't a puppy. But this time, she accepted his offer and slid from between him and the counter.

Coward.

Maybe.

Okay, definitely. But his unexpected displays of tenderness and the potent, dark sexuality that he emitted like pheromones combined to undermine every guard she'd erected since that night he'd so coldly rejected her after giving her devastating pleasure.

She went in search of the restroom, and after locating it and washing her hands, she continued her tour of his place. At least the downstairs. A formal dining room. A bedroom done in soft blues and cream. Maybe this was where his sister, Olivia, slept when she came over; he'd said the T-shirt and leggings he'd given Shay were hers. Until that moment, she hadn't even known he had a sister. But he didn't offer more information, and for the sake of their temporary cease-fire, she didn't ask.

Another bathroom. A study. A den.

She paused at the open door of that last room. With its two couches, love seat, numerous end tables, large coffee table, massive television screen mounted above the fireplace, this space appeared more lived-in than the rest of the penthouse.

She glanced behind her, but the hallway remained empty. *Just a peek*, she promised herself, then she'd leave. Moving into the room, she stroked a hand over the leather couch that bore a distinct imprint in the middle cushion.

Must be where Gideon sat the most. She could easily imagine the man she'd spent this evening with—in his black, long-sleeved, V-neck sweater, black jeans and bare feet—relaxing in this room. Feet up on the table, remote in hand, scanning through the no-doubt-numerous channels before deciding on...what? Funny. She knew how he had sex, but had no clue about his favorite TV shows or movies.

For some reason, that struck her as sad.

It also lit a hunger to discover more about him. Some things they'd shared in the blackout, but not nearly enough to satisfy her curiosity. What was his favorite color? His favorite band? Snack? Boo—

Oh God.

Breath trapped in her throat, she crossed the room toward the instrument that had captured her attention. No, *instruments*. Plural. A glossy black stand with padded interior cradled six guitars. She knew nothing of guitars, but she could tell the three acoustic and three thinner, sleeker electric guitars had to be expensive. And obviously well cared for.

A flutter tickled her stomach, launching into a full-out quake. She reached a slightly trembling hand toward the guitars.

"Do you play?"

She whipped around, guilt snaking through her. "I—I'm sorry," she stammered, backing away from the instruments. Damn, she was a sneak. And not even a good one. "I didn't mean to snoop, I..." She paused and inhaled a deep breath. "I was taking a self-guided tour of your house and saw the guitars. They're beautiful," she whispered. "I don't play, but obviously, you do...?"

He nodded, crossed the room on silent bare feet and halted next to the stand.

"For years," he said, brushing an affectionate stroke over the gleaming wood of an acoustic guitar. Her thighs tightened, the touch reminding her of how he'd caressed her skin. A lover's familiar caress. "We didn't have a lot of money when I was growing up. But when I showed an interest and aptitude for guitar, my mother somehow managed to scrape enough together for lessons. I didn't find out until I was a teenager, but my father played the guitar, too. I don't remember it, but I like to think I inherited my love of music from him, as you did cooking from your mother."

"Will you—" She broke off. God, she was pushing her luck. From his explanation, she sensed he didn't share this part of himself with many people. It didn't line up with the image of ruthless business tycoon. But in this moment, she wanted to see his clever, talented fingers fly over those strings. To witness him coax beautiful music from that instrument. To watch him lower that damnable shield and let her in. "Will you play for me?"

He stared at her, and her heart thudded against her rib

cage. Finally, *finally*, he dipped his chin and reached for the acoustic guitar on the far end. He almost reverently lifted it off the stand and carried it to the love seat. She trailed behind him, not saying anything. Afraid if she uttered a word, he might change his mind. Once he perched on one end of the small love seat, she sank to the other.

Propping the instrument on his thighs, he plucked a few strings, turned the knobs at the top. Once he seemed satisfied, he cupped the neck, fingers at the ready there. And the other hand hovered over the big, rounded body.

Then he started to play.

And... *Jesus.*

She'd expected something classical, reserved. But no. Passion flowed from beneath his fingers. Passion, and anger, and joy and grief. So many emotions soared from the music, which sounded almost Spanish, but bluesy and a little bit of rock. It was fierce, soul-jarring and...and beautiful. So. Beautiful.

Pain swelled in her lungs, and she expelled a huge breath, just realizing she'd been holding it.

When his fingers stilled, and the music faded away, she remained speechless, breathless. Like she'd been transported to Oz and offered this rare peek behind the wizard's curtain. Only she didn't find a fraud, but a rare, wonderful truth about this man. One that few people were gifted with seeing.

He lifted his head, and those fathomless black eyes studied her. A faint frown creased his brow, and he reached for her, swiping his thumb under her eye.

"You're crying," he murmured.

"Am I?" she asked, shocked, wiping her fingers over her cheeks. Well, hell. She was. "I didn't notice."

"Was I that bad?" he teased, with a soft smile she'd never witnessed on him.

"You were—" *are* "—amazing," she whispered. "Thank you for sharing that with me."

The smile disappeared, but his midnight gaze glittered as if dozens of stars lay behind the black.

"I shouldn't want you." She blurted out the confession. "I shouldn't. But… Even knowing who we are… Even knowing this can only end one way, I still want to grab on to those moments when we're just Gideon and Shay, not someone's enemy or sister. When we're being honest with each other the only way we truly can."

Sex. Need. Passion—they're honest. The body can't lie. Lust is the great equalizer regardless of social status, race or tax bracket.

It was a risk saying those words to him, since he'd uttered them to Camille, not her. And from the gleam in his hooded gaze and the tightening of his sensual mouth, maybe he remembered giving them to another woman.

Honesty. Though her pulse slammed her ears, she had to drag her big-girl panties on and tell him the truth. She couldn't justify keeping it from him anymore, especially when he'd offered her the gift of playing for her.

"There's something you should know," she murmured. "I've been keeping something from you. The night of the blackout, Bridgette had come down with a bad cold and asked me to take her place at a job so she wouldn't lose it. Gideon, that was at the Du—"

"Shay, I already figured it out. You're Camille."

Her lips parted with a gasp. She blinked, staring at him. How had he…?

"Did you really believe I could be inside your body and

not remember?" he murmured. "Not remember every detail of how tight and sweet you are? No, moonbeam." He shook his head. "I'd never forget that."

"Wait." It suddenly made sense now. His rejection afterward. "Is that why you were so cold to me? Because I hadn't told you?"

He studied her for a long, quiet moment. "It wasn't so much that you lied, but wondering *why* you were at the gala and why you kept the truth from me."

"Bridgette would've lost her job if she'd called in on such short notice, and with her business just getting off the ground, she can't afford that. And I had to use a disguise and a fake name. I've attended the gala in the past, and my brother also..." She trailed off, a dark inkling beginning to stir in her head. "My brother," she whispered. "Did you think I'd been there because of him? That I sought you out for him?"

After a slight hesitation, he nodded. "The thought occurred to me."

"Someone must have hurt you terribly for you to be so mistrusting and suspicious," she continued softly. And she had an idea about the identity of that "someone."

"Trevor had no clue I was there. There were only two people in that break room, Gideon—you and me. What happened between us was the scariest and most exhilarating, *freeing* thing I've ever done. That's what you make me feel. Terrified out of my mind because no one has ever affected me so viscerally I don't recognize myself. While at the same time, I'm excited because I like it...crave it."

As soon as the confession escaped her, she recognized that he could use it to his advantage. But she mentally shook her head. Gideon wasn't like her brother. He might utilize blackmail to gain her compliance, but never once had he tried to use her passion against her. He might be ruthless, but he possessed his own code of honor.

Sex. Desire. It was their Switzerland.

And she'd seek asylum there for a while before they found themselves on opposite sides of a war again. Because that was inevitable.

But for now...

She shifted closer to him, covered the hand that still rested on the body of the guitar. Lightly, she explored those fingers, amazed at how they could draw such magic out of the instrument and her. She wanted him to cradle, strum and play her.

She trailed a caress up his arm, over his shoulder and neck, until she reached his jaw. Cupping it, she mimicked the many times he'd held her in the same grip. She swept her thumb over his full bottom lip.

His gaze never leaving hers, Gideon carefully set the guitar on the table, then clasped her hand in his. He turned his head, placing a kiss in the center of her palm, then tracing a path to her wrist. His lips pressed there over her pulse, and her lashes fluttered down. But at the damp flick of his tongue, she gasped, eyes flying open. Liquid heat pooled between her legs, and she didn't even try to contain her whimper.

He rose, gently tugging her to her feet. Without releasing her hand, he led her out of the room, down the hallway and up the curving staircase. They entered a cavernous bedroom lit only by a single lamp on a nightstand. Not just any bedroom—his. The big king-size bed covered in a black spread and white pillows, two chairs flanking a large, freestanding fireplace, a couple glossy bedside tables, a rug—the almost austere decor was relieved by the breathtaking view of the Chicago River and city skyline through the three floor-to-ceiling windows, and the one wall that bore a black-and-white mural of a bare, leafless tree on a lonely plain. It was gorgeous. It was him.

Turning to her, he captured all her attention by cradling her face between his palms, tilting her head back and claiming her mouth. Slow, tender; raw and erotic. His tongue relayed all that he wanted to do to her—would do to her. And as she cocked her head to the side, granting him deeper access, she consented to it all.

"I've had you on a couch and in the back seat of my car. I want to take you on a bed," he muttered against her lips. "*My* bed."

As soon as her whispered "Please," passed her lips, he stripped her, haphazardly tossing her borrowed clothes to the floor. His clothes followed and, hiking her in his arms, he carried her to the bed. Her back hit the covers and his big, hot body pressed her into the mattress. He kissed her harder, wilder, more insistently, as if that leash on his control had unraveled. She dug her fingers into his hair, yanking off the band that corralled it and freeing the strands so they tumbled around both their faces. With a hot, low rumble, he kissed her again, then every inch of her received attention from his mouth, his fingers. By the time he tugged open the drawer on a bedside table and pulled a condom free, she shook with need, twisting and aching for him to fulfill his promise and take her.

Linking their fingers, he drew her arms up, their joined hands bracketing her head.

"Open for me, moonbeam," he murmured, desire burning hot in his dark eyes. The head of his erection nudged her entrance, and she willingly, eagerly widened her thighs and locked them around his slim hips. "Thank you, baby."

He groaned as he sank inside her, not stopping until her sex fully sheathed him. She arched under him, grinding her head into the pillow. God, he stretched her, filled her. Branded her. When he started to move in long, hard thrusts that rocked her body and her soul, she felt claimed. And when her channel clenched around him, and she hurtled into an orgasm that threatened to break her apart, she shut her eyes and became a willing sacrifice to it.

Soon, the aftershocks rippling through her eased, and the fog of ecstasy started to fade. She tensed, waiting for him to roll away from her, to reject her. But when he drew her into his arms, his still-labored breathing bathing her neck, she slowly relaxed.

Right before she drifted away, his low, hoarse voice penetrated her heavy blanket of drowsiness.

"Don't let me break you, Shay. Protect yourself from me."

She didn't reply, but carried that warning with her into sleep.

Chapter 15

Shay nabbed the slice of bread out of the toaster and spread avocado on it. She ate it leaning against the counter, alternating between sips of fresh coffee. Gideon had already left for the office, and with a glance at her wrist, she realized she didn't have long before she had to leave, too. Since she no longer had a position at RemingtonNeal, she'd scheduled a meeting with a potential client.

Staying the night hadn't been in the plan. But when he'd curled around her after he'd made her body sing its own special melody, she hadn't wanted to go anywhere. And then he'd woken her with a cup of steaming coffee, keys to one of his cars and a sweet but wicked kiss that left her toes curling into the mattress.

But those lovely gestures couldn't completely erase the kernel of apprehension that lingered at the edge of her consciousness.

Don't let me break you, Shay. Protect yourself from me.

His murmured warning stayed with her, and dread wormed its way through the warmth. He didn't caution her to be careful because he might hurt her, but because he would. And she would be foolish to ignore that truth. Real life was blackmail, revenge, vendettas and pain. Only in fairy tales did frogs turn to princes. Or wolves to heroes.

Cold seeped into her veins. Suddenly losing her appetite, she dumped the remains of her breakfast. She needed to get going and return to the real world outside this penthouse.

She was heading toward the closet to collect her wrap and dress when the front door opened. Startled, Shay stared as a woman who looked to be about her age entered. With wavy black hair that tumbled over her shoulders, smooth, unlined skin and a tall, slender frame wrapped in a camel cashmere coat, she was obviously too young to be the housekeeper Gideon mentioned last night. Jealousy, unbidden and bright, flared in Shay's chest. Whoever she was, she must be close to Gideon to have a key to his penthouse.

But then the other woman lifted her head, and the truth slammed into Shay. With those heavily lashed, beautiful onyx eyes, she had to be related to Gideon. And considering her age, she was most likely his sister.

"Oh, hi," Olivia said, arching a dark eyebrow in a manner so similar to Gideon's, it confirmed her identity. "I'm sorry. I didn't know Gideon had company. I can come back."

"No, you're fine," Shay objected, finding her voice as his sister half turned to grasp the doorknob. "Gideon's not home, and I was just leaving, too. You must be Olivia." Shay moved forward, her hand extended. Gideon's sister stepped away from the door with a smile, her arm lifting. "My name's Shay. Shay Neal."

Olivia froze, except for the arm falling woodenly back to her side. "Neal?" she repeated in a tremulous whisper. "Are you related to Trevor Neal?"

Unease crawled through her. "Yes. Do you know him?"

Olivia paled, her eyes widening. Visibly trembling fingers lifted to her lips and pressed against them. "I didn't— no, he wouldn't—"

Her fractured sentences made little sense to Shay, but the woman's obvious distress amplified the dread until it was full-out fear. "Olivia, are you okay?" she asked, risking moving closer.

Olivia jerked her head from side to side, tears glistening in her eyes. "Why are you here?"

"Gideon and I are…" She paused, unsure of how much to expose. "…seeing each other. Would you like to sit down? Can I get you anything?"

Again, Olivia shook her head, the tears streaming down her cheeks now. Unable to stand the woman's pain, Shay reached for her, wrapping her in a hug. She half expected Olivia to shove her away, but instead, the woman clung to her, sobbing now.

God. Shay tightened her embrace, her own eyes stinging. What kind of agony must Olivia be in to cause this kind of reaction? It burrowed inside Shay, and she wanted to soothe it, to take it from her. Gently, she guided the crying woman to the living room and lowered them both to the couch. She continued to hold Olivia, gently rocking her as her mother used to do when Shay ran to her in need of comfort.

She didn't glance at her watch to see how long they sat

there. If Olivia needed her to remain the whole day, she would. Anything so those awful, tearing sobs would stop. Gradually, Olivia calmed, and only when she went silent and the trembles eased did Shay slip her arms away. Her shoulders twinged, but she ignored the slight ache. She left for the bathroom. Minutes later, after a quick stop in the kitchen, she returned with a box of tissues, a warm, damp cloth and a bottle of water.

"Thank you," Olivia whispered, her voice hoarse from her tears. "I—I'm sorry. I didn't mean to—"

"Please don't apologize. It's okay," Shay assured her. The woman's clear air of fragility stirred a sense of protectiveness in Shay. "I'm a stranger to you, and you don't have to talk if you don't want to, but I'm here. And whatever you say will stay between us."

For several moments, Olivia clutched the bottle between her hands. Though she'd wiped her face with the cloth, her eyes remained stark, her cheeks and lips pale. Shay waited, ready to listen if Olivia chose to confide in her, ready to just sit with her if she decided not to.

"I know your brother," Olivia finally said, haltingly at first. "I met him a year ago, and we…we fell in love. Or at least I did. I don't know if he ever did love me. But he told me so. And I believed him. I would've done anything for him—and I did. He asked me to keep our relationship a secret because he and Gideon were business rivals, and he didn't want any of that interfering with us. I'd heard Gideon mention Trevor before and knew he had no love for him, so I agreed. Also, I figured once he saw how much we loved each other, he would come around. Especially since I became pregnant."

Shay gasped, unable to contain her shock and dismay.

At the sound, Olivia lifted her gaze from the water bottle. The grief and unadulterated pain there shook Shay, and she wanted to gather the other woman in her arms again. But she didn't, sensing Olivia needed to get this out, like lacerating a festering wound so it could heal faster.

"I thought he would be happy about the news. I was overjoyed. All I dreamed about was marrying him and starting a family. We would be doing it a little out of order, but I didn't care. But—but..." She paused, and a sob escaped her.

Shay grabbed her hand, offering her support, and Olivia went on. "When I told him about the pregnancy, he told me he didn't want me or the baby. To get rid of it because I was no longer useful to him. Then he walked away, like I was garbage he'd tossed out the window. He used me to get back at my brother. At the time, I worked at Gideon's company as his executive assistant. I was so naive, so snowed by Trevor, that when he asked me questions about Gideon's agenda, who he was meeting with, I gave him the information. He worded it to make it sound like he was only asking about my day, what I had on my plate, but he was pumping me for inside information. He never loved me, never had any intention of creating a family with me." She shook her head, her throat working, as if swallowing back another sob. "I refused to end the pregnancy, but it didn't matter. I miscarried and lost the baby."

Shay remained sitting next to Olivia, but inside she reeled, enraged screams slamming against her skull. Part of her longed to deny the story, to label Olivia a liar, but she couldn't. Not only could she not violate this woman all over again by not believing her, but deep inside her soul where only honesty existed, she knew Olivia wasn't lying. Her utter agony bore witness to it, and Shay believed her.

Grief assaulted Shay, welling up in her, and she silently wept. For Olivia. For her pain. For Shay's own pain. For Trevor's coldness, controlling behavior and dismissal of her hopes, dreams and needs. For her disillusionment about her brother. If Trevor could treat his own sister so callously as well as do something as despicable as take advantage of this woman for personal gain, then what else was he capable of? Maybe those things in Gideon's dossier?

Gideon. Was Olivia the reason behind his plans? The night in the restaurant, when he'd first showed her the incriminating file, he'd scoffed at her claim that Trevor wouldn't care who she was dating.

Oh yes. Your brother will care. And he'll understand.

Then, his assertion had been cryptic, but now, understanding dawned on her. No wonder he hated Trevor and had no qualms about blackmailing her. This was more than a business deal; Trevor had come after Gideon's family. If she'd harbored any fledgling hope after waking up in his bed this morning that maybe they could have something more than a truce, this knowledge obliterated it. She would always be a living reminder of the harm and damage her brother had inflicted on his sister, his family.

There was no forgiveness for that. Not for her brother. And not for her, being guilty by association.

Chapter 16

"I still don't think this is a wise decision."

Shay stared out the rear window of Gideon's Town Car at the Gold Coast historic mansion lit up with a cheerful glow. A steady stream of people climbed the front stone steps of the place she'd called home for nearly twenty-six years, entering for Trevor and Madison's engagement party.

"You and Trevor might not be seeing eye to eye right now, but I'm sure he wouldn't want to celebrate his engagement without his sister," Gideon said from beside her.

She glanced at him, irritation and something deeper, sadder pressing against her breastbone like a large boulder. "You won't pass up an opportunity to turn the screw, will you?"

With his aloof mask firmly in place, he met her gaze, onyx eyes steady and unblinking. "No."

She faced the window again, that heaviness gaining weight. It'd been a week since she'd walked out of her childhood home. A week since her and Gideon's truce, which had stretched longer than the next morning. A week since she'd held Olivia as the woman broke down in her arms and revealed Trevor's betrayal.

Yes, now Shay understood the motives behind Gideon's blackmail. And a part of her couldn't blame him. But another part—the part that remembered the man who'd played guitar for her, the man who'd cuddled her close in his bed after tearing her apart with pleasure—longed for him to put all of this aside.

For her.

To want her more than revenge.

She shut her eyes, making sure to keep her head turned away so he couldn't glimpse the yearning that she was certain leaked into her expression. In spite of knowing it was the epitome of foolishness, she'd started to fall for Gideon.

No, that was a lie. The fall had started some time ago, at what moment, she couldn't pinpoint. Maybe when he'd revealed his own pain to her in the back seat of the car. Maybe when he'd raced to Bridgette's house and decided to place her comfort above putting on another episode of the Gideon and Shay Show at the ballet. Maybe when he'd sat on that couch with his guitar and revealed a part of himself that he didn't with most people.

Not that narrowing down the exact instant mattered.

The truth was she loved Gideon Knight.

His fierceness. His heart, which he tried to hide. His passion. His love for his family.

Yes, he was a hard man, a merciless man, but never a cruel one. And when she looked at him, gazed into those midnight-and-stars eyes, she dreamed. She stupidly dreamed that he could love her as he'd once adored

Madison before she'd scarred him with her disloyalty and infidelity.

Maybe she did believe in fairy tales, after all.

The door to the car opened, and with a sigh, she climbed out, murmuring a thank-you to the valet who stood next to it. Seconds later, Gideon's body heat warmed her back, and his palm settled at the base of her spine. A spine she straightened.

No time for self-pity now.

She had the performance of a lifetime to give.

Because she was walking into the lion's den knowing her arrival on Gideon's arm would announce her decision to her brother—she'd chosen his enemy over family loyalty. That's how Trevor would see it.

And she wasn't naive; there would be consequences to her decision. No job at RemingtonNeal. She would most likely have to find a place to live because she couldn't stay with Bridgette forever. And, most importantly, Leida Investments and the businesses she'd invested in would be affected. Especially if Trevor followed through on his threat of tampering with the start-ups she'd funded. She had savings, and she could use most of it to provide capital. But the possibility of having to scale back or rebuild her company was very real without her salary.

The cost of loving Gideon was high.

And, God help her, she was willing to pay it.

Gideon walked silently beside her, but the tension rolled off him, and it ratcheted higher when they entered her home and handed their coats to a waiting servant.

She seamlessly fell back into the role of Chicago socialite and, pasting on a smile, mingled with the other guests. Many of whom didn't seem surprised to see her with Gideon, so the gossip about them as a couple must've made the rounds. Still, they were aware of the enmity between Gideon and Trevor as business rivals, and watched her and Gideon with an avid, greedy curiosity.

Especially when a path seemed to open, and they stood only feet away from Trevor, Madison and Senator Reus. Shay looked up, and her gaze connected with her brother's. Though he smiled for the benefit of those around them, fury blazed from his hazel eyes, so like hers. His glare shifted from her to Gideon, and a frightening rage hardened his expression before he controlled it.

"Stand tall, moonbeam," Gideon murmured in her ear. His big palm slid up her back and under her hair, curling around the nape of her neck. "He can't hurt you."

But you can. The words rang in her head, her chest. Tipping her head back, she said, "That's debatable. Cutting me off emotionally and financially and targeting my company definitely falls under the 'hurting me' category."

"Correction, then," he growled. "I won't let him hurt you."

That ship had sailed and was a faint glimmer on the horizon.

She straightened her shoulders and added a little more wattage to her smile. "We should go greet the happy couple."

"You mean, get it over with?" he retorted, dark eyebrow arched. She'd once detested the gesture, but now counted each one.

"That's what I said."

His low chuckle tripped over her bare arms. Inhaling a deep breath, she allowed him to guide her over to the trio who stoically watched their approach.

"Trevor, Madison, congratulations." She leaned forward and stiffly kissed Madison's cheek. Although she did return the feigned embrace, most likely for those closely observing them, Madison's rigid posture didn't relax. Straightening, Shay nodded to her brother's future father-in-law. "Senator."

"Shay," he murmured coldly.

"Your sister wanted to see you, wish you well," Gideon said to Trevor, his tone frigid, but she detected the undercurrent of anger. Of hatred. "She has a forgiving heart considering you put her out of her own house."

Oh God.

"She left by her own choice," Trevor snapped, the fury in his eyes leaking into his face. His lips twisted into an ugly snarl. "But come now, Gideon. We both know how trying *sisters* can be."

Nausea churned in her belly and raced for the back of her throat.

Dark waves of rage poured off Gideon, and he moved forward. Terrified, she latched on to his arm, fearful of what he might do to her brother. And she feared *for* Gideon, for the consequences he might suffer for his actions. She harbored no doubt that Trevor would enjoy pressing charges and using it against him.

"Gideon, no," she pleaded softly. "It's what he wants."

Trevor sneered. "Shay, I need to speak to you. Alone," he stressed.

"Fine," she agreed, more to separate Gideon from Trevor than to be amenable. "Gideon," she whispered. When he tore his still-frightening stare from her brother, she squeezed his arm. "I'll be right back."

"You don't have to do this," he reminded her, just as softly, but the fury still vibrated in his voice.

"Yes, I do," she returned. Rising onto her toes, she

placed a kiss on his jaw. "They're not worth it." She waited for his abrupt nod before she turned back to her brother. "In the study, I assume."

Not waiting for his confirmation, she strode toward the rear of the house. Anger bristled under her skin, poking her like thousands of tiny needles. When she entered her brother's domain, she could barely look at him.

"How dare you bring that asshole into my house?" Trevor ground out through clenched teeth as soon as he closed the study door behind them.

"Your house?" She crossed her arms. "You were right when you told Gideon that I chose to leave. Chose. Because this is *our* home, Trevor. I can bring whoever I want here, and you have no say. I don't need to ask your permission."

"I would've never thought you were a traitor," he snarled. "Mom and Dad wouldn't recognize you right now."

She absorbed the power of that blow and fought not to stagger from it. But the pain ebbed and flowed inside her.

Stand tall. He can't hurt you.

Inhaling a deep breath, she pushed past it.

"You're such a hypocrite," she said, surprised at her even tone. "So righteous and high-and-mighty. And to think I defended you. Believed in you. Trusted you. But you didn't deserve any of it."

"What the hell are you talking about, Shay?" he demanded. "I've done nothing but honor this family, the Neal name, *you*. You, baby sister, betrayed me."

"By thinking for myself, wanting something for myself? For daring to defy you? I'm not a sheep, Trevor. I have a mind. I have feelings. I have a heart, but there's only one Neal who can claim to possess the last two. Because somewhere along the way, you lost them to jealousy, pettiness and hate. No, *big brother*," she said, throwing his taunt back at him. "I've done nothing but stand by this family. I've protected it when you would've destroyed it with your greed and ambition."

"You need to stop right there," he warned in a dark growl, taking a step forward.

But he didn't intimidate her. Didn't control her. Not anymore. She didn't wait for him to advance, but marched forward and met him halfway.

"No, you stop. And listen. I know what you and your precious senator are up to," she said. "Insider information. Fixing contracts. Kickbacks. Illegal campaign contributions. And that's just the tip of it." When he rocked back in shock, his eyes flaring wide, she nodded. "Yes, Trevor, I know about it all. Because Gideon has a file on you, inches thick. I've seen it, read it. I'm aware of all your dirty dealings, which if made public could topple RemingtonNeal, ruin the Neal name and send you and Julian to jail."

"How long have you…?" His voice trailed off, but she understood his question.

"Weeks. Since before the Grace Sanctuary fund-raiser. I made a deal with the devil to save you. I agreed to pretend to be in a fake relationship with him so he wouldn't expose you. That's why I couldn't break things off with him. Because if I did, you would've been destroyed. But that's not all," she whispered, eliminating the small space between her and the man who wore her brother's face, but was a stranger. "He did all this because of Olivia. You remember her, don't you?" At his stony expression, she nodded again. "Of course you do. The woman you seduced, used to get back at her brother, impregnated, then tossed aside. All for your petty hatred and resentment. Now, who wouldn't Dad and Mom recognize?"

"You don't understand," he spat, but the anger in his eyes had been overshadowed by worry. By fear. Because he understood that his greatest enemy had the dirt on him, no doubt. "You could never understand..."

"Not understand what? How hard it is to live up to our name? To live under the yoke of it for so long that sometimes you feel like your back's going to break from the burden? Yes, Trevor, I do. The difference between you and me is that I'm choosing not to let it poison me until I make unconscionable decisions that hurt other people. I decided to help people rather than harm them. But just to get your way, you would steal that from me, too."

For too long, she'd allowed him and the duty of being a Neal to dictate her life, her behavior, her decisions. No longer. She might have been quiet, but she'd learned from the best.

Not him. Gideon.

"I love you, Trevor. For the brother and man you were, I'm giving you a choice now. Come after Leida Investments or any of the businesses I've invested in, or my trust fund, and Gideon won't have to leak any of that information to the press and SEC. I will. He gave me a copy of the file, and right now, it's tucked away safe. But if you dare touch anything that's mine—and when I say mine, that includes Gideon Knight and everything he loves—I'll take you down. And I won't lose sleep over it."

Trevor stared at her, shocked. But she didn't wait for his response. He couldn't say anything that would fix what he'd broken. She would just have to accept that some men changed for the worse instead of the better, and as much as it tore her heart apart, Trevor was one of them.

* * *

"I have to admit, Gideon, I never expected you to go to *these* lengths." Madison tsked, appearing at his side, her familiar scent teasing his nostrils.

At one time, he'd found the floral fragrance alluring. Now it was just cloying. She trailed fingertips down his arm and over the back of his hand. Tilting her head to the side, she offered him what she probably considered a coy smile. She didn't pull it off. Not when he knew the real woman behind the mask.

He shifted his arm, knocking her hand away. Foolish as hell of him to think he could slip unseen into the closed-off room that reminded him of his den. He'd needed space and time to walk off the killing rage that had consumed him when Trevor had alluded to Olivia.

If not for Shay, he would've put that bastard through the wall, his hands around his throat, and damn the consequences. But his name in that soft voice and the fear darkening her lovely eyes had stopped him. He'd put that hated emotion in her gaze, and he detested himself for it. Still, even with rage roiling inside him like a volcano set to blow, he would've accompanied her to that meeting with her brother. He hadn't wanted to leave her alone. That protective streak toward her had only widened and deepened in the time they'd spent together. Yet he also understood she needed to have it out with Trevor, to stand up to him on her own. And she couldn't do that with his life in imminent danger from Gideon.

But right after he marched into an empty room to cool off with a glass of bourbon from the bar, Madison had appeared.

Goddamn, he didn't have the patience to deal with her machinations right now.

"What lengths, Madison?" He lifted the tumbler to his

lips, downing the last of the dark alcohol before setting the glass on the mantel. "I don't have time for your games."

"Time for me," she corrected, assuming a hurt expression. "That's what went wrong with us, you know? You spent so much time at the office or out of town at meetings, I felt neglected. I missed you and couldn't stand the loneliness."

He snorted. "Is this your way of trying to explain why I walked in on you sitting on Trevor's dick? Forget it, sweetheart. This guilt trip not only isn't going to work, but it's months too late. I don't give a fuck now."

"We both know that's not true, Gideon," she crooned, clutching his arm. He stiffened, hating her hands on him. It felt...wrong. There'd been a time when he'd enjoyed her teasing caresses, her heated strokes. But now? Now his skin prickled and crawled as if his very body rebelled against her. These days, he welcomed the touch of only one woman. Shay.

Again he shifted away, dislodging her touch.

"If you'd answered any of my phone calls this week, you'd know—"

"I didn't answer them because we have nothing to talk about," he said.

"So you're going to tell me that your love for me just died? Went away just like that?" She snapped her fingers, eyes flashing. "I don't believe it."

"Believe it," he growled. "You killed it. And you don't get a do-over. Get it through your head, sweetheart. I. Don't. Want. You."

Tired of this, he went to move around her, but she sidestepped, blocking him. Unless he wanted to grab her, pick her up and shift her out of the way, he couldn't pass. And at the moment, the thought of putting his hands on her caused his stomach to curdle.

"Then what was this whole...act with Shay about? You

don't expect me, or anyone for that matter, to actually accept that you're madly in love with her? The sister of the man who stole the woman you love? You don't have to continue this silly pretense anymore, Gideon." She shoved into his personal space, so her perfume clogged his nose, crawled down his throat. He grabbed her shoulders to prevent her from coming any nearer. She flattened her palms on his chest. "I love you. I made a mistake leaving you for him. It's been you all along. And I know you still love me if you'll go to these lengths."

Screw this. He tightened his grip on her, prepared to move her. "Madison…" he growled.

"Yes, Gideon." She moaned, and shooting up on her toes, wrapped her arms around his neck and crushed her mouth to his.

Shock froze him. But just for a second. Bile scorched a path to the back of his throat. Muttering a curse, he jerked his head back, circled her wrists and yanked her off him.

"Dammit," he snapped. But any more words died on his tongue.

Shay stood in the doorway to the den, her shuttered gaze on them.

"Oh, Shay," Madison cooed, panting lightly. "We didn't see you there." Perverse satisfaction threaded her tone.

"Shay," he breathed, already leaving the unfaithful bitch he'd almost married behind, forgotten, and moving toward the woman with the wounded eyes.

"I'm ready if you are," she said, her voice flat, hideously polite.

She turned on her heel and left, leaving a void in his gut.

Chapter 17

Shay stared out the window of the Town Car, watching the landmarks that defined Chicago passing by in the distance. What she wouldn't give to be in one of those monuments right now. Just anywhere as long as it wasn't here, sitting in the back of this car, tension thick, her pain crushing her chest like an anvil.

Tonight had been a special hell. Between the confrontation and probable loss of her relationship with Trevor and walking in on Madison and Gideon kissing, she just wanted to hole up somewhere and wait out this pain. But how could she hide from it, when she embodied it, breathed it?

Next to her, Gideon was silent, brooding. She'd never seen him brood. Distant, yes. Taunting, yes. Passionate, God yes. But never this dark heaviness that seemed to reach out to her, wrap around her.

Hold on, she reminded herself. Just hold on until she

could get out of the car and into her temporary home,
where she could break down. But not now. Not in front
of Gideon.

"Shay."

His deep, silken voice stroked over her skin even under
her coat, and she flinched away from it.

"I didn't kiss her, Shay," he rasped.

She squeezed her eyes shut. As if she could block out
the sight of Madison, her arms thrown around him, her
mouth pressed to the one that she adored, needed. But that
image would no doubt be branded onto her brain for all
eternity. As well as the slashing pain on her heart.

Yet... "I know, Gideon."

A pause, and then an audible exhale. "You believe me,"
he stated.

She nodded. "Yes."

"Then, baby, look at me. Please." It was the "please"
that had her turning her head and meeting that midnight
gaze. "Then what's wrong? Why haven't you spoken to
me, looked at me since leaving the party? Tell me what
I've done and let me explain it."

"You haven't done anything," she said, scanning his
features. Committing them to memory. "But I can't go
through with this charade. Our agreement is over."

His head snapped back, his eyes narrowing on her face.
"Why? Did your brother convince you to leave me?"

"Leave you?" She chuckled, and it grated her throat
raw. "You once accused me of being blind, Gideon. It
seems to be contagious. You can't see that I would do
anything to stay with you. But not as a pretend girlfriend
or a lover-for-now. I want the real thing. I *deserve* the
real thing."

"Shay," he said, and her heart squeezed so hard, she placed her hand over her chest. "What are you saying?"

"I'm saying I love you. Desperately. Completely. Finally. There's no going back for me. There's no one else. And that's a problem, because you don't love me. You don't want me other than as a bed partner and a means to an end."

"That's not fair," he rumbled, the skin tautening over his cheekbones, anger diamond-bright in his eyes. "You mean more to me than a fuck. I've never treated you like that. I never would."

"No," she agreed. "You've been one of the few men in my life who saw past the socialite, the family name and money. You saw the business owner, the capable woman. When no one else respected me, you did...even as you used me to get back at my brother. And that's the problem. Because above all, the first thing you will always see is Trevor Neal's sister." She hesitated, but in the end, she had nothing to lose in laying it all out there. "I know about what he did to Olivia," she said.

Gideon transformed into living stone. Except for his eyes, which blazed with anger and another darker, more heartbreaking emotion.

"How did you find out? Surely *Trevor*," he spat her brother's name, "didn't confess his sins to you."

"No." She shook her head, hurting for him, for Olivia. Shame for Trevor's despicable actions coating her in grime even though she wasn't responsible for him. "I didn't tell you, but Olivia came by the morning after I moved out of my house. She broke down when she realized who I was, and she ended up revealing everything to me. She's the reason behind the file, the blackmail, the revenge, not

Madison. Your hatred goes much deeper than him cheating with her."

"Yes," he confirmed, still cold, still impenetrable. "You saw for yourself what he did to Olivia. She's been emotionally fragile ever since he left her, and she lost the baby. The morning after the blackout, she'd found out about his engagement to Madison. And it sent her to the hospital. She's recovering, but she hasn't been the girl I remember since before your brother came along."

"And you'll never be able to get past that. Not that I blame you. He crossed an unforgivable line, and there's nothing that could justify it. But even realizing this, I can't waste one more day hoping you will let it go. Not one more day living a lie. It's time for me to live for me, to determine and shape my own future, and I can't do that with a man who insists on remaining in the past. A man for whom revenge is more important than love...than me."

"I didn't ask for your love," he snapped, and the tone, razor sharp, flayed her already wounded and bleeding heart. "I told you not to let me break you, Shay. I warned you."

"And I didn't ask for your permission to love you," she countered softly. "Don't feel guilty, Gideon. I'm used to not being enough for the men in my life. But the difference—what you've taught me—is I no longer give a damn. I'm enough for *me*."

At that moment, the car stopped in front of Bridgette's house. Shay didn't wait for the driver to come around and open her door. She unlocked it and did the honors herself. It was like a metaphor for her new life. She was tired of waiting on others. She was in control of her own fate; she could open her own doors.

And she would.

Starting now.

"Shay." Gideon's strong fingers grasped her wrist. "Please."

"Goodbye, Gideon," she whispered.

Then, pulling free, she stepped out of the car.

And didn't look back.

Chapter 18

Gideon entered the numbers into the spreadsheet, then several seconds later swore under his breath and deleted them. *Dammit*. He'd been doing a repeat of this same thing for hours now.

Hours, hell. His fingers fisted on top of the keyboard. Days.

His concentration had been shot for five nights and six days. Since the five nights and six days ago when Shay got out of his car. When she'd announced she loved him, then walked away without looking back. As an image of her leaving him, spine ramrod straight, glide elegant and proud, wavered in his head, he squeezed his eyes shut. Bowing his head, he didn't will the mental picture away. No, he conjured it up over and over, punishing himself with the memory of the pain and soul-deep sadness that had darkened her eyes, of the words that had driven daggers into his chest.

Of the resolve and strength radiating from her that let him know if he didn't say something, *do* something to prevent her from exiting the car, he would never see her again. Never inhale her rain-and-roses scent. Never hear her husky voice. Never have her body pressed to his, fitting like a missing puzzle piece.

But he'd done nothing.

That grab at her wrist had been weak, and they'd both known it.

"Damn you, Shay," he whispered harshly. "Damn you."

Like he'd told her that night, he hadn't asked for her love. Didn't want it. He'd earned a PhD in how faithless love was. People threw that word around to abuse, betray and abandon others. Madison had claimed to love him. Trevor had vowed the same to his sister.

Love deceived, used and...died. It left pain and disillusionment and loss behind. It changed people for the worse, not the better. Intuition had warned him that if he allowed Shay in, if he risked opening to her, when she left—because experience had taught him the leaving was inevitable—the wreckage would be much worse than the damage Madison had inflicted. Shay would level him.

He refused to be played for the fool by *love* again. Ever.

With that "ever" ricocheting off his skull, he turned back to his computer screen and the report he'd been trying to finish for the past two hours.

His desk phone buzzed. "Mr. Knight, there's a Mr. Trevor Neal here to see you. He doesn't have an appointment—"

"Send him in," Gideon snapped.

What the hell was Trevor doing here? Scratch that. He didn't give a damn.

For the first two days after dropping Shay off, Gideon had tried to drown her out with alcohol. When that had failed, work had been his next attempt to erase her from his mind. Apparently, that wasn't succeeding, either. While meeting with Trevor was most likely a terrible idea, he was also spoiling for a fight. A grim smile stretched across his mouth. For the first time in days—six days and five nights, to be exact—he looked forward to something.

Seconds later, his office door opened, and the man he'd resented for thirteen years and actively hated since he'd harmed Olivia stalked inside. Harsh lines etched his forehead and bracketed his mouth, and his eyes, so like his sister's, blazed with anger. His hands curled into fists at his sides. Seemed like Gideon wasn't the only one looking for a fight.

His smile widened.

"Good afternoon, Trevor. I'd say it was nice to see you again, but we both know that would be bullshit. So we'll skip the pleasantries and get to what are you doing here." Gideon leaned back in his desk chair and templed his fingers beneath his chin.

"You son of a bitch," Trevor snarled.

"Well, that didn't take long," Gideon drawled with a sigh, his voice heavy with mock disappointment. Rising, he flattened his palms on the top of his desk. "What the fuck do you want?"

"Where's my sister?" Trevor demanded. "I checked with Bridgette. She's no longer staying there. So where is she?"

"I don't know," Gideon replied calmly. Though inside, alarm clanged in his head, his chest. As far as he'd known, she'd still been with her best friend. *Was she okay? Was she safe?* The questions barraged him, but he forced his focus back to the man across from him. "Why do you care? You let her leave the only home she ever knew because she wouldn't bend to your demands. Are you suddenly having an attack of conscience?"

Doubtful, since the man didn't have one.

"Not that it's any of your business, but I need to speak to her. Last time we spoke, she made some...irrational accusations and threats. We need to clear this up. As a *family*," he sneered.

Gideon arched an eyebrow. "Threats?" Pride and admiration warmed him. "There's an interesting turn of events."

"You would find it funny." Trevor scowled. "She wasn't like this before. I'm thinking it's the company she's been keeping."

"Thank you." Gideon dipped his head in acknowledgment. "And just for the record, your sister has always been strong. You were just too busy playing lord of the manor to recognize it. If you had, maybe you would've used her brilliance for the advantage of your *family* company instead of sticking her in some bullshit position. Then she might not have had to go form her own business, but could've helped yours grow."

"You know nothing about Shay," Trevor growled, shifting forward as if ready to leap over the desk. "Don't pretend that your *relationship*," he spat the word, "was real. She told me the truth about your blackmailing her into pretending you two were a couple. She also informed me about the file of lies you have on me."

Shock reverberated through him. When she'd claimed she wouldn't go one more day living a lie, had she been referring to confessing to her brother about their arrangement?

Flipping these new revelations over and over in his mind, Gideon returned his attention to Trevor. "You might have tried that argument with Shay, but don't bother with me. Everything listed in that file is the least of your crimes. We both know who you are, Trevor. We both know what you're capable of," he growled. "You used my sister, then tossed her aside like she was something beneath your shoe. No, I take that back. You would've at least paused and scraped something off the bottom of your precious loafers. You didn't even give her that courtesy. And for what? A grudge against me from high school? You broke her, and for you it was business as usual."

"Like you broke my sister?" Trevor accused. "Eye for an eye? Don't stand there and preach to me like you're so self-righteous, when you turned around and did the same thing to Shay. You used her to get back at me. That doesn't make you the hero in this story."

"You're right."

Trevor's mouth snapped closed, his eyes flaring in surprise at Gideon's quick agreement, before narrowing. He was probably wondering what Gideon's game was now. But there wasn't any game. There wasn't any trickery to slide another point home as if this was a contest to be won.

He'd used Shay. Oh yes, he'd justified it as righting a wrong against Olivia, as protecting future women from being hurt by Trevor. But the truth couldn't be denied any longer. His actions hadn't been noble—they'd been selfish, vengeful...and reprehensible. Maybe unforgivable.

Not because of Trevor. He still had zero fucks to give about Trevor. But because he'd dragged an innocent into it. As blameless as Olivia had been in Trevor's schemes, Shay had been just as blameless. His mother's warning haunted him, ringing in his head like a premonition that had come to pass. He *had* ended up hurting others. And the most important person he'd hurt was Shay. No, he wasn't Trevor—could never deliberately deceive and devastate someone, then walk away from a child he'd created—but he'd also blackmailed, hurt, then turned his back on the woman he loved.

God. He loved her.

The force of the revelation struck him with the blow of a mallet to the chest. He sank to his chair, staring blindly ahead.

He loved Shay.

Somehow, despite every wall, every barrier and shield he'd thrown up, she'd wedged herself into his heart, his soul. No wonder he'd felt so empty these past days. The one who'd given him life again was gone. Because, yes, she'd resuscitated him, jolting his heart so it beat again. She'd given him more than work to be excited about— she'd given him her quiet humor, her defiance, her wit, her loyalty, her body…her love.

And what had he done? Thrown it back at her like it meant nothing.

Don't feel guilty, Gideon. I'm used to not being enough for the men in my life.

Pain, razor sharp and searing hot, razed his chest. He gasped at the agony of it. Nothing—absolutely nothing—could be further from the truth. She was more than enough. She was *everything.* But he'd been willing to throw away a future with her for revenge.

"Gideon," Trevor snapped, hauling Gideon out of the hell he'd plummeted into.

He jerked his head up, blinking. God, he'd forgotten all about this man standing in his office. And now he didn't have time for him or the vendetta that had brought both of them low. Urgency spiraling through him, Gideon shot to his feet and strode across the room. Removing a large picture from the wall, he revealed the safe behind it and quickly punched in the code to open it. He withdrew the thick, brown file inside, then slammed the safe door shut, not bothering to replace the painting.

"Here." He marched over to Trevor and shoved the dossier containing all his damning information into the other man's chest. "Take it. There aren't any more copies other than the one I gave your sister."

"What?" Trevor gasped. He clutched the folder, glancing at it before his gaze whipped back to Gideon. "What's your angle now? You can't seriously just hand this over to me without wanting something in return."

Gideon stepped back, shaking his head. "No angle. No ulterior motive. But you're right. I do want something in return. Or rather, someone. I want Shay. More than that file or revenge against you. But that's for me to fix, not you."

How he'd go about doing that, he had no clue. Hell, by all rights, she shouldn't forgive him. But he needed her. He loved her.

And he'd fight to have her. Harder than he'd ever fought to pay back Trevor.

Because winning Shay was more important than any battle he'd ever faced.

Chapter 19

"Order up, babe."

Shay turned around and rushed across the minimal space inside the food truck to grab the two cartons of larb served over thin noodles. Snatching up napkins and plastic utensils, she placed everything in a bag and handed it to the waiting customers through the window. Smiling and thanking them, she turned to the next person and took his order for green papaya salad.

Bridgette had called that morning, asking if she would help her out on the truck again. Though Shay suspected her friend had arranged this sudden lack of help to keep her busy and her mind off a certain person, she'd jumped at the chance to get out of her newly leased, empty Edgewater apartment. More specifically, she'd been eager to get out of her head.

In the almost two weeks since she'd walked away from Gideon, she'd found an apartment—despite Bridgette's argument that she could stay with her as long as she wanted—located a small office space for Leida Investments, officially resigned from RemingtonNeal, opened a safe deposit box for the damning file on her brother and done more research on start-up companies that she could invest in.

Yes, her family and love life had exploded, but she refused to stop living. A gaping hole existed where her heart had once been, but that didn't mean she would roll over and give in. She'd meant every word she'd uttered to Gideon.

This was her time. Her life. And no one but she was in control of it.

She might have lost the man she loved because he wanted revenge and hate rather than her, but for the first time in longer than she could remember, she loved herself. She *valued* herself. And she was demanding it from everyone in her life.

As Bridgette had put it, Shay was a boss.

Dammit, yeah, she was.

She'd learned something in the last couple weeks. She would've loved having Gideon in her life. But he *wasn't* her life.

And she was okay with that.

"Have another order for the larb, but by itself, without the noodles," she called out to Bridgette over her shoulder before returning her attention to the window and the next customer. "Hi, how can I..." She trailed off, the sudden lurch of her heart to her throat preventing the rest of the words from escaping.

No.

No.

She stared into midnight eyes with stars and the scream inside her head increased in volume. It wasn't fair. What the hell was he doing here? Telling him she loved him and having him reject her had been agonizing, humiliating. How did he not know that? Was he a sadist getting pleasure from her pain?

Well, *screw that.*

She schooled her features into the cool, polite mask she'd mastered since she'd been old enough to sit at the adult table. He wouldn't get anything else from her. She didn't have it in her to give.

"What are you doing here, Gideon?" she asked, proud when not so much as a tremor shook her voice.

Behind her, Bridgette appeared next to her elbow like a bodyguard. "What the hell is this?" she demanded, spatula still in hand.

"I got this," Shay murmured to her friend. "We're busy, as you can tell," she said to Gideon. "And you and I don't have anything left to say to each other."

Again, she sounded calm even to her own ears. Sounded as if her fingertips didn't tingle with the need to touch him.

But inside...

Inside she quaked. Love, hurt, yearning, desire—they all coalesced and swirled in her chest, leaving almost no room for air. She dragged in what little she could and waited.

"You don't have to say anything, moonbeam. All I ask is for you to listen."

"Don't call me that," she snapped, and silently cursed herself for betraying that much emotion. She shouldn't care if he murmured that endearment. It shouldn't affect her.

"Two minutes, Shay." His dark gaze searched hers. "Please."

Please.

Like before, it gave her pause.

"Two minutes. That's it," she agreed.

"Thank you," he said, then hesitating, he dragged his hands over his head. Taken aback by the uncharacteristically nervous gesture, Shay narrowed her eyes on him. Noting for the first time the faint smudges under his eyes, the two-minutes-past-five-o'clock shadow that darkened his jaw. Where was the clean-cut, reserved man she'd known?

He gave a rough, abrupt chuckle. "Now that I'm here, I don't know where to begin." Sighing, he dropped his arm. "First, I should apologize. And I am sorry, Shay. I used you. There's no getting around that fact. I rationalized and defended my actions by claiming I wanted justice for Olivia. That your brother had gotten away with hurting people long enough, and if no one else would make him pay, then I would. But what I didn't want to admit is that I blamed myself.

"I hated myself as much as, if not more than, him. It was my job to protect my sister, and I failed. If I'd been a better brother, she would've felt free to tell me about the relationship with Trevor instead of keeping it a secret. And most of all, if not for me, she wouldn't have even been on his radar. Me. It all came back to me, and I couldn't bear the guilt, the shame and, God, yes, the anger. It was that anger that led me to do what I had judged him for— ruthlessly using you to get to him. I convinced myself I was more honorable than him, but in my rage, I'd *become* him. And worst of all, I hurt you. That, I will never forgive myself for."

Soul-deep shock robbed her of speech. Even the long line of people behind him had stopped grumbling and were quiet. A few even had their phones out. She mentally winced. Gideon wouldn't be happy to know he was probably live-streaming on social media.

"Gideon, you don't have to—" she began, only to be cut off.

"Yes, I do. I'm desperate, Shay. I don't have any pride left. Not when it comes to you. And I don't want it. Don't need it. Not when it kept me from telling you how important you are. God, baby, you're *vital*. Nothing is the same without you in my world. Before you, work, family, money, success—those were priorities. Hell, they were everything. But since you walked away from me, I still have all of those, and aside from my mother and sister, they don't fulfill me anymore.

"I can't concentrate at work because I'm wondering where you are, what you're doing…if you're thinking about me. I could escape into all the things wealth buys, I could travel to the most exotic places on this earth, but I'd see nothing, appreciate nothing, because you wouldn't be there with me. Success?" He held up his hands, palms out. "Until you, I measured success by how many clients I had, the profits, how many doors opened for me. But now? Success is how many times I can make you smile. How many times I can hear you say I love you. How many nights I can fall asleep beside you. How many ways I can prove to you that you're loved. So far, I've been damn unsuccessful."

"Wow," Bridgette whispered beside her. Shay shot her friend a look, and she shrugged, smiling sheepishly. "I mean, bastard."

Shaking her head, Shay returned her gaze to the man who'd captured her attention and that of an increasingly growing lunch crowd in Hyde Park. She blinked back the tears stinging her eyes, and her heart pounded thickly against her rib cage. Hope tried to rear its foolish head, but she slapped it back down. She'd been stupid enough to spin impossible dreams around this man once, even though he'd never made promises to her. And that was just it. She could no longer afford to pin nebulous hopes on a man who refused to put her first. No matter how lovely his speech.

"Thank you for the apology, Gideon. I really do appreciate it. But I can't risk taking a chance on you. How long before you realize you're sleeping with the enemy—literally—and resent me for it? I can't live waiting for that day to happen."

"You don't get it, moonbeam," he said, moving closer to the service window. And in spite of her resolve, she leaned forward, a part of her—the part that woke up aching for him every night, the part that refused to stop believing in fairy tales—desperate to hear what she didn't get. "I love you. I don't know when it happened. When I sat down across from you in that restaurant and you essentially told me to go to hell? When you refused to answer my phone call and cater to me because you were helping a friend? When I played my guitar for you? Maybe…" He hesitated, swallowed hard. Then whispered, "Maybe the first time I saw you as Camille."

"Saw you as Camille? What kind of kink are y'all into?" Bridgette muttered from behind her.

Shay ignored her, latched on to every word falling from Gideon's lips. Ensnared by those onyx eyes that she couldn't tear herself away from.

"I don't deserve you. But there's no man on this earth who does. But that won't stop me from fighting for you. From fighting for *us*. From begging you to not throw me away, even though I almost did. Moonbeam, you complete me in a way revenge never could. Without you as my conscience, my lover, my friend, I'm empty. I want to be full. I want to be found. Please, don't leave me out there again. I love you, Shay Neal. Desperately. Completely. Finally. There's no going back for me. There's no one else."

He gifted her with the words she'd given him. Only this time, he was the one standing on the ledge, hoping she would grasp his hand and pull him back to safety, to love. He'd pushed her over that night. And now, she could do the same. Pay him back. Turn away to a future that he wouldn't be in, but would still be good. Or she could reach across, risk her heart again and jump off the edge, trusting him to catch her. And hold her forever.

There was no choice.

Running, she barreled out of the truck, but before she could round it, she crashed into Gideon. He hadn't waited, but met her halfway. That's what they would always do— meet each other. Never fail to be there for one another.

Dimly, she heard a roar of applause and cheers, but as his arms closed around her, and she wrapped hers around his neck, everything else ceased to exist. He captured her mouth in a kiss that stole her breath and sent heat roaring through her. But most of all, it shattered every remnant of fear and doubt, promising her with the thrust of his tongue, the molding of his lips, that he would love her, cherish her, worship her. And she returned the vow.

"I love you," she whispered, peppering his mouth, jaw and chin with kisses. "I love you so much."

"I thought I'd never hear you say that again," he rasped, pressing his forehead to hers.

"I promise you I'll never stop telling you." She took his mouth this time, leaving them shaking against each other. "I love you."

"Forever?"

"Forever."

Epilogue

One Year Later

"Mrs. Knight, your husband's here to see you."

Shay smiled, pressing the speaker button on her desk phone. God, she never tired of being called that. "Please send him in, Jackie." Seconds later, her executive assistant opened the door, grinning as Gideon strode past her. Leida Investments was still small, but now Shay could afford a staff. Even if that staff was just Jackie. Still, the business was steadily growing, and Shay couldn't be happier.

Well, she took that back, her smile warming as Gideon crossed the room and took her into his arms. With the news she'd just received not minutes ago, she could indeed be happier. And she was.

Her lips parted under his, and as always, his kiss kindled the desire that only he could stir within her. She tilted her head back farther, opened her mouth wider, and he dived deeper. By the time he lifted his head, their rough breaths echoed in the office.

"I'm supposed to be taking you to lunch," he reminded her with a sensual smile that was reflected in his eyes. "But with you kissing me like that, hell, moonbeam, you might *be* lunch."

She chuckled. "You're bad. And I refuse to keep your mother and sister waiting. I had to twist Bridgette's arm to let me have Olivia for an afternoon, so nope, not missing lunch."

Gideon's eyes brightened at hearing his sister's name. And no wonder. Olivia had come a long way in a year. After hearing the whole story about what Trevor had done to her, Bridgette had decided to take her under her wing. And Olivia hadn't had much of a choice. Bridgette had bulldozed her way into Olivia's world, and assumed the role of big sister, as Shay had. Soon, she had Olivia in the food truck, working beside her, and to Olivia's surprise, she'd enjoyed it and was wonderful with people and the business side of it. Bridgette had taken her on as a partner, and now the two of them were planning to buy another truck.

And Trevor... A sliver of sadness wormed its way into Shay's happiness. It happened whenever she thought of him. She hadn't shared the file she had on him; he was her brother, and no matter what he'd done, she couldn't destroy him. But things like that had a way of exposing themselves. He and the senator were in trouble with the law and SEC now. Soon, Trevor would lose not only his wife, the family business and reputation, but also his freedom. He'd caused a lot of pain and loss to people both emotionally and financially, and now he faced the consequences of his actions. She loved him, but she also hadn't seen him since the night of his engagement party.

"Are you sure about lunch?" Gideon asked, cupping her chin and tipping her head back for another press of his lips to hers. "I'm sure Mom and Olivia would understand."

"Yes." Shay laughed, then cradled his cheeks between her palms. "I'm hungry." She paused. "And especially since I'm eating for two now."

Shock blanked his features. Slowly, understanding dawned, and his black eyes glittered.

"What?" he rasped. "Are you telling me that we're... that you're..."

"Pregnant," she finished with a wide grin, slipping her arms around his neck again. "We're going to have a baby."

"Moonbeam," he whispered, awed. With a reverence that brought tears to her eyes, he stepped back, and her arms fell to her sides. He knelt in front of her, his big hands spreading over her still-flat abdomen. "Jesus, Moonbeam. How can you continue making me the happiest, richest, most loved man in the world?" He dipped his head, brushed his mouth over her belly. Rising to his feet, he pulled her into a tight, hard embrace and buried his face in her neck. "I love you, Shay. I love you so much."

"I love you, too. Forever."

* * * * *